P9-BZK-122

ALSO BY JULIAN STOCKWIN

KYDD

ARTEMIS

A NOVEL

JULIAN STOCKWIN

SCRIBNER

NEW YORK   LONDON   TORONTO   SYDNEY   SINGAPORE

SCRIBNER
1230 Avenue of the Americas
New York, NY 10020

First Scribner edition 2002
Originally published in Great Britain in 2001 by Hodder and Stoughton,
a division of Hodder Headline

SCRIBNER and design are trademarks of Macmillan Library
Reference USA, Inc., used under license by Simon & Schuster,
the publisher of this work.

For information regarding special discounts for bulk purchases,
please contact Simon & Schuster Special Sales at 1-800-456-6798 or
business@simonandschuster.com

Designed by Colin Joh
Set in Galliard

Manufactured in the United States of America

1 3 5 7 9 10 8 6 4 2

Library of Congress Cataloging-in-Publication Data
Stockwin, Julian.
Artemis : a novel / Julian Stockwin.
1st Scribner ed.
p. cm.
1. Great Britain—History, Naval—18th century—Fiction.
2. France—History—Revolution, 1789–1799—Fiction.
3. Sailors—Fiction. I. Title.

PR6119.T76 A89 2002
823'.92—dc21   2002019686

ISBN 0-7432-1460-9

To the mistress of my heart

ARTEMIS

CHAPTER 1

≈≈≈

Thomas Kydd stood awkwardly on the deck of the frigate with his few possessions at his feet. A bare hour ago he had been an ordinary seaman in the old line-of-battle ship *Duke William*. Now, somewhere off the enemy coast of Revolutionary France, he was gazing back at her from a crack frigate as an able seaman, a replacement for prize crew.

A hand lifted in farewell in the boat pulling back to the big ship-of-the-line. It was Whaley, and with a lump in his throat Kydd realized that he would probably never see his broad smile again or share a grog with his other old shipmates. It had started hard—as a young perruquier from Guildford, Kydd had been seized by the press-gang six months before, but despite all he had suffered, he had come to admire the skill and courage of the seamen. And now, as a sailor himself, he was parting from the ship that had been his home for so long.

He waved in return and forced his attention back inboard.

Men were waiting on deck—a weatherbeaten older man in plain black and a much worn tricorne, a hard-looking lieutenant in serviceable seagoing blues, a childlike midshipman without a hat, and the man at the wheel, stolidly chewing tobacco. Next to Kydd, Renzi gave a conspiratorial grimace. They had been through much together, he and his friend. The others in the little party looked equally bemused: Stirk, the tough gun captain; Doud, the devil-may-care topman; Doggo, a ferally ugly able seaman; Pinto, a neat and deadly Iberian; and Wong, the inscrutable circus strongman. But there would be no complaint; service in a fast frigate ranging the oceans for prey and prize money was infinitely preferable to the boredom of a big ship on blockade duty.

"Brace around that foresail—run away with it, you damn sluggards!" The hard bellow from behind startled Kydd. "Away aloft, you dawdling old women—lay out and loose!" The officer was dressed in austere sea rig, only faded lace indicating that here was the most powerful man aboard, a post captain in the Royal Navy and commander of the frigate.

The men leaped to obey. Kydd saw that they moved with enthusiasm and speed, quite unlike the heavy, deliberate movements he'd been used to in the battleship. Some made a race of it, sprinting along the top of the swaying yard before dropping to the footrope in a daring display of skill.

Artemis responded immediately, the chuckle of water under her forefoot feathering rapidly, the creaking of cordage and sheaves as more sails were sheeted home soon rewarded with an eager swoop across the broad Atlantic swell. Kydd felt the lively response with a lifting of the heart. To windward, in the *Duke William,* the ponderous spars were still coming around, but the frigate was already stretching over the sparkling sea, impatient to be away.

Turning to them, the Captain roared, "Lay aft, you men!" He stood abaft the wheel: with no poop in a frigate the spar deck swept unbroken from the beakhead forward in a sweet curve right aft to the taffrail.

Kydd and the others moved quickly. This was Black Jack Powlett, the famous frigate captain who already had five prizes to his name safe in English ports. There was no mistaking the quality of the man, the hard, penetrating stare and pugnacious forward lean of his body.

He looked at them speculatively, hands clasped behind his back. "So you're all able seamen?" His eyes flicked over to the fast receding bulk of the three-decker astern. "Goddamn it—I'll not believe Caldwell has only prime hands to spare." His voice was cool, but there was a restlessness in his manner, a coiled energy that seemed to radiate out to those around him. His hand stroked his close-shaven blue-black jaw as he tried to make sense of the gift. "You, sir!" he snapped at Doud. "Pray be so good as to touch the sheave of the flying jibboom."

Doud gaped, then turned and darted forward. He was being asked to touch the very tip of the bowsprit eighty feet out over the sea.

Powlett drew out a silver watch. "And you, sir," he rounded on Renzi, "both stuns'l boom irons of the fore t'gallant yard."

The restless eyes settled on Kydd, who tensed. "To touch the main truck, if you please." The main truck—the very highest point in the vessel. Kydd knew that his standing as seaman rested on his actions of the next few minutes.

He swung nimbly into the main shrouds, heaving himself up the ratlines and around the futtock shrouds. On and up the main topmast shrouds he swarmed, conserving his strength for the last lap. At the main topmast top the ratlines stopped. He stepped out onto the cross trees and looked down. Already at a height of one hundred and thirty feet, he was as far aloft as he had ever been before. But still above was the royal yard—and beyond that the truck.

He grasped the single-rope topgallant mast shrouds firmly. At this height the pitch and roll were fierce and he was jerked through a vertiginous seventy-foot arc. His feet pinioning the tarred rope, and hands pulling upward, he made his way to the light royal yard and past that to the seizings of the main royal backstay. The truck was only a matter of a few feet farther, a round cap at the very tip of the mast—but now there was nothing but the bare mast.

The motion was alarming, a soaring through the airy firmament before a whipping stop and surge the other way. The pole mast was only a few inches thick and he locked his legs around it securely before transferring his grip and hauling himself upward. Not daring to look down he watched the truck come closer—nearer, and then it was within his reach. Something rattled on the far side of the mast. He followed it up and saw that it was a stout chain

clamped to the round of the truck. A newfangled lightning con-
ductor. On a crazy impulse he transferred his hands to the chain
and drew himself up to the truck itself. A strong copper rod continued in the thin air beyond the truck.

It was the work of moments to heave himself up and past the
cap—and then he was standing erect on the bird-slimed truck,
trembling with fatigue and exhilaration and holding the lightning
rod in a death grip. He flung up an arm to indicate his position,
but before starting his descent he snatched a look at the panorama.
Every part of the vessel was now at a level below him, decks,
masts, sails. Not a single thing intruded to spoil the totality of his
three-hundred-and-sixty-degree view.

Carefully lowering himself back down the mast, he slid the
few feet to the royal backstay. Transferring his grip from mast to
stay he soared hand over hand down the backstay to the deck
again.

"I do confess I am at a stand. It's no parcel of lubberly landmen
we have here, Mr. Spershott," Powlett said to the lean officer next
to him.

It took a moment or two for Kydd to realize why the mess deck
was so different. There were the same mess tables and ship's side
racks for cutlery and mess traps, but here there were no massive
cannon regularly spaced along the sides. Aboard the battleship
Kydd was used to having his living space between a pair of massive
thirty-two-pounder long guns, sharing his domestics with the
smoke and blast of broadsides, but here there was only a single
function.

It was noon and the berth deck was alive with gossip and laughter after the issue of grog. A ship's boy had shown them to their
new mess, half the party to a starboard mess, the other to larboard. They stood awkwardly.

"Hear tell they's promising ter send us some real man-o'-war hands," said a thin-looking older man at the ship's side. Kydd knew enough about unwritten mess etiquette to realize that this was the senior hand of the mess. Like the others, he deliberately chose not to notice the newcomers.

A handsome, well-groomed sailor replied, "As long as they're not ship-of-the-line jacks is all I asks. Them big-ship ways—no room fer marching up an' down in this little barky."

The older man snorted. "Nor all that there flags an' buntin' all th' time. An' yer've gotta be slow in th' wits to be big ships, else yer intellects rot, waitin' while the ship wants ter tack about."

"Has t' be a big ship," came back the other, "all them pressed men—why, they has to batten 'em down when they makes port, else they'll think to ramble off home, like."

The older man started, as though seeing the arrivals for the first time. "Well, look who it ain't. A parcel o' *Royal Billy*s! Sit yerselves down then—grog's up."

Self-consciously Kydd edged over and sat next to a neat, slightly built sailor who held out his hand with a pleasant smile. "Guess we have t' take ye aboard, we being grievous shorthanded 'n' all!" he said. "Adam—Nathan Adam."

"Kydd, Tom Kydd." He flushed with pleasure, quite uncon-scious of the striking figure of a seaman he now made. His dark, strong features were well set off by the short blue jacket, white duck trousers, and a red kerchief knotted carelessly over a blue-striped waistcoat. His ebony hair gleamed in a tight clubbed pig-tail, his tanned, open face bore a broad white smile.

Sliding in easily next to Kydd, Renzi sat opposite. Curious looks met his from around the table, for he was most definitely at vari-ance with the usual man-o'-war's man with his careful, intelligent dark eyes and a face with incised lines of character suggesting dangerous mystery. Renzi's black hair, short to the point of monas-ticism, also hinted at an inner discipline quite unlike the carefree sailor's.

He was next to a well-muscled black man, who turned to greet him. "Never bin in a ship-o'-the-line, meself," he said. "Guess there's plenty more room in them big ships."

"Know where I'd rather be," Kydd said.

The senior hand interrupted. "Got yer traps?" Kydd fished around in his ditty bag and drew out his tankard, an old brass-strapped wooden one that had once belonged to a close shipmate, now dead.

"Me apologies about the blackstrap," the man said, upending a bottle into the tankard. "Cap'n thinks to give us this'n instead o' the right sort." He shrugged. "Took a thousan' off a Frenchy last week."

Renzi's eyes widened. He picked up the bottle eagerly and stared at the label. "My God!" he said. "Haut Brion, *premier cru,* the seventy-nine no less!" His beautifully modulated patrician tones took them aback quite as much as his words, but in the age-old custom of the sea, no obvious notice was taken of a character quirk.

"Hey, now, yer mate likes our grog, then," the black man said happily.

The senior hand banged on the table with his grog can, a little of the rich dark wine spilling. Mature and lined, with an oddly soft voice, he announced, "We has new chums, mates." The others paid attention. "Name's Petit, Elias Petit, 'n' yer already knows Nathan. Yon hulkin' blackamoor—we call 'im Quashee, 'n' if yer wants ter raise a right decent sea-pie, he's yer man."

Kydd nodded. "Tom Kydd, an' Nicholas Renzi," he said, gesturing toward Renzi. He noticed the curiosity that Renzi's manner had evoked, but continued, "and Pinto, er—"

"Fernando da Mesouta Pinto, at your service," the wall-faced Iberian added smoothly.

"Pinto is a Portugee," Kydd said, "and Nicholas is my particular friend," he concluded firmly.

A thatch-haired lad brought up two kids of food and thumped them on the table.

"Thank 'ee, Luke," Petit said. The lad upended a wooden tub to sit on and looked at the newcomers with the frankness of youth. Petit lifted the lid of one wooden container. "'Tis poor stuff only," he announced defensively, and began doling out the food.

Kydd could hardly believe his eyes. Real china plates instead of squares of dark wood, a pewter spoon and even a fork. And the food! The oatmeal was not only seasoned with herbs but the meat was pig's trotters with collops of real meat—this was a feast.

Petit looked at Kydd curiously. "So yer likes our scran too," he said.

Kydd thought of the single galley in the ship-of-the-line serving eight hundred men. You could have anything so long as it could be boiled in the vast coppers. "Yessir!" he answered. "We has a saying in *Royal Billy* which we hear before we begins our salt beef." He assumed an air of reverence.

> *Old horse, old horse, what brought you here?*
> *You've carried me gear for many a year!*
> *An' now wore out with sore abuse*
> *They salt you down for sailor's use!*
> *They gaze on you with sad surprise*
> *They roll ye over and bugger y'r eyes*
> *They eat y'r meat and pick your bones*
> *And send the rest t' Davey Jones!*

Laughing, they fell upon the food. Kydd glanced across the width of the deck to the mess opposite. Doggo, Wong and the others were clearly enjoying their change of fortune also, and a slow wink broke Stirk's oaken face.

"Hear tell as how y'r Black Jack is a tartar," mumbled Kydd, his mouth full.

"Not as who would say," Petit replied. "The cat ain't seen th' daylight this five weeks or more—Cap'n, he knows it's us what fights the ship for 'im, 'n' so he treats us a-right, does he."

"What about the first luff?" Kydd asked, absentmindedly tapping a piece of hardtack on the table. To his surprise no black-headed weevils squirmed out.

"Spershott? Don't say much. Keeps station on the Cap'n always, he does," said Petit dismissively. "It's Parry yer wants ter watch. Second luff. Thinks he's goin' to make his mark b' comin' down on Rowley, the third—it's Devil-bait agin Harry Flashers all bloody day long."

"An' Neville," prompted Quashee.

"An' Neville," agreed Petit. "Kinda fourth luff, but supernumer'y—wished on us b' the Admiral who wants to put him in the way of a mort o' prize money, my guess." He grunted and added, "But a square sort, I'll grant yer."

Kydd took another pull at his tankard. The wine was rich and smooth. Adam seemed not to relish it. "Not to y'r taste, Nathan?" Kydd asked amiably.

The courteous expression did not change. "Christ abstained."

"Blue light sailor," said Petit, wiping his mouth. "But he dursn't top it the preacher wi' us."

Kydd nodded, and looking at Adam continued with a smile, "Aye, but Christ made damn sure the wedding wasn't dry, though, didn't he!"

Adam looked at him steadily and sipped his drink.

"Where are we headed, do you believe?" Renzi asked.

"Where there's a Frenchy what swims." Quashee chuckled. He aped a prize agent reluctantly doling out the guineas—so ludicrous was the sight of his bulk going through the motions that the mess fell about helpless.

Petit clapped him on the back. "True enough, yer black bastard. That is ter say that we're raidin' commerce, which is ter say that ev'rything what is under sail has ter loose tops'ls to us, 'n' we has first pickin's."

At the fore-hatchway the squeal of a boatswain's calls cut through the sociability. Reluctantly the sailors rose.

Evening quarters was exercised every day at sea in *Artemis*. At four bells in the last dog-watch, the entire ship's company closed up for action to the stirring sound of "Hearts of Oak" on the fife and drum.

Lieutenant Rowley had the gundeck, and stood impassive at the fore-hatch. Kydd noted the puffs of white lace that emerged at each sleeve and the luxuriant hair, carefully styled in the new Romantic vogue. His fashionable cynical mannerisms gave the impression of hauteur, heightened by the faultlessly cut uniform. His orders were resonant enough, however. "Exercise of the great guns—gun captains, in your own time . . ."

Stirk mustered his gun crew. His previous ship experience had ensured a rate of gun captain, and with Kydd and Renzi there were three other *Royal Billys*, Wong, Pinto and Doggo.

That left two of the original frigate crew on this gun—Gully, a bushy, round-faced man, and Colton, the second gun captain, a shrewish man with an uneven temper.

The twelve-pounder was only belly-high where the great thirty-two-pounders aboard the lower gundeck of *Duke William* were chest-high. Other than that, the cannon were nearly identical, and Kydd saw that the only real difference was in the number of men. Up to twenty men were needed to serve the big guns. Here, there were but three, together with a gun captain and his second, and the powder monkey.

Stirk was equal to the challenge. "Right—different ships, different long splices. This barky likes it b' numbers, so 'ere's how we go." He considered his men. "Doggo, you're number one, load wad an' shot. Kydd, number two, want you to sponge 'n' ram.

Renzi, number three, get the wad an' shot to number one. Gully, is it? Number four on the side tackle, please, mate, with Pinto an' Wong as number five 'n' six on the tackle. Oh, yeah—five an' six as well works the handspike, 'n' everyone bears a fist on the tackle falls runnin' out the gun."

"An' me, Mr. Stirk!" called the gangling boy at the hatch gratings amidships.

"An' Mr. Luke, 'oo'll be doin' the honors with the powder," he added gravely.

He stepped back, bumping into Colton. There was a moment of tension as Stirk stared him down. "An' the second captain overhauls th' trainin' tackle."

The routine of loading and firing was simple enough—the gun was run out and fired, then recoiled inboard. The cannon was sponged out, and a cartridge and wad rammed home. A ball was slammed in the muzzle, another was followed, rammed firmly in place, and the gun was run out again ready for firing. It was teamwork that counted, not only with the danger of naked powder brought close to gun blast, but the whole effectiveness of the gun depended on knowing what to do, and keeping out of the way of others when they did their part.

"We does it slow time first, lads," ordered Stirk.

This was Kydd's first time on the rammer. It was confusing that the rammer and sponge were at either end of the same stout wooden stave. He laid the stave down, sponge inboard, and joined at the side tackle. The gun was run out. The noise seemed more of a heavy rattle than the bass rumble of the three tons of the larger gun.

"Gun 'as fired," Stirk said laconically. He looked pointedly at Colton, but Wong and Pinto thrust past and seized the training tackle at the breech end of the gun to make it "recoil." Kydd had the sponge ready in the bucket, and lifted the dripping sheepskin. Passing the rammer end out of the gunport to get more room, he plunged it into the muzzle.

Renzi, across from Kydd, had an imaginary "cartridge" and "wad" ready for Doggo, who stuffed them into the muzzle. Kydd quickly had the cuplike end of the rammer stabbing down inside the muzzle; Doggo took the shot and another wad and slammed them into the maw. Kydd repeated his ramming and the gun crew hauled together on the tackles to run out; Stirk performed his priming and pointing, and the cycle was over. "We does it now in quick time!" he growled.

They did it again, causing Stirk to groan with frustration. Kydd, in his enthusiasm, had his rammer flailing straight after Doggo's cartridge but before his wad could be applied, and Wong, used to the huge inertia of larger guns, tripped over at the side tackle and sent his side down in a tangle of cursing men. At that moment a single squeal from a boatswain's call pierced the din.

"Still!" cried Rowley, striding aft to meet the Captain with his first lieutenant. Rowley removed his hat as Powlett stepped onto the gundeck. All movement ceased.

"Where are our *Royal Billy*s, if you please, Mr. Rowley?" Powlett demanded.

"This way, sir," Rowley replied, and with a graceful gesture moved forward.

Kydd watched them approach. Rowley was short enough to stand upright and stepped carefully, as if distrustful of where he trod. Powlett stooped slightly and ranged like a wary lion. Spershott hurried on behind.

"*Duke Williams*, sir, Tobias Stirk, gun captain."

Kydd sensed a cold ferocity behind Powlett's eyes and felt his back stiffening.

"Your men up to service in a frigate, Stirk?" Powlett rasped.

Stirk hesitated.

"Very well—we'll have the measure of you nevertheless." Powlett drew out his watch. He swung round to the twelve-pounder next along. "Symonds!"

"Aye, sir?" the other gun captain said carefully.

"You and the *Royal Billy*s will exercise together."

He turned back to Stirk. "Run out. On my mark!"

Stirk spat on his hands and glared at his crew.

Powlett consulted his watch. "Now!" His arm swept down and the gun crews leapt into action.

With Wong's great strength at the training tackle the recoil was accomplished rapidly. With nervous energy Kydd sponged and withdrew, Doggo's cartridge instantly ready at the muzzle. Kydd returned with the stave—but Doggo hissed savagely, "Fuckin' rammer!" Kydd had made a stupid mistake. He had not reversed the stave and the wet sheepskin was still inboard with the rammer gaily poking out of the gunport. He tried to turn the stave outside the port but he fumbled and it fell away, tumbling noisily against the ship's side and into the sea, sinking in the wake astern.

Symonds and his crew laughed cruelly. Spershott stepped over, scandalized. "Crown property! This will be stopped from your pay, you rascal."

Powlett held up a hand. "No. *Royal Billy*s will carry on with their exercise. And the rest of you may secure and stand down." He spared just one glance for the furious Stirk and returned up the ladder.

Liberated from duty, the *Artemis* hands gathered for the entertainment, and for the rest of the dog-watch the red-faced Stirk drove his crew mercilessly to the jeers and laughter of the others.

The days that followed were not easy for the *Royal Billy*s. Things moved faster in a frigate. It needed agile feet to get out on a slender yard and back, and her speed of response at the helm took even Stirk by surprise. It was sailoring on a different and more challenging plane, but stung by the element of competition they responded nimbly.

It was six weeks he had been in *Artemis,* and Kydd now felt he had found his feet. The middle watch was going slowly. As lookout,

Kydd could not pass the time companionably with Renzi, and must occupy himself for an hour staring out into the night. Kydd drew his grego closer about him, the coarse wadmerel material warm and quite up to keeping out the keen night winds. The fitful moon was mostly hidden in cloud, leaving an impenetrable gloom that made it difficult even to discern the nearby helmsman. Kydd gazed out again over the hurrying seas, fighting a comfortable drowsiness.

Something caught his eye, far out into the night. A blink of paleness, suddenly apparent at the extremity of his vision then gone. He stared hard, but could not catch it again. There it was once more! A momentary pallid blob appearing and disappearing in one place.

"Officer o' the watch, sir!" Kydd called. A voice replied from the other side of the deck, and a dark figure loomed next to him.

"Kydd, sir, larb'd after lookout. Saw something way to loo'ard, flash o' white or so."

"Where away?" It was Parry's hard voice.

The pale object obliged by winking into existence in the general direction Kydd indicated, remaining for a brief space before it disappeared.

Parry had his night glass up instantly, searching. "Damn it—yes, I have it." He snapped the glass down. "Pass the word—my duty to the Captain, and a sail is sighted." With a captain like Powlett there could only be one response. They would close on the sail, and take their chances.

In the short time before Powlett hastened on deck *Artemis* had braced around and begun bearing down on the strange sail. "I'll trouble you to take in the topsails, Mr. Parry—no point in alarming them unnecessarily." The pale blob steadied and remained. "We keep to windward. Stand off and on until dawn."

After an hour it became clear that the stranger had sighted them and changed course toward them. *Artemis* followed suit to retain her windward position. The stranger soon tired of this and eased away off the wind, and the two ships spent the remaining hours of darkness running parallel under easy sail.

The stirring rattle of the drums died away, and with every man closed up at his post, they waited for the darkness to lift. *Artemis* always met a new day with guns run out and men at quarters: they would never be caught out by the light of day revealing an enemy alongside ready to blow them out of the water.

The stranger was still there at daybreak five miles under their lee, the summer dawn languorously painting in the colors of the day— darkling sea to a vivid cobalt, lilac sky to a perfect cerulean with vast towers of pure white clouds to the south. It also revealed the sleek low black and yellow lines of a frigate, quite as big as they, and in the process of shortening sail.

Artemis bore down on the vessel, every glass trained on her. The quarterdeck grew tense. "She does not throw out her private signal, dammit!" grunted Powlett. If this were a Royal Navy ship there was a need to establish the relative seniority of their respective captains. But on the other hand she might well have thought that *Artemis,* end on, could be a French ship and feel reluctant to deter the approach by showing her true colors too soon.

The sailing master, Mr. Prewse, took off his hat to scratch at his sparse hair. "Don't know as I recognizes her as a King's ship at all."

The boatswain took a telescope and stared at the stranger for a long time. "Could be a Swede, but my money's on her bein' a Frenchy."

Powlett's response was quick. "Why so?"

"'Cos, sir, she has squared-off hances, much less of a sheer, an' as you can see, sir, the fo'c'sle rail is never carried forrard of the cat-head—she's French-built right enough."

"Thank you, Mr. Merrydew," Powlett said quietly.

"If you please, sir." Parry stood patiently before Powlett, his expression as uncompromising as ever.

"Mr. Parry?"

The second lieutenant motioned forward a sailor.

"What is it, Boyden?"

"Sir, that there's the *Sit-oy-en*," he said definitively.

"The what?"

"*Sit-oy-en*. Seen 'er in Toulong. We was alongside, takin' in wine, we was, sir, last days o' the peace, 'n' she takes a piece outa us comin' down with the tide."

Powlett stiffened. "The *Citoyenne*, you mean. You're sure? What is her force, man?"

"Thirty-six long twelves, sixes on the quarterdeck, don't remember else. Ah—she's big, an' has a consid'rable crew—"

Powlett nodded. Unlike the world-ranging British frigates, French vessels could re-supply at any time and as a consequence were crowded with fighting men. This one was also smart and confident, and presumably did not have prize crews away.

"And, sir."

"Yes?"

"Her cap'n is a right tartar, beggin' yer pardon, like, sir. Our second lootenant, he 'eard him ter say that if the new crew didn't shape up sharpish, he promises ter turn 'em over inta the galleys— an' that more'n six months ago."

Lieutenant Neville cleared his throat and said lightly, "Then we can expect a warm welcome."

No smile broke Powlett's expression.

"Eyes of the world, I rather fancy." Rowley's musing was ill-timed, but ignoring Powlett's glower he pursued the thought. "For the first time in this war—here we have a match of equal force. The only thing to tip the scales will be the character of the nation. Will hot-blooded revolutionary zeal triumph over the lords of the sea? Or does right prevail? It will be a tournament that

I rather think will mean more to the country than a single lonely battle far out at sea."

Parry turned on Rowley. "Are you in any doubt of the outcome, sir?"

"I would be a fool were I to think other than that it will be a hard-fought contest—but it will go hard for us at home should fortune deny us the victory."

Powlett broke clear of the group. "Give 'em a gun and tell 'em who we are, Mr. Parry."

A gun to weather banged out. Overhead the battle ensign broke out, its enormous size streaming brazenly in the breeze.

Powlett bared his teeth. "Rig the splinter nettings, Mr. Parry, and we'll have barricades in the tops." He glanced at the heavy frigate riding the waves ahead. "We're going to have to earn our honors today."

Leaning out of the gunport below, Kydd and Stirk tried to make out the ship ahead. "He's a Frog, 'n' we's invitin' him to a tea party," Stirk said, pulling back inboard. "An' it looks to be a right roaratorious time, he bein' at least our weight o' metal."

Kydd looked at the enemy again. There was activity at the braces as the ship began a turn. Her profile shortened as she fell away off the wind, showing her ornamented stern and gathering way as she fled from them. Kydd was incredulous. "She's running!"

Renzi's cool voice from behind answered him. "As she should, of course, dear fellow. Her captain knows his job is to fall upon our merchant shipping, our commerce—that is the greatest harm she can do our cause. We are of the same force. If he engages, the best he can expect is a costly battle. He will be damaged and cannot proceed to his real work. He must preserve his ship."

Stirk looked at him in contempt. "Preserve 'is ship? No man preserves 'is honor by runnin'. Not even a Frenchy!"

Renzi shrugged.

"*Haaands* to make sail!" Powlett wanted royals loosed. *Citoyenne* was shaping a course that took the breeze on her quarter, but *Artemis* was not accounted a flyer for nothing. Taut and trim, she sped along.

Kydd joined the others on the foredeck, watching the chase. Foam-flecks spattered up from the slicing stem, streaming air thrumming gaily in the rigging. The weather was perfect for *Artemis,* and she drew closer; *Citoyenne* was now some small miles ahead and downwind.

Without warning *Citoyenne* angled over, to come as close to the wind as she could lie. *Artemis* followed suit immediately to keep to her weather position, and the two sped over the lifting seas. Powlett rapidly had bowlines fast to their bridles, stretching the forward edges of the sails to their utmost in a hard straining of every stitch of canvas.

"*Haaands* to quarters!"

Kydd clattered down the fore-hatch and closed up at his gun, heart thudding. He pulled down the rammer stave from its beckets at the deckhead and stood clear while Stirk checked gear.

Renzi looked calm and flexed his shoulders. Others finished folding and tying their kerchiefs over their ears. Most stripped to the waist, while some tested the wet sanded deck to decide whether bare feet would give the better grip.

Stirk made a fuss of securing Luke's ear pads. The boy stood wide-eyed on the hatch gratings and from the tone of Stirk's murmuring Kydd guessed that he was doing his best to ease the lad's fears. He wondered what he could think of to say in like circumstances. The gundeck settled, the guns long since run out ready for the first broadside. Stirk waited patiently at the breech with the lanyard from the gunlock coiled in his hand.

Kydd, now perfectly competent at his task after long hours of practice, was icily aware that this was not an exercise. He remembered his previous brush with the enemy, but that had been in a powerful ship-of-the-line; he had seen blood and death but it had ended brutally and quickly. Now, he wondered how he would perform in a much smaller ship, at closer quarters. He shuddered and looked about him. Doggo, his station at the muzzle, was leaning out of the gunport, gazing steadily ahead. Renzi stood with his arms folded, a half-smile playing on his lips. On the center-line, Luke waited with his cartridge box in his hands, anxiously watching Stirk. Kydd knew that he was more worried about letting down his hero than possible death or mutilation.

The gundeck was strangely quiet, odd shipboard noises sounding over-loud, the cordage tension in working so close-hauled producing a finely tuned high frequency in the wind. Suddenly dry in the mouth, Kydd crossed to the center of the gundeck, and scooped at the scuttled butt of vinegar and water.

Relatively shorthanded, they had crews to fight the guns on one side only, but with a single opponent this was no disadvantage. Rowley paced at the forward end of the gundeck with a London dandy's nonchalance. His action clothing was plainer than usual, but Kydd noticed just a peep of lace at the sleeves, and his buttons gleamed with the glitter of gold. His sword, however, held an air of uncompromising martial serviceability.

"What'n hell?" Doggo shouted.

They crowded to the gunport.

Citoyenne was shortening sail and slowing. As they watched, she relaxed her hard beat to windward into a more comfortable full and bye, and soon lay quietly under topsails. She was ready to turn on her tormentor.

"No—you will await my order!" Powlett's roar was directed at Parry, who had drawn his sword and was pacing about like a wild animal. *Artemis* surged on, the distance rapidly closing. "Shorten sail to topsails, Mr. Prewse. Lay me within pistol shot to windward of her, if you please," Powlett ordered.

The big courses were brought to the yards and furled, seamen working frantically as if determined not to miss the excitement to come. *Artemis* slowed to a glide.

The ships drew closer. "Damn me that he doesn't risk a raking broadside," muttered Merrydew.

As *Artemis* turned for the final run in to place herself parallel to the *Citoyenne* she would necessarily expose her bow to her opponent. Even one round-shot passing down the length of the vessel could do terrible damage, smashing through the guns one after another, maiming and killing in an unstoppable swath of destruction.

But there was no cannon fire. In silence *Artemis* glided toward the enemy frigate, her own broadside held to a hair trigger. Parry glanced at Powlett, who stood foursquare on the quarterdeck, facing the *Citoyenne* as the two ships converged. "On my signal," snarled Powlett.

At a walking pace *Citoyenne* slipped forward, enough way on for the rudder to answer. Men crowded on her decks, the knot of officers on her quarterdeck clearly distinguishable. From her open gunports the muzzles of cannon menaced, each one ready to deliver a crushing blow. But still they rested silent.

"Their captain," Parry whispered.

The blue and gold figure opposite stood erect and proud. His arm swept up and he removed his hat with a courtly bow.

"My God!" Parry blurted.

"Shut up!" Powlett snapped. He removed his own hat, sweeping it down in an elegant leg, then stood tall and imperious. "Long live His Majesty King George," he roared. "Huzzah for the King!" Dumbfounded, the group of officers removed their hats at the wild cheering that erupted from all parts of their vessel.

Opposite, the French Captain waited patiently for the sound to die. Now the ships ran parallel at an easy pace some two hundred yards apart. The Captain turned to one of a nearby gun crew and seized his cap, holding it aloft. It was a Phrygian cap of liberty.

"*Vive la République!*" The emotion in his voice was evident even across the distance. A storm of hoarse cheering broke out. The Captain clutched the cap once to his bosom, then thrust it at a sea-man. Followed by cheering acclamation the man swarmed up the main shrouds, and at the masthead nailed the cap in place.

Powlett straightened. "Enough of this nonsense," he snorted, and clapped his hat back on his head. It was the signal. After the briefest of pauses *Artemis*'s broadside smashed out in a brutal, thunderous roar, instantly filling the space between the two ships with acrid rolling gunsmoke.

The first broadside was an ear-splitting, mind-blasting slam of sound, choking the gundeck with writhing masses of smoke. Immediately *Citoyenne*'s broadside answered. It arrived in a storm of violence, iron round-shot beating into *Artemis*'s sides and deck—smashing, splintering, killing.

"Load, yer buggers!" yelled Stirk. The gun crew threw them-selves at the task.

There was no time for Kydd to look around, to discover the source of the terrible shrieking nearby. No time to ponder the ori-gin of the heavy clattering overhead, or the strange quiet of the gun next to them. It was impossible to see anything of the enemy through the gunport. They remained unseen under the double volume of gunsmoke.

He wielded his dripping sponge-rammer with a nervous fury, plunging it into the still smoking maw of the twelve-pounder, deep inside with a couple of twists to the left, and out again with twists to the right. Doggo was there in an instant, with the lethal gray cartridge and then a wad into the muzzle. Kydd had the stave reversed and savagely stabbed the rammer down. He caught Stirk's eyes as he looked down the gun from the breech end, his thumb over the vent hole to detect when the cartridge was truly seated, but there was no hint of recognition.

Then the ball, clapped in by Doggo and followed by a final

wad. Kydd's movements on the rammer were fierce and positive. If they could get away another broadside before the enemy, it was the same as doubling their firepower.

"Run out!" Stirk shouted hoarsely. The gun bellowed and slammed in.

Kydd leapt into action again, the same motions. The work, the need to intermesh his movements with the others, meant there was no time for fear.

The second broadside from *Citoyenne* came smashing in, a long roll of terrible crashes instead of the massed simultaneity of the first. Kydd froze as they beat in on his senses. To his left, next to him, Kydd saw Gully drop to his knees with a muffled cry. In the smoky darkness it was difficult to see the cause, but the spreading dark stain under him was plain enough. He fell to his side, and scrabbled at the fat of his upper thigh. Kydd stared at the foot-long splinter, which had been driven up by a rampaging ball and transfixed him. Gully wept with pain and crawled away in a trail of blood. Stirk's eyes searched wildly for a replacement.

Kydd glanced across the gun and saw Renzi, his face grave, and thought how easy it would have been for his friend to be a victim instead. He crushed the thought, and shoved the side tackle rope into the hand of the unknown seaman who was taking Gully's place.

The enemy were pacing them; there would not be any doubling of firepower—it would be a fight to the death among equals.

Powlett strolled slowly and grimly on the quarterdeck as debris rained down from above. Only the sails of the enemy were visible, but in her fighting tops above the smoke, moving figures could be seen leveling muskets at *Artemis*'s quarterdeck.

Neville clasped his hands firmly behind him and paced slowly on the other side of the deck.

Parry had his sword out and was gripping the mizzen shrouds as he glared across at the enemy. Merrydew had disappeared into the hell forward with his mates, and the young midshipman attending on the Captain was visibly trembling.

A second broadside from *Citoyenne* crashed out into the thinning smoke between them. As the awful onslaught struck, Powlett was enveloped for a moment by the powder smoke. Then a sudden shock was transmitted through the deck planking. A thin scream came from out of nowhere and Neville was struck violently, sent sprawling by the flailing limbs of a man falling from aloft. Neville picked himself up; the man now lay untidily, dead.

A round-shot had nearly severed the driver gaff between the throat and peak halliards. The long spar began to sag. Then, in a slow rending, it fell apart. Without support the big sail first crumpled then ripped from top to bottom, the heavy boom and rigging crushing and entangling the larboard six-pounder crews.

"Can't hold 'er!" the helmsman shouted, spinning the wheel fast to prevent the ship sagging to leeward and the enemy.

Powlett turned to the midshipman. "Tell 'em to get in the headsails!" he snapped. *Artemis* slowed, her fine sailing qualities useless. Without a driver sail aft if she showed canvas forward they would pivot around in a helpless spiral.

They could neither maneuver nor run away. The smoke drifted over the bright sea, revealing *Citoyenne* pulling triumphantly ahead. The sun caught a quick flash of glass on her quarterdeck as her officers eagerly inspected the damage to *Artemis*.

It was obvious that there was no way they could effect a battle repair on the driver quickly—it was a unique fore-and-aft sail that needed special gear to set it out from the mast. And without maneuverability they could only take what was coming . . .

After a few hundred yards *Citoyenne* began her turn into the wind. This would take her across the bows of *Artemis*, and would let her rake her adversary as she tacked around. This nightmare of a full broadside smashing headlong into her bows and down the length of the vessel was now upon them.

Forward the experienced fo'c'slemen saw the danger and frantically re-set the headsails—jib, staysails, anything. *Artemis* responded,
falling away off the wind; but in so doing she kept her broadside to bear, turning in time with *Citoyenne*. With all the fury of
helplessness *Artemis* thundered out her broadside again, strikes on
Citoyenne visible now from her quarterdeck. The reply was thin and
ragged, but this was only because most of the experienced French
seamen would be at work putting the ship about.

Citoyenne completed her tack and was now ready to pass back
in the opposite direction, poised to deliver her next broadside
with full crews. Her tactics had also given her the weather gauge,
an upwind position, which would allow her now to dictate the
conditions of the battle. The French frigate began her pass, but
there was one advantage that had been left *Artemis*—*Citoyenne*'s
battered side faced them once more, but it was their own undam-
aged opposite side that awaited the clash.

As the two vessels passed, guns crashed out as they bore, no
pretense at disciplined broadsides. Like the potshots of a crazy
drunk, the cruel iron shot pounded into *Artemis* as the ships
slipped past.

At one point, Spershott, emerging from below, was flung across
the deck like a child's discarded rag doll. He did not move where
he sprawled. Two sailors took him by the arms and legs and
dragged him below.

Powlett did not pause in his calm pacing.

Citoyenne ceased fire as she reached beyond *Artemis*. The enemy
frigate wore around, so sure of her victim that she eschewed the
faster tacking in going about for the more deliberate but less tax-
ing wear. In wearing ship, *Citoyenne* would now pass much closer.
This was the act of a supremely confident commander, who
wanted to finish things quickly.

"Mr. Neville!" roared Powlett, from the other side of the deck.
"Repel boarders!" He was grimed in smoke but stood stiff as a

ramrod. The French frigate was pressing close because she was coming in to board. With her superior weight of numbers she was going to end it all with a final broadside before boarding *Artemis* in the gunsmoke. "Aye aye, sir!" Neville yelled back.

Powlett cracked a grim smile. "Go to it!"

The gundeck was a pit of horror. With the space wreathed in thick choking powder smoke, shot through with screams and cries, Kydd knew only the unvarying cycle of load and fire. The wet sheepskin of his sponge met the blistering iron each time with a mad sizzle.

At each pass of the enemy there was a monotonous crashing and thudding of round-shot strikes.

The guns fell silent. It seemed on the gundeck that *Citoyenne* was taking time wearing around instead of tacking. The smoke gradually cleared, and those who could peered from the gunports. The enemy was returning, closing, with the clear intention of finishing *Artemis*.

"Repel boarders! *Awaaaay,* first division of boarders!"

Kydd hesitated.

"Off yer go, cock," Stirk said, in a hoarse voice. "An'—best o' luck, mate."

With his heart pounding with dread, Kydd rushed up the forehatch. On deck the ship was in ruinous condition—shot-through sails, ragged and unraveled rigging hanging down and swinging in the breeze, and scored and splintered decks littered with blocks and debris. The last act had begun.

He stumbled across to the foremast and yanked away a boarding pike from its stand. A boatswain's mate directed him aft where he joined the little group on the quarterdeck. Lieutenant Neville was there with drawn sword. He had thrown off his coat and now stood dramatically in front of them. "We shall meet the French like heroes and we will drive them back into the sea."

There was a prickling in his right leg that distracted Kydd. Below the knee a splinter had torn his trouser and had penetrated his flesh before ripping its way out again. It was the coagulated blood sticking and pulling at his leg hairs that annoyed him. He allowed a twisted smile to acknowledge his first wound in battle, then cut away his duck trousers above the wound.

Astern, *Citoyenne* took in sail preparatory to coming in. On her fo'c'sle her boarders were massed, a menacing, shouting crowd.

"Pikemen at the ready!" Neville called loudly. "To the bulwarks, advance!"

"Belay that." It was Powlett. "Madness—on the deck, get down! They'll be using grape, you fool."

They fell to the deck, behind the low bulwarks. The forward guns of *Citoyenne* were charged with grapeshot and they unleashed their hail of deadly small balls. The shot battered and tore at the nettings and side, but did not find flesh to tear.

It was a different matter for the carronades on *Artemis*. These ugly little weapons, short and stubby cannon on a slide, could bear aft, and when they replied it was with canister, a sleeting cloud of musket balls, which found targets aplenty in the bodies of the boarders. Shouts and jeers turned instantly to shrieks and cries, and to Kydd's horrified fascination, runnels of blood began coursing down the bow of the ship as it passed by their quarterdeck.

"Silly buggers," grunted the carronade gun captain.

The other carronade had held its fire and its captain was fiercely concentrating on the changing angle. *Citoyenne*'s bow swept by, but still he did not fire.

"Men, he will attempt to board in the smoke of his broadside," Neville called loudly. His voice broke with the intensity of his warning.

Kydd understood and rose with the others to the ready. Grounding the butt end of the boarding pike he thrust it forward and outward and tried to remember all he had been told. Soon there would be a final broadside and somewhere from the powder smoke would come a screaming pack of Frenchmen. He had to be ready to meet them.

The enemy boat-space passed with still no firing, but *Citoyenne* was slowing for the kill. Kydd held his breath. Suddenly the remaining carronade blasted off. It caught Kydd unawares, but its shot, a twenty-four-pounder round-shot, was well aimed. It smashed squarely into the base of the enemy's mizzen mast, which slowly fell toward them, bringing down the entire mass of sails, spars and rigging—and the hapless men in the mizzen top—over the side.

But there was an additional and crucial injury. The shot that had chewed a fatal bite from the mizzen mast had first smashed the ship's wheel. Without helm *Citoyenne* was out of control. She surged away for a short time but then swung toward *Artemis*. The angle opened but they were so close that the result was inevitable— the long bowsprit of the French ship speared across the decks of *Artemis* between the foremast and mainmast and the frigate thumped heavily to a stop, her bow hard up against the midships of her prey.

Kydd watched, appalled. Inertia drove at the French frigate, but her locked fore-end prevented her completing the move: hundreds of tons forced the big bowsprit against *Artemis*'s mainmast. It stopped dead, then strained and creaked noisily under the pressure.

Something had to give—either *Artemis*'s mainmast or *Citoyenne*'s entire bowsprit and forward gear. Both ships seemed to hold their breath. There was a series of thunderclap cracking noises. Then French fir gave best to British oak, and in a deafening, splintering surge the bowsprit broke and the whole fore assembly of *Citoyenne* gave way. Her bow dissolved into a tangle of spars, rigging and sails, most of which lay draped on *Artemis*'s midships. Relieved of the frenzy of forces, *Citoyenne* swung into *Artemis* and came to rest alongside.

"Stand to!" yelled Neville.

This was now the decisive time—no more maneuvering, no more waiting. The battle had reached its climax. Seamen spread out along the bulwarks, pikes resolutely outward, but they were so pitifully few.

Powlett stood stock still, staring at the *Citoyenne.*

"Sir?" said Neville.

"There's something wrong aboard the Frenchy," Powlett muttered. There seemed to be confusion, a turmoil of directionless men. A number had begun swarming up the rigging on some desperate mission, but angry shouts indicated that the order had been countermanded or misunderstood. Some milled about the decks but nowhere were boarders massing for the attack.

"Her captain has fallen," Powlett said in a low voice. Then louder, savagely, he said, "And we have our chance, Mr. Neville." He drew his sword. "*Awaaaay,* boarders!"

Neville looked thunderstruck—then grinned. "Aye aye, sir! Boarders away!"

A full-throated cheer roared up from the men. This was better than waiting tamely for the enemy. Pikes were thrown to the deck; men raced to the arms chest and snatched their weapons—a brace of pistols, a cutlass, some took a tomahawk. Kydd stuffed a pair of pistols into his wide belt and also grabbed a cutlass, which he held as naked steel. Tensing nervously, he turned back to Neville. The man seemed strangely serene. His eyes flashed then he turned to his men. "Boarders to the fore—advance! God save the King!" With his sword stabbing ahead, he plunged forward. The first division of boarders followed him.

Men scrambled on and up to the remains of the bowsprit. It lay across the battered-down bulwarks of *Artemis* amidships, a perfect bridge into the heart of the enemy. With mad cheering and wild waving of cutlasses they were soon on the broad top of the big spar. Slashing at the entangled rigging, Neville forced his way across to the fo'c'sle of the other ship, to the rapidly gathering band of enraged French. Kydd stumbled and charged with the others, his thoughts a mad whirl of the imperative for victory—and survival.

The gundeck cleared of smoke, revealing the wreckage of battle. The occasional cannon crashed out from their foe, but with the ruin of *Citoyenne*'s fore-rigging there was a pause in the fighting. The after end of *Citoyenne* completed its swing, and the shot-scarred side of the frigate filled the frame of the gunport. Above them on the upper deck came a roar of British cheering.

Renzi looked at the smoke-begrimed Stirk, who met his gaze with a tired smile. "Looks like we got ourselves a tartar by th' tail," he said. The slight relative motion of the vessels brought their gunports into line. With men away repelling boarders the British guns could not be served: they had to stand silent until the tide of battle had turned.

Through the port Renzi could see erratic movements in the other ship. Then he understood. The thumping of feet on the deck above was *toward* the ship's side—it was *they* who were boarding! With a breaking wave of emotion he screamed, "We're boarding! By God, it's us!"

Stirk glared at him—realization struck and he threw himself at the midships arms chest, and brought out a cutlass. "Move, you bastards!"

Renzi hurled himself to the chest and snatched up a cutlass for himself, jostled impatiently by others.

With a bull-like roar Stirk lunged into the gaping gunport, through and on to the enemy gundeck. Renzi followed close behind, and jumped into the hostile deck, fetching up next to a dismounted gun. The scene was a crazy impression of bodies, live and dead. The low deckhead left no room for subtleties—the swordsman in Renzi sank to butchery, the robust greased steel of the Sea Service cutlass cleaving and plunging.

Their bold attack was unexpected, and opposition melted as

more British seamen poured through the gunports and battered a path toward the cabin spaces aft.

Jumping to the enemy foredeck Kydd nearly impaled himself on a pike shoved at him by a fearfully pale young man. Kydd's cutlass came up and being inside the long pike he turned its length to his advantage—it was easy to force the pike aside, leaving the man at his mercy.

The face sagged in sudden realization. Kydd's blade slashed forward and with an inhuman shriek the Frenchman crunched and gouted blood. Kydd drew the cutlass back, the gray steel now streaked red.

The man was already at Kydd's feet, a spreading pool of blood under his jerking body. Kydd looked up. A larger seaman with a mustache threw himself toward him, his cutlass ready at point. Kydd clumsily came to an outside half-hanger and felt a violent clash of steel. The cutlass flashed back and Kydd's inside guard was only just in time and instinctive. The assault ended in a deadly slither along his blade to the hilt. It banged against his forehead and he felt the hot burn of a wound.

The man was overbearing, thrusting, slashing—Kydd gave ground. Suddenly his antagonist slipped on the spreading pool of blood, and reflexively threw out his arms. Kydd thrust out and felt his blade jar against bone before sinking deep into softer tissue. The cutlass was jerked from his hands, but it was the man falling to his knees, Kydd's blade jutting from his chest.

Kydd looked around wildly. It was impossible to make sense of the mêlée, and he caught the flash of movement of a French officer who lunged toward him with a rapier. Horror seized Kydd, but in a frenzied split second he remembered his pistols and drew one from his belt. At the full length of his arm he shoved the heavy weapon straight into the face of the officer and pulled the trigger. The man's face became a mask of blood and bone and he crashed to the deck in front of Kydd.

His first victim still lay sprawled on his side. Kydd stamped his foot on the body of the other seaman and heaved out his cutlass. He looked around. Men were fleeing, general confusion. He heard Neville's shouted orders from ahead, and hurried forward to the scrimmage by the boat-space. It had broken up by the time he reached it, but re-formed farther aft.

Abreast the main jeer bitts a wall of the enemy had formed across the deck and was pressing the seamen from *Artemis* hard. Surrounded by enemy, Neville was in the front, his blade faster than a snake's tongue. Kydd fell back, arms exhausted and burning with fatigue, but there was no retreat. He slashed and parried, swaying forward and back, weariness blunting his skills. Stubbornly he called on his last store of strength, furious that things had to end in this way.

Suddenly, gloriously, there was the sound of wild cheering as Stirk boiled up from the after hatchway in the enemy's rear. He whirled his blade like a lunatic and close behind him were Renzi and the others in a triumphant assault.

The French broke, then ran. Screaming harshly Kydd flailed after them, but they bolted down the hatchway and into the rigging, leaving the British in possession of the deck.

"Follow me!" screamed Neville. Kydd stumbled after him, a huge grin at the sight of Renzi alongside him. They reached the quarterdeck. Neville's sword slashed at the clumsy attempt the French had made to keep the *tricolore* hoisted high on the stump of the wrecked mizzenmast, and the enemy colors tumbled down. He held them aloft in his hands, an ecstatic expression on his face. Insane cheering broke out, again and again, and echoed from *Artemis*.

Kydd stopped and lowered his stained weapon in a daze. It was victory! A swelling pride swept over him suddenly and he looked down the long deck of the enemy ship with its piled-up ruin of rigging and bodies, a battlefield of blood and desperation—and knew the warrior's pulsing triumph.

Around him others had come to a stop, as did the French. Sullen and tense, first one, then the rest of the enemy let their pikes, tomahawks and cutlasses drop to the deck. A strange silence hammered at Kydd's ears after the furious clash of battle. Then the sailors began to move again at the shouts of petty officers as they directed their men to surround the prisoners.

Renzi appeared, his smoke-grimed figure and apologetic half-smile making Kydd feel guilty that he had not spared time to think of his friend as he had hewn and slashed his way along the enemy decks.

Beside him Neville staggered then steadied himself against the fallen mizzen. He seemed to be working under some emotional burden. "Well done, you men. I—I'm proud of you all," he said huskily. Sheathing his sword clumsily he looked up to where the ensign of the Royal Navy floated free above the French on the stump of the mast. His eyes did not leave the flags; he seemed to sag.

Worried, Kydd then noticed the deck beneath Neville—bright flowers of scarlet blossomed on the planking. Neville slid down to a sitting position, looking oddly preoccupied. Kydd moved to his side and steadied him, but Neville shrugged off his support irritably. "S-secure the prisoners," he ordered no one in particular. His eyes had a glassy look.

No one moved: they were staring at him. "A-and cu' away thi' raffle," he said, in a pitiable version of his usual crisp delivery. The eyes focused. "Abou' y-your duty, m-men!" he ordered, in a querulous tone. Kydd felt at his side—his hand came away steeped in blood. Neville's eyes turned to him, puzzled, then his body seemed to collapse inwards of itself and, with Kydd tenderly supporting, Neville subsided to the deck. He lay still on his back, but his eyes moved, seeking out the ensign, which they fixed and held. For long moments he did not move, then gently, his body relaxed and stilled.

Kydd waited, but the mantle of death was unmistakable. "He's gone," he murmured, and closed the still open eyes. He felt an upwelling of emotion, which threatened to overwhelm him.

A voice spoke next to him, a cool, steadying voice. "As of this moment there is no British officer aboard," said Renzi. Kydd looked up at him, grateful for the intervention but not sure what he meant.

"We must find the enemy captain at once," Renzi went on. Of course—the capitulation could not be completed until the Captain had yielded his sword. Renzi crossed over to one of the growing numbers of disarmed French sailors. The man looked dazed as he questioned him, then pointed toward a knot of bodies draped around the base of the mainmast.

The imperatives of war meant that the corpse must be found and deprived of its sword, and Kydd reluctantly approached the charnel house, where men had been dragged to die. Movement caught his eye. Propped up against the mast was a hideously wounded man with his left hip and part of his back blasted away by a round-shot. The man was doggedly biting and tearing at papers, his eyes rolling in unspeakable pain.

Kydd knelt down and saw gold lace beneath the clotted blood. He realized that this was the Captain. Overcome with compassion, Kydd reached out to stop the manic activity.

He was pushed aside by Parry, who grabbed uselessly at the paper fragments. "Damn him!" he said in disgust.

The Frenchman smiled, and passed from the world.

"The Master believes we shall descry St. Catherine's at seven bells," Renzi said. His tone was guarded, but Kydd could tell he was charged with feeling. They were sitting on the fore-hatch, busy with other seamen on endless coils of shot-riven rope. It was not unpleasant—the morning sun was warm and beneficent, their progress a crawl under the jury driver, an ingenious contraption of spare topmast and leather butt lashing.

Kydd had lain sleepless in his hammock all night, trying to put the nightmarish, jerking scenes of death and peril from his mind. Time and again the piteous pale face of the youngster he had slaughtered cringed and begged. Kydd questioned his own humanity until his brain staggered under the weight of his doubts.

Wallowing astern, the *Citoyenne* pumped ship every hour, her hull and rigging a crazy patchwork of hasty repair, but above the tricolor floated *Artemis*'s battle ensign.

"Did you notice?" Renzi said, in a low voice.

Kydd knew that his friend would now reveal what was troubling him.

"The French captain, Maillot," Renzi said quietly.

Kydd remembered the gory corpse, the manic biting. "What about him?"

"The papers he was destroying."

"Yes?"

"It was his commission."

"But all officers carry theirs on them in battle—in case they're captured."

"Parry found it amusing," Renzi said drily. "Said it was a fine time to find it a worthless Jacobin scrap of paper, that he must destroy it."

"But—"

"Exactly. I do not believe a man in his last minutes would think to commit such an act."

"Then why—"

Renzi looked away. "It was an act by the bravest man I know," he said softly.

Kydd sighed with exasperation. "Why so?" he said.

Renzi opened his mouth to speak, but changed his mind. "You will forgive me, but at times my philosophies lead me down strange paths." He picked up his splice and continued his work.

"Damn strange, if y' asks me." Kydd snorted.

Renzi's face lifted—it was troubled. "Would you have me take the last mortal act of a gallant man and turn it to ashes? Or do I honor his memory and remain silent?"

There was no doubt in Kydd's mind. "If it is a matter touching on the safety of England then y' have no choice—y'r logic will say, you are overborne by the higher."

"Yes."

"Would you be so timid, were you to make the decision under stress o' battle? You would not—the matter is not decided till the flag is down."

"You are in the right of it, dear fellow." Renzi stared down for a moment. "Come," he said.

He went to the shrouds, pretending to be passing a line. Kydd joined him, understanding that Renzi needed to be away from the ears of others.

"His commission, he would not destroy it—but he would if in his final agony he believed it to be some other paper, one that was of vital urgency to the security of his nation. I believe that in one of his *other* pockets we shall find this paper, whatever it might be."

Kydd stared at him. "We must tell this."

"And have Parry admit his contempt was misplaced? I think not. We find it ourselves, if indeed it is there."

The body of Captain Maillot was laid out in the orlop, on the main-hatch. It would be given a funeral with full honors when they reached England in one or two days, but meanwhile it would rest below, sword and cocked hat laid carefully upon it.

A single lanthorn shed a soft light on the still form, and on the marine sentry loosely at attention at the foot of the shroud.

They approached and the sentry snapped awake. "Gerroff!"

"This the Frog captain?" Kydd asked.

"Yeah—now yer've clapped peepers on 'im, bugger off!"

Kydd sauntered up to the sentry. "Last chance we gets, y'know. Seein' his face an' that," he went on. The sentry didn't reply, stiffening his posture.

Renzi glanced meaningfully at Kydd, who tried again. "It was we who got to him first, you knows," he said. "There he was, all gory an' all, we were the ones who saw him, there dyin'."

The sentry shifted slightly and said from the corner of his mouth, "Saw yez do yer boardin'. That wuz a plucky do—bad luck to me if it ain't."

"Then let's see his face, pay our respects like," Kydd wheedled.

The man looked nervous. "Me sergeant catches me . . ."

Kydd eased a black bottle from inside his waistcoat. He started, as though noticing the sentry for the first time. "Why, there's m' bad manners. You've been down here, looking after his Nobbs, with never a drop—here, take a rummer while we have a quick peek."

The sentry offered his musket to Kydd to hold, and took a long pull. Renzi quickly undid the lacing at the head of the shroud to reveal the pale face and staring eyes of Maillot. A sickening odor drifted up.

"'Ere, yer can't do that!" The sentry had noticed Renzi move the sword and hat and continue unlacing down the length of the corpse.

"Have another pull if ye likes," Kydd urged.

Renzi found nothing in the pockets. If there had been an alternative paper it was not there anymore. He knew that if they were found, any explanation would be futile. It would be assumed they were robbing the corpse—a hanging offense. He threw a despairing glance at Kydd, then clamped his kerchief to his face and burrowed deeper into the dead captain's inner clothing. He tried to ignore the coldness of death.

"Hey, stop that, yer thievin' sod!" The sentry had come to his senses, and tried to pull Renzi off the body. Kydd held him back, and at that moment Renzi froze. His hand withdrew. In it was a single sheet of closely written paper. He held it to the light, and Kydd could see his eyes gleam. "Set him to rights, Tom. We have it."

The paper was stuffed back and the body restored to a state of proper reverence.

Snatching back the bottle, Kydd hurried after Renzi to the open air again.

"Secret coast signals—priceless," whispered Renzi. "But how—"

Kydd grinned back at him. "Easy! Let's say you overheard the French prisoners talking among 'emselves, thought it proper to lay it before Black Jack that he might find somethin' interesting should he rummage the body."

CHAPTER 2

≈

"God rot their bones for an infernal set of useless lubberly rogues!"
exploded the Admiral, his face reddening at the pressure of the
starched collar at his neck.

His wife sighed in exasperation. "Now, John, you well know how I
disapprove of your sea language in the house."

The Admiral held his tongue, acutely aware of how very little it
would take to provoke him to indulge his rage. He took some satisfaction
from casting loose the fastening of his high collar, hoping it would be
concealed under the snowy lace cravat. "You would bear me some sympathy, m'dear, were you to know the very considerable vexations I
endure as a consequence of His Majesty's unexpected decision to visit,"
he growled. He would get the sympathy, he knew, but not the understanding. King George's sudden decision to leave the capital, to witness
personally the triumphant entry of the battered victor and her prize,
was causing untold difficulties for the Port Admiral.

"Of course, my love, it must be a grievous trial to you." Lady Clowes
had her own views on what constituted a vexation: she was personally
responsible for the success of the royal entertainments, and if they were a
failure in any way it would be held against her, but if they passed off
without drama she would be forgotten. She had only that odious flag
lieutenant to assist her, and he a simple sea officer with no appreciation
of the subtleties of Court etiquette. "Try not to think about it too much,
dear," she added absently. Her thoughts were more on what to do with
the ambitious Lady Saxton. The Dockyard Commissioner's wife was
married to a mere post captain but he was a baronet: if these ambitions
were to be contained she faced a nice dilemma of precedence at the
Court presentations.

"I beg pardon, sir." The flag lieutenant appeared at the doorway.

"Damn you, sir! When we are—"

"My earnest apologies, sir, but we have had word from Brigadier Crossley," the lieutenant broke in carefully. *"He desires you to know that the press of people now is such that he fears for the safe progress of the King's procession."* He waited, his eyes averted from Lady Clowes.

"Ah." The Admiral felt his choler rising once more. So much for the Army—nothing to do but march up and down all day and now they couldn't be trusted to clear a path through the crowds. *"I shall attend in my office within the hour. I'm sure they'll hold till then,"* he said testily.

"Sir," the lieutenant acknowledged, and vanished.

"John?" His wife had seen the signs and moved to head off the storm.

"Yes?"

"Be so good as to rehearse with me why this event is so glorious at this time," she said demurely.

"It's simple, my dear. We're at war with a mad parcel of rascals who are unstoppable on land. This is the first time we've been able to try their mettle at sea as equals, and now we've proved they can be stopped. The country has good reason to be grateful to Captain Powlett, I believe." The Admiral said no more, but he found he was rather looking forward to hearing about the now famous engagement at first hand.

Kydd slipped hand over hand down the fore-topgallant backstay to the deck, arriving breathless. "Something amiss—I c'n see quantities of people, Nicholas, all th' way fr'm Portsmouth Point along t' the old castle."

Renzi performed a neat belay on the line as he contemplated Kydd's excitement. If there really was any civil disturbance in Portsmouth they would not be proceeding calmly into harbor with their prize.

"There is talk that the French contemplate a landing," he said.

Kydd looked at him sideways. "There's something happened," he retorted stubbornly.

They had reached a point some five miles off the Nab and the brisk northeasterly was making it tricky for them to gain ground toward Spithead, hampered as they were by their jury rig and *Citoyenne* under tow astern.

Sailors gathered on the foredeck to try to make sense of the tumult ashore. "Fleet's still at anchor," observed Adam, adding that this would not be the case were there any real threat.

Petit paused in his work, and tried to make out the anonymous multitude of humanity up and down the distant shore. "Ain't never seen a crowd like it since the last age."

"'Oo's that, then?" said Stirk.

As *Artemis* approached St. Helens, first one, then several small craft came around the headland. From their press of sail they appeared to be in some degree of commotion, their fore-and-aft canvas straining perilously in the sea breeze.

Artemis opened the angle into the last stretch before Spithead, the sailing boats pressing forward fast, with several larger hulks and lighters also creeping out toward them.

The first of the boats reached them. It was a small yawl, crammed with passengers who waved energetically. The boat hissed past and tacked smartly about, dangerously close. A second arrived, with figures clinging to the shrouds shouting a frantic welcome. Soon there were dozens of sailing craft, weaving and dodging, the raucous whoops from their passengers leaving no doubt why they had come.

"Well, glory be," Petit breathed. "It's fer us, mates."

On the quarterdeck Captain Powlett emerged from the hatchway and paced slowly with a fixed expression. He wore full dress uniform with sword and decorations, a resplendent figure compared to his usual Spartan sea rig.

The far-off bark of a gun broke through the hullabaloo, the smoke eddying away from the bow of a naval cutter trying to break through the scrimmage. It fussed its way alongside.

The group of seamen forward watched as an officer clambered aboard and a polite exchange followed on the quarterdeck. Then things moved swiftly. The tow was cast off, and lighters and hulks gathered about to take the prize in hand, leaving the battle-pitted *Artemis* to proceed on alone under easy sail. Their salute to the Admiral at Spithead banged out regularly, but they passed the great fleet at anchor without stopping—they would enter the harbor itself.

Artemis shortened to topsails for the last mile into the narrow entrance, the line of passage taking her parallel with the shore a bare couple of hundred yards to starboard, past the furiously cheering crowds that swarmed over every imaginable viewpoint. Grateful that his station in the foretop allowed him to witness these marvelous events, Kydd looked out on a scene that he knew would stay with him all his life.

A gun went off below him. It startled him: they had no reason to salute. Then a seaman pointed out the colorful standard hoisted on the dockyard signal tower. "'Is Nibs," he said laconically.

The salute banged on—the full twenty-one for the King of England. They were now passing through the close entrance. They glided past the rickety old buildings of Portsmouth Point close in to starboard, every window full of cheering figures. On the opposite side of the entrance was the darkened brick solidity of Fort Blockhouse, and beyond it Haslar Naval Hospital. As many wounded and sick sailors that were able to had hobbled down to the water's edge, and a military band thumped out "Hearts of Oak."

On they sailed, past the low white medieval turrets of the gun wharf, then where the harbor inside widened again, to Portsmouth Hard with its taverns and hostelries alive with crowds. Two men-o'-war moored midstream had manned ship. Hundreds of men lined along bare masts and yards gave full-throated cheers to the now famous frigate.

Abruptly they were upon the long dockyard buildings. There was a flurry of activity as *Artemis* swung about into the wind and slowed. Her sails were brailed up and lines were relayed ashore by waiting boats and they were warped in alongside the dock.

Aware of the official welcoming party on the quay, Kydd felt uneasy and self-conscious, on the one hand wishing that the assembly of pomp and finery could be somewhere else, and on the other seized with a thrill of expectation.

With her sails in a harbor stow and the running rigging secured and flemished down, a special gangway was positioned from the quarterdeck to the dock. It had white canvas-covered rope hand-lines, and on each supporting post there was a small royal crest.

"Into line, Kydd!" The harsh whisper from the Master-at-Arms caught him by surprise. "Sideboy!" the man snapped, seeing that Kydd did not react immediately. He was pushed into a double line of men at the head of the gangway after the boatswain's mates. At the inner end of the line the Captain and officers waited, their tension evident. On the wharf a similar line of redcoats formed facing each other with muskets rigidly at the present.

"Stand by!" snapped Rowley, the officer-of-the-watch. The boatswain's mates whipped up their silver calls to the ready. There was silence throughout the ship. The noises of celebration outside the dockyard gates sounded even rowdier.

"Pipe!" Rowley rapped. The calls blasted out together and Kydd's eyes slid to the small group who slowly mounted the gangway. In the lead was King George and behind him, the Queen.

When the monarch reached the deck the piping ceased. No one moved a muscle. Genially, King George looked about him, not more than a few feet from Kydd. He paced forward a step or two, glancing around with interest, then turned to his aide-de-camp. "Soon took the gloss off the sides of the Frenchy, showed him the way into Portsmouth Harbor, hey—hey?" His large rubicund face lit up.

"Indeed so, sire."

The kindly eyes turned to Kydd.

A voice from behind murmured, "Thomas Kydd, foretopman, sir."

The King nodded. "Where are ye from?"

Kydd's heart stopped. "Guildford town—er, Y'r Majesty," he said, touching his forehead automatically in a naval salute. Too late he realized that kings would probably expect something more in the way of a bow.

The broad white eyebrows rose. "Fine place f'r turnips, very fine! An' sheep too—prime sheep, y'r Surrey cross." He looked at Kydd somewhat bemused, as if finding it hard to reconcile farming talk with the strong young sailor before him.

Before Kydd's frozen brain could think of a reply, his sovereign had moved on to address others, but Kydd was content simply to stare ahead, suffused with happiness. Nobody at all in his acquaintance, high and low, had ever claimed an introduction to the King himself!

There was a murmuring of the most elegant politeness as Powlett's officers were introduced and the party moved down the main hatchway to view the scars of battle.

Kydd heaved a sigh of relief, but by this time others had mounted the gangway, and the quarterdeck was getting crowded. With a rustle of material a vision in light rose and cream paused in front of him. The girl pouted and fingered the sturdy black anchor buttons on his jacket. "You lif on the schip all zer time?" she uttered, in thick German-accented English. Kydd could only nod while he thought frantically how he should address a foreign princess. His brain could only come up with half-remembered stories of princesses in fairy tales.

She was a good head shorter than him, and her clear pale eyes looked up at him through extraordinary long eyelashes. Her hairstyle was markedly plainer than the other women's, and was not caked in powder. "Pliss to show me your brafe schip," she begged, and smiled winningly.

She would only be about seventeen, what remained of his objective mind observed. Reddening to the roots of his hair, Kydd mumbled something and pushed through the gawping crowd forward. To larboard of the mainmast was a stubborn darkening of the deck planking. "Where our first lieutenant, er, fell."

Her hand flew to her mouth as she took in the implications of the stain, then she turned back to him.

"He lives yet," Kydd stuttered, "he is below at this, um, time." He tried a bow, but his body was not the willowy type, and it turned out an awkward jerk. Her long gloved hand touched his arm as she pealed with laughter. After a moment Kydd joined in.

"Ah, Sophia, there you are." A tall hussar in dark green uniform, gold frogging and ornate hat slipped neatly between the two of them, his back to Kydd. "Allow me to escort you around the boat," he said, offering his arm.

She pulled free, and defiantly dropped Kydd a magnificent curtsy. She held it, her eyes locked on his. The moment passed, then she laughed delightedly, and took the soldier's arm. She moved away, throwing a single glance back at Kydd, who stared after them, afraid to break the spell.

"All the haaaands! All hands on deck—lay aft!"

Kydd, at the fore-royals, had caught a glimpse of his princess as the party went ashore. She was looking up, as if searching among the hundreds of cheering men.

The ship's company had only just come down from manning the yards for a three times three for His Majesty. The King had paused on his way back through the lines of redcoats and turned, clearly affected. He bowed this way and that while the huzzahs echoed from the buildings, the sailors redoubling their efforts at his unfeigned pleasure.

They assembled now on the main deck below the boat-space, and on the gangways each side, some hanging in the rigging to get a better view. Powlett stood forward of the wheel, his face working under evident emotion.

Kydd waited impatiently for Renzi. It was with the utmost

pleasure that he told him of his meeting with a princess. His friend stared in frank amazement, and then rubbed his chin. "That would probably have been Princess Sophia of Mecklenburg, I believe." His face held every indication of envy, causing great satisfaction to Kydd. Then Renzi chuckled. "You should keep an eye to windward, my dear fellow, for after the unfortunate passing of the Duke of Buccleuch's eldest, she is now an unattached maiden." Kydd's smile broadened.

Boatswain's calls piped the still, and the men quickly fell into silence.

"His Majesty is—pleased," Powlett said, seeming to have difficulty with the words. "And he has—will be doing me the deepest honor, in conferring on me a knighthood." He paused and looked down at his spotless court shoes. The ship erupted into cheers upon cheers.

He looked up, the hard face mobile. "He has also been so kind as to present me with a purse. In it is a golden guinea for every man. His Majesty commands that with this his honest tars shall drink his health in a bumper." The cheers were genuine and long.

Powlett's voice strengthened. "In the matter of prize money . . ." he grinned, knowing the interest his words were creating ". . . I have to tell you that I have been led to understand that, subject to survey, the Frenchman will be bought into the Service!" A wave of muttering passed among the assembly. Prize money was a subject for intense satisfaction, not cheers. "And as a result, and in view of our previous successes, it is my intention to make a preliminary award now, while your liberty tickets are being prepared."

There was no stopping it. "Three cheers an' a tiger fer Cap'n Powlett!" came a roar from the throng. The hoarse cheering went on and on, emotion from the battle finally released in a flood of affection for the tough Captain. "Carry on!" Powlett said, and abruptly turned on his heel and went below.

*   *   *

The golden orbs above the old dockyard gate seemed to draw the people like a magnet, all of them eager to catch a sight of their famed hearts of oak. Beside the marine sentry were soldiers, shoving back at the crowd. Kydd was astonished at the press of people, the riot of heaving, jostling humanity. "What ship—what ship?" The cries were insistent.

An elderly seaman from another vessel answered nervously, indistinct in the clamor. With shouts of derision he was shouldered aside. In their turn Kydd and Renzi were challenged. "*Artemis!*" they replied, and were instantly swept off by the adoring crowd, faces on all sides babbling and shouting, alive with joy and drink. It seemed that their escort meant them to go no farther than the Admiral Benbow close by the Hard.

There was a deafening uproar inside the taproom; red faces and blue smoke, sweating men and flashing-eyed femininity along with the sickly sweet smell of beer and wet sawdust. "*Artemis!*" The shout was relayed around the room, and without delay a barmaid arrived to press tankards of foaming dark beer on the pair.

"To the sons o' Neptune 'oo are Old England's right true glory!" A generous roar followed, and tankards tilted. Kydd flushed with pleasure and raised his own.

Renzi noticed a calculating gleam in several female faces. Like birds of prey they detached from their perches and sidled across. The two sailors found themselves with a brace apiece, one on each arm. Renzi skillfully disengaged, but Kydd did not seem to be in any hurry to part.

"Gave 'em a right quiltin', did yer not, darlin'?" one said, her face flushed and hair peeping out from under her mob cap. She looked up at Kydd's face and said huskily, "Wager you didn't hang back, me lovely, when the call ter duty went out."

The other fingered his jacket. Defying the venomous looks of the first, she said, "Why doesn't you an' me take a short cruise? I c'n show yez a time as'll keep yer warm for a year." The first raised her leg gently and caressed Kydd's thigh. He colored and pretended to enjoy his beer while she teased him toward her.

The tug-of-war continued until a thin-faced man in drab shore clothes appeared, and plucked at Kydd's sleeves. "Ben Watkins— mizzen topsailman o' the *Duchess* as was," he said, against the din. "Heard tell it was a near-run thing, mates."

The pulling and tugging subsided a little. "Yes," said Kydd shortly, but with a smile.

"Know somethin' about it, me bein' aboard when we took the—the *Majesté* that time," Watkins said. Kydd looked at him. The man's voice lowered. "See, mates, has ter bear up for Poverty Bay like, see, and I needs an outfit afore I ships out agen, and . . ."

Kydd felt inside his waistcoat and came out with a crown piece. Renzi grabbed his hand, but Kydd pressed it on the man. He looked at Renzi. "I know," he said, "but I'm feelin' flush."

Renzi realized that Kydd knew the man to be a fraud—there was no such thing as a "mizzen topsailman" and he had never heard of a *Duchess* or of a *Majesté*. It was Kydd's simple generosity, and Renzi felt mean. "Let's cruise, shipmate," he said, and disengaged Kydd from the harpies' embraces. They shouldered through the noisy crush, seeing Petit being borne in, laughing and shouting.

Outside they paused in the bright sunlight. The water was alive with small craft, and a light frigate was making her way slowly past in the summer breeze, outward bound. The street was a kaleidoscope of color.

As a pressed man in the old battleship *Duke William,* Kydd had never before had the opportunity to enjoy shoreside pleasures and he looked keenly about him—the hucksters, gentlemen and their ladies, sailors ashore and the vivid splash of red of an officer of a foot regiment. A cart trundled past, piled high with barrels. The sweat of the two horses was sharp in his nostrils; there was something about the purity of the sea air on a long voyage that made the scents of the shore so much more pungent.

Without a word they turned to the left, away from the dockyard, and made their way down the street. Sailors were shouting to each other and rolling down the way in fine style. Impecunious lieutenants heading for the dockyard from their cheap lodgings in Southsea crossed to the other side to avoid confrontation, but most passersby grinned conspiratorially at their antics.

At the first corner Kydd and Renzi headed down the maze of smaller lanes to wander among the shops and hostelries. The aroma of mutton and onions hit them. "My dear fellow—" began Renzi, but Kydd, with a quick grin, was already on his way into the chop house. They slid into place in a high-backed alcove and loudly demanded service.

"A brace of y'r shilling mutton pies an' not so damn near with y'r trimmings," Kydd began.

"With pork chops on the side, if you please," agreed Renzi.

"An' onions all over, with a jug o' y'r best stingo."

"To be sure—and if your vittles isn't of the first quality then we shall tack about and make another board."

An hour later, replete, they eased out into the street again. The day was cheerful in every particular, the noises in the thoroughfare busy and jolly, and the two friends wandered along, mellow and happy.

A tattoo parlor attracted Kydd, who suggested that a bright blue anchor on the back of each hand might be the very thing. "Leave it till later," Renzi advised quickly, and pulled him across to an agreeably decorated bow window where sailors' knickknacks were on display.

The corpulent shopman sized them up. "*Artemis,* if my eyes do not deceive," he burbled, fussing at his stock. "Just the wery thing for a gentleman mariner," he declared, sweeping forward a deep blue seaman's jacket. It was ornately finished in white piping and boasted a splendid superfluity of white buttons. "Yes? Then you will without doubt need a waistcoat of the true sort—and 'ere I 'ave the harticle in question. I see you have already noticed the genuine pearl buttons and extra-fine stitching."

A short time later the pair emerged from the shop in fine attire, complete with the latest style of round hat with a dashing curled brim. Wiggling his toes in his smart long-quartered shoes, Kydd laughed with the sheer delight of being rigged out like a true-born son of the sea.

Their steps took them past the anachronistic yet charming white stone walls and turrets of the gun wharf. They turned right toward Broad Street, Kydd's rolling walk just a little exaggerated. In Old Portsmouth a sailor was a natural denizen among the crazy, rickety buildings of the narrow spit of Portsmouth Point.

At the lowering ramparts of King Henry's fortifications they turned right, past the Sally Port, where boat crews came and went from the great fleet at anchor at Spithead. The massive dark stone arch they passed was the last part of England that would be seen by the wretches condemned to transportation to Botany Bay. Kydd shuddered. The last time he had seen these old stones was from seaward, as a new-pressed landman on the foredeck of a line-of-battle ship.

In the narrowing confines it seemed as if the whole sea world had converged on the place. There were seamen in every rig imaginable and from every maritime nation, all brought together by the need to know something other than their harsh sea life.

"Avast there, yer scrovy swabs!" Stirk's familiar bellow broke in on Kydd's musings. He came striding across, his face creasing in delight. Behind him was Doggo, who pointedly lifted a bottle. Stirk stopped, and looked askance at Kydd. "Well, bugger me days—flash as a rat with a gold tooth!" he said, still grinning. He nodded politely to Renzi, who had chosen more plainly.

"We gotta blow out our gaff, then—shall we lay course to board the Lamb 'n' Flag, me hearties?" The four passed along the street companionably, with the old houses and taverns pressing in on both sides to the end of the spit. There, a shingle beach offered a view into the harbor with *Artemis* alongside at the dockyard.

Kydd caught the powerful odor of seaweed, wet ropes and tar.

But he hadn't long to reflect as they swung through the dark oak doors of the tavern. "Hey, now! Toby Stirk! Warp yerself alongside, mate." The roar came from a knot of men at a table to the left. A vast, red-faced seaman laughed and beckoned them over.

"Yair, well." Stirk strode across and took the man's hand and pumped it for a long time. Remembering himself, he gestured at Kydd and Renzi. "'S me shipmates, Ralf, in *Artemis* frigate we is, see." Kydd had never seen Stirk so touched, and wondered what poignant tale was behind it.

The saloon was dusky but comfortable. In the light of the candlesticks Kydd's gaze took in the exotic mix of characters from half a hundred men-o'-war. Dusty artifacts from the seven seas adorned the walls; wicked lances from the South Seas, faded coconut monkeys from the coast of Africa and the mysterious gold-on-red lettering of the Orient.

The beer was good—very good, Kydd decided, and he sank another. He was happy to let the wizened sailmaker opposite make the running in the conversation. Out of the corner of his eye he noticed Renzi puffing contentedly on his clay pipe, also allowing the talk to flow over him.

Stirk leaned back. "Sportsman's Hall in business?" he asked.

"Millers, is all," he was told.

"That'll do, mates."

The group moved to the brightly lit back room, where snarling terriers, restrained by thick leather straps, bayed loudly when the rat cages were brought in. The hubbub rose to a crescendo as bets were laid, Stirk and Doggo to the fore. Kydd held back, he had no real taste for the sport. With his head a-swim with ale he watched the terriers furiously flailing about, biting and worrying at the darting black rats.

Renzi caught Kydd's eye, his slow, regular puffing adding to the blue haze in the room. "Shall we withdraw, do you think?"

Outside the fresh air discommoded Kydd. The excitement of the day had its inevitable effect and he staggered over to the low seawall, and heaved onto the rocks below. Renzi stood back until it was all over. As Kydd recovered, he went into the tavern and reappeared with a pan of water. Kydd accepted it gratefully. Dusting off his new rig, which had miraculously escaped being soiled, he stretched, then looked at Renzi. For no logical reason he felt resentment, not at Renzi but at the world, at things.

It grew and burned, and gradually took focus. "I need—a woman," he said thickly, glaring into space.

Renzi's expression did not change. "Do you not feel a slattern's lues a hard price for the joy of the moment?"

Kydd's feelings erupted. "D'ye think to preach at me? I do as I will!"

Looking at him dispassionately, Renzi knew there was no dissuading him. Kydd would have his way, and some raddled trull would know his youth and innocence.

"And, pray, what shall I tell Princess Sophia?" As soon as it was uttered, Renzi regretted the unworthy spite that made him say it, but it was too late. Kydd turned abruptly and disappeared into the crowds.

Renzi stood still and watched him go. The coolness of his logic was slipping: he needed to rationalize recent events, to process them into tidy portions fit for inspection by a rational mind. He needed to get away. He trudged north, away from town, with no clear purpose in mind. Before reaching Landport Gate, the landward entrance to Portsmouth, he heard the grinding of an oxcart behind.

It was a farm worker in embroidered smock and shapeless hat driving two hand of oxen, returning after delivering his produce. Renzi stopped him. "I'd be obliged were you to offer me passage."

"Oi has no truck wi' deserters, tha knows," the man said doubtfully.

"Do I sound like one, my friend?" Renzi said, offering silver. The man bit the half-crown piece and grinned widely, patting the bench beside him.

At the Landport Arch they were stopped by a sentry. Renzi pulled out his ticket-of-leave, and waved it at the soldier. The sergeant ambled over and took a look. "Ah—this 'ere is a Jack Tar orf the *Artemis,* lad. Come t' raise the dust after their 'orrible great battle."

It was pleasant in the hot afternoon sun. The farmhand was not given to idle chat but had a steady grin of amusement on his homely face. They left Portsea Island and approached the foothills, joining the highway to Petersfield for a short while before taking the steep Southwick road to the summit of Portsdown Hill.

Bidding the man a courteous farewell, Renzi alighted there, and stretched out on the chalky grass. It was a superb view, high above the coastal plain, looking out over the town and dockyard for miles. The sunlit sea stretched out, the fleet at Spithead dark models against the sparkling flat sea.

He plucked idly at the grass and let his thoughts run free. He had been taken by surprise at the ferocity of his feelings as they boarded *Citoyenne,* equally as blood mad as any of his shipmates. The hopeless bravery of the French Captain had impressed him greatly, and he had been touched to hear that Powlett had taken steps to remit a competence to his widow in recognition of this. The value of the coast signals lay in the secret of their recovery, and the world would never know of Maillot's gallant failure.

Now he also realized that for all his carefully erected barriers there was a personal vulnerability, an unguarded breach for which his own weakness was to blame. Kydd and he had endured and laughed together too many times for the friendship to be cast aside, and therefore he had to face the fact that through Kydd he was vulnerable. The thought of Kydd's clumsy attempts at a woman made him wince, as much at the memory of his own past concupiscence and willfulness as anything, for in his own case there had been no excuse.

The sun beat down and he lay back, letting the tension seep from his bones. He tipped his hat over his eyes. An occasional insect buzz reached him over the gentle sough of the breeze. He lay there, drowsy and tranquil.

Faint shouts wafted up on the late afternoon breeze, difficult to decipher. Behind closed eyes he tried to make sense of them. Then he heard the vexatious whinny of a horse and the unmistakable gritty progress of carriage wheels.

Renzi sat up. Bursting into view came a coach, the horses snorting and nodding after the long haul up. But this was no ordinary conveyance: it was fitted out for a cruise by a crew of enterprising sailors. With a flag hoisted at the main, a cargo of a stout keg aft and the inn sign of the Lamb and Flag forward for a figurehead, she was manned by a cheering, drunken crew of seamen from *Artemis* bent on a roaratorious frolic.

The coach pulled up and painted doxies fanned out decorously to sink relieved to the grass. Renzi stood up in amazement. The keg was tapped again and again and pots waved assertively in the air as bets were laid on the race down the long hill and back into town. The browbeaten driver nervously checked the traces.

"Why, damn me eyes if it ain't Gennelman Jack hisself." A quartermaster's mate of Renzi's slight acquaintance pointed at him in astonishment. Others joined to peer in his direction. Renzi gave a diffident wave and approached. Then from the other side, buttoning the flap on his trousers, came Kydd. He stopped dead.

For a moment Renzi stood nonplussed, then clapping his new hat over his breast, he loudly declaimed,

> *"While up the shrouds the sailor goes, or ventures to the yard*
> *The landman who no better knows, believes his lot is hard*
> *But Jack with smiles each danger meets . . .*
> *. . . and drinks his can of grog!"*

Inwardly flinching at the populist doggerel, he was nevertheless met with a storm of cheers. "Welcome aboard th' barky, shipmate." A dusty, well-used tankard was thrust at him and he joined the riotous crew, winking at Kydd as he passed to climb inside.

The coach jerked off down the road, drunken sailors aloft and alow. "Whoay, mateys!" said one, left astern as he scrambled to reach his post aft on the postillion's seat. The coach rattled and shook in a cloud of dust as it plunged madly down the road, a fiddler scraping a jig alongside the terrified driver. Renzi smiled at the apprehensive women opposite, dust streaked over their caked rouge, their mob caps askew. "Your acquaintance, ladies!" He bowed. Their eyes flashed white as they strove to make sense of it all, the rattling coach now violently swaying.

The most worldly-wise looked at him in suspicion, his manner so utterly at odds with the open hilarity of the sailors outside. Eventually she appeared to make up her mind and, lifting her chin, stared out determinedly.

Cheers and whoops came from outside as they plunged past a startled populace, and an upside-down face suddenly popped into frame at the window. "Me pot, Jack," it said. Not understanding, Renzi hesitated.

The lady seized a tankard from the apparition and fumbled under the seat for a bottle, which she skillfully upended with only the minimum of slop. She handed it up and glared at Renzi. "These 'ere sailor boys 'r' all 'ut stands 'tween us an' the Frogs, matey. You'd begrudge 'em their spree?" Hesitant smiles appeared on other faces—Jack Tar ashore was popular in this part of the world.

"Indeed no, madam," he said, sincerely. He glanced out again and saw the town ramparts flash past, sentries scattering. Past houses and cheering taverns they flew. The sailors above kicked up a deafening hullabaloo as they neared their goal, the coach careering dangerously around every corner.

An excited roar arose, the wheels juddered under locked brakes—and they teetered to a stop, horses a-tremble and the driver with his head in his hands. The crew piled out, arguing loudly, but without a timepiece between them judgment as to records was academic. The keg was unlashed and the driver mollified with silver.

"Rare time!" said Renzi lightly to Kydd, who had jumped from the roof of the vehicle.

Kydd brushed himself down, delaying a response. Renzi saw that his eyes were bloodshot and he moved carefully. "Yes," Kydd said neutrally.

"Should you desire a roborant, it would be my pleasure to find you one," Renzi said.

"Thank ye, that will not be necessary," Kydd replied. He made no move to walk away, and when Renzi began to walk across the Common, Kydd fell into step next to him.

"Mrs. Jordan is in town, I understand," Renzi tried. There was no response, then Renzi saw that it held no particular meaning for Kydd. "She is playing Maltravers in *The Fair Dealer of York,* apparently," he continued. Kydd grunted, but Renzi detected a thaw of mood.

"At Thornton's," he added, "on Gosport side." A quick glance, and he continued, "It could prove a most satisfactory ending to the day were we to experience her talents at the first hand," he said.

Kydd cleared his throat. "Is she accounted good?"

"The very first of the age."

Their pennies were refused by the boatman who stretched at his oars with a will. Golden lights sparkled over the harbor and along the lines of ships at Spithead. Occasional bursts of fireworks exploded, the shore still seething with excited crowds.

Crossing to Gosport, the slop and hurry of waves against the wherry sides was hypnotic and Kydd felt a lifting of spirit. He would never tell Renzi, however, that his gibe about the princess had struck hard and true—he had felt the sweet pain of frustration but he had not surrendered his will to a whore.

The theater was packed and restless, the heat of the chandeliers and burning lime nearly suffocating. They were not the only sailors in the audience: most in the gallery with them were from *Artemis* and another frigate, happily chaffing while waiting for the curtain.

A thin orchestra in the pit struck up, the stridulations of the strings setting Renzi's teeth on edge, then one by one the chandeliers were lowered and snuffed. The audience stirred expectantly. The curtain swept aside to reveal an impossibly baroque drawing room, white in the glare of the lime light. Patrons quelled the rowdier elements of the audience, and a quiet spread out.

The silence lengthened. Vague scuffles sounded offstage, and eventually a disheveled reprobate figure shot on, to stand swaying resentfully before the crowd. He staggered over to the high-backed chair and collapsed in it, to the vast delight of the sailors. Hastily, a flourish from the orchestra cut across the jeers and laughter, and onto the stage swept a voluptuous mannish figure. Clad in silk breeches with an exaggerated wig and fashionable cane, the figure acknowledged the storm of applause with dignified bows.

When the noise had died away the figure advanced to the front of the stage. Absolute silence.

"Prithee, sir, art anguished at Maltravers's summons?" was demanded of the recumbent form. The voice was female, husky and powerful. The form continued to stare.

"Art thou not?" The imperious tone had a venomous edge. There was no response. Suggestive catcalls broke the silence.

"Sir!" the voice continued silkily. "I see thou art in liquor!" The cane flashed out and caught the form in the midriff, doubling him over.

"But stay, this do I well comprehend!" The shouting died away. With dramatic intensity Maltravers strode to the edge of the stage. "What man, a drop of English blood in his veins, can stand unmoved at the news—the thrice welcom'd news—that the dastardly French have been bested at sea! By *Artemis* frigate in a duel at arms at which there could be but one victor—bless'd Albion it was . . ."

The rest of the extempore speech was drowned in an avalanche of cheering, wild, unashamed exultation. Bowing left and right, Maltravers held up "his" hands for silence. " 'Come cheer up, me lads, 'tis to glory we steer . . .' " The whole theater stood and broke into the Garrick favorite, feverishly accompanied by the orchestra. Kydd's face flushed as he sang along with insatiable pride.

The play moved on in a wordy stream. Renzi looked to see its effect on Kydd. To his amused dismay he saw that his friend was no longer concerning himself. He was slumped in his seat, fast asleep.

CHAPTER 3

≈

Next day the men moved slowly and stoically, stripping *Artemis* of her guns and stores preparatory to her docking. Her grievous wounds were laid bare, and her injured spars sent down to a dismayed clucking from boatswain Merrydew.

Noon came, but few could stomach the cold rations supplied by the receiving hulk lashed alongside. After an all-night-in, Kydd was feeling better, and when the day was done and liberty was piped again, he felt ready to step ashore with the larbowlines once more.

He sat quietly as Renzi plaited his glossy pigtail. He had cleaned his new rig carefully for who knew what adventures lay ashore, and with prize money still to spend they would take their pick of the pleasures of the land.

"Hoay, Tom!" The hail from the hatchway was Doud, looking for him.

"What cheer, mate?" Kydd called back.

Doud had an expression of marked curiosity. "Officer o' the day passes the word for Tom Kydd." He paused for effect. "It's a visitor at the brow askin' after you, my frien'. A lady visitor."

A rumble of ribald interest from around Kydd made him ask, "Should y' call her, might we say, taut rigged?"

"As saucy and trim a barky as ever graced the seas—an' a fine figurehead with it," Doud acknowledged. This did not at all sound like a common drab, should one be bold enough to seek him out.

"Spread more sail, mate, an' yer'll soon board her in rollicking style," urged Petit, with a huge grin.

Hurriedly checking his rig, Kydd leapt up the hatchway ladder, closely followed by half the mess deck. Striding up to the master's mate he demanded, "Where away, Mr. Shipton?" With a grin, the man indicated a dark young lady standing diminutive and lonely on the dockside.

It took a few moments, for it had been another place, another lifetime—but he recognized his only sister, Cecilia. Impetuously, he clattered down the gangway to the stones of the dock and crushed her to him.

"Oh, Thomas, my dear, my very dear . . ." She wept, and clung to him, her femininity utterly disarming. She pushed him away and dabbed at her eyes. "Thomas! Look at you! I would never— you are a man!"

Kydd blushed, and she giggled at his discomfiture, but did not let go his arms. Her eyes flashed in that familiar way; she swung him round to face the ship again, her arm through his. "Do introduce me to your ship, Thomas."

In earlier years this imperious behavior would have resulted in an instant squabble, but now Kydd could think of no easy rejoinder. He looked up and saw the line of men at the deck edge gazing down. Slowly they mounted the gangway, her arm primly on his, her manner decidedly possessive. The men looked on with interest. They reached the bulwarks, the men fell back into a semicircle, and she accepted his awkward assistance to the deck with a dainty "Thank you, Thomas."

The sight of his shipmates, sea-hardened and battle-proved to a man, so transparently agog, was too much for Kydd. A smile pulled at his mouth. "Now, please behave y'rself, sis," he whispered.

Renzi stood back, impassive.

Kydd took off his hat and held it across his chest. "Gentlemen, I have th' honor to introduce Miss Cecilia Kydd, my worthy an' only sister."

A sigh went through the group. Renzi performed an elegant

leg, but in the main hats flew off and there was a gawky shuffling from men quite unused to ladies of Cecilia's evident quality.

Kydd watched his sister's gratification in amusement. She was perhaps too strong-featured on her smaller frame, but her dark looks were appealing in their directness and she was undeniably handsome. She curtsied to Renzi and gave him a dazzling smile. She nodded to the others, instinctively giving best to Petit, who fawned on her ridiculously.

Kydd had the sense to move her forward to Shipton, who exchanged bows and polite courtesies. Of course it was in order for Kydd to show her the ship. A veiled reference to the cockpit was a warning that the midshipmen would perhaps be entertaining women of quite another sort, and the boatswain would, by now, be indisposed.

There was little to see in a frigate stripped of most of her guns and fitments, but enough remained to give an idea of life aboard. Accompanied by the enraptured men Kydd escorted Cecilia forward. "That there's where we keep the boats," he said, pointing to the skid beams straddling the open space of the spar deck amidships.

"Where th' seaboat is kept, if't please yer, miss," Petit added.

"An' the longboat, in course," Adam said eagerly.

"When it ain't a launch," growled Stirk, who had heard of the visitation and had hurried up on deck.

"How interesting," Cecilia murmured, gazing blankly at the empty space.

They moved on to the forward end of the boat-space. "What a dear little bell," she exclaimed, catching sight of the ship's bell in its ornate belfry.

"It's how we tells the time," said Gully eagerly. Cecilia looked closely but could find no sign of clock hands or any such.

The men crowded around. "Like, we strikes it every glass, see, so we always knows when ter go on watch," explained Stirk, his tone a peculiar mix of tender attention and awkwardness.

Cecilia replied faintly that she was sure, but felt that the glass might suffer overmuch in the striking.

"Ah, our gun captain, Tobias Stirk," Kydd said, trying to regain center stage. He led the way down the fore-hatch, resolutely keeping the men clear while she felt her way down to the main deck.

At the sight of the remaining twelve-pounders Cecilia paused. The heat of battle had boiled away the gun blacking to a patchy metallic graininess, and they looked what they were, lethal engines of war that had so recently taken an enemy warship and the life of her captain.

Scars of the desperate conflict were easy to find—long, splintered furrows in the pristine clean deck, daylight through smashed-in side timbers and suggestive dark stains in more than one spot. An insistent rank odor of stale gunsmoke still pervaded the air along with the vinegar-sulphur mixture used to remove dried body parts.

"And, Tom, pray where . . ." She tailed off, her hand over her mouth, eyes opened wide.

Kydd showed her, not speaking.

She looked around wildly, the alien grimness of the scene visibly crowding in. "Thomas, I—I—if you please, might we . . ."

Concerned, Kydd led her up to the open air again. Another colorful sunset promised, and he remembered Renzi's plans for a splendid meal. He addressed the adoring throng: "Avast there, y' cod-eyed lubbers, we have business ashore now." Beckoning to Renzi he announced, "We dine as planned, Nicholas, and with company."

Cecilia hesitated, then whispered up at him. Kydd smiled. "We shall make a rendezvous for eight, but it seems my little sister wishes time with me first." He turned and they went ashore, arm in arm.

Her lodgings were a tiny room in Southsea. She put down her hat and began to comb her hair before the hinged mirror. Kydd watched the familiar ritual fondly, the brush going *swit-swit* in regular strokes to her waist. He caught her eyes in the mirror and smiled. Quickly she averted hers and stared woodenly ahead, the brush continuing its monotonous rhythm. Taken aback Kydd wondered what he had said. Then he saw her eyes glisten. Stubbornly she stared into the mirror, the brush smoothing her hair in long strokes, and then the tears came. He held her as emotion shook her small frame, frightening him with its sudden onset. "It wasn't so bad, Cec," he mouthed softly, "it was over in an hour or two, I swear."

She didn't answer and he held her away from him, searching her face. "It's not that, is it?" he said, a cold dread beginning. "It's Mother, isn't it?"

"No," she choked.

"Papa?" he said.

"No, Tom, all are well," she said, her voice muffled. She dried her eyes and turned on the stool to face him. "I am a silly billy," she croaked. "Please forgive me, Thomas." She tried a smile and Kydd laughed quietly.

"The twins have breeched, you know," she said, in a stronger voice. "And Mrs. Mulder is to wed again in the autumn." She hesitated. "It's only been half a year—does it seem long to you, Thomas?"

Kydd thought of the incredible events and changes that he had endured. "Er, yes, I suppose it does."

She surveyed him at length. It was nothing short of magical, the change in him. The pale, earnest perruquier had metamorphosed into this strong, oaken-visaged sailor with the ready smile and lean body, fitting his colorful seaman's dress as though born to it.

"We didn't get your letter until March," she said, omitting the details about the frantic worry that had preceded it, "and that short one came in May."

Kydd remembered the scrap of letter he had dashed off to his mother at sea in a battleship, forty miles off the French coast on the day before he was due to go ashore with the doomed landing party. Apparently another two letters were still on their way, but at least they had had word of his transfer.

"We didn't understand the bit about a frigate, but Lady Onslow was so sweet about it," she said. Sir Richard was himself at sea at that very time, Rear Admiral of the White.

So they would have known about his transfer to *Artemis,* and therefore would have been horrified when news of her dreadful battle had become known.

Cecilia flopped onto the bed like the child she so recently had been, and looked up at him with shining eyes. "Tell me, what's it like to be a sailor? Really, Tom, no gammon."

Kydd felt a wave of affection break over him, her childish glee touching his heart. He told her of the sea, his lofty world of perils and adventure, skill and honor; the first sight of a sea-tossed dawn, the deep experience of feeling a deck heave, a comber bursting against the bow in a sheet of rainbow spray. He spoke of his friends—his shipmates, and their rough, simple gentleness.

She listened speechless, carried by his words but never gulled into underestimation by their simplicity. "Oh, Tom, who would have thought it?"

Kydd had never experienced hero worship from his sister, and reddened. "When I spoke with the King, he remembered Guildford, Cec—"

"The King!" she squealed. "Never! You never did!"

"And with a beautiful princess—a real one, mind you."

Her speechless admiration made him feel a poltroon. Guiltily he glanced around. "What o'clock is it, sis? We mustn't be adrift for Nicholas."

The dancing light faded from her eyes. She looked away, her body sagging.

Kydd felt the cold dread returning. "What is it, Cec?" he said softly.

"Oh, Tom, I—I feel so dreadful!"

He put his arms around her shoulder. "Tell me."

She looked deeply into his eyes as if to spare him what she could. "It's Father," she said carefully. "His eyes are failing."

He sat back, confused.

Brokenly she murmured, "Tom—how can you . . ." Her hands twisted together. "When I looked up at that great big ship and saw you there, my heart nearly broke. You looked so—right as a sailor. So handsome! My big brother!" Her eyes filled. "And now we are asking you to give it all up—Tom, he is making mistakes, the customers are complaining. If the shop fails . . ."

They were asking him to return home, to resume his place behind the counter of the old shop, talking wigs with customers. He gulped, and looked sightlessly out into the night and past the celebrations. His sister gripped his hands in hers until they hurt. Renzi and he would part, he would no longer know his dear friend, who would go on to better things in another world.

"Tom . . ."

It was not her fault: it must have taken real courage to make the journey alone to this notorious naval town, but only now was she understanding the true cost of her appeal. He got heavily to his feet, and balled his fists in silent agony. There was no decision to make. Without him, the family would slide into destitution, the debtor's prison and worse.

"This war, Tom, it's ruinous for the business. Everyone is asking for bob wigs only, and some are even refusing to wear any. It's a new fashion."

Kydd remembered his father's endless but nearsighted primping and sewing of horsehair at the carcass of full-bottomed wigs, and his retort died before it was uttered. He took a deep breath. "I have prize money," he said, but Cecilia cut him off quickly.

"Tom—it's not just for now," she said firmly. "You must face it, we need you to provide for us in the future. We need you, Tom."

"Yes," he muttered. "Yes, I know—I know, I know, *I know*, damn you!" he choked out in his pain.

She said nothing and waited.

He looked up miserably. "We'll go to Nicholas now."

The darkness outside was split with bonfires, fireworks and excited people hurrying this way and that with blazing link torches, candles in colored glass and all manner of festive flame. They trudged silently along the seafront. The dark offshore shapes of the fleet had needlepoints of light on deck, which Kydd knew were lanthorns strung over the fo'c'sle and quarterdeck. A regular deep thump of minute guns from somewhere out there struck him viscerally.

Kydd didn't notice the gang of rowdies until they had surrounded them both. He stopped, Cecilia gripping his arm apprehensively.

"Dursn't show a light, then?" One swaggered up to him, demanding he show illuminations in patriotic celebration.

They closed in menacingly. "Tip 'im a stoter, Jem, 'n' then capsize 'im in th' sea!"

"Don't you dare, you ruffians!" shouted Cecilia. "He's from *Artemis* and he's been in a terrible battle, you scoundrels."

They fell back under her anger, and changing tack began shouting, "*Artemis!* An *Artemis!*" Hoisting Kydd up, they carried him shoulder high, cheering and whooping, not noticing the anguish in his face.

Renzi waited outside the Queen, concerned at Kydd's lateness. When he saw the two come into sight he hailed briskly. Kydd did not respond at first, then he said quietly, "Nicholas, come walk with me a spell, I have—some news."

CHAPTER 4

≋

Kydd slumped back in the coach as it bucketed northward along the London Road. Next to him Cecilia held a small book as though reading, wise enough to leave him to his thoughts. The initial sharp pain had dulled. He knew that Renzi, with his fine logic and learning, would have a philosophy to suit, but in the last few minutes they had spent together, dividing the contents of the sea chest they shared, it did not seem to be the thing to talk about. It had seemed so casual, the farewell, so matter-of-fact. They had stood in the 'tween decks; there had been a reluctant shaking of hands, a banal comment or two, and then he had turned his back on the only true, deep friend he had ever had.

There would be no problem about his departure—a famous frigate captain like Black Jack Powlett would find a score of volunteers eager to step into his place. He had left without delay, unable to face the leave-taking, letting Renzi tell the others. He hoped he would be missed as much as he missed them. The lump in his throat tightened.

They drew into Guildford in light drizzle. As he stared moodily from the coach window he saw that the country town had not changed in his absence beyond an imagined wartime unkemptness. They clattered into the old timbered passage of the Angel posting house and finally came to a halt. He handed Cecilia down, ignoring the gaping ostler who had never seen a proper sailor before.

He knew the way, of course, up the high street and under the great clock to the family shop. With his seabag comfortably over his shoulder and Cecilia's luggage under his arm, he swung into the accustomed gloom of the shop. The smell of musty horsehair and pomatum took him back but the room seemed smaller than he remembered.

There was a scream of delight as his mother appeared. She clung to him as though he would vanish again before her eyes. His father stood at the door but held back. "Welcome home, son," his mother said tearfully, her eyes running over his lean figure. "Get your sailor costume off, dear, and I'll have such a dish ready for you as will warm the cockles." Her hands went to his jacket, working at the buttons. Something in Cecilia's manner communicated itself to her, and the fussing turned to flustered prattle. His father remained still, staring at him.

Kydd took a deep breath and strode over to him. "I hope I find ye well, Father," he said.

A smile broke the deep lines of his father's face, and his hand came out, hesitantly. Kydd's generous nature surged to the fore— it was not the man's fault that mortal weakness was laying its hands on him. The room burst into excited babble; Kydd was back in the bosom of his family, and they all wanted to hear of his awful adventures.

Once again the rightful inhabitant of the tiny room above the shop, he peeled off his seaman's rig—for the last time. He laid it down tenderly, smoothing the folds, then pulled on his knee breeches and snuff-colored ruffled waistcoat. It felt flimsy, constricting, after his stout sailor's wear. He felt contempt, hatred for it building.

There was a tiny knock at the door. Cecilia stood there, small and vulnerable. Struggling, she spoke in an unnatural voice. "Tom—thank you." Wrestling his thoughts he crossed to her and hugged her tight. "Need t' get used to it again, is all," he mumbled.

The days passed with leaden steps. One by one reminders of his sea life faded into the past. The softness of his bed had been suffocating, and he slept on the floor for the first few nights; his mother had quietly got rid of his seaman's knife, which had been at his side every waking moment before, and his wooden ditty box containing his personal treasures was replaced by a sensible porcelain dish.

His pigtail did not last either. Cecilia chopped and scissored at its gleaming length and it fell forlornly to the floor. As a perruquier, it just would not do not to wear a wig himself. What was left of the prize money was gratefully accepted, but by unspoken consent after that first night, his time at sea was never again mentioned.

Kydd took to walking alone. It was possible to make the journey from Pewley Downs to Shere along the crest of the North Downs, and in the summer warmth it was a bright and pretty sight. His thoughts were free to roam wherever he wanted. The North Downs had a dual view with a certain meaning for Kydd. On one hand, to the northeast there was the flat plain that led to London, its presence betrayed by a distant pall of dun-colored smoke. The fleet anchorage of the Nore, where as a pressed man he had spent his first days in the Navy, was not so very far beyond. Over in the other direction was the road south, to the many seaports of the coast, where as many as two hundred sail at a time could be seen from the white cliffs. Unlike any of the others he met on his walks, he knew full well what lay beyond the gray waves breaking ashore.

In the shop, business was not good. Cecilia had been right: the fashion sweeping in from revolutionary Europe for unrestrained hair had a strong hold now and the future for wig-making looked bleak. There was still a small but reliable demand from physicians, the richer merchants and the like, but the Kydds had to compete against a larger establishment in Godalming that could deliver faster.

Kydd's days were now circumscribed by long hours in the workshop punctuated by periods of soul-destroying inactivity behind the counter, waiting for custom. The days turned to weeks and he felt his soul shrivel.

After listlessly serving ribbons to the voluble Mrs. Coombs he looked up from the counter at the person who had just entered—dusty and travel-worn, carrying a ragged bag and in a worn blue sailor's jacket. It was Renzi. He held out his hand.

Kydd couldn't respond at first; it was like seeing a ghost. He was caught utterly off-balance. "W-well met, sir," he stuttered, not knowing how to deal with a man he knew to be well-born, but in quite different circumstances his particular friend.

Renzi reached out, took Kydd's hand and shook it warmly. He was shocked at the changes he saw, the slow responses, the downcast look. It was also a grievously sad travesty, seeing Kydd's broad shoulders and lithe foretopman's body draped in wig and breeches and the tight, faded brocade waistcoat. "Were I to beg shelter for the night, I fear I would sadly inconvenience," he said, and watched anguish chase delight on his friend's features.

"Nicholas—but o' course! But—"

"I have a story to tell, but it must wait. If you would be so good as to conduct me to a tailor's I will do my best not to shame you to your family—and then we will dine."

Renzi became another being in long clothes. In anonymous black, a severe and unadorned black, his natural patrician authority readily asserted itself. Other clients in the saloon respectfully made way for them both and they sat down to a dish of salmagundi.

"You'll be stayin' long in town?" Kydd asked, fearful of the reply.

"No plans at the moment, my friend."

"Then you shall stay at home—my room is yours." A bed could be made on the floor of the shop for himself.

The cured fish went down rapidly, as did the jug of porter.

"You wonder at my visitation," Renzi said finally. Kydd smiled, so he went on. "*Artemis* is still in dock, we are sent away on leave," he said, playing with a fork. "I thought it proper to visit my family. I posted to the village and walked to the estate." Renzi seemed to have some difficulty with the tale. Kydd recalled that after a particularly harsh Act of Enclosure by Renzi's father, a tenant farmer's son had committed suicide. Out of the highest sensibility and purest logic, Renzi had taken this personally as a moral crime by his family and, in expiation, had sentenced himself to five years' exile at sea, an extraordinary act of self-denial.

Renzi leaned back with a twisted smile. "At the boundary of the last field I—remembered, saw again the body hanging in the barn." He looked intensely at his fork. "I could not go on. I tried, but could not." His voice was thick, the first time Kydd had heard it so overborne by emotion. "The nights I slept under a hedge—it was nonsensical, and so here I am." His eyes glimmered.

He signaled to the pot-boy. "Well met—indeed it is!" He smiled, and saw Kydd's fumbling. "In the article of prize money," he said gently, "except for a slight indulgence in poetry I have not had the opportunity to get rid of it before now. Allow me to . . ."

The claret was passable and under its influence Renzi heard Kydd's story. His heart went out to his friend, for there was little that he could do himself, cut off from his own family and wealth. It needed a long-term solution, but in the time before he must repair back aboard his ship there was little chance that one would be found.

Kydd's mother was surprised at her son's general rally, and therefore looked at his visitor with some interest. Cecilia's hand flew to her mouth when she recognized him. Renzi's impeccable manners and kind attentions quickly charmed the house and he was warmly welcomed.

On occasion Renzi caught some thoughtful looks from Kydd's father but on the whole it was accounted that Kydd's guest was a fine friend to the family. Cecilia was beside herself with curiosity, but was always courteously deflected, to her considerable chagrin.

Renzi, however, sensed Kydd's desperation; the strong likelihood was that when they parted, the next cruise could span years, and by then—he forced down the thought and bent to the task of making the days as agreeable as he could for his friend.

"Do you wait for me a moment, dear fellow," Renzi said, outside the bookshop at the top of the high street. Sated with depressing news from the *Anti-Jacobin Review* he longed for a new volume from the young iconoclast Wordsworth.

Kydd entered too, and watched as Renzi took down volume after volume in their fine-tooled leather bindings. An odd clunking sound intruded from behind, but it was only a shopman approaching; he had a wooden leg. Kydd did not know him—he must be a new assistant.

"C'n I help ye?" the man said. His voice was strong—in fact, it was hard and had a strength Kydd recognized instantly.

"Do I fin' myself addressing a gentleman o' the sea?"

The man stopped, and stared suspiciously. "Are ye lookin' for somethin' special?" he said.

"I'm sorry, I thought—"

"Then y' thought right. So?"

A corpulent, worried-looking man bustled up and said loudly, "Is there any problem? Are the gennelmen being attended to, Mr., er, What's-y'r-name?"

They left without the book. Outside, the summer afternoon bustle of the high street eddied around Renzi as he and Kydd walked back the few steps to the wig shop. Its crabbed windows and general seediness clutched at Renzi's heart. Kydd clapped him on the shoulder and disappeared inside, leaving Renzi alone.

Renzi could feel a gray depression settling. He could not interfere, it was Kydd's decision, a good and noble decision for the sake of his family, but it did not alter the fact that the price was ruinous—it was costing Kydd his spirit and therefore his soul; in twenty years he would be an old man. Renzi sighed heavily. A careless grocer carrying a basket of greens on his head cannoned into him, interrupting his train of thought. He shot the man a glance of such venom that he recoiled in fright and dropped his load.

Reason was not enough in this situation: soon Kydd and he would part. He himself would be back at sea in his self-imposed exile, but without his friend, a true and understanding companion in a perilous and exciting following.

He passed by the open door of the Red Lion at the top of the high street. The dark interior was warm, odoriferous and in a convivial hubbub. On impulse he entered and found an empty high-backed cubicle. Perhaps he could loosen his mind with ale and think of something he could do for Kydd before he left. The pot-boy arrived, looking curiously at his featureless black long clothes—it was seldom that the quality patronized this pothouse.

Renzi ordered a Friary ale, the local dark bitter brewed here since the Middle Ages. He sipped slowly, staring into space as once more he went over the available alternatives. They were pitifully few. His own means were slender; returning to his family to claim his own was out of the question, and his recent acquaintances did not in any wise include men of substance. But this was not a matter of a few guineas' loan, this was an entire family's future. Reluctantly, he conceded that Kydd's act was the only one that had any practical consequence for his family, and it was probably kinder to take his leave quietly—and forever, knowing that their lives had now irrevocably diverged.

Renzi became aware that someone was standing next to him. He looked up. At first he could not place the man, then remembered the assistant with the wooden leg in the bookshop. The man's hard face rearranged itself into an ingratiating smile. His worn but serviceable tricorne hat was in his hands. "I begs yer pardon, sir," he said. Kydd had been right, Renzi thought, this was a seaman; by his bearing probably a petty officer—a quarter-gunner, quartermaster's mate or any one of the band of men rightly termed the backbone of the Navy. "Perrott, Jabez Perrott, if'n yer pleases. If I c'n have a few words, like."

Renzi felt a surge of irritation. He had no coins to spare—Kydd would get all he had when he left. He did not invite the man to sit, and stared back.

Perrott stood resolute and pressed on. "Yer in the Sea Service."

It was a bald statement, and surprised Renzi. He knew he did not have the born-to-it strength and character of a seaman that Kydd so obviously had, but for some reason he motioned Perrott to sit opposite. "What can I do for you?"

The man's hat appeared on the table, the strong hands twisting it, an unaccountably poignant sight for Renzi. What encounter far out at sea had ended for him with his leg under the surgeon's blade, screaming pain and a severed limb tossed bloodily into the tub?

"If yer could see yer way clear, sir . . ." Perrott was clearly unused to pleading.

Renzi waited.

"Like, if yez has need of a sea-cook, sir, aboard yer barky, well, I'm a-sayin' as how I'm yer man . . ."

Perrott evidently thought he was an officer, a captain. Irony twisted at Renzi's lips.

"Or mebbe cook's mate, even," Perrott added, seeing the expression, "an' get an actin' warrant, like."

It was certainly the practice to employ maimed seamen as cooks, but this required an Admiralty warrant of appointment. No captain, certainly no officer, could simply take on a man without this necessary document. "You mistake me, I am no naval officer," Renzi said, his pained amusement not shared by Perrott.

"Since swallerin' the anchor, sir, it's been hard—cruel hard. Had t' bear up fer Poverty Bay, like."

Renzi could only guess the difficulties to be faced by a proud, self-sufficient seaman cast ashore in a cold and indifferent world. The man was either too proud or without the interest to secure a place at Greenwich Hospital, the home for crippled seamen without family.

"I say again, I am not a naval officer, and even if I were, without an Admiralty warrant you may never ship aboard as sea-cook," Renzi told him.

Perrott allowed a glimmer of a smile to surface at Renzi's unwitting use of Navy terms. "Aye, sir, if you sez, youse ain't a naval officer." He allowed a moment's pause and continued, "But if yer could have a word with the pusser, an' tell 'im that I'd divvy on th' slush . . ."

Perrott was clutching at straws if he imagined that a promise to the purser to share in his perquisites as cook would get him a berth. "What are you doing in Guildford?" Renzi asked. The quiet rural town was far from the sea, in deep farming country.

"Mem'ries," said Perrott immediately, his face blank.

Renzi felt a pang of sympathy—Perrott obviously meant memories of the sea and ships, where he had been a prime seaman, a whole man with pride and confidence, not a hobbling cripple with a bleak future, dependent on charity. There would be no reminders in Guildford. Despising himself, Renzi got to his feet to bring the conversation to an end.

Perrott rose also, his wooden limb clattering against the bench. "C'n I call on yer for y'r decision?" His eyes were opaque, the body tense.

"I cannot give you any hope in the matter, Mr. Perrott," Renzi snapped, angry at himself for allowing sentiment to cloud his reason. He left Perrott at the door of the alehouse staring after him and his anger turned to self-contempt—the very least he should have done was leave him with a pot of beer.

By degrees his depression turned black. The beauty of the summer evening was in sharp contrast to his mood and he felt a need to allow its languorous warmth to enter him without the distraction of others. The high street ran steeply down to the river Wey; along its pleasant banks was a path overhung with willows. He walked slowly there, thinking of nothing, letting his soul empty of its gross humors. Insects circled in clouds in the stillness, individually gilded by the setting sun; a flock of ducks paddled lazily along.

He had his solitude; by the first bend of the river he was feeling better, and around the curve, with something approaching equanimity, he was able to smile at the sight of a woman on a footbridge upbraiding two children. The two small boys were quite out of hand, shouting across at each other from either bank. The mother's voice shrilled in vexation.

Renzi had it in mind to cross the footbridge and return by the other bank, and mounted the bridge. The woman saw him and grew flustered. "Oh! I do declare, these infants are impossible." Renzi did not reply, but bowed civilly. Encouraged, the woman continued, "I am truly at a stand, sir. These—these monsters are trying my patience sorely."

The bigger of the two boys looked at him speculatively, then quickly returned to his baiting of the smaller. "Young people today are so dreadfully ill-mannered," the woman continued, "and since my dear husband requires to spend so much of his time in London, in his absence they are quite unbiddable. I am vexed to know just what to do in the matter of discipline."

Nodding pleasantly, Renzi let the woman pass, and began his return by the other bank. He would not allow Kydd to discover his mood, and deliberately put aside thoughts of his friend's fate.

He had not gone more than a few yards when an idea formed, grew and burst into expression. It was merely an idle thought, but it developed swiftly—and with what possibilities! His depression lifted instantly and he found it difficult to sleep that night.

Early in the morning Renzi mysteriously excused himself and

vanished into town on undisclosed business. He was back at noon, and lost no time in finding Kydd. "I'd be obliged to you, should you spare me the odd hour, Tom," he said, with peculiar intensity.

They passed to the left of Holy Trinity Church, up past the glebe cottages to the open fields beyond. Here, at Renzi's urging, they turned down the dusty lane to the slate-covered buildings at the end. "Take a look, Tom."

Cautiously picking their way over the rubbish in the small courtyard they entered the main structure. It was sturdily built of stone, but decay had allowed the roof timbers to give way and they lay in ruins inside. Nettles populated the rubble.

Kydd looked doubtfully at Renzi's wild expression, but held his tongue.

"There! You see in front of you the fruit of an enlightened intellect."

Mystified, Kydd tried to make sense of Renzi's ramblings.

Renzi continued, "Two disparate thoughts, leading inescapably to a fine conclusion—to a *practical* conclusion such as you will bless me for."

Fearing for his friend's sanity, Kydd took Renzi's arm.

"No! You don't understand," Renzi said, pulling away. His eyes shone. "Here we have it. A solution—I have the school building, I have the schoolmaster, we want but resolve."

The chance meeting with the woman and her children had given Renzi an idea. He had returned to the bookshop and approached the one-legged assistant and determined he was essentially free for other employment. Adding the other side of the equation, Renzi explained, "Your revered father need fear no loss of visual precision as a schoolmaster, it is not needed, but the worthy citizens of Guildford need a school for their infants that accentuates discipline in these tumultuous times."

He smiled happily. "So we establish a school on naval lines—a captain assisted by a strict bo'sun and capable quartermaster. You see, your father will be the principal, your dear self as his assistant and your mother to provide for the infants. And we have a bo'sun with a wooden leg who shall rule all aboard with silver call and cane, showing neither fear nor favor to any."

Touched by his friend's thoughtfulness and privately reserving judgment as to his suitability as a schoolmaster, Kydd suppressed a stab of excitement at the stability and hope that the plan promised. Affecting reluctance, he growled, "An' the money? What kind o' plan is it without a pot o' money at the back of it?"

Renzi had plans for this, too. "You will tell me that Guildford is a strange town, a wicked place that does not give a fair price for a desirable shop in the high street, and places wild value on a pile of stones high and dry away from passing trade." He feigned dejection, and said, "So I am undone, my plan is worthless. Let's return to the Red Lion and console ourselves in drink."

Kydd felt a bursting elation, but determined not to show it. Instead he said grumpily, "We had best first tell them where we have been wastin' our evening, then."

"You will know that I've been in the trade since before I was breeched, Thomas, as was my father before me." Kydd's father was obdurate. "A Kydd does not abandon all this for the sake of some wild adventure, my son."

Renzi interjected gently: "Then what Thomas told me of his uncle in Canada, your brother, is nonsense, then, Mr. Kydd?" It served to bring some sense of proportion to the discussion, and they went to bed on the promise of a serious look at the plan in the morning.

The "boatswain" attended at the inaugural meeting in the front room of the closed shop the next day. Despite his wooden leg, it was the glint in his eye and his iron-bound manner that inspired the group as nothing else did, and the day was carried.

Within the week, Kydd and Renzi were standing in the grounds of the Kydd schoolhouse.

" 'Cry havoc! And let slip the dogs of war!' " exclaimed Renzi, and fell upon the ruin, tugging masonry and wizened balks of timber clear. It was hard work, and sweat streamed from them under the summer sun. Cecilia kept up a running supply of lemon shrub, Kydd's father remaining in the shop to complete outstanding orders.

First, the interior was cleared, and the walls set to rights. The next stage brought out the boatswain with his tackle. He took charge immediately, and with hard, seamanlike orders, perfectly understandable to a brace of foretopmen, had them "swaying up the yards" and "tailing onto the topping lift" until the roof beams were all safely in place.

The boatswain pressed some hands for the roof tiling, and before Kydd's amazed eyes, a trim little classroom appeared. A schoolmaster's study and other necessaries were next, and soon a central plinth in the tiny quadrangle was seen stepping a mast—complete with topmast and all the standing rigging proper to such an edifice.

The day came when the mayor was prevailed upon to open the schoolhouse. Three soldiers and a fife arrived from the Royal Surreys, and to the grave glee of the children of the town, they marched about then stood to attention in strict line in front of the mast.

Fine and earnest words were said, and then in this country town, far from the sea, the good folk were treated to the exotic spectacle of the boatswain in his best seagoing gear, solemnly piping a salute to the Union flag of Old England, as it was hauled slowly and impressively up the "mizzen halliards."

There was something suspiciously like a tear in Mrs. Kydd's eye as the guests—and prospective parents—inspected the neat buildings. And there was more than a little of the man-o'-war about the scrupulously clean rooms, the squared-off desks and Spartan appointments. The boatswain stumped about, fierce and strict, his silver call around his neck, and Mr. Kydd in the unaccustomed black breeches of a schoolmaster did his best to look severe. Cecilia went up to Renzi and enveloped him in a hug, which went on and on, until she released him, eyes sparkling.

Kydd frowned. It was not so much having to spend such a fine day inside, here alone in the new classroom, it was the impenetrable obtuseness of the book he was trying to get his head round. It was a standard grammar, Lowth, and it would be the one he would have to teach, but he had only the sketchiest dame school education to meet it with.

Without thinking he had sat not at the high, severe teacher's desk at the front of the room, but at a child's desk facing it. His head was a-swim with words. An adverb? What the devil was that again? Wasn't it something that ended with *ing*? But surely that was an adjective? He sighed in despair. And what if one of the pupils asked him the question he dreaded more than any other: "If you please, sir, what *use* is an adverb?"

He ground his teeth with frustration. "The adverb (Lat. *adverbium*) as the attribute of an attribute doth occur in divers forms, cf. adverbiation, the phraseological adverb . . ." What possible value could that be to anyone in real life? To a sailor, for instance, out there on a topsail yardarm in a blow, fisting the madly flogging canvas to a reef while the ship rolled wildly. He leaned back in vivid recollection. And what would Stirk say if at quarters, the gun loaded and run out, he reminded him, "It is of the first importance to apprehend the singular difference between the two distinct families of nouns—the *nomen substantium* the first, the *nomen adjectivum* the second. On no account should these be confused . . ." He smiled at the thought.

"Then you do not find your lot uncongenial?" He had not noticed Renzi entering the little classroom.

"Be damned—how this mumping rogue c'n cackle his grease like this, I'm beggared t' know."

Renzi's eyes softened. "A utile article will always prove perdurant to the mind," he said enigmatically. Kydd threw him a frosty glance and bent again to his book.

"I proceed to town this afternoon. There are some articles I must have when—when I return aboard. Do you wish anything for the school?" Kydd looked up. Renzi was saddened at the bleakness in his expression. Kydd's family future was now secure, but the family's only son most surely was not intended to be a crabby pedagogue.

"Thank ye, no," Kydd replied, and quickly bent to his work.

Renzi left noiselessly. There were now only days left on his ticket-of-leave, at which point he must go and, in accordance with his resolve, for good.

The bookshop still had not the new Wordsworth in stock, and he turned to leave.

"Why, Mr. Renzi, what a pleasure." Renzi faced a well-proportioned woman in the latest high-waisted fashion and fussily ornate reticule, her face just a little too ruddy for the elegance of her attire. It crossed his mind that this was one of the mothers who entrusted her child to the Kydd school—her name eluded him—and he politely inclined his head.

Her eyes roamed over his austere black, and an impish smile appeared. "You are a man of mystery, I do declare, Mr. Renzi," she said, eyes a-twinkle. "You appear suddenly from nowhere, and not a soul knows aught of you! Pray, where are you spending your leisure?"

Daryton, that was her name. And with a daughter to provide for, he remembered with sudden caution. "Do not, I beg, concern yourself on my account, Mrs. Daryton," said Renzi coolly. "I have reasons enough to visit this charming town, but when these are concluded I must return."

There was a brief hesitation, but then she continued brightly, "Yet even the man of business must seek diversion, or the spirit must wither." Her eyes remained watchfully on his.

He allowed a brief smile to show, then bowed and made to leave.

"Oh, Mr. Renzi," she called, "it has just this moment crossed my mind—silly me, it seems I may have omitted to let you know—that we are holding an assembly next Tuesday. Mr. Budsoe will perform on the flute and Miss Eccles has promised her new poem for me on that very night. Can you find it in your heart to forgive my lapse and accept my invitation? I know Letitia is beside herself to meet you."

No doubt, thought Renzi wryly. He opened his mouth to refuse, then found himself saying, "Indeed. May I inquire who will be attending?"

"Why, His Worship, of course," she began.

The mayor must have been a coup for her, Renzi mused.

"And Major Summers of the militia, Mr. Beddle—the one that owns the mill, not the other one—and . . ."

"Quite so," said Renzi smoothly, "and of course Mr. and Mrs. Kydd," he added, without change of tone.

Mrs. Daryton stopped, shocked. "A tradesman! Mr. Renzi, you . . ."

". . . who now owns the new town school, a man of business, a professional gentleman," he continued.

"But he was . . ."

"And who is considering extending his holdings to a Godalming establishment of the same nature in the future, I understand," Renzi continued, inspecting his cuffs disdainfully.

"My *reputation* . . ."

". . . who some would consider it folly to disregard."

Mrs. Daryton stared at Renzi with barely concealed frustration, then began with finality, "Mr. Renzi, I cannot—"

Renzi drew himself upright. "Mrs. Daryton, I thank you for your kind invitation—I will consult my engagements, and hope they will allow me to accept." He fixed her eye with an uncompromising determination.

"Very well, Mr. Renzi," she stuttered.

Renzi relaxed his expression. "I do recall, however, that in the event, Tuesday will be available to me, Mrs. Daryton." She returned his gaze with puzzlement—even a small country town had its delicate social snobberies of which pedagogy came perilously low on the social scale, and just where did Renzi fit in the scheme of things with his effortless sophistication?

It would, of course, be expected that a daughter of marriageable age attend, and therefore it would be impossible to refuse the son—Renzi felt a twinge of amusement at the thought of Kydd in a social situation, but this was his future, and it was the least he could do to set him up in this way. The Darytons were some sort of merchants, he couldn't quite recall, and therefore the occasion would not be high, but it would serve to set the Kydds one step up on the social scale.

"They have a son and daughter, I believe," Renzi said.

"But of course," said Mrs. Daryton faintly. "But was he not at one time a common sailor?" she added more strongly.

"He was most untimely taken up by the press, if that is your understanding," Renzi admonished, "and now he has been able to establish his credentials and return to the bosom of his family."

"How dreadful," she replied, eyes wide.

"Until Tuesday eve," Renzi prompted unctuously.

"Tuesday, then, Mr. Renzi."

The hired carriage ground on briskly toward Merrow Downs, the four passengers in a companionable crush inside. Mr. Kydd had a slightly bemused air, Cecilia was serene, and Mrs. Kydd fidgeted with the fan in her lap. "Do remember, Cecilia, that it is not seemly to be seen to accept a dance with a gennelman too quick. When he says, 'Do you want a dance?' you make him wait," said Mrs. Kydd.

Cecilia flashed a guarded look of amusement at Renzi, sitting opposite, and murmured, "I will remember, Mama."

Renzi returned a faint smile, knowing the impossibility of conveying the byzantine subtleties of social interplay to someone without the breeding to have absorbed it from birth. He felt sure, however, that Cecilia could be relied upon to give a spirited account of herself. "I rather fancy that the formalities in this instance will not necessarily be observed to the full," Renzi said. That would certainly be the case—discreet enquiries had revealed that the Darytons had done well only recently in the coach trade to Brighton, and had since set up in a fine house out of town.

"I just know I should have worn the mauve crêpe," fretted Mrs. Kydd. "Cambric will not answer, but it is the fashion—what will Mrs. Daryton think?"

"Now, Mama, please don't fuss. Think of the hours we spent at the needle and goffering iron. We are now in the first rank of the fancy. Set your cares at rest and enjoy yourself tonight, dear Mama."

The carriage swayed at a corner. "Tell the driver to have a care, Walter," Mrs. Kydd instructed, shrilly. Mr. Kydd obediently banged at the roof. An upside-down face suddenly appeared at the window, grinning devilishly; the ladies screamed.

"T-take care, if you please, driver," Mr. Kydd said to the apparition.

"Aye aye, sir!" said the boatswain, and winked at Cecilia but remained inverted, grinning inanely.

"Mr. Perrott, you are in drink," said Mrs. Kydd frostily.

"*All the haaaaands* to dance and skylark!" the boatswain roared happily.

"You are quite betwaddled, Mr. Perrott, and—my God, who's driving the carriage?" she suddenly screamed in terror.

The boatswain winked again. "Why, Mr. Thomas—'e's 'ad the ribbons this last mile 'n' a half." He seemed to recollect something and disappeared abruptly.

Shaken, Mrs. Kydd turned to her husband. "I knew we shouldn't have let Thomas ride outside," she muttered. The carriage turned abruptly, and swung in through a wrought iron gate, rolling grittily up the driveway. "We're here, Walter," she exclaimed, in consternation.

They drew up at twin sconces that flamed each side of an impressive doorway. Even before the carriage had come to a stop, Kydd dropped lightly to the ground and was at the door, lowering the step. Muffled sounds of gaiety and music from within raised the pitch of excitement to an exquisite expectation.

"Milady." He grinned at Cecilia, who accepted his hand daintily in much the same way as she had boarded the frigate at his side in Portsmouth. A special, soft look was Kydd's token that she had not forgotten either.

The party stood outside, uncertain. The carriage stood also. Mrs. Kydd dug her elbow discreetly into Mr. Kydd's side until he blinked and spoke up to the figure at the reins. "Er, please to await our pleasure, er, you may proceed, Mr. Perrott."

The boatswain leaned down puzzled, then looked mystified at Kydd. "Oh—he means, lay off to loo'ard but stay within hail," Kydd explained. The boatswain grinned and jerked the carriage forward.

At the door, a harassed footman appeared. Renzi guessed that the household did not run to over-many servants but approached with good grace. He was in his plain black, his only concession to the evening a borrowed silver-gray waistcoat. The footman, expecting something by way of a cloak, stood confused.

"Mr. and Mrs. Kydd, Miss Cecilia Kydd, Mr. Thomas Kydd—and Mr. Renzi," Renzi said quietly.

Kydd's own raiment was of an altogether more flamboyant nature. Growling that he wanted nothing of coats and breeches he had finally succumbed, and at the last minute wore a brave show of bottle-green coat, blue breeches and tasseled yellow waistcoat. Renzi had shuddered at the sight, but loudly approved Kydd's snowy white lace cravat.

The footman led them into the house to what would serve as the assembly room for the night. It was ablaze with candlelight, mirrors at each end placed cunningly to make the room seem even larger, and filled with people chattering delightedly. Beyond were large French windows open to the warm darkness of the garden beyond. Packed into the corner a string trio sawed away and a shy maid bore around a tray of sweetmeats.

"Oh, Mr. Renzi," said Mrs. Daryton warmly, advancing on Renzi. "I am so glad you were able to come." Her gown gave ample prominence to her bosom, and her exuberant display of jewelry glittered in the candlelight. "You must meet Letitia, she has been talking about you—and Mr. Bedsoe says as how he is sure you are in the diplomatic line," she added.

Renzi stood his ground, and with a perfect bow stepped aside to reveal Cecilia, eyes wide and looking striking in the ivory dress, with her strong features and dark looks. "May I present Miss Cecilia Kydd," he said, signaling discreetly to the motionless Cecilia to step forward. Renzi caught faces turning appreciatively in her direction as the men took her measure.

"My dear, I hope you will enjoy this little evening, I'm sure," Mrs. Daryton murmured. Renzi hung back discreetly, and she moved on to Mrs. Kydd. "I don't think I've had the pleasure," she said, in a silver-cool voice.

Mrs. Kydd flushed, but Mr. Kydd stepped up manfully. "Mrs. Daryton, may—er—might I present my wife, Fanny." To Mrs. Daryton's infinite satisfaction, Mrs. Kydd bobbed her a quick curtsy. "And my son, Thomas." Raising her eyebrows at Kydd's interesting appearance, she nevertheless took in thoughtfully his manly strength and direct gaze.

Renzi watched the proceedings and when honors had been

duly done, assumed a polite smile and moved forward into the noisy throng.

"I say, you, Renzi!" A short man with a flushed face and sharp flinty eyes confronted him. "D'ye think we don't know what y'r about?"

"I am afraid you have the advantage of me, sir," said Renzi.

The man flashed glances around the room. "Bedsoe, sir, and it's a guinea to a shillin' you're in gover'ment business, an' diplomacy at that. Right?"

Renzi gave a short bow. "I am desolated to contradict you, Mr. Bedsoe, but I am far from being a diplomat." Another two men, one with an interested lady on his arm, joined the conversation.

"Ah, but still on government business, I'll be bound," one said.

His lady looked at Renzi boldly. "You will forgive us quizzing you, sir, but you do present as a man of some mystery," she said, her eyes on his.

"I vow I am not on government business," Renzi deflected urbanely.

"He is a man of business," the other man said to the lady, "I heard Mrs. Daryton say."

"Oh—then it must be, let me see, in banking, foreign money, secret arrangements." The lady's eyes sparkled.

"No, no!" Renzi laughed.

"Then what, pray?"

"Er, all that I am permitted to say is that as of this moment I am on the King's Service," Renzi said.

"Ah! The King! And—"

"I am not at liberty to say anything further, madam."

The group fell into a silence, looking respectfully at Renzi. "These are fearful times, my dear," the first man told her, "uncommon dreadful things happenin' everywhere in the world. I'm sure Mr. Renzi is involved in these at some peril to himself, in our interest—is that not so, Renzi?"

*   *   *

Kydd felt more awkward than ever he had felt before. He hung back from the crowd, watching the backs of men as they chatted amiably with the women, some of whom threw him curious glances. He was left alone in his misery—he knew no one and could think of no easy conversational *entrée*.

"What have we here, Charles?" To his right, two men strolled toward him, their gold quizzing glasses and tight buckskin breeches proclaiming them dandies. A quizzing glass went up and the taller man swept Kydd up and down. "Such a fopling, Charles—but I do believe it is our new word-grinder at this Navy school."

The other dandy's eyebrows went up in astonishment. "By Jessamy, an' I think you may be right, dear fellow."

Kydd glowered, but could not think of what to do in the situation.

"I say, Mr. Schoolman, do you realize you'll be learnin' young Brenton his gerunds from his gerundives?" The two dissolved into elegant fits of the giggles for some reason.

"If y'r Brenton needs his jerruns he'll learn his jerruns, right enough," Kydd said stiffly.

The two broke into howls of laughter, and sauntered off. Kydd's face burned, and he yearned with all his heart to be back in the clear salt air of the sea, where men about him were honest and direct.

The hum of conversations rose and fell, and he watched Cecilia playing complex games of coquetry with her fan to a circle of admirers. Renzi was backed into a corner by a group of what seemed to be local businessmen, and his mother sat in animated conversation with other mothers of an age in the chairs along one wall.

A silvery tinkle sounded above the hubbub. It persisted, and the noise died. It was Mrs. Daryton in the center of the room, looking about her primly.

"The gentlemen may now find their partners for the quadrille," she announced.

A happy burst of chatter erupted and Kydd was shouldered unceremoniously aside by excited couples. He flattened himself against the wall and saw Renzi stride through the crowd to Cecilia. "Shall you dance with me, Miss Kydd?" he said, raising her hand to his lips.

Cecilia dropped her eyes and said modestly, "My mama tells me never to accept a man's invitation too precipitately." Then the eyes flicked up and filled with laughter. "Of course, dear Nicholas."

Renzi led her out to the center of the room, and they assumed one side of the square of four couples. He smiled—he had prudently enquired about Daryton evenings and had found that Mrs. Daryton favored the formality of a quadrille to open the entertainments. Cecilia had proved an apt pupil, and he would now claim his reward.

The string trio handled the rondo with aplomb, neither too quick nor too tiresome, and Cecilia clearly reveled in the gay rush and stately retreat, a *baloté* followed by the *pas de basque,* a fetching blush rising to her cheeks. Renzi warmed to her vivacity, the sparkling eyes unaffected by pose or affect, and he felt oddly moved by his remembrance of her visit to the frigate to claim her brother.

A twinge of guilt had him looking about the room for Kydd. He finally caught sight of him behind the crush, bent down in trying to make a deaf old lady understand something. He realized what was happening but shrugged mentally: Kydd would have to make his own way in this world now—if he could.

The dance ended. Cecilia laughed with pleasure. "That was the most enormous fun," she said, "but I am quite out of breath." She swayed dramatically against him, clutching at his arms, and seeming quite unaware of the electric effect on him of her breasts against his chest. "May we cool off in the garden for a spell?"

Renzi had been propositioned as brazenly before, but sensed that this was a far more innocent invitation. Again he warmed to her. "But of course, my dear," he said, offering his arm.

The garden was not large, but dark and scattered with well-tended shrubs and rockeries. They strolled together, Cecilia's arm on his. Renzi's thoughts swelled and deepened—but this was no time to be interested in a girl, no matter how high the sap had risen. "You danced divinely, Cecilia," he said, quite truthfully.

"Why thank you, Nicholas," she replied happily, squeezing his arm. "It is my first essay," she said shyly, "but thanks to you . . ."

"Cecilia . . ." he began, but cold reason came unbidden to destroy the thought.

"Nicholas?" she said, sensing something and stopping to meet his eyes.

Renzi could not let even Kydd know of his thoughts—in any case they were too complex: the return to polite company after so long, the impossibility of explaining the effect of experiencing war at the first hand to this innocent country society, the presence of a handsome beauty of such touching ingenuousness, it was too much. He swung her round to face him, her other hand went up to meet his and she searched his face. "Cecilia!" he began again, thickly.

Her expression tautened, then softened to an exquisite longing. "Nicholas," she said, her voice low and throaty. Her hands gripped his. "Nicholas—it's . . . Thomas, isn't it?"

Renzi froze.

"It's Thomas—you're worried for Thomas, you think he'll be unhappy, don't you?" she breathed. Her eyes glistened. "That is so sweet of you, Nicholas, so like you." She disengaged and dabbed at her eyes. "But don't worry, I pray—we are going to take good care of him for you." At Renzi's stricken look she hurried on, "I know he would probably be a wonderful sailor, to sail the seas and see strange lands and fight in dreadful battles, but—" She broke off and hugged Renzi with all her might. "I do pray you will come back to us, and tell of your adventures on the high seas. You will, won't you, Nicholas? Promise me."

Renzi nodded. "I promise," he said softly.

She sighed, linking her arm in his, and they walked on back to the house.

Suddenly the string trio stopped playing and the happy confusion of chattering and laughter died away. Then a general roar of approval met the musicians getting to their feet and taking position for country dancing.

Cecilia gave a squeal of delight. " 'Shepherd's Hey!' " she exclaimed. In dismay Renzi saw the couples forming up. Too late, the reel was quickly taken by three couples, and the dancing began again, much more boisterously than before with flushed faces, happy calls, whispered asides.

"I do apologize, Cecilia, I fear I am not accustomed to these particular steps," Renzi said quietly. A slight shadow passed over his features.

"Then we shall sit, sir," she said.

"On no account—be so good as to rescue poor Thomas." She left, but Kydd had already cheered up at the rustic dancing and was striking the hey with the best of them, at last enjoying himself.

A sudden commotion at the end of the line of men resolved itself into a loud clunking. Renzi knew what it must be; the boatswain had been drawn to the joyous sound of the dance and had joined in. With his red face split by a huge smile, first one leg then his wooden peg rose and fell with a clunk as the line advanced and bowed, advanced and reared. The assembly roared with good-humored laughter and the violinist redoubled his efforts.

The evening wore on—Mr. Bedsoe performed most creditably on the flute, and Miss Eccles was greeted with much polite applause on presenting her new poem. Then, after more dancing, it was clear that the evening was drawing to a close. Renzi sought Cecilia again, and found her in conversation with her brother. "I find this is the final dance. Should you stand up for me, I would be obliged," he said.

"Oh, stuff and nonsense, Nicholas, of course I shall." She laid her hand in his and they moved out onto the floor again. She looked up at him—fondly, he thought.

The dance began, the couples swirled and exchanged. His new partner prattled on, clearly flattered at partnering Renzi. The arches formed, the girl went through with a giggle, and another presented herself to be exchanged, grinning vapidly up at him. His eyes strayed about, looking for Cecilia. On the opposite side he saw her, twirling around a serious young man he had seen her with before and who obviously knew her.

The music skirled on heedless, and it was time to exchange again. But Cecilia did not—the young man had whispered something to her and she had stopped dead, staring at him. Renzi missed his step in his concentration and had to apologize to his partner. When he looked again, it was to see the pair disappearing into the garden.

With rising feeling he endured the wait, mechanically stepping out the measures. Eventually they returned, hand in hand, Cecilia's face a study in happiness. Impulsively, she pulled down the young man's shy face and kissed him, looking up at him intensely.

Renzi stopped dancing, letting his hands fall to his sides. A welling bitterness rose, not at Cecilia but at life—existence itself.

Astonished, his partner stared at him in dismay. He mumbled his excuses and left the floor, enduring the stares and muttered comments of the other dancers. He took a glass of shrub and downed it quickly. Kydd was over in the corner, reclaimed by the deaf old woman who was maundering on at him. Renzi strode over and interrupted, "Brother, I crave fresh air. The evening is over. Do you wish a walk home, or . . ."

Kydd looked at him in surprise, but quickly recovered. "O' course, m' friend." Renzi noted with relief that he needed no explanations. Courteous but firm, Renzi paid his devoirs to Mrs. Daryton, explained their intent to a puzzled Mrs. Kydd, and they were soon afoot on the three-mile stretch back to Guildford.

Silent, they tramped back in the warm darkness, past fields of sleeping oxen and sheep, hayricks looming rickety and large. Kydd was aware that something untoward had occurred to trouble his friend. "Is anythin' amiss, Nicholas?" he asked in a low voice.

Renzi did not answer at first, then said harshly, "Know that I must depart for Portsmouth these three days."

"I know," said Kydd softly. He had often wondered, over the last few weeks, how he would take the actuality of Renzi's departure, the blankness in his life where his friend had been.

"Then I shall not allude to it further," Renzi said, in an affected voice.

Kydd felt a lump rising in his own throat, but knew that any display of emotion on his part would alienate Renzi. "O' course," he said.

They preserved silence the whole way back, finally reaching the schoolhouse. It was in darkness; the carriage must have long since passed them on the other road, and everyone would now be abed.

"There is a light in the kitchen," Kydd said quietly. They climbed over the low garden fence and made their way to the back. A single candle lay on the kitchen table, and they entered, the door squeaking noisily. They tiptoed in, but they had been heard, and Cecilia appeared in a nightgown with a candle, her face alight with excitement. "Thomas—Nicholas," she whispered, as loudly as she could. "You'll never guess what happened tonight."

Renzi's face set like stone. Kydd frowned in bafflement. "What is it, sis?" he asked.

"No—really, the most wonderful news!" she squealed.

Kydd snorted impatiently. "What is it then, if we c'n ask?"

She pouted prettily. "Then I won't tell you, you horrid man."

There was a stirring next to Kydd. "Do I take it that we must offer our felicitations?" Renzi said woodenly.

Cecilia stared at him. "I—I don't know what you mean, Nicholas," she said uncertainly.

"The young man—he and you . . ."

"Roger Partington, and you'd never conceive—tonight he confessed to me that it would make him the happiest man in the world if I could grant his dearest wish."

She turned to Kydd, oblivious of the look on Renzi's face.

"Thomas, he wishes so much to be a teacher, a scholar, and wanted me to intercede with Father in this. But then I thought, why should he not take your place, dear brother, and then you can go back to sea?"

She watched, delighted, as her words rendered the two men equally thunderstruck. "Well, Thomas, can you bear after all not to be a teacher? Shall you pine after the grammar, yearn for your figuring again?"

Kydd and Renzi stood frozen.

"I shall return presently," Cecilia whispered, and swept up the stairs. In a few minutes she was back. At the stupid look on Kydd's face she threw her arms about his neck. "You darling boy! You wonderful, silly brother—can you not see?" Handing him a brown paper parcel she said, "I have saved your precious sailor rig for you. I hid it from Mother as I knew you would need it someday. You are a sailor, Tom, you're different from we land folks." She lowered her eyes. "Go with Nicholas, Tom, you must. And may God bless you and keep you, and bring you safely back to us."

"God *damn* it!" Kydd exploded. He was sitting on the grass verge of the road, shaking out yet another stone from his shoe. It was wonderful to be back in his loose-swinging sailor's rig, but his feet were sore, they had not brought drink and the sun beat down on them.

Renzi looked up resentfully. "If we had kept back just one . . ." he began, in an uncharacteristically morose tone.

"And if *we* had thought t' ask the other . . . !" Kydd snapped back. It was the fault of both and neither: in their plan to avoid the wounded looks of his mother they had, with Cecilia's reluctant connivance, sneaked out before dawn for the journey south.

Independently, they had emptied their pockets of their remaining money, leaving it as a peace offering on the mantelpiece of the drawing room. The driver of the mail coach at the Angel had adequate experience of sailors and their prodigal habits ashore, and was scornful of their entreaties. The coach lurched off without them, down the high street and away with a splendid cracking of whips and deafening clatter of wheels on cobblestones. There was no way they could return home, not after Cecilia's generous but stricken farewell.

Kydd felt warm at the memory of her shyly producing his sea clothes, sweet-smelling and neatly folded. He had stowed them in his seabag, together with the meaningful gift of an ingenious portable writing set: quills, ink block and penknife in a polished wooden box.

Renzi softened too—there had been a kiss for them both, for him the moist warmth had been placed rather closer to his mouth than was customary, and her head had not been averted suffi ciently to avoid his chaste return peck landing perilously close to her own parted lips. Goethe's "Prometheus" in the Hallstadt edition was her gift to him; its restless subjectivity was not altogether to his taste, but he would persevere for the sake of her kindness.

A bishop's carriage prepared to leave, and they gratefully accepted his patriotic offer. The kindly gentleman had taken them as far as Petworth, provided they rode outside and promised to behave themselves with sobriety and decorum.

They were now on foot, six miles beyond on Duncton Hill and halfway to their goal of Chichester and the coast. There, they hoped the busy coastwise roads would provide transport.

Renzi was only too aware that he was not as inured to walking as the country folk, who would quickly starve if they insisted on coaches wherever they went. On the road they met several who waved curiously at the exotic pair. He muttered under his breath, and humped his seabag once more, but a distant movement and dust haze on the winding road caught his eye. Some sort of empty hay wagon; there was a blotch of red in the front seat, unusual where faded fustian was more the rule.

Seeing Renzi pause, Kydd glanced back. "You think . . . ?" he said.

"In our direction, and without a load," Renzi replied.

Without discussion, they dropped their bundles and waited for the wagon to approach. The horses toiled listlessly up the hill, and it became clear that there were objects in the body of the wagon.

"That's a lobsterback!" Kydd burst out. As the wagon approached they saw that the marine was a guard for the press-gang, the objects in the wagon his luckless catch.

Kydd laughed. "If we don't leg it smartly, we could fin' ourselves pressed."

Renzi smiled wryly. They were in no danger—real deserters would be in disguise and heading *away* from the seaports.

They waved down the wagon. The marine was dusty and bored, and saw no reason why they should not share a ride to Portsmouth. They clambered gratefully into the wagon with their bundles, and found themselves a place among the dozen or so victims of the press, who were handcuffed to the outside rail.

There were two sailors also, members of the gang, comfortably wedged at the forward end, enjoying a bottle. They looked up in surprise as Kydd and Renzi boarded. "Yo ho, shipmates, what cheer," the older one said.

"*Artemis,*" Kydd said briefly, swelling with pride.

The sailors sat up. "No flam! Then ye'll need to clap on more sail, mates, should yer wanna be aboard afore she sails."

"What?"

"She's sailin', mate—another of yer vy'ges with a bag o' gold fer yez all at the end," the younger said enviously.

So her battle damage had been made good already; there must have been some ruffled feathers in the staid world of the dock-yards. But would they make it in time?

"She out o' dock yet?" Kydd asked.

"Dunno—we're *Diadem*s at Spithead, mate, how would we know?" The older man was short with them. *Diadem* was an old-fashioned and slow sixty-four-gun third rate, which could neither catch a frigate nor really keep the line of battle.

The bottle was passed over as the wagon ground off, and as Kydd took a pull at the liquor he noticed one or two resentful looks from the prisoners, who lolled pitifully, their hands clinking the iron cuffs that held them.

There was one young man of an age with himself, sitting miser-ably with his head back. He stared up into the summer sky with an expression that spoke of homesickness, fear and helplessness. Kydd's own dolorous journey as a pressed man was only a little more than six months before and so much had happened since—adventures that would have seemed terrifying if he had known of them beforehand.

He flashed a comradely grin at the lad, who turned away in his misery, not wishing to talk. Kydd shrugged. There was an unbridgeable distance between them. He raised his bottle. The raw gin was heady but did nothing for his thirst. He wiped his mouth and passed it to Renzi.

It was a serious matter if they missed *Artemis*. They would have no option but to ship out in another unknown vessel, which as volunteers they would have the privilege of choosing. But Kydd had been much looking forward to meeting his old shipmates again, and the frigate was of the first order as a fighting ship—lucky, too.

The wagon swayed on, the wheels grinding monotonously as the hours passed, the heat tedious to bear without any shade. Finally they passed on to Portsea Island and began the final stretch to Portsmouth town. The gaiety and feverish celebrations of before were now well over, replaced by a purposeful wartime hurry.

The downcast pressed men stirred when they realized their journey was concluding, and at the sight of the grim lines of ships at anchor a youngster began to whimper and the older ones turned grave.

Kydd's heart leapt, however, as his gaze took in the scene. His nostrils caught the fresh sea air breezing in, and he eagerly observed the ships at anchor—the bulk of *Queen Charlotte,* Admiral Howe's flagship; the *Royal Sovereign* of equal size; and he thought he recognized old *Duke William* farther down the line.

The wagon stopped at the Sally Port—the prisoners would wait shackled until the boats came for them, but they were free to bid farewell and tramp up the well-remembered road across to the dockyard.

The dock and the berth alongside were empty. There was no sign of *Artemis,* and Kydd's heart sank. They were too late. Depressed, they hunkered down on the cobblestones as they thought about what to do. It was a keen loss, which Kydd perceived came from a sense of homelessness, when hearth and home now sheltered someone else.

Renzi first spotted her. End on, she was over at the other side of the harbor, at Weevil Lake off the Royal Clarence Victualling Yard, taking in casks of salt beef and ship's biscuit. But how were they to get out to her?

Almost immediately they saw distantly a boat put off from the stern of *Artemis.* It slowly crossed the bright water toward their dockyard jetty, resolving into the Captain's barge.

"No way, Jack," the coxswain of the barge replied to their entreaties. "Cap'n's orders," he said impatiently. "We 'as a full crew, 'n' don't need no more volunteers." He unshipped the rudder and heaved it into the boat, and came up to where they were standing. "Yer knows she's goin' foreign?" he said, looking at them knowingly. The information would deter some. At the expression on their faces, the man softened. "Look, mates, tell yez now—barky closed books on 'er ship's company sennight since, ain't taken a soul after. Sorry."

They didn't speak, so the coxswain shrugged and left them to it.

Lifting his seabag Kydd muttered, "We'll need t' find a ship, Nicholas, or we're like t' starve."

Renzi nodded agreement, and got slowly to his feet.

"Oars!" bellowed the coxswain. In the boat the men tossed their oars to the vertical and assumed a reverential dignity. "Bugger off," he whispered harshly.

With his head bowed in concentration, Captain Powlett strode forcefully down to the jetty. A gray-haired lieutenant talked to him urgently until they reached the boat. The coxswain saluted, and took the Captain's plain leather dispatch case.

Powlett began to descend the stone steps to the boat when Kydd pushed forward. "Sir!" he called. Powlett looked up irritably, without pausing in his motions. "Sir—you remember me?"

The Captain stopped and glanced up in surprise. "Ah, yes—one of the *Royal Billys*." His eyebrows contracted in an effort of remembrance. "And one of the first boarders," he added, in satisfaction.

"Sir, we want t' ship with you."

There was a hiss of indrawn breath from the Captain's coxswain.

The moment hung. The pair's travel-worn appearance and something about Kydd's intensity moved Powlett. "Very well. Get forrard, then."

The scandalized coxswain glared, the bowman grinned and shifted over, but Kydd obstinately remained standing. "We both, sir."

Powlett glanced at Renzi. "The odd one, but quick with a blade—through the gunport, was it not?" he asked.

"Sir."

"Then we can find a place for them both, Mr. Fairfax?" Powlett said to the lieutenant, with an unmistakable edge.

"Aye aye, sir," the man said.

"So yez had enough o' them 'long shore ways," Petit rasped.

"Couldn't stomach the shoreside scran," grumbled Kydd, fighting down a grin.

"A bag o' guineas says yer *did* jus' manage to get outside a dark ale or three." This was Billy Cundall. He had moved into their mess in place of Adam, who had decided for no special reason to move across to another mess.

Kydd's smile was broad and open, his white teeth showing in the dim gold light of the lanthorn above the table. He raised his grog can in salute and swallowed. While in port, the small beer was quite acceptable, brewed specially in the dockyard for the fleet. It was only after weeks at sea that the sourness and metallic aftertaste became apparent.

Luke came with a mess kid of steaming pottage. He still had the hollow eyes and withdrawn air that he'd had since the battle.

Quashee broke off his conversation with Petit. "What ho, Luke, is it to me exactin' standard, or shall we have ter send it back?" There was no answer from the boy, and Quashee glanced at Petit.

"Leave 'im be, mate," Petit muttered.

Renzi made a characteristic deprecating gesture, and the mess knew that he had something to say, and waited expectantly. "We shall within this week be outward bound—to the far side of the world." He drew himself up and intoned

> *"On burning coasts, or frozen seas,*
> *Alike in each extreme*
> *The gallant sailor's ere at ease,*
> *But floats with fortune's stream . . ."*

"Clap a stopper on it!"

"Avast th' jabber, shipmate!"

The good-natured chorus drowned Renzi's attempts, and in mock disgust he drank noisily from his pot.

"What's y'r meaning, Nicholas?" Kydd prodded.

"Well, *if* you will allow me," he said, and leaned back.

"Get on with it, damn you for a shab!"

Kydd's eyebrows contracted at Cundall's ill-judged words to his friend.

Renzi seemed not to have heard. "It will not have escaped your notice that the officers are laying in stores, a good deal. This voyage will not be a simple one." The table exchanged looks. It was widely believed that Renzi had second sight, such had been the accuracy of his predictions in the past.

"What do ye mean?" Petit said carefully.

"That mayhap we should follow suit—in our little way, of course."

"We?"

"Can you conceive a span of six months at sea, nothing new, always the same food, the same company? We will rue it, I believe, were we not to take a precaution."

The thought had clearly not entered their heads.

"Only one kinda stores we better 'ave—an' if the kegs run out, then it'll have ter be bottles." Cundall had a handsome face: he took care to flare his side whiskers to frame it.

"Aye, but ye knows that in th' Indies it's like to be arrack—made outa rice. It'll bowse up yer jib in a brace o' shakes right enough, Billy boy." Eyes turned to Petit, who leaned back innocently.

"Come on, mate, you've bin out there afore, ain't yer?" Quashee said.

"Yair, but I wanta hear what Renzi is a-sayin'," Petit said.

Renzi continued, "Only little things, I grant, but I have the feeling they will be deeply appreciated in the future. I say that we empower Quashee to step ashore to make purchases for the mess in general as he sees fit, some condiments, some—"

"Some 'oo?" Cundall said.

"Conweniences!" said Quashee happily. "He means conweniences! A rub o' ginger, dried 'erbs, a jar o' molasses, that's the ticket."

"Just so," Renzi said. "But we also need amusements. I have made my preparations, but could I suggest it be taken under general consideration?" The concept of preparing for recreation was a novel matter: it caused the table to go quiet.

Pinto spoke up for the first time. "*Padrino,*" he said to Petit, "what you do, when you sail to the Indee?"

Petit toyed with his pot. "Renzi's right, o' course. Three, four year back it was, if yer recollects, we went ter Batavia to pick up Bligh 'n' his crew 'oo stayed with 'im in the *Bounty* launch. Took 'em back to Portsmouth." Kydd remembered reading about it in the news; it had a different meaning now.

Petit had their attention and carried on with his yarn. "Illtempered sod, was Bligh—noo his rights as a grunter, did he, 'n' him only a jumped-up master's mate. Useta strut up 'n' down the quarterdeck, never goin' forrard, ever."

There was a stirring around the table. Opinions in the Navy were divided between admiration for Bligh's undoubted feat of seamanship—four thousand miles in an open boat without losing a man—and contempt for his equally undoubted senseless brutality to his men. "Long v'yage, yair, but don't recollect we 'ad troubles findin' things to do," he ruminated.

"Well, what did y' do in th' dog-watches each night?" prompted Kydd.

"Usual kinda things. Yarns, dice, fancy work with th' rope. Oh, yeah, makin' things!" He fumbled and pulled out his seaman's knife. "Like this I done." The handle was beautifully carved, the hand-filling curve of a leaping dolphin in ebony.

"'N' others, they like ter scrimshander—carvin' whale's teeth an' that."

Kydd thought of Wong and the intricate nude Oriental females he always fashioned. "Yeah, I seen that."

Petit scratched his head. "'Bout all I c'n say—you makes yer own amusements, mates."

It made Kydd thoughtful, and he broached the subject with Renzi later.

"Food for the intellect, dear fellow. Turn time to account. He who kills time is a murderer." Renzi had no doubt about it. Kydd guessed that soon a significant amount of space in their shared sea chest would be taken up with books.

There was no way of avoiding it—the ship was under sailing orders and could sail imminently: Kydd had to write a final letter to Cecilia. Reluctantly he found his portable writing kit and set it up.

He tested the sharpness of the quill nib with his thumb, and settled his paper and ink once again. The noise of the mess deck around him was unsettling, the building excitement making it difficult to concentrate—and, of course, he was no taut hand with words, it was quite outside his character.

"*Artemis,* at anchor, Spithead," he began.

He sucked at the tip of the quill until it began to look bedraggled and sorry, and he glanced around despairingly. The lanthorn set on the table next to him guttered and radiated a hot candle smell.

"The 15th day of August, 1793. Weather: Cool westerlies, slight chop." This was better, it was beginning to flow.

"Dear Sister"—or should that be "Cecilia"? He had never written to her before in his life.

"I trust I leave you, as our mother and father, in good health." Clever one, that—women always set great store by such things.

"We sail for India now. Nicholas says it will be 13,000 miles. We have been taking in stores. It is hard work, and you would stare at the strange kinds."

His mind reviewed the last sentence. Some were passing strange—a mysterious canvas mailbag with a heavy padlock through the cringles at its mouth and guarded by sour-faced red-coats; the heavy rectangular bundles requiring special dry storage that turned out to be scores of newspapers; the chickens and goats that would be looked after at sea by the peculiar Jemmy Ducks and slaughtered in turn—she obviously wouldn't be interested in these arid details.

"We will be at sea for many months or a year, or more than a year. Today is dry and cool. Elias Petit says that around the Cape will set us at hazard this time of the year. *Daemon* frigate was there lost with all hands in the year '86." It was difficult to think of anything else that might interest her, and when Renzi arrived, he looked up with relief. "Nicholas! What should I write to my sister? Here is my paper, and it's not yet half written."

Renzi looked over his shoulder, then sat opposite, quite blank-faced. "Do you understand, Thomas, that the ladies are on quite another tack to us in the matter of communications?" he explained. "They are illogical, flighty and strangely interested in the merest details, you know."

Kydd had never considered the matter before.

Renzi waited, and thought of Cecilia, the intelligent, darting dark eyes, the sturdy practicality giving backbone to the appealing childish warmth of her femininity. Unaccountably he felt a pang. "Would you be offended were I to offer my suggestions?" he found himself saying.

"O' course not, Nicholas! Give us a broadside of 'em, I beg."

"Very well." Cecilia was practical, but she would want to know personal details. "Are you ready?"

" 'It is the eve of great adventures—to the fabled court of the Great Moghul, the sacred groves of Calicut—yet must I look to the needs of the voyage! Therefore, dear sister, I have . . .' " Those eyes, softening under his gaze. She would want to know of feelings; fears, hopes . . . " 'At the signal on the morrow we spread our sails and disappear from mortal ken into the Great Unknown, the vasty deep. I cannot but feel a quickening of the spirit as I contemplate the asininity of man's claims to dominion, when he but rides above the . . .' "

"Wait! This pen is scratchy. Do ye think she'll suspect that it's not me, I mean, writin' like this?"

"Of course she will not, brother. '. . . if you give thought to me, dear Cecilia, be certain that my image is foremost in your mind when . . .' " It would be months before there would be chance of a mail passage back to England in one of the stately East Indiamans; this letter would have to last.

"*Haaaands* to unmoor ship!"

The anchorage was the same, the view of the low, dark green coast and white slashed downs was the same, but the feeling was definitely different.

Kydd waited in the foretop to go up to lay out and loose the foretopsail; he had possibly the best view in the ship. Impulsively he reached for one of the brand-new lines from aloft, and took a long sniff. The deep, heady odor of the tar was a clean sea smell, and it seemed to Kydd to symbolize his break with the land.

His heart beat with excitement at the thought of the epic voyage ahead, to lands strange and far. What singular sights would he see, what adventures would he undergo, before he would be back here again? He gulped but his eyes shone. Deep-sea voyaging was never anything but a hard, chancy affair. Death from a dozen causes lay in wait—a helpless fall from aloft into the vastness of the sea, malice of the enemy, shipwreck, disease. His eyes might at this moment be making their last mortal sighting of the land that had given him birth.

On deck below, officers paced impatiently as the cable slowly came in at the hawse, and Kydd blessed his fortune once again at being a topman and therefore spared cruel labor at the capstan.

"Lay out and loose!" The voice blared up from Parry's speaking trumpet. It was common knowledge that he had been mortified when Fairfax had been brought in as first lieutenant against his expectations. It was usual for wholesale promotions to follow a successful bloody action. Some officers might take their disappointment out on the men; time would tell.

The frigate cast effortlessly to starboard, quickly gathering way. The fo'c's'le guns banged out the salute, eddying puffs of a reduced charge from the six-pounders reaching him with its memory of battle.

On deck again, Kydd heaved a deep sigh, gripping a shroud and looking back on the still-detailed shoreline. He thought of the small schoolhouse that perhaps he would never see again. A tremor passed over him, a premonition perhaps. Had this all been a mistake?

The yards trimmed, the anchor at last catted and fished, *Artemis* settled down for the run out to sea. Kydd busied himself at the forebitts, anxious for some reason to keep the land in sight for as long as possible. Details of the shore diminished and blurred into insignificance as it slipped away astern, and the land began to take on an anonymous uniformity.

As they passed beyond the seamark of Worsley's Obelisk, *Artemis* duly performed her curtsy to Neptune, the first deep sea swell raising her bow majestically and passing down her length until at midpoint she fell again in a smash of spray. The motion made him stagger at first, but the live deck once more under his feet was glorious. Glancing aloft he drank in the curving of the leeches of the sails, one above the other in exactly the right blend of curves and graces, the bar-taut new rigging in its familiar complexity as an elegant counterpoint.

With no raised poop the deck edge was a sweet line from where he stood right aft, and he marveled anew at the natural beauty of a ship: no straight lines, no blocky walls, she was much closer to a sculpture than a building.

He looked back to the land. Within the span of a deck watch it had transformed from the solid earth from where before he had his being to the graying band now about to leave his sight and consciousness. In a short time they would be alone, quite alone in the trackless immensity of the ocean.

CHAPTER 5

≈

Staring at the empty horizon where England had been, he didn't hear the footsteps behind. A hand clapped on Kydd's shoulder, snapping him out of his reverie. "No vittles fer you, then, lad?"

He followed Petit to the fore-hatch, and joined the others with mixed emotions at dinner. The lines beside Renzi's mouth seemed deeper, his expression more set than Kydd could remember having seen it before. He realized that Renzi must feel the same way as he, but with the added force of an intelligence that had no control over its destiny, no chance to affect its onward rush into whatever lay ahead. It was a somber thought.

"So it's farewell t' Old England!" Kydd tried to be breezy, but it fell flat. The table lapsed into silence; no one wished to catch an eye. It might be years before they saw home again, and with the certainty that some would not make the happy return.

Cundall slammed down his pot. "An' not too soon, mates—me dear ole uncle just got scragged at Newgate fer twitchin' a bit o' silver, me aunt needin' the rhino 'n' all."

There was murmuring; justice shoreside was far worse than at sea. Kydd sat for a while, letting the conversation ebb and flow about him, listening to the regular creaks and swishes of a ship in a seaway, and felt better.

"Why we goin' to India, Mr. Petit?" Luke's treble voice sounded above the talk.

Petit shoved away his plate, and thought for a while. "Why, can't say as 'ow I has an answer fer that, Luke. We threw out the Frogs fer good not so long ago . . ."

"Nicholas?" Kydd prompted.

Staring at the timbers of the ship's side, Renzi didn't speak. At first Kydd thought he had not heard, then he said quietly, "I cannot say. True, the French have been ejected, but there are native rajahs who see their best interest in stirring discord among the Europeans, and are probably in communication with the French—but this is small stuff." He settled back and continued, "I can't think what there is in Calcutta that would justify our presence, especially a crack frigate of our reputation."

That was the sticking point: *Artemis* was not just any frigate but at the moment the most famous in the Navy. Loosed like a wolf on the French sea-lanes she was a proven predator, and if a frigate was wanted in those seas then others could be spared.

"Coulda got wind of a Frog ship come ter ruffle feathers like, those parts." Doud had drawn up a tub to join the group. He always respected Renzi's pronouncements for their profundity.

Renzi shook his head. "No, wouldn't be that, Ned. Bombay Marine will settle their account. Seems we have a mystery, shipmates."

Artemis made a fast passage south, through Biscay and on into sunnier seas. At one point they were reined in by an irascible captain of a passing seventy-four-gun ship-of-the-line, but under Admiralty orders they could not be touched, and once more spread canvas for their far destination.

Kydd was surprised at how the immediacy and movement of his life on land froze so quickly, was packaged into a series of static images, then slipped away into the past, to become a collection of memory fossils. His immediacy was now the rhythm of sea life—the regular watch on deck, an occasional fluster of an "all hands" to take in sail for a squall, and the continual ebb and flow of daily events, each as predictable as the rising sun, but in sum a comforting background against which Kydd grew and matured as a seaman.

His oaken complexion was renewed in the sun, and work aloft restored his upper body strength to the point at which he could have swarmed up a rope hand over hand without using his feet to grip.

Renzi envied Kydd's easy development, his agility aloft, his natural gifts as a sailor. Kydd's splicing and pointing were meticulous, while his own was adequate but lacked the regularity, even technical beauty, of Kydd's work. His own body tended to the spare, whipcord wiriness that went with his austere temperament, and where Kydd gloried in the dangers lurking aloft, Renzi was careful and sure in his movements, never taking uncalculated risks or making an unconsidered move. Kydd soon caught up and overtook him in these skills but, as Renzi reminded himself, his own objective was to serve a sentence, not to make a life's calling.

He recalled what had passed when they were tasked off to bowse down the gammoning around the bowsprit. Suspended on opposite sides, under the gratings and walkways above, they were as close to the exact point at which the stem cleaved the water as they could be. It was mesmerizing, seeing at such close quarters the cutwater dip slowly and deeply into the ocean, scattering rainbow jewels of water, pausing, then making an unhurried rise, as regular and comforting as the breathing of a child at a mother's breast. It took an effort of will for them to finish the job and return.

And at night, the startlingly bright moonpath of countless gleaming shards, which continually fractured and joined, danced and glittered in a spirited restlessness. The reliable winds at this latitude left little for the watch on deck to do, and they would stare at it for long periods. Under its influence they considered the mysteries of life, which the normal course of existence on land, with its ever-present distractions, would never have allowed. Time at sea had a different quality: it required that men move to its own rhythms, conforming to its own pace.

"Night's as black as ol' Nick hisself," said Doud, finishing hanking the fall of the weather fore-brace. The usual trimming of sails at the beginning of the watch was complete now and they would

probably be stood down. Only voices in the dark and passing
shadows on the glimmering paleness of the decks were evidence of
the existence of other beings. A low cry came from aft: "Watch on
deck, stand down."

They would remain on deck ready, but they could make themselves as comfortable as the conditions would allow. Soft talk
washed around Kydd; old times, old loves. Drowsily, he looked up
at the sky. It was easy to be hypnotized by the regular shifting
occlusion of sails and rigging across the star-field as the vessel
rolled to the swell.

"What's down there?" he found himself saying.

The talk trailed off. "Yer what?" said one voice.

Kydd levered himself up while the thought took shape. "I
mean, at the bottom o' the sea—we're only on th' top, must be all
kinds'a things down there." His mind swam with images of
sunken ships, skeletons of whales and the recollection of a diorama
he had once seen of Davy Jones's Locker. It seemed reasonable to
expect the muddy seabed that their anchor gripped to extend
indefinitely in all directions, coming up only for land. "How deep
does it get?" he asked.

A deeper voice answered, "Dunno. That is ter say, no one
knows. Yer deep-sea lead is eighty, hunnerd fathom, an' it gives 'no
bottom' only a few leagues off Scilly. After that, who knows? It's
as deep as it is."

Six hundred, maybe a thousand feet, and straight down. Kydd
remembered the purity and crystal clarity of deep seawater in the
daytime with the sun's rays reaching down in moving shafts of
light, and even then he had never seen the bottom.

"Nighttime, that's when yer thinks about it—what's there
movin' about under our keel, mates, a rousin' good question," the
voice declared.

A buzz of animated conversation started.

"Ship goes down with all hands in a blow, stands ter reason,
they're down there still."

"Naah—sharks'll be at their bones quicker'n silver."

"What flam, Jeb! Where's yer sharks in th' north?"

"There's other things, mate, what likes ter eat a sailor's bones. Things 'r' down there a-waitin' their chance."

"What things?" Kydd asked, apprehensive of the reply.

"Monsters, mate! Huge 'n' bloody monsters."

This provoked a restless stirring, but the voice was not contradicted. The cheerful slapping of ropes against the mast and the unseen plash of the wake shifted imperceptibly to a manic fretfulness. A new voice started from farther away: "He's right there, has ter be said. Some as say there ain't no monsters, but yer've got ter agree, a sea this big c'n hide more'n a whole tribe of 'em."

"Sure there's monsters," an older voice cut in. "An' I seen one. Two summers ago only. We wuz at anchor off Funchal—'n' that ain't so far from here—had fishin' lines over the side, hopin' fer albacore, so 'twas stout gear we had out." He cleared his throat and continued, "Nearly sundown, 'n' we was about to haul th' lines in when comes such a tug on one it nearly took me with it inter the 'oggin. Me frien' who was alongside me saw the line smokin' out like it had a stone weight on it plungin' down, an' he takes a turn on a cleat, slows it down a bit. Then th' line slackens an' he hauls in."

There was total quiet.

"Sudden-like, there's a shout. I goes ter the side an', so help me God, I sees there somethin' I don' never want ter see again!"

Kydd held his breath.

"Red eyes 'n' fangs workin' away, there's this great long dark green serpent. An' I mean long! Me frien' worked it aft by tyin' off on the pins one be one, an' I'm here ter tell yez, mates, it stretched out from abreast the foremast all the way aft ter the quarterdeck. Squirmin' and thrashin', right knaggy it was, thumpin' the side until officer o' the deck told us to cut him loose ter save the ship."

A younger voice interjected, "Yer c'n be sure that's nowt but a tiddler, Lofty. Bigger ones down there, yer just don't know."

"An' they ain't the worst of 'em—it's them what the Norskeys call the Kraken, they're the worst."

"What 'r' they?"

"It's yer giant octopus, mate, big as yer like, loomin' up outa the sea at night, eyes as big as a church clock a-starin' up at yer—an' that's when you knows it's all up, 'cos it feeds on sailors what it sweeps up orf of the deck with its slimy great arms forty fathom long, with these 'ere suckers all over 'em."

Apprehension spread over Kydd. As they spoke there might be one directly in their path, lying in silent anticipation of its meal, just at this moment noiselessly rising up from the depths. He shivered, and hunkered down in the blackness as low as he could. Renzi was out of reach, now at his trick on the wheel, but in the forenoon they would certainly talk together.

The prevailing westerlies died and from the other direction the northeast trade winds began: pleasantly warm, vigorous and exhilarating, the best possible impetus for their southward voyaging. The sea turned ultramarine under the azure sky, and with hurrying white horses below and towering cumulus rising above, their sea world was a contrasting study in blue and white.

On the sun-dappled main deck Petit paused in his seaming. "Yez knows what this means."

Kydd looked up and waited.

"These are the trade winds, 'n' that means we now got Africa ter larb'd."

It was a thought to conjure with. The fabled dark continent, its interior unknown to mankind. Jungle and swamp, the whole mystery lying just over there from where the winds were blowing. Kydd was seized with a yearning to glimpse it, just once.

The weather grew from warm to hot; pitch between the deck planking became sticky to the touch where the sun beat down on it, and Kydd had to cover his torso with an open shirt; his bare feet had long ago become strong and toughened.

*   *   *

Below decks it was too hot to sleep. Kydd and Renzi sat on the fo'c'sle, off watch, Renzi with his clay pipe drawing contentedly and Kydd staring up dreamily. The stars were out, and of such brilliance they appeared low enough to touch. Along the eastern horizon, however, was a dark line. Curious, they watched it take shape. As the hours wore on it extended gradually on both sides and fattened to a bank of darkness. Lightning played within it, a continuous flickering that illuminated tiny details of the cloud mass in tawny gold.

The heat of the day was still with them, the air breathy, heavy. They looked toward the bank idly, fascinated by the primeval sight. It was now moving toward them from the beam. As it drew nearer the distant flashes of lightning became more separated and distinct, and after a long interval an answering sullen rumbling of thunder could be heard floating toward them over the water.

"All the hands! All hands on deck—*haaaaands* to shorten sail!"

There was no apparent change in the immediate weather; the wind was the same streaming easterly, but for the first time Kydd could detect a scent, a heavy humid rankness of rotten vegetation and stagnant pools—the heady fragrance of Africa.

They took in courses, then topsails. Powlett, it seemed, would not be satisfied until the yards were at the cap and all they showed were staysails fore-and-aft. Their speed fell off, and the roll of the ship changed in character: the Atlantic swell passed them by to leave the ship wallowing in long jerky movements, an unsettling sensation for a fast frigate.

Drawing closer, the dense cloud bank increased in height and width, its dark pall gradually snuffing out the stars until it loomed high over them. Men did not return below, they lined the side and watched. The lightning became more spectacular, the thunder a spiteful crack and pealing roar. Then came a darkness more intense than ever.

Kydd felt something elemental stealing over him; the towers of blackness glowered moody and threatening, fat with menace. The wind died; in the calm the flashing and banging of the lightning filled the senses. There was a breathless pause as the last stars flickered out overhead. In the ominous calm it seemed that the fluky winds were in dispute for the right to turn on their prey.

A gust, then others. The wind picked up in violent, shifting squalls, sending Kydd staggering. The wall of blackness raced across toward them—and they were hit. In an instant it seemed as if the heavens were afire. The lightning coalesced into one blinding, ear-splitting blast of thunder, which ripped the air apart. The squalls tore at Kydd's grip in a nightmare buffeting and all he could do was stand rigid, stupefied. The ship reared and shied like a frightened horse, deafening volleys of thunder entering the fabric of the vessel, transmitting through to his feet. Worse by far than any broadside, the sound smashed at his senses. He fumbled for half-remembered prayers. They jostled in his mind but focus was impossible under the assault.

And the rain came down. Walls of warm, gusting tropical rain in quantities so huge that it forced Kydd down as though he were caught in a waterfall. Breathing was almost impossible, and he lowered his head to avoid the worst of the water tumbling down on him. Hair streaming, clothes plastered to his body, his mind went numb. It went on and on, the ship trembling and directionless, heading for who knew what inevitable destruction.

Kydd felt a grip on his arm. Through blurred vision he saw Renzi and, to his astonishment, realized that the man was laughing. He felt anger welling up, an indignant resentment that Renzi was enjoying the experience, no doubt adding it to his store of philosophic curiosities. He tore away his arm and resumed his posture of endurance, but it was no good, the spell had been broken. Reluctantly he had to concede that if modern learning could proof a man against nature's bluster then perhaps it had some merit.

He looked up again and grinned slowly. The heavens rattled

and roared but in some way the storm's sting had been drawn, and within the hour its fury had moderated. The rain petered out, and the blackness began to dissolve, the lightning spending itself in vicious flickers that whip-cracked right across the sky.

The last of the darkness was passing overhead. Rueful, soaked figures fumbled about on the streaming decks.

"*Haaaands* to make sail!"

Kydd moved to the larboard fore-shrouds and swung himself up for the climb into the foretop. But before he had risen a dozen feet there was a single dazzling flash and a clap of thunder so tremendous that it shook the ship with its concussion.

Deafened, he clung to the shrouds, shaking his head to clear it. As his eyes tried to adjust to the dark and his ears stopped buzzing he became aware of a commotion on the opposite side. The shrouds there gave off wisps of steam along their length. Still muzzy from the shock of the discharge Kydd couldn't understand. Then he realized—there had been one last spiteful play of lightning, and it had struck the foremast but by chance had passed down the opposite shrouds, to the iron of an anchor and into the sea.

Trembling at the thought of his near escape from an unspeakably violent death Kydd dropped to the deck and went over to see the results of the strike. The lines of rigging were randomly patterned with steaming black. Above, still clinging to the shrouds, were the silhouettes of three men, ominously still. Others climbed up beside them. There were shouts, high-strung and chilling—Kydd knew with a sinking inevitability what they had found.

By the light of a lanthorn they crowded round the stiff, discolored corpses as they were lowered down. Even the eyeballs had burst in the white heat, and the bodies had swollen to grotesque proportions. There was the sound of retching before canvas was brought to cover the indecency.

Dying rumbles followed the black mass as it fell away to leeward as rapidly as it had approached, leaving the stars to resume their calm display.

"No, me boy, we sank Africa astern three, five days ago," said Merrydew. For him the heat was a trial, his corpulent figure sweaty, his movements slow and reluctant.

Kydd found it confusing. From his barely remembered geography lessons he recalled that Africa was a fat pear shape running north and south. If they were to round its southern tip to reach India, why were they heading away?

"Because we're makin' a westing, that's why," the boatswain explained. To Kydd it seemed as nonsensical as ever. Patiently, Merrydew carried on. "These latitudes, why, much farther the wind gives up altogether, none to be had. Bad—we calls it the doldrums. We wants to avoid 'em, so we makes a slant over to t' other side o' the ocean afore it gets too bad. We then crosses the Line into the south half o' the world and slants back with an opposite wind—see?"

It was wearisome, life in the tropics aboard a frigate. The hardest thing was the intense humidity below decks, only partly relieved by wind scoops at the hatches. The next most difficult thing to bear was the food. Their molasses ran out, and the morning burgoo tasted of what it was, oatmeal months in the sack, malodorous and lacking flavor but for the insect droppings. Quashee did his best with the little store of conveniences, occasionally reaching heights of excellence. In the flying fish belt he produced a legendary gazy pie, the little fish heads peeping up through the crust all around, and flavored with hoarded garnishings.

The wind had been light and erratic for days now, a trying time when the hauling on lines had to be done under a near-vertical sun beating down, which blasted back at them from the water.

One morning the wind died away entirely, the sea disturbed only by a long but slight swell. The heat was close to intolerable, despite the awnings, and the boatswain's red face swelled. The sails hung in folds from the yards, barely moving; the ship, with a sluggish roll, was without any kind of steerage way. *Artemis* drifted aimlessly in the mirrorlike sea.

Nobody spoke, it cost too much effort. At three in the afternoon, a flaw of wind darkened the water. On the quarterdeck Powlett in his thin, threadbare shirt looked meaningfully at the figure of the Master.

It was what they had been waiting for. A wind—but from the southeast! They had already reached the winds of the south. The change in spirits aboard *Artemis* was remarkable. Although they had to wait until evening for the winds to reach a point where the sails began to fill and the rudder to bite, all talk was on the future.

"Got our slant—gonna be shakin' hands with them Kidderpore fillies in a month."

"Hassuming that we get in afore the monsoon shifts about."

Happy chatter swelled, but Petit remained serious as he cradled his pot.

"Anythin' amiss, Elias, mate?" Stirk asked. His powerful body was, as usual, naked from the waist up, an expanse of damp mahogany muscle.

"Yes, mate," Petit replied quietly.

The talking stopped and the group on the fo'c'sle looked over at him in the lanthorn light.

"How so, cuffin?" Stirk said softly.

"You knows, Toby, youse a man-o'-war's man an' unnerstands." Stirk didn't reply, but a frown lined his face. "Recollect, shipmate, we're in th' south now, and we ain't never had a visit from 'Is Majesty."

Stirk's face eased fractionally. "But o' course," he murmured. When Kydd looked again he had disappeared.

It looked as though the wind would hold. The morning breeze had stayed and strengthened just a little, and with the lightest possible canvas spread abroad they were making progress. Powlett stood with his arms folded, squinting up at the undulating sails as they played with the breeze. The Master was next to him, willing on the winds.

Kydd was tricing up the after end of the quarterdeck awning and could hear the pleased conversations—whatever was in those secret orders, he guessed they must include every stricture for speed.

The boatswain came aft, and touched his hat. "Sir," he said, "with m' duty, just found this paper near the quarterdeck nettings, thought you'd want t' sight it."

Taking the paper, Powlett's face hardened. The ploy was often used to allow crew members to convey discontents anonymously aft. He read on, his expression grim. "King Neptune? It's a nonsense, Mr. Merrydew!" he roared. The boatswain stiffened. "And a damnable impertinence!" Powlett snapped, and ripped the paper in two. The pieces fluttered to the deck. The boatswain's chin jutted belligerently: the customs of the Sea Service were not so easily to be put aside.

Turning to the Master, Powlett said loudly, "Mr. Prewse, pray tell us our position."

Rubbing his chin, Prewse looked up at the sky. "Well, sir, near enough . . ."

"Our position, sir!"

"Our longitude was thirty-two degree an' seventeen minutes west, noon yesterday."

"Latitude, Mr. Prewse?"

"An' nought degrees an' fifty-four minutes—north!"

Powlett whirled back on the boatswain. "There you are. North. Do you propose, sir, that we enter King Neptune's realm early? That is to say, precipitate, like a damn-fool set o' canting lubbers who can't work a sea position to save their skins?"

The boatswain's face eased into a smile. "Aye, sir, we'd best not set His Majesty at defiance!"

*   *   *

Kydd could hardly wait to relay the conversation to the mess, who were taking their victuals in the shade of the main deck.

"Yair, well, it's no small thing, mate, to enter hupon his realm," Petit said portentously.

Cundall leered evilly at Kydd. "An' it's bad days fer them 'oo 'aven't been welcomed inta it yet."

Realizing that he would be made sport of whatever he did, Kydd just smiled.

Doud's grin was devilish. His gaze slid to Quashee, who winked at him, and he affected a kind, considerate manner. "Could be the best fer any who don't know the rules to steer a mite clear of the ceremonies," he told Kydd. "'Is Majesty don't stand fer no contempt ter his person."

Kydd resolved to be conveniently absent when King Neptune came aboard.

"Should be hearin' from 'im soon!" Stirk said, his black eyes glittering at Kydd. "'Oo is it that ain't been admitted to 'is kingdom, then?"

That night, at seven bells of the first watch, *Artemis* was boarded by a messenger from King Neptune himself. Or, at least, a man looking just like a ragged sea sprite and dripping seawater suddenly appeared before the starboard fo'c'sle lookout from outboard, clambering rudely over the fife rail.

"What ship?" was demanded, and when the hapless lookout stuttered an answer, he was pelted with a rotten fish. "Down, yer scurvy shab, make yer respects to one o' King Neptune's crew!"

The officer-of-the-watch was summoned; it was Rowley. He doffed his hat, and courteously enquired of the stranger.

"'Is Majesty requires of yer a list of all 'oo have not yet bin truly welcomed inter his realm," the officer was told in lordly tones. By this time curious sightseers had gathered around, including some from the wardroom.

"Of course," said Rowley, "but I beg you, be so good as to take a glass while you wait. A rummer of brandy will, I believe, keep the damp from your bones."

Well satisfied but grumbling mightily, the sprite later eased himself over the rail and disappeared.

On the following forenoon, the masthead lookout hailed the deck. "Sail, ho! Strange sail right ahead, standin' fer the ship."

"What ship?"

"More like a boat wi' a lugsail."

Telescopes flashed on the quarterdeck. The boatswain turned importantly to the Captain and said, "It's very like King Neptune, sir!"

"Very well," said Powlett. "Make ready his carriage—heave to and prepare a welcome, Mr. Parry."

The boat was secured to the forechains and King Neptune was swayed aboard in a chair suspended from a whip rove at the fore-yardarm, followed shortly by his wife. His courtiers scrambled up the side and quickly took possession of the foredeck. They were a motley crew, rigged in a wild assortment of regalia: colored rags and old sailcloth decorated with seaweed, seagull feathers and wigs of oakum. The King's conveyance turned out to be a twelve-pounder gun carriage, with a suitably comfortable leatherbound chair lashed to it. Neptune assumed his rightful position, acknowledging the murmurs of awe in regal fashion with his trident.

Captain Powlett hurried to greet his august visitors, making a fine leg with his gold-laced hat sweeping down. "Well pleased are we, Your Majesty, that you have deigned to welcome us. Pray accept a glass of Western Ocean punch."

Neptune was certainly an imperious sight—a mighty beard of tarred oakum, long, flowing wig, striped toga, a trident and flaring golden crown. The glass was immediately to hand, and after draining it in one, the King addressed the party in a deep, rich voice. "What ship?"

"*Artemis* frigate, s' please Your Majesty," replied Powlett, in his usual worn shirt, but with his gold-laced cocked hat in honor of the occasion.

"Whither bound?" demanded King Neptune.

An expectant hush fell. "To the far Indee, the land of the peacock and elephant, rubies and gold," answered Powlett.

"What do ye there?" Neptune would answer to his shipmates later were he to pass up his chance.

Powlett's eyes glinted. "Nothing that would interest the puissant Sovereign of all the Seas!" he growled.

Neptune's wife adjusted her breasts. "Now, dear, we mustn't be late for the mermaid's dance," she said, in a beautiful falsetto that only a singer's voice like Doud's could produce. In her long flowing hair of teased-out manila, cheeks thick with red ocher and petticoat of yellow bunting she drew admiring looks, which she played upon shamelessly. Coquettishly she fingered the King's chain of office, a string of seashells, and the crowd roared.

"Badger Bag!" Neptune thundered.

His chamberlain stepped forward, an unmistakable hard figure with glittering black eyes under the fish scales and sacking. "Sire."

"Yon land toggies have no respec' for my royal person!" Neptune gestured angrily at the grinning officers.

Badger Bag reached into his large sack, but there was no need: the officers hurried to render elaborate obeisance to His Oceanic Majesty.

"Is my court prepared?" Neptune demanded.

"Of course, Your Majesty," said Powlett.

"Then forward!"

Flogged on by Badger Bag with a rope's end of stout sargasso seaweed, and with the maximum of horseplay, his courtiers trundled the haughty Neptune aft to the main jeer bitts, where his grand throne of a cunningly sawn large cask took pride of place.

"Where's 'is sea?" Badger Bag demanded, outraged. Quickly a kid filled with seawater was brought, and Neptune sat on his throne with a theatrical sigh, able to keep his feet at the very least in his natural element. Western Ocean punch flowed freely—it would be a sad thing indeed if *Artemis* could not right royally entertain their regal guests.

Neptune wiped his mouth after his third glass, dislodging his beard somewhat and revealing that his black complexion owed more to nature than artifice.

"King Neptune is black?" an amused Rowley said to Badger Bag.

"O' course" was the reply. "'Is Majesty is in mournin' fer his first wife—caught a mortal chill off the Newfie banks, sucklin' their child. 'E's minded ter blockade the Shetlands an' force the mermaids ter suckle the next one." For his temerity Rowley was struck roundly on the ear with a large fish drawn from the sack.

"Avast!" bellowed Neptune. "Bring forth the pollywogs."

Badger Bag fumbled in his sack and extracted a parchment. "Midshipman Titmuss!" he thundered. The youth in question, a dreamy boy with golden curls, was set upon by his assistants, the bears, who hauled him forward.

"Is this scrawny mortal worthy of entry to my realm?" Neptune demanded.

"Stands accused of leavin' his mama a-weepin' on land while he sails orf over the briny deep," Badger Bag said, "an' seen ter take soft tommy when 'e could've supped on hardtack," he continued remorselessly.

The bears began capering immediately. "Guilty! Guilty!" they crowed, scampering about the deck.

"Hold!" Neptune said. "In m' mercy, he shall be admitted—but not in them there awful whiskers! Shave 'im!"

The golden down could hardly be termed whiskers, but nevertheless a blindfold was clapped on and the youth frogmarched to the after end of the quarterdeck, where a huge canvas tub of seawater waited. He was guided to a chair on the edge of the tub. A bucket of water was dashed into his face, and the bears set to work with large wooden razors and carpenter's paste mixed with rancid butter. The youth struggled and yelled in desperation, but it only resulted in his mouth being choked with more of the foaming paste. At the height of his struggles, the chair was tipped over and the victim tumbled into the water.

Others were summoned and given summary justice, varying in their reactions from resignation to fighting like tigers, but all ending the same way, water flying everywhere and not least upon the bystanders.

Neptune sat back enjoying his judgments, but suddenly he stood up and flourished his trident. "That man there!" he said, pointing at Lieutenant Parry. "He smiled!"

Knowing looks were exchanged. The dour Parry was tight and grim in his dealings, humorless to a degree, but contempt of court could not be lightly dismissed—this would be interesting.

"Therefore he must be sick!" The court fell about in laughter. "Summon my doctor!" An elderly bear, slightly the worse for wear and Western Ocean punch, swayed forward. "What have you ter cure 'is mullygrubs?" Neptune ordered.

The bear blinked and then leered, pulling out a dark green bottle. "This'll cure anythin', sire."

The bears closed in. Parry drew himself up, his jaw hard. "Enough—hold your nonsense, you swabs." To the bears, who had seen him enjoy the torments of others, this was an invitation. Parry looked despairingly at Powlett, who seemed suddenly interested in the condition of the mizzen staysail downhaul.

"Sir!" he called, but it ended in a yelp, as he was borne to the deck by weight of numbers, and to the cheers and delight of the court was helped to liberal doses of "saline."

The jollity increased. Buckets of water, strategically placed in the rigging and operated by a twine trip-line, ensured that those looking to escape by keeping clear of the scrimmage received attention as well.

From his hiding place in the forepeak, Kydd thought the world had gone mad. Sitting cramped on smelly sea stores in the stifling heat, he heard the roars and unknown thuds and rushes overhead. At least he felt safe where he was, a place kindly suggested by Doud: the only entrance was through a small hatch. When a thump of feet sounded above he waited for them to pass but the hatch was thrown open and four bears with evil grins looked down on him. What Kydd hadn't reckoned on was the jigger tackle they had brought, which made easy meat of hauling out their victim.

He flailed wildly as they hoisted him out, but his struggles were ineffective. He was blindfolded and manhandled on deck to the riotous applause of the court seated in the chair of justice. The dread tones of Badger Bag sonorously announced his misdeeds. "Did fail to wind up the middle watch, in course o' which his shipmates did double tides."

"Guilty! Guilty!" slurred the gleeful bears.

"How dare he appear before me li' that!" The punch was having its effect on Neptune also. His wife now had baby Amphitrite to comfort, which she did vigorously, then dangled the odd creature from her harpoon.

Needing no prompting the barber's crew went into action. The shock of the seawater thrown in his face made Kydd open his mouth in protest. This was all they needed, and Kydd found himself choking on a revolting paste.

"Hold!" called Neptune, barely heard by the helpless Kydd. "Case dismiss'd on account 'e's a iggerant pollywog," he ordered.

Relieved, Kydd tried to remove his blindfold, but was stopped. "No, cully, this way."

He was guided to a plank spanning the water tub and ordered to cross. After some perilous swaying Kydd found himself inevitably plunging in. A generous tankard of punch was thrust at him as he surfaced, and the merriment transferred to the next victim, leaving Kydd rueful but relieved. He drank deeply, and noticed Renzi, also soaked and disheveled. They roared with laughter together.

The rampageous saturnalia cleared the air, and it was a happy ship that caught the next morning's breeze, when they resumed their southward plunge through deep blue seas and cloudless skies.

The frigate made magnificent sailing, the southeasterly trade winds strong and sure, an exhilarating sail, day after sunlit day, tight to the wind with bowlines on courses and topsails. With six months' sea endurance and a good amount of water from rain-storms, *Artemis* had no need to touch at the Cape. The only indication they had of reaching the southern tip of Africa was when, within a few days of each other, the southeasterlies had diminished, the chill Benguela current had turned the sea from blue to green, and the globe-encircling westerlies had taken them in hand.

They entered the great Southern Ocean, and for nearly a week they foamed along before the wind, marveling at the massive undulating swells and the albatross that followed in their wake, barely moving, staying aloft day after day. When at last they altered course northward, the Master's face cracked into a smile, and he and Powlett were seen to shake hands. They were in time to catch the last of the summer monsoon to speed them on to their destination.

As they passed deeper into the Indian Ocean it seemed an anti-climax. Sighting Madagascar, a faint blue-gray smudge far away to larboard, they crossed the Line to the north once more, but this time under a full press of sail.

It couldn't last, however: some days from their destination, after a particularly unpleasant tropical storm, they emerged into different airs. The heavy humidity and sultry heat had been replaced by a definite coolness, and the sky was a pearly cast of uniform dull lightness. The wind had changed from the urging southwesterly to a light, breathy breeze—in their teeth from the northeast.

Artemis braced up sharp, but it would not answer. She had a foul wind for Calcutta and must tack against the wind in long boards alternately, their rate of advance now cut by more than half. It was becoming a soul-deadening tedium.

As they worked closer to their goal they glimpsed tantalizing promises of their fabled destination. The floating remains of palm trees, a pair of vultures soaring out from the Deccan, the bloated body of a water buffalo; all were exotica to marvel over. Nearer still, ships were sighted daily: stately Indiamen, the first of the winter monsoon trading season, putting to sea with precious Darjeeling tea; humbler traders with jute—and warlike vessels crammed with opium on their way to the far Orient. There were also Arab dhows, their sweeping diagonal sail and rickety hull looking curious to an Atlantic seaman, and there were other, even stranger coastal craft.

It was enthralling—Kydd was excited by the sights and couldn't wait to see his first truly foreign shore.

"Heard th' Master say we should raise land in a coupla days," Doud said idly. The cool damp even reached down into the berth deck, and where it was allowed to remain mold grew and made objects slimy and rank.

"An' not before time," Kydd said. It felt a lifetime since they had left England, under sail the entire time, watch by watch, the days passing in regular progression; days, weeks, months at sea, until he knew every part of the ship with an intimacy he had never thought possible. "Be good t' know how things are at home," he mused.

Cundall laughed sharply. "Don' be stoopid—only way they gonna have word here is with the noospapers we took aboard in Spithead."

Kydd resented Cundall's tone, but he was the only one of the mess who had been to India before, and Kydd had questions for him.

Renzi stirred. "Fascinating—in the months we've been at sea, anything could have happened. The war might even now be over, King Louis avenged. And yet, like ripples on a pond, we are our own news . . ."

"So yer've been this way before, Cundall?" Petit said. It was curious, Kydd thought, that nobody called him anything else.

"Yair, bin here once or twice," he replied smugly.

"Yer like it?" Petit persisted. Cundall's pot went forward meaningfully. Petit filled it and listened.

"Aye, it's a rare enough place ter step ashore—more o' them Injuns yer'll ever dream ter see, thousands of 'em, an' all dirt poor 'n' poxy. Yer falls over 'em in the street, yer hears 'em yak away in this 'eathen talk—place is jus' swarming with 'em."

Kydd took it in, but his mind was on the wonders of Calicut. "Thought it had these golden temples, an' elephants, 'n' heathen idols, an' things," he said.

"Yeah, well, they has them as well, o' course, but this I tell yer now, here the cuntkins are yours fer a coupla annas fer a short time—an' they knows *all* about it, mates, nuthin' they don't know." He winked. "An' best o' it is they're all young—bantlings all, no more'n ten, twelve years, tight as yer'll get, an' all tricked out in this fancy long red 'n' gold." He licked his lips unconsciously, causing a wave of revulsion in Kydd.

Cundall mistook the look and continued, "Don't worry—they knows all th' tricks, jus' like th' old 'uns."

The talk petered out, most of the men simply wanting to get ashore and see for themselves. Vaguely unsatisfied, Kydd got up and left. He reached the upper deck just as dusk settled in. Somewhere over the horizon was India, and very soon he would be the only one of his family to know an exotic shore.

CHAPTER 6

≈

Two mornings later the foredeck was crowded with men when they raised land. Kydd watched as it took form over the horizon. This land rimming the northern reaches was low lying, in fact so low that not a single mountain or even hill disturbed its monotonous green flatness. As they drew nearer, Kydd's eyes searched in vain for some evidence of the fabled East, but all that was in prospect was the vast estuary of the khaki-colored river up which they were headed and the green of endless vegetation.

The great river was several miles across, but as its banks approached on either side Kydd had a closer view. Its promise still failed to materialize: the river was swarming with small craft, strange but decrepit, and the lush green just went on and on.

At a wide bend in the river the order to moor ship was passed, and when they made it around they saw lines of vessels at anchor along the outer bank. This was as far as oceangoing vessels could venture.

Artemis glided to a stop and the anchor splashed into the turbid water. Almost immediately she drifted downstream in the tumbling, muddy current, and when she came to her anchor the frigate snubbed to the cable sharply and swung to face unwaveringly upstream. After nearly two months of sea, and more than ten thousand sea miles, *Artemis* was finally at rest.

Kydd joined the others aloft, furling the sails. To his exasperation, there was no sign whatsoever of anything that could remotely be termed fabulous. From this height he could see the tops of palm trees stretching unendingly away, the odd clearing here and there, while nearby the dun-colored tops of huts peeped above the sea of green. He could make out no elephants or palaces, still less any exotic girls.

On deck a damp heat had descended on the stationary vessel, now so quiet that the restless whispering of the river's passage past and the harsh crying of a bird was all that intruded. As if by magic river trading craft, garish colors on their canopies and peeling sides, appeared from nowhere making for the new-moored ship. The boarding nettings were quickly rigged and hung below the line of gunports, opened to the sullen airs. The craft lay off, waiting it out.

Wiping his forehead, Kydd watched Renzi staring out. "Is this your East, Nicholas?" he asked ruefully.

Renzi grinned. "Apparently the city lies more than a hundred miles beyond, up the Hooghly to its confluence with another river—that trip would set your Gosport boatman at a stand, I believe." Scratching at his itching body, Renzi felt similarly cheated. Privately he was excited; he would see the native peacock, the golden domes of the Hindoo, and the naked holy man, but here?

Kydd's mind ran on more practical lines. "So we are to warp upstream a hundred miles? I think not."

"Then what are we here for?" Renzi said, perplexed. "We have arrived and not arrived. This is vexatious in the extreme."

On the quarterdeck the Captain and a midshipman stood next to a small amount of baggage. A sudden flurry from the waiting craft followed the boatswain's signal, and one was permitted to come alongside to pick up the officers.

"Now there's a thing," Renzi said, looking intensely at the boat shoving off, its odd sail rising up the mast in rapid jerks.

A sudden pealing of boatswain's calls broke out. "*All haaaands! All the hands! Hands to store ship!*"

*   *   *

Hatches to open right down to the hold, yardarm stay tackles, parbuckles—all the preparations for storing ship. What was going on? Why the hurry? Kydd could see no point in it. Ships usually took the opportunity after a long voyage to refit and repair and, of course, sailors relaxed ashore, yet here they were preparing to lay in stores as though their lives depended on it. What did the Captain's rapid departure mean? Parry's scowling face on the quarterdeck gave no sign and by the time the first store-ships arrived, Kydd was none the wiser.

These were flat barges fitted with long sweeps, creeping around the bend like water beetles. Kydd watched as they approached, not at all looking forward to laboring work in the clammy closeness. The barges secured alongside, several abreast, and gangplanks were placed over them to the ship's side.

"Hey, you—Kydd!" It was Gant, the tall boatswain's mate. "Didn't ya hear? Stand fast, topmen!" He grinned. "You swabs are gonna fettle the barky ready for sea agen."

Relieved, Kydd joined Renzi at the splicing, pointing and re-reeving of lines, which were jobs requiring real seamanship skills, and left the rest of *Artemis*'s crew to the storing. It seemed that rumor had substance: they would put to sea before long. But it stood to reason that they would be given time ashore first.

Long lines of gray-brown lascar stevedores patiently padded over the gangplanks bringing their heavy loads aboard. Kydd looked at them curiously—lean, impossibly stringy, there was not the slightest bit of fat on them. Their eyes showed no interest, no recognizable humanity he could relate to; the men simply plodded on in regular, economic movements.

Renzi went below to find some rope yarn, and Kydd lost interest in the stream of brown figures and pressed on with his work.

"If yer'd help us, friend, oi'd be roight grateful!" a hoarse voice said. Kydd looked up sharply, but there was no one, only the stream of lascars under the watchful eye of their *serang*. He looked around warily. If that was a joke, it was a pitiful attempt. He shrugged and continued at his marline spike and splice. "Loike, we'em desperate." The hoarse voice was close, very close. Kydd stood up angrily.

The boatswain arrived from below, puffing like a grampus. He stood at the rail, gathering his breath, and watched the line of native laborers. "That slivey dog," he said to Kydd. "No, t'other one—mark his motions. Lazy fellow thinks to take it easy, an' he so well fed."

The lascar indicated was indeed better nourished than the others. Instead of the sculpted angular ridges of hardness, there was a definite rounding of flesh; possibly the man was of superior caste.

"Hey, you, the *serang*," the boatswain shouted across at the overseer. "*Jowla, jowla*—him!" he ordered, pointing at the offending individual.

The *serang* looked at him doubtfully, and raising his rattan gently rapped the man over his naked shoulders.

"Good Christ!" the boatswain said in astonishment. "That wouldn't wake a sleepin' dog." He snorted in disgust and stumped off below again.

Curiously Kydd watched the lascar trudge to the barge, lift a bale of dry goods awkwardly to his shoulders and turn to trace his steps over the gangplank and back aboard. As the man came over the bulwark he saw Kydd, and stumbled on a ring-bolt. The bale came down, bouncing along the deck, fetching up against the hatch coaming. Their eyes met—and Kydd saw real fear.

Kydd got to his feet. "You savvy—no one hurtee you, this ship," he said loudly. The man looked at him, then seized the bale and dragged it over.

"Thank Chroist!" the lascar said. "Oi'm bleedin' well at t'end of me senses."

Snatching up a rope's end, Kydd slashed him over the shoulders. "Wha—" the lascar cried piteously.

"Shut up 'n' move!" Kydd hissed. Driving the man down the

fore-companion to the gundeck, he pushed him past the canvas screening that concealed the sick quarters in the bow—he knew the three sick had been landed and the space was clear.

He spun the man round savagely. "I've heard o' men doin' things t' run, but this is the first I heard someone wantin' so bad to get 'emselves *aboard* a King's ship!"

The man's voice caught in a sob as he crumpled to his knees. "S' help me, frien', oi don' know how t' thank ye!" His brimming eyes looked up at Kydd. Taking a gulp, he continued, "Fort William— 'tis a hellhole loike yer worst dreams. Oi joined t' foller the colors an' a shillin' a day, not sweat in this black stink-pit."

His face worked in a sudden paroxysm. "This now's the cool o' the seasons—while yer wait fer the monsoon t' break, whoi, it's hotter 'n a griddle in hell—an' full uniform on parade or Sar'n't Askins'll 'ave yer!" His head dropped, and he stared hopelessly at the deck.

Kydd thought quickly. "We sails soon, need t' get ye out o' sight." His eyes strayed over the man's dark skin. How would it be possible to conceal such a color? "No idea where we're bound, but y' can get ashore easy enough—we got no pressed men aboard."

The man caught Kydd's look. "Ah, me dark skin. Walnut juice."

Kydd smiled. "Wait here."

"Look, Oi know this looks bad, but ye've got t' unnerstan' what it's loike—"

Clapping him on the arm, Kydd stepped outside. He cannoned into a lascar waiting there, who had obviously followed them down. He gestured at the fore ladder. "Up! You gettee up there!"

"'Eard what yer said ter Ralf," began the lascar.

Kydd groaned. "Not you as well!" He should have known by the pale eyes, incongruous in the dark brown face.

"Well, yeah, but only the pair o' us, mate—Ralf Bunce and me, Scrufty Weems," the man said.

"Get in there with y' chuckle-headed frien'," Kydd told him, and shoved him forward.

*   *   *

To his credit, Renzi only hesitated a moment when Kydd told him. Aiding a deserter was a Botany Bay offense in England; here it might be worse. There was no way the soldiers could mix in with the two hundred odd of the ship's company, for every face was familiar after the long voyage. They would have to be found a hidey-hole until they made port.

"The orlop," Renzi suggested.

"No—mate o' the hold checks every forenoon, bound t' find anything askew." Kydd remembered his hiding place from King Neptune's bears. "The forepeak?"

"In this heat? Have mercy, Tom!"

However, even for this, the soldiers proved pathetically grateful and dropped down the tiny hatch into the malodorous darkness without a word.

Storing complete, the ship's company looked forward to liberty ashore, but instead they were set to scraping and scrubbing, painting and prettying in a senseless round of work that sorely tried their patience. Tales of shoreside in India grew in the telling, but Parry gave not an inch. The ship was to gleam and that was that.

Kydd and Renzi knew it was impossible to keep their secret from their shipmates. The others found it amusing that deserters from the Army thought they could find sanctuary in a man-o'-war, but in the generous way of sailors, they made their guests welcome.

Immured in the forepeak during the day, they could creep up to the fo'c'sle under cover of dark and join the sailors in a grog or two. They talked about the boredom and heat, the dust and disease of a cantonment on the plains of India. They told also of their struggle to the coast and their final bribing of the *serang*—and his confusion when told to beat a white man.

The sailors heard of the other side of life in India, the bazaars and what could be bought there, the heartless cruelty of the suttee funeral pyre and the deadly thuggees. Their desire for shore leave diminished.

Bunce heard Kydd recall his experience on their first morning at anchor. Sent down as part of the duty watch to clear the hawse, he had looked over the side of the beakhead forward and seen an untidy bundle wrapped around the anchor cable. He had slid down to clear it away, but closer to, it took form—a grossly mis-shapen corpse bleached a chalky white, barely recognizable as a young woman. It belched pungent death smells when he tried to pry it away, the sickly gases catching Kydd in the back of the throat, and there were ragged holes in the face where the kites had been tearing at it. When he prodded with a boat hook parts of it detached, floating away in the muddy river. Every day there were always one or two to clear like it.

Bunce had just nodded. "When y' dies in India, proper drill is t' burn th' body on a pile o' wood. But there's some uz are so dirt poor, they has t' wait until dark an' then they heaves their loved 'un in th' river."

The seamen, no strangers themselves to hardships, shuddered and vowed to see their guests safely ashore in some haven far away rather than return them to such horrors.

Two days later when the Captain returned he immediately disap-peared below with Fairfax. Within the hour boatswain's mates were piping at the hatchways.

"Clear lower deck—all the hands! *Haaaands* t' lay aft!"

The rush to hear the news caused pandemonium, but Powlett's appearance on deck brought an immediate expectant hush. He turned meaningfully to the sergeant in charge of marines. "Sergeant!"

"Sah!"

"A sentry at the boats, another on the fo'c'sle! No one to leave or board the ship without my express permission."

"Sah!"

Unbelieving looks and an exasperated grumbling spread over the assembly.

"Silence!" Powlett roared. The muttering died down. He stood near the deserted wheel with a forbidding expression. "I am now able to tell you of our mission and why we have been at such pains with our ship."

He paused and let his words sink into the silence. "*Artemis* has been honored to be chosen as the vessel to convey a special envoy from His Majesty King George to the Emperor of China in Peking."

CHAPTER 7

≈

That evening Lord Elmhurst and his retinue arrived, plunging the man-o'-war into a state of confusion. Eighteen souls were more than it seemed possible to cram into the spaces aft. All officers lost their cabins, but even so, with Lady Elmhurst, her daughter and maids to find privacy for, it was a near insurmountable task.

Fairfax hurried about late into the night, pursued by the shrill, demanding voice of Lady Elmhurst. The seamen retired to the forward end of the ship and let the upheaval spend itself—there would be no interference in their way of life, although in deference to the quality aboard, they would have to don shirts and for the time being forswear curses.

The frigate would sail in the morning at first light, ready or not, for there was no time to lose. There would be no touching at land *en route,* their first port of call would be Canton in South China, the only touching point allowed for vessels trading with China. It hardly seemed credible—a voyage to China! There was no more distant or exotic land; there were few aboard who had ever been as far east as this.

At dawn the anchor was won from the sticky mud. What followed was a particularly difficult and perilous piece of seamanship. The problem was the rapid current. The Hooghly was wide enough, but with so many other vessels at anchor it was necessary to get control on the ship as fast as possible after she was freed of the ground. But she had a leeward tide—the northerly monsoon wind was in the same direction that the current was drifting the ship. This meant that although they were moving smartly relative to the river bottom, they were not actually moving through the water. The rudder, therefore, could not bite and the ship had no steerage way—she would drift out of control in the crowded fairway.

The solution was not obvious and Powlett's seamanship caused dismay to some but a growing respect from others. With topgallants and courses hanging in the brails, the frigate set topsails, jib and driver, with the main topsail backed. Trimmed this way *Artemis* drifted broadside to the current, apparently helpless. But at every obstruction, an anchored vessel or a creeping line of barges, either the foretopmast staysail forward would be hoisted or the driver aft would be hauled out. This would send *Artemis* slowly across the breadth of the river and the hazard would be cleared. For those spectators on deck it was a tense time, but where the estuary widened as it met the sea, the current slowed and it was then possible to cast to the right tack and shape their course, at last outward bound.

Passing the Sandheads and with the mangroves and lush jungle slipping away astern, the deck began to crowd with strangers and parasols, chattering and promenading, an amazing thing in a warship. Once again the harried Fairfax made the rounds, and the sightseers were given to understand that their territory would be aft, around the wheel and the neat expanse of the quarterdeck abaft.

The tall figure of the dour and abstemious Lord Elmhurst was easy to spot, pacing slowly in conversation with Powlett, obstinately in full breeches and frock coat in defiance of sea conventions. Lady Elmhurst, a somewhat mannish figure with a fan constantly at work, always seemed to be the center of attention, a formidable woman who looked quite as capable as her husband.

Once in the open sea, *Artemis* hove to, drifting quietly, as she waited for the stately East Indiaman that would accompany them with the rest of the envoy's entourage.

The *Walmer Castle* emerged from the Hooghly and stiffly

acknowledged their presence as she fell in astern. The two vessels foamed ahead.

At the end of the afternoon watch Kydd went to go below, but Renzi caught his sleeve. "You will scarcely credit what I have been able to borrow."

Kydd had not seen him the whole afternoon, but guessed where he had been. "What have you got then, shipmate?"

"A treatment of the metaphysick of China in four volumes," he said triumphantly. It had cost him dear, an hour of sympathetic weaseling of a crabbed old savant, but it was a thousand times worth it. "There are learned men and counselors in the entourage, sadly overlooked." He sighed happily. "Now I shall know the truth of the soul-stealers of the Kao Hsuang and the greatness of the saintly Confucius."

Kydd couldn't help smiling. He had never seen Renzi so animated, and was happy for him. No doubt in the fullness of time, there would be a watch on deck in the tropical dusk and he would hear Renzi exploring these philosophies. He would use Kydd as a foil to worry happily over some arcane point, and then with dawning comprehension Kydd would see it slowly unfold into an important point and then a great truth, and they would both end up deeply satisfied. They clattered down the fore-hatchway for their evening meal, pleased to be away from the deck with its high-born passengers and awkward atmosphere.

"Hey, Wong! How d'ye say in Chinee, 'Come under m'lee, me lovely, an' I'll steer ye fer a safe port'?"

"Wong, mate, is there a reg'lar-built tavern, be chance, in Peking?"

"Tell us—do yer Chinee fillies like it, you know—"

Wong sat rigid, a dogged frown on his glistening face. Suddenly, he slammed his fist on the table and shouted hoarsely, "*Da choh, lei kau tik!*" The mess table subsided.

"Woulda thought he'd be happier, the sad dog," Doud said, in puzzlement. "Goin' to visit his folks, like."

Wong rose, knocking over the other seamen of the mess on his way back on deck. "Heathen prick!" Cundall snorted.

Kydd saw that Wong had more than paying a call on his family on his mind: normally impervious to lower-deck banter, he was now touchy and morose. "We got other things t' consider right now, mates," Kydd said seriously. They looked at him. "Yon lobster-back friends o' ours," he said. In the tropics the men could not survive for long in the stifling heat of the forepeak, and strangers aboard would be spotted as soon as they set foot on deck.

"He'll 'ave ter set 'em ashore, first port o' call, o' course," Cundall said, dismissively.

"Yeah—which is China, ain't it?" Doud retorted. "Nah, he strings 'em up as Army deserters, o' course."

"What? Wi' women aboard ter see? Don't give me that. He'll 'ave t' put 'em in bilboes an' send 'em back fust ship he sees," said Petit.

"Steerage 'as all the women in, anyways—d'ye like ter 'ave them trippin' over the condemned men every time they goes topside?"

"Condemned?"

"Yair—in course, they gets topped soon as they gets sent back ter the barracks."

Kydd leaned forward. "Not if Black Jack don't know. Look, we finds 'em in the forepeak. They're stowaways, see, wants to ship in *Artemis* 'cos they've heard we're famous, an' wants a piece o' the prize money."

"What prize money?" grunted Cundall.

"We rigs 'em in sailor's gear, teaches 'em the lingo and I'll wager Black Jack'll snap 'em up."

Doud laughed. "Yeah, he could at that—we landed sick more'n a brace at Calcutta."

Petit looked doubtful. "Aye, but y'knows that a sojer is always a sojer. How, then, are yer goin' ter make sailors outa them?"

*   *   *

The breeze freshened on the open ocean, and the blue sea with its hurrying white horses seemed to sense the urgency of the mission. The frigate's movements became more lively, a barreling roll in the following wind and sea, and the deck gradually cleared of passengers, returning to its usual seamanlike expanse.

Reveling in the crispness of the air after the heavy humidity Kydd went forward. They loped along under easy sail down the long swells of the ocean, the Indiaman trying its best two miles astern. Kydd went to the ornate voluted beakhead and leaned on the rail. Below him the bow-wave foamed and roared, a broad swash of white spreading out each side from the stem. The figurehead, the chaste white figure of Artemis, thrust out a hunting bow as if to urge the rest of the ship to follow, a splendid icon for a prime predator of the seas.

The sea was much closer than in his previous ship, the big three-decker, and the sensation of speed was thrilling. Everything about the frigate suggested speed—her sails were perfectly cut to the yards and sheeted in so taut they hardly bellied. Her clean lines resulted in a fine-drawn wake and the jib and fore staysails flying down to the bowsprit seemed to arrow the ship forward. Reluctantly Kydd made his way back: this was his favorite place.

He stepped behind the canvas screen of the sick bay and groaned at the sight of the two soldiers. "Now y' please to pay attention." They looked eagerly up at him from their cross-legged position. "Y' didn't do so well on th' last sea word I gave ye—here's a new one, see if y' can do a bit better. Show th' Captain how you know y' ropes."

Their guileless expressions made Kydd sigh, but he persevered. "Th' word 'start,' we uses it with care, f'r it has more'n one meaning. If we use it about a cask o' water, this means t' empty it, see, but if we talks about our anchor, then o' course it means to move it a piece. An' to start bread has the meaning f'r us to turn it out of its bags and casks an' stow it together in bulk—but when we talks about t' start a butt-end of a plank, why, that's serious, it means that the seas have sprung it an' we're takin' in water fast." Kydd tried to ignore their glassy stares. "On deck, if we starts the tack or sheet, it means t' loosen it, like 'raise tacks an' sheets' when we goes about. An' the carpenter, when he wants t' move a contrary bolt, he starts it with a starting bolt."

Scrufty Weems muttered, "If this is yer 'start' then God 'elp us at the 'finish'!"

"An' if you're slack in y'r ways on deck, you c'n be sure there's a bo'sun's mate'll start ye with his rope's end, sure enough."

Kydd knew they had to get the two soldiers before the Captain very shortly, for any real stowaways would have shown themselves as soon as the ship reached the open sea. "Now, c'n ye tell me, what are the sea watches in order, startin' with the middle watch?"

With the northerly monsoon driving boisterously at them from astern, and the positive effect of the clockwise ocean vortex of the Bay of Bengal, they made excellent time south, aiming for the Malacca Strait, the narrowing passage between Malaya and Sumatra.

"Down, y' scurvy dogs!" Kydd thrust the two soldiers at the feet of Captain Powlett, who had just begun his morning pace of the quarterdeck.

"What the devil?" Bunce and Weems had on old sailors' gear, but their walnut juice disguise had faded to a scrofulous blotchy streaking.

"Stowaways! Found 'em in the forepeak, sir."

Powlett stared. The men got to their feet, staggered slightly at a playful heave of the deck, but touched their foreheads smartly enough.

"Aye, sir, we'em from the old *Mary Jane* brig, 'n' we want t' be part of the crew o' the famous *Artemis*."

Powlett glowered. "So you thought to desert your shipmates and join the King's Service when it suited you."

"Whoy, no, sir!" Bunce replied. "The boat is in, er, ball'st, waitin' this two month fer a cargo, an' we're rare flummoxed as t' how to get out ter sea agen."

"What rate are you?"

"Sir?"

Kydd said quickly, "Claims they're able seamen, sir."

"Oh, yez, that's what we are, then," said Bunce.

"Then be so kind as to climb the larb'd mizzen shrouds and touch the cro'jick tye block," said Powlett lazily.

Bunce caught Kydd's hurried hand signal. "Ah—we would, er, do that if'n we worn't so bad in th' back. See, we had to 'aul up on this mast thing, an' it did fer me back, it did. Be roight in a coupla days, I guess."

Powlett's smile thinned. "And you?" he asked Weems, who started with apprehension.

"Me too, yer honor, I wuz with 'im when we both did in our backs."

Fairfax pushed forward. "Wharf rats, that's what they are!" he spluttered. "They're no seamen! We must put 'em ashore, sir, before—"

"No—recollect, sir, we are on a mission of some delicacy," Powlett said. "No one goes ashore."

He paced around the pair, jaw clamped. "We landed three sick at Calcutta, I must allow as the appearance of this pair is not unwelcome." He stopped, and a thin smile appeared. "Mr. Fairfax, rate these two Landman, but as Mr. Kydd found them, he can be responsible to see they measure up."

The two soldiers snapped to attention, saluted smartly Army fashion and doubled away forward. Jaw dropping, Powlett stared after them; Kydd quickly touched his hat and mumbled, "T' see they measure up, sir," and hurried after them.

A bare week later they had passed the new settlement of Penang to larboard, keeping close in with the land to catch the useful southward current, and entered a different, more airy kind of tropical regime. The sailing master had not passed this way since his youth, but his memory was sure, and they sailed on confidently past Malacca.

At almost the line of the equator they approached the southern tip of Malaya. *Artemis* ghosted along in the sultry stillness preceding the usual regular dog-watch deluge. Under the awning aft muslin clung damply to female limbs as the women chattered excitedly, exclaiming at the riot of jungle greenery and coconut palms.

Over the still water came the clatter of wings as a covey of parrots rose into the air, their squawks ignored by the troop of monkeys swinging through the dense foliage underneath.

"Enchanting!" said Lady Elmhurst. "I say, Mr. Prewse," she said to the Master, "have we time, do you think, to take a small picnic on the land over there?"

"My lady, I don' think it so advisable, if you takes me meaning," Prewse said, removing his old tricorne to mop his forehead.

"No, I do not at all take your meaning," Lady Elmhurst snapped. Her fan increased its tempo as she turned to Powlett. "Captain Powlett, surely an hour or two on the land will not discommode you—we have after all been cooped up in this little ship for weeks now."

Powlett removed his cocked hat with a pleasant smile, but thwacked it at his side. "Mr. Prewse, do you think it advisable for the ladies to step ashore in this *particular* place?"

Prewse rubbed his chin. "It's a lovely part o' the world, that I'll grant, but there's a mort o' bother ashore. First, we have the tigers."

"The tigers? This seems—"

"The tigers, milady. Over there they runs free, an' you can't see 'em in these woods until theys on you, all roarin' and big teeth. Then there's y'r snakes." He paused—the fan stopped. "Biggest in th' whole world, they is here, long as y'r main yard," he said quietly, pointing out the largest spar in the ship. "Hides near a brook, hangin' down from the tree quiet like. Eats a whole goat at one gulp when it comes down t' drink."

He scratched his head. "Then you've got y'r Dyaks. Bad joss, is they. Nasty cannibals they are, saves the head f'r to decorate their homes, but eats the rest on a slow fire. Comes down the coast fast in their three-piece canoes, on y' quick, 'cos you can't see 'em in this. S'pose I could land a party of marines, armed seamen, with ye. You'd have a good chance then—"

"Thank you, there will be no need. I now recollect that my husband has impressed upon me the need for dispatch. We need to press on, I believe."

Once around the peninsula they were in the South China Sea. Imperceptibly, the seascape changed. The glaring equatorial seas gave way to a hard cobalt blue, and then by degrees, as they progressed northward against the winter monsoon, to a particular shade of jade-green.

The fishing boats they encountered as they tacked toward the China coast were of an unknown appearance. Their keel-less hull form, more like a banana than a sea boat, had a baleful multicolored eye painted on the bow. Kydd's seaman's eye, however, saw that the violent bobbing and rolling was an effective method of keeping the craft dry. There was not an inch of water shipped, despite the considerable seas, and the tiny fisher-children were entirely at home in the tumultuous motion. Closer to the mountainous gray-green seaboard there were more of the strange three-masted craft, their ribbed sails distinctive against the coastline.

The winter monsoon was cold off the sea, and had the seamen rummaging in their chests for Channel warmers. *Artemis* closed with the anonymous shoreline, bound for the Pearl River and Canton, their landfall in China.

"What does it all mean, Nicholas?" Kydd asked over his grog, pointing at Renzi's book. There was a real need for rum to warm the cockles, the streaming northwesterly monsoon being so stern. He had seen hardly anything of his friend since Calcutta: Renzi's interest in the Orient was insatiable and he had spent every spare minute with his volumes and in discussion with the savants.

"To understand this, my friend, you must know that the Chinese have now the most mighty civilization on this earth."

Kydd opened his eyes wide. Others were not so sure, and looks were exchanged. "You're saying as . . ."

"Yes. They can trace their history in a straight line from before the ancients of our race right up to the present Emperor, Ch'ien Lung. You may believe that in that time they have learnt something of the arts of civilization. And its size! A hundred or more times ours, stretches from the frozen north to the tropics, and from the Pacific half across all Asia. It's amazing! The people—why, there are so many that it is thought that one out of every three or four souls on earth is Chinese."

The mess members paused in their meal to stare at him blankly or with troubled expressions. This was not a subject that was often brought up at mess table in a man-o'-war.

"Then tell me this, mate," said Cundall, waving his grog can in Renzi's face, "why ain't they conquer'd the world, then, if it's like you said?"

Renzi recoiled from the can with faint distaste. "I said a mighty civilization, and that is what it is. Their government under the Celestial Emperor is a just one, for it requires every officer to compete for his post by written examination—everyone, from beadle and magistrate to general and governor. This makes certain that only the very best can reach the high offices of the land, and true and just governance is the sure result."

"Cundall has a point," Kydd pressed.

"Therefore they have disdain for lesser attempts at civilized conduct, and have withdrawn from the world. They have no need for its paltry achievements, and so they keep the world at a distance—and that is why we are quarantined in Canton, to keep their civilization pure."

The table broke into indignant rumbling.

Kydd snorted. "Be damn'd to the scrovy crew! They got no right—"

"They have every right! It's beholden on us to step quietly in their land—if nothing else, I would not like to be the one to tread on the Dragon's tail."

"Sounds jus' like you're one o' their yeller stripe, Mr. Chinaman," Cundall spat, the grog thickening his voice.

Renzi looked at him speculatively. The mess fell silent, for Renzi as an aggrieved party was still an unknown.

"Nicholas . . ." Kydd began.

"No, fair question." Renzi looked down at the table, and when his face looked up again, it was with a smile touched with a degree of serious introspection, a look Kydd recognized immediately. "I do confess to a liking—no, a respect and honor for their metaphysick. They approach matters of logic in a curious and obscure way, and I am determined to learn of it at origin. And I am not too proud to say that it may reveal truths that might in fact reflect ill on our own polity." He drained his pot and left.

The final approach of the two vessels as they stood toward the coast saw a strengthening of the wind and a steepening of the waves, which obliged them to shorten sail. On deck foul-weather gear made its appearance in the thickening spray, and the few sightseers disappeared below.

Next to the Master was the stumpy figure of the just-boarded China Seas pilot, who looked more confident than the near proximity of a rocky coast would have seemed to justify. In sight there were only islands dark green with bamboo clumps interspersed with gray rocky outcrops, against which the seas surged in soundless white explosions.

The brisk gale whipped the wave-tops to an angry white, leaving tiger claws in their wake, and the vessels lurched awkwardly. Even the doughty fishing junks were retiring toward the land, and the two foreign ships found themselves converging with them on an obscure passage opening up to leeward.

Helm over, *Artemis* bore away downwind, and slipped down the narrow channel between the steep sides of a large island on one side and the mainland on the other. A cluster of hovels, a small jetty and bobbing sampans of a tiny fishing village and they were through. The seas moderated, and the ship settled for the run into a fine harbor of at least five miles of roadstead sheltered on three sides.

Apart from one or two more of the stilted fisher-villages there was nothing to break the barren appearance of the steep rocky island, but ahead there was a flat peninsula pointing directly at the center of the island.

"Pray, what is this place?" said the envoy.

The pilot started, then gave a jerky half-bow. "They calls it Heung Kong, m'lord, means 'Place of the fragrant waters' on account o' the good waterin' to be had after a long sea v'yage."

There were masts and yards visible beyond the peninsula, and Lord Elmhurst gestured at them. "It would seem that we are not the only mariners to appreciate its qualities," he said.

"Well, now, m'lord, that's 'cos we have here a port o' refuge that's good enough even f'r a *tai fung*—what they calls a regular-goin' hurricane hereabouts." The pilot noticed the envoy's eyebrows rise and hastened to add, "Not as we're likely to get one this late in th' season."

They passed the tip of the peninsula and its scattering of huts. The harbor opened up spectacularly, steep islands and sea passages in a maze on all sides. Sampans and fishing junks passed them by with not even a curious look at the trim and deadly frigate.

"*Haaaands* to moor ship!" With best bower anchor cleared away, *Artemis* took in sail and glided to a standstill, her anchor tumbling down into the jade-green waters and leaving the man-o'-war to her longed-for rest.

"Mr. Merrydew."

"Sir?" The boatswain touched his hat unwillingly. There was much to do in a ship that had traveled so far.

"Lord Elmhurst will proceed upriver to see the Chinese Viceroy in Canton. As you know, the navigation is hazardous for great ships—sandbars and shoals—so he will instead take passage in a John Company cutter. We will provide the crew. Find five men you *know* are reliable and tell them to muster in the waist at six bells in their best rig." Powlett's head thrust forward and his eyes narrowed. "And should they be taken by barrel fever and bring dishonor to this ship, I will personally see their liver at the gangway. Do I make myself clear?"

The East India Company cutter *Leila* leaned to the keen wind, slashing through the waves like a knife. It was Kydd's first experience of true fore-and-aft rig—the tiny square topsail did not really count   and it was a revelation. There was no way the craft could take to the open ocean, but inshore its speed and ability to lie close to the wind made it ideal.

Now on their way up the Pearl River, Kydd saw ahead: where the two sides of the bay rapidly swept together into twin high bluffs, the river constricted to less than a mile. High above, frowning down from the eminence of the craggy rock face, were two facing forts exceptionally well placed to command the approaches.

"Chuen Pi," the pilot said to Lord Elmhurst, who sat in an ornate canvas chair on the afterdeck. "Or, as the Portuguese have it, Boca Tigris—the tiger's mouth."

Kydd, tending the mainsheets with Adam, was able to take in every word. He would try to remember the details, for Renzi had not been selected for this duty. "Like a pusser's shirt on a marline spike" was the boatswain's unkind comment; the tropics had indeed left Renzi thin and rangy. With a twinge Kydd remembered the forlorn devastation on Renzi's face as he had left to go on to witness the marvels of the Orient at first hand without him.

A puff of smoke jetted from one fort, followed a little later by a hollow boom. The sound reverberated between the high sides of the passage and Kydd thought he could detect the almost tuneful resonance of bronze cannon.

Minutes later, the gaudy ribbed sails of a war-junk appeared from behind a prominence. The three lateen-rigged sails worked against each other to achieve remarkable maneuverability.

"Back yer topsail an' brail up!" growled Quinlan, the Master's mate at the tiller. The cutter slowed to a stop as the sails were dowsed, and she wallowed uncomfortably.

"Shouldn't have any trouble," the pilot said. "We does the run every week, an' there's no squeeze unless y'r carryin' cargo."

The war-junk dipped and plunged toward them, pennants and streamers in the wind, a big painted eye on each bow. It passed down one side; Kydd saw weeds and sea growth hanging long and unkempt, the sailors in their curious conical hats lounging, bored.

Going about, the vessel came up the other side of them; on the turn there was the same wild rocking to the waves as the fishing boats he had seen earlier, and the same astonishingly dry decks. It passed close by, and Kydd could see guns on deck, green-streaked bronze cannon with muzzles in the form of rudimentary dragon mouths. It passed ahead, and from its leeward guns came a perfunctory three-gun salute.

"Let go an' sheet in," snapped Quinlan, and shaped course to follow. They passed between the bluffs and into the land beyond. The cliffs gradually subsided and the river widened to a quite different prospect; hummocks and the flatness of paddy-fields stretching away to the gray-blue of distant mountains. The river slowed and dissipated into a maze of sandbanks and waterways. Two merchant ships lay at anchor in a tidepool, their sails carelessly draped in a loose furl, men hanging listlessly over the rail.

"C'n only get over at the top o' the tide, deep-sea vessels," the pilot said. "With three sandbars, means ye can't make it up in under two days."

They pressed on, the pilot standing close to Quinlan and muttering instructions. It was physically strenuous negotiating the tortuous bends, with the sudden tacking and gybing. Kydd worked hard at the mainsheets. As he hauled, he couldn't take his eyes off the land. It was outside his experience: subtly foreign vegetation, an exotic cooking smell in the air and the uniquely Oriental sights—stilt houses, a blindfolded water buffalo driven by a small boy in an endless circle, a monstrous-sized waterwheel, and dotting the paddy-fields inland, several many-storyed pagodas.

Lord Elmhurst remained on deck, choosing not to join his equerry in the comfortable half-cabin. With his face set in a frown he scanned the unfamiliar panorama. "How far is it to Canton?"

The pilot swung round. "In large, it's forty-three miles from Boca Tigris, m'lord, but we notes that deep-water packets can only reach to Whampoa, jus' a dozen miles short." He smiled and added, "An' we'll be takin' our vittles there within the hour."

The river narrowed again and as they surged past a stilted village Kydd heard for the first time the garrulous, noisy chatter of the Chinese against the lowing of water buffalo and squealing of pigs. Around the bend the river widened considerably. A large island occupied the middle of the river and anchored all along its shoreline were merchant ships, loading bales. From the shore rickety jetties ran out to the ships.

"Whampoa, m'lord," the pilot said unnecessarily.

Neatly, *Leila* ran alongside an Indiaman. Stirk expertly dowsed the headsails and, turning quickly, grappled the boat hook to her main-chains. It became apparent that Lord Elmhurst would not be swarming up the rope ladder to get aboard the merchant ship, but would be dining aboard *Leila*.

"Two hours to find scran," warned Quinlan, who lost no time getting himself over the bulwark. The Indiaman's hatches were off, and a continuous line of coolies brought cedarwood tea chests for loading; others were in the hold stowing, tomming down the cargo securely for the stormy trip home.

A man in breeches and shirtsleeves glanced at them curiously, his eyes following every move of the coolies. Quinlan nodded to him and crossed the deck to the precarious planks of the brow down to the jetty.

Kydd's mind whirled at the impact on his senses—an unmistakable sickly stench from the vegetable plots, the charcoal smell of cooking fires and the sheer rich stink of land after months at sea. The flank of the central spine of the island was one long alley with shanty shops on both sides, each with its blank-faced proprietor in white gown, shaved head and slender pigtail to the waist. There was every kind of knickknack and curio.

"Keep together," Quinlan muttered. He seemed to have directions, and strode forward purposefully. There were occasional European sailors, but they were of another world, the merchant marine, and were in loose, serviceable sea clothes that were as different from their own smart man-o'-war's rig as they were from the Chinese. Some even wore the baggy petticoat breeches of a previous age.

At the natural boundary of a stream they turned right and soon were in much more congenial surroundings: notwithstanding the bamboo walls and matshed roof it was unmistakably a tavern. In fact, there were several—and more! They wasted no time and crowded into the first. The Cantonese pot-boy seemed to understand their needs and scurried away. Before they had chosen their rattan table and settled into the odd straight-backed chairs he was back, whisking foaming tankards before them.

"Well, stap me!" Stirk marveled. "Died 'n' gone t' heaven!" The pot-boy remained, standing quietly. His eyes were fathomless black buttons.

"Er, yair—anyone got some loot?"

Quinlan held up a Spanish silver dollar. "This makee two

rounds, you savvy, John?" he said, making a twirling motion with his finger. The man glanced back, with considerable dignity, thought Kydd. Apparently the answer was an affirmative for he nodded and left soundlessly.

It was nectar, the first beer ashore. The taste was more watery than their English palates would have preferred, but it was fresh and went down very rapidly.

"Hey, John! Next round—chop-chop!"

As swiftly as the first, another round was before them, and they raised their tankards. "T' the poor bastards back aboard, an' workin' their hearts out."

Kydd raised his tankard, thinking of Renzi. He didn't notice the men looming behind until one spoke. "An' what are King's men doin' here, c'n I ask?" The speaker was bulky, unshaven, and there were several others with him.

"Yes, yer might ask, mate," Stirk said mildly.

"Well?"

"Well, cully, we're not the press-gang—but we could make an exception in your case," he said, with a chuckle.

"Don' you chouse us, matey—we tips the Hoppo an' he'll settle yer soon enough." He folded his arms. "Whampoa's fer merchantmen only—what're yez doing here?" The man's hectoring tone annoyed Kydd, who got to his feet.

Stirk interrupted him. "We're here on a mishun," he told the merchant sailor softly.

"A wot?" he replied mockingly. Kydd stiffened.

The man's lips curled in a derisive sneer. "We don' hold with no pretty boys in sailor suits here—it's men only."

Kydd's fist slammed out. The man fell back, roaring. Instantly, everyone was on their feet, defensively grouped behind Kydd.

The man felt his bloody nose. Snarling, he drew his knife. Kydd's heart thudded, but he was elbowed aside by Stirk, whose own blade was across his palm, held loosely forward.

"Seen 'is kind afore, mate—can't take a joke." Stirk glanced behind, quickly. "About time we weren't here, mates. Let's head back."

Pitching his voice toward Kydd as they withdrew from the tavern the large man shouted, "You watch yer back ashore, mate. You 'n' me got somethin' t' settle."

Stirk slid his knife back, and chuckled grimly. "Merchant jacks—got me sympathy, always shorthanded an' that, but pickin' a man-o'-war's man, they'd 'ave t' be pixy-led!"

Kydd winked at Stirk. "Insultin' the King's uniform—couldn't help m'self."

The last stage to Canton was through perfectly flat rice fields that seemed to stretch away forever into the immense unknown of Asia, an alien vastness that made Kydd shiver. Abruptly the last bend straightened and within sight of the city walls the northern bank opened up, with wide buildings fronting the river. In front of each was a flagpole with a national flag firmly in place.

The largest and most central had the Union flag of Great Britain, and they headed toward it. Respectfully, Kydd handed the envoy up the wooden steps to the small group at the top.

The sailors waited in the cutter until the formalities were complete. The envoy's small party moved off, and a figure appeared at the edge of the wharf. "Hey, you lot, up here, chop-chop!"

The seamen looked at each other, shrugged and clambered up. The young man at the top was in white silk breeches and loose shirt, and was coatless. He surveyed the group in surprise, their trim appearance apparently a novelty. "So, Lord Elmhurst has given instructions that you shall be the, er, guests of John Company while he is in Canton." There was a noticeable hesitation. "And it seems I shall be answerable for your conduct while he is here."

The young face had a patrician stamp and an easy confidence, but it was clear that its owner was unsure of a situation that placed him with the responsibility for a crew of hard-looking naval seamen.

Stirk folded his arms and stared at him, while Quinlan stepped forward to the front and tugged his tarpaulin hat to an aggressive tilt.

The young man seemed to come to a decision. "I'm Jamesen, supercargo in John Company for my sins." The tone of his voice suggested that he had decided to take them into his confidence rather than attempt to lord it over them. "Now, Canton is different from any place you've ever been to, and there's rules here which are stupid, childish and cruel—but this is China, and we have no choice. There's a hundred million Chinese over there," he said, waving toward the endless paddy-fields, "and we are a few hundred. Do you get my drift?"

The interior of the mess was airy and cool, the furniture spare. With the seamen incongruously clutching an eggshell-like teacup of transparent green tea, Jamesen explained further. "Trade is everything—we buy tea, they buy . . . not much. They think they're the center of the world, and everyone else is a barbarian and needs to be kept at a distance, so all trade with the biggest country in the world is through the one place, Canton!

"Now, I warn you in all sincerity, if you cause an incident, we can do nothing to save you. All dealings are through the Hoppo, a greasy, fat and entirely corrupt chief of the Co-Hong, which are a scurvy crew appointed by the Viceroy to deal with the barbarians and save him getting his hands dirty—as long as he gets his cut." He finished his tea and refilled his cup. "The season finishes soon, and we all have to fall back to our families in Macao, until March."

He paused, and grinned. "Your envoy will find that he will get his audience, and his presents will be graciously accepted, but he will have to wait for his reply at Macao like the rest, so I doubt you'll be here long. There's shops and things around here, we're pretty self-contained. Wouldn't advise going off on your own. Be in the mess by sundown, don't get fuddled with drink, beware of everything and everybody."

They nodded. They were not about to go on the ran-tan ashore hereabouts.

Jamesen softened a little. "If there's any wants a stroll, it's my practice to take a turn around the city walls before dark. Anyone want to come?" Stirk and Kydd were the only takers.

They stepped it out, down the narrow alleys and along the sandy northern banks of the Pearl River. Much closer to the city the bustle increased. Flooding the pathways were Chinese of every description, carrying trussed chickens, yokes suspending large dark jars and huge clusters of unrecognizable vegetables. Their constant chattering was deafening.

"You know, it's instant execution for any Chinese teaching the language to a foreign devil," said Jamesen. "*Tui m syu!*" he added politely, stepping around an old lady struggling with a bound piglet.

A palanquin with oiled-paper windows swayed toward them, preceded by a lackey in an embroidered gown banging a gong to clear a path. There was no sign of the occupant.

Kydd noticed a ragged bundle floating in the river. "Ah, that you'll find is a female baby—up-country they want strong sons, not useless girls. Easiest way to solve the problem," Jamesen explained.

Just before the dilapidated walls was a small sandy beach, and a crowd gathered around some officials. A large drum pounded monotonously. "You may be interested in this," Jamesen said languidly.

They hovered on the edge of the crowd and watched two men being brought forward. They had signs in Chinese characters around their necks, and their heads hung in listless dejection. "They're pirates—probably peached on by their friends." The men were thrust to their knees, facing the water. Reading from a scroll, an official chanted loudly, then suddenly whipped it down and stepped back. From the crowd came a man bared to the waist, carrying a highly polished Oriental sword. He swaggered up to the first pirate and stood ready. The noise from the crowd buzzed on without change.

At a screamed order from the official the executioner made ready, slowly and deliberately. Kydd went cold. The sword went up, the crowd's chatter continued to wash around unabated; the victim had nothing but a blank look on his face but tensed slightly. The sword blurred down and connected with a meaty crunch, the head bounced twice on the sand while the torso toppled slowly, gouting blood from the neck.

"Doesn't seem to deter them," Jamesen commented. "The pirates, I mean."

There was no variation in the cheerful hum of conversations in the crowd. The seamen watched as the second pirate lost his head. Stirk looked at Kydd, but didn't speak.

The city walls were decrepit and crumbled at the edges. "Never really needed these since the Ming dynasty was overthrown," Jamesen said, kicking away a half-eaten gourd from some strange fruit.

They paced along slowly, deliberately ignoring the small barefoot boys who tagged on behind chanting, "*Faan kwai! Hung mo-tik faan kwai lo!*"

At Kydd's look, Jamesen explained, "Seems you're the usual sort of a hairy foreign devil."

On the way back, they wended through a market, a riotous mix of women bargaining shrilly and vociferous stall-keepers. Edging around them, Kydd had never in his life felt so conspicuous, and was not helped by the many darting looks, some curious, most sullen and venomous.

"'Ere—rum dos!" Stirk had seen a movement in a large wicker basket and was standing over it, pointing. Kydd crossed to see and was shocked to see that it contained a human being, tied in a fetal position.

"It's not—"

Jamesen cocked an eye, then grabbed his arm. "Leave now!" His voice was urgent. The talking had died away around them, and there was hostility in the air. They hurried off, pursued by derisive shouts.

"What?"

"Not your fault," said Jamesen breathlessly. "They're on display." He paused to recover.

"Don' tell me!" Stirk growled.

"Yes. If they're found guilty, they're on display at the scene of the crime until sunset, then they're taken out and strangled on the spot. Silk rope, of course."

"O' course," Stirk said hoarsely.

Jamesen sniffed into a handkerchief and went on. "They don't like the foreign devils to get involved—I'll be glad to get back to the compound. A few years ago they got hold of a gunner of a Bristol packet caught in an accident." He looked back furtively, and went on. "They tortured him publicly in front of the family concerned before strangling him."

In the factory Jamesen found some wine. "Has to be drunk anyway before we retire to Macao. China is old and ancient," he mused. "Decaying on the inside and out. If some country knocked on the door hard enough, it would come crashing down and let some fresh air in. And trade." He drained the glass expertly. "As near eighty per centum of trade goes in English bottoms, I guess it'll be us doing the deed some day—and I hope soon."

Hearing curt voices outside, Jamesen got to his feet. "Stay here," he commanded. He was back quickly. "As I thought. You'll be going downriver tomorrow to await the Viceroy's reply. I'll see to your sleeping arrangements."

Renzi said nothing, simply puffed quietly on his long clay pipe and sat back on the foredeck of *Artemis*. Kydd tried to provoke him, but could not break his composure, only a slight smile betraying anything of his feelings. The others had left the deck when the chill of evening crept in, leaving the two alone.

"An' you are telling me this is th' mark of civilization?" Kydd continued, with heat.

Renzi stirred and knocked out his pipe on the planksheer. Red sparks of dottle cascaded prettily into the gloaming. "My dear fellow, how can I say? I was not there, I was never a witness to these . . . untoward events." Inwardly he was hot with indignation that he had not been able to see for himself. He was sure that the savant would not lie, and that the precepts of Confucius did indeed inform the actions of the ruling class, but this?

Kydd snorted. "If you had seen f'r yourself only—or, better still, smelt f'r yourself! It's a—a beast of a country." He longed for the words to put into stark, unmistakable perspective for Renzi what he had experienced: the stink, the cacophonous noise, the unconcern for life.

"If we remain for long here, I've no doubt I shall. But I hear tomorrow we shift berth to Macao." He looked sideways at Kydd. "Which, as you will know, is a Portuguese territory, and therefore an ally of ours in this war, and I have no doubt will give us a warm welcome."

Kydd grunted. "It'll still be the same as the rest of China."

CHAPTER 8

≋

The opposite side of the Pearl River was nowhere near as spectacular: in place of the deep clear green were the muddy shallows of the estuary, and around them craggy islands lay subdued and sleepy. However, where their great anchorage was nearly bereft of human habitation, Macao offered a compact, pleasing prospect of familiar buildings from the home continent. As their anchor splashed down, it was possible to make out dark stone forts, the façade of a cathedral, state buildings in a comfortable pink wash and all the appurtenances of a sane world.

Kydd's heart lifted. It would be good to step ashore here. "Do we get liberty soon, d'ye suppose?"

As they spoke, a nineteen-gun salute puffed out in distant thuds from the fort commanding the town below, to be returned with the sharper report of the frigate's bow deck guns as she glided to a stop. Boats were quickly in the water and the envoy, in plumed cocked hat and sword, went down the side to his waiting barge for the steady pull over to the quay and the guard of welcome.

The boat secured to the landing stage, and in dignified silence the envoy of His Britannic Majesty mounted the steps. Harsh shouts from the waiting Portuguese guard commander brought his men to attention.

Lord Elmhurst and his equerry turned—and stopped. The formed-up ceremonial guard that stared back at them was of every possible tint of mestizo, undersized and with threadbare regimentals. Their European officers wore ornate uniform that, however, drooped sadly. But there was no mistaking the warmth of the welcome. With earnest cries of welcome the *desembargador* advanced on them.

The envoy, deciding that there was no deeper meaning to the astonishing sight, moved forward, to the almost perceptible relief of the Portuguese.

"So it's leave t' both watches," Doud said, with relish. "An we're gonna be here fer ever, if it's ter be believed," he added contentedly.

"Aye, but without s' much as a single cobb in me bung, what's th' use?" said Cundall ungraciously.

Petit had a long face. "What's amiss, Elias?" Kydd asked.

Stirring in his seat, Petit said dourly, "It ain't good fer a man-o'-war ter stay too long in port. Seen it 'appen in foreign parts, y' gets all the sickness 'n' pox goin' from off of the land. Sea, it's clean 'n' good, land . . ."

"Yeah, well, no harm in a frolic ashore," laughed Doud. "A cruise with a right little piece sets a man up fer his next v'yage."

Kydd was stitching carefully at the fluting of the smart blue jacket Renzi had last worn in celebration in Portsmouth, on the other side of the world. "Seems regular enough, buildings and such," he said, biting off the thread and picking up his own jacket.

"They've been here since before the age of old Queen Bess—plenty of time to make themselves comfortable, I think," Renzi replied, and put on his jacket.

"What d'ye think to find there, Nicholas?"

"I'd be content to see where Camões wrote the immortal *Luisiadas*." At the dry looks this received, he persevered: "Grievously shipwrecked, then manages to get himself banished to here. The poem is about one of the greatest of sailors—Vasco da Gama."

There were no sudden cries of understanding although Petit nodded wisely. "But, mark you, Kydd's right—this's still China, 'n' Toby 'as told me a piece about what he saw in Canton. I'd steer small were I ashore, if I wuz you."

* * *

With the *Walmer Castle* on her slow way up-river to Whampoa to discharge and load, and the rest of the envoy's party safely conveyed to their lodgings, the ship prepared for the wait. Even with the busy China trade vulnerable, for some reason the French had not reached this far across the globe, perhaps distracted by the work of the guillotine and the frenzied mob at home. It was considered therefore that the threat was low, and that the frigate could remain quietly at rest.

Artemis lay in harbor to two anchors. Her sails were thoroughly dried, naked topmasts sent down. Communication was set up with the shore for a daily supply of victuals, and soft tack was on the table for the first time since England. With the frigate as trim and shipshape as could be found in any top naval port it was time to step ashore.

The leafy sweep of the Praia Grande gave the appearance of some comfortable Iberian town but for the fact that the majority of the population was not European. Besides the ubiquitous Chinese there was the black of Negro slaves, the varying shades of brown of half-castes, and only occasionally the short, dark, compact figure of a Portuguese.

The gaudily colored buildings were Portugal transplanted, and Pinto's eyes glistened with emotion. He stopped a Portuguese striding past and babbled to him, a curious thing for his shipmates to witness. The man looked at him contemptuously and gestured eastwards into the crowded city. "He say all sailor go to Solmar to get hickey," Pinto said happily.

"So we claps on all sail 'n' shapes course for th' Solmar!" Stirk said, to general approval.

"Perhaps we will join you later, Toby," said Renzi diplomatically, catching Kydd's arm, and they plunged into the unknown inner city. The streets were steep and impossibly crowded. It was as if every square inch was valuable, and they were soon lost in the maze of ancient shops and anonymous structures seething with humanity.

They emerged suddenly from the press toward the top of a rise at the stone face of a cathedral, glowering down the hill at them, it seemed to their Protestant sensibilities. From the dark interior a priest emerged, a neat goatee beard flecked with gray on his sensitive lined face. He paced down the hill toward them, clearly in deep thought.

"*S'il vous plaît, aidez-nous, mon Père!*" Renzi tried, his Portuguese nonexistent.

The man's head jerked up in astonishment, and his hands fluttered in noncomprehension. "*Non,* er, *non!*" he said, his voice high-pitched and agitated.

Renzi tried again. "*Bitte helfen Sie uns, Hochwürden.*" The language of Goethe would be an unlikely acquisition for a Portuguese, but Renzi felt that his Latin would not be equal to the strain, and he was now at a loss.

"Do you have any Englis'?" the priest asked hopefully, his eyes darting between the two of them.

"Ah, sir, then you are a scholar?" Renzi said politely.

The priest flashed a quick look at him and smiled. "Where there is trade, you find the Englis' and there is much trade here."

"Then, sir, if you could assist me in a small way, we seek Camões, the soldier-poet of the last age. Is there trace of him still?"

The priest's face turned from astonishment to bewilderment, and then satisfaction. "*You,* sir, are then the scholar!" He shot a speculative glance at Renzi and ventured carefully, "Περι δε της μαντικης της 'εν τοις 'υπνοις . . ."

"Aristotle—prophecy in sleep? Sir, I am no friend to his position, but I will gladly debate the matter at—"

He could go no further. The priest grasped his arms and held him at length. "*Meu Deus!* You are sent to me on this day of days.

Pray walk with me to my *residência* and we will sup together the lunch." Recollecting himself, he turned to Kydd. "You gentlemen are mos' welcome, and you shall see the *casa* of our Luis de Camões presently."

Kydd sighed. Neither the prospect of a discussion on Aristotle nor the inspection of this revered *casa* article was maintaining his spirits, which had looked forward to tasting the more direct pleasures of these foreign shores. Still, it was kind of the old fellow, and they did need something now, at noon. In any event, he had an hour or two to think of a ploy to raise the state of play to a more satisfactory level.

The priest's modest cell was close by, and they entered the cool room, tastefully set off by the hand-painted blue and white tiles covering one entire wall. The furniture was commodious, in the Chinese style. The chairs were tall and square-backed in dark wood, with a carved central panel. Across one corner of the room was a beautiful black and gilt screen fully six feet high, with an iridescent shell inlay of butterflies and bamboo.

Seated at the round table, sipping their green tea, they waited respectfully. The room smelt of the layered odors of untold centuries, and was redolent of peace.

The priest smiled at them. "My name is Nuñez—my flock call me *Honrar.* It has been my good fortune to follow in the shadow of Matteo Ricci and Adam Schall here in the College of São Paolo for thirty-eight years. You are sailors, no?"

"From the British frigate *Artemis,*" said Renzi.

"Macao is very old, very set in her ways," he said seriously. "We Portuguese, it must be faced, have now passed the time of our greatness. For us, history has ceased."

Renzi made a gesture, but the priest was looking at Kydd. "But you, the British, are a race that has found itself in these troubling times, and greatness lies waiting before you." His face was difficult to read. "Thus you will pardon me if I make myself clear. Do not expect us to like you. Your manners are turbulent and thrusting, you are impatient with the old ways, you are confident—very sure—and we are afraid of you."

Renzi stirred. "But surely you can see that as a nation we trade, we do not conquer?"

"Trade always brings a domination in its wake!" Nuñez did not smile, and the two sailors sat uncomfortably.

"We do not allow any of your trading hongs to own land or dwellings in Macao, only to rent. This is because, as you will surely see, you British are rich and powerful and we—are not. You are growing restless at your lack of a trading port and may seize our own."

Hesitating, Kydd spoke awkwardly. "Sir, I'm only a seaman, but I c'n see that Macao is too small for y'r deep-sea vessels—we saw a rattlin' good place for a port over the other side, Heung Kong its name."

The priest's eyes glimmered. "A bare rock on which you will have to build houses, docks, roads—I don't think even the British would do that if there is another for the taking." Unexpectedly, he got to his feet. "But I am ungracious! Perhaps it has been so long since—excuse me."

He swiftly left the room, his dark gown swishing. Kydd turned to Renzi, but at his look did not speak. The priest returned with a bottle and three glasses. "I hope you will join me at wine, *cavalheiros*."

It was a musky Sercial, mellow and gentle. From somewhere inside the house floated a tantalizing odor of food, but even in its richness there was nothing they could identify.

"We eat in the Chinese style. It is cheaper and more convenient," Nuñez said apologetically. The odor took form and strength, of a potent but mouthwatering character. "Oh, yes, I hope you do not mind, but it is my regular practice in this season to offer hospitality to another at noon—she will join us soon."

Renzi seemed not to have heard. His face grew in intensity and leaning forward he asked, "The soul-stealers of the Kao Hsuang! Can it be that they have overthrown the sacred precepts of Confucius, or do they bend him to their philosophy?"

"Ah! You know of these?" Nuñez asked, in amazement. "Your answer is that in their deviltry they have their own philosophy, and it is based on the Janus-faced sayings of Hsun-tzu, who teaches that—"

The door opened and a figure appeared, limned in the sunlight from outside and therefore difficult to see.

"Oh—*Honrar!* You have guests. I . . ." It was a young woman's voice.

"No, no, child, you are welcome. Please come in and take your place."

The door closed and Kydd watched a young lady unlace her bonnet to let her auburn hair tumble down in lazy waves. She stood uncertain, a petite but self-assured girl of less than twenty years, with an elfin face and large eyes. She looked directly at Kydd. She was pretty rather than beautiful but the strength in her features and the sharp sculpted curving of her face had its effect on Kydd—a sharp and uncomfortable sensual shock.

Gracefully she sat down at the table, next to Kydd, managing to do so without looking at him again.

"*Minha cara,* these are my guests," Nuñez said. "They are sailors from the British warship . . ."

"Nicholas Renzi and Thomas Kydd, from *Artemis* frigate," Renzi offered. Kydd caught his look of interest in the girl.

"Miss Sarah Bullivant," she said, sitting straight-backed, her hands firmly in her lap. "I trust your visit will be a pleasant one," she added, her eyes falling carefully between the two of them.

"It could prove a lengthy one by all events," said Renzi. Kydd thought that his manner was unnecessarily unctuous.

She looked up. "Pray, why will that be?"

"Why, I stand amazed the world does not know of it—His Britannic Majesty's envoy Lord Elmhurst awaits a reply from the Viceroy of Canton touching on his mission to the Emperor in Peking."

"Then be assured, sir, the wait could well be a protracted one." The coy flutter of her eyelashes as she engaged Renzi in conversation did not escape Kydd.

"It suggests that the British are attempting a separate agreement as to trade," Nuñez agreed.

Just inches from her body, Kydd felt his own respond, and a betraying dull heat crept up his neck. At sea, with not the slightest femininity to trigger sexuality, desire subsided, a quiescence not troubled by ribaldry or images, but the first woman encountered ashore, by her sensual proximity, provoked an immediate awakening. Kydd could detect Miss Bullivant's faint scent, and sensed her body outline beneath her dress.

"Not the odious opium trade, I do sincerely pray." She dabbed at her generously curved lips.

There! Kydd exulted. Her face was still turned toward Renzi, but her eyes had flicked sideways.

"I am in full accord with you, Miss Bullivant," Renzi said elegantly. To Kydd's savage delight his slight pause was not rewarded by a bidding to continue. "Yet there are some who point out that we English regularly consume opium without ill effects—laudanum, your Godfrey's cordial. Could it possibly be that the Chinese character is weaker, less in control?"

As the food arrived, Nuñez grunted. "It is well known, saving your presence, that the English have long sought a species of trade that can balance the books for all the tea they must have—and they care not for its origin."

There was an uncomfortable silence, the clatter of crockery sounding overly loud. Nuñez handled the chopsticks like a native; Sarah was capable but without elegance, and Renzi fumbled.

Kydd surveyed the cluster of little dishes and resolutely abstracted the flat-bottomed spoon from a dark sauce dish, which he then proceeded to wield on everything.

"Ah, yes, my friend!" Nuñez turned to Renzi. "The Casa Camões." He laid down his chopsticks on their little rest. "It lies within the grounds of a *residência* which is let to Mr. Drummond, of your East India Company." He smiled. "I do believe that were a young lady to desire entrance then you would more readily gain admittance. Sarah, would you . . ."

Sarah's face tightened. "Sir, it is not my practice to be observed in public with sailors."

Kydd flushed. But there was no avoiding it—a woman with Jack Tar ashore had only one purpose.

Nuñez's face creased in amusement. "In that case, let me be of assistance. I have . . . what do you say? The walking-out clothes. They are perhaps unfashionable in these days, and are in the older style, but they would fit you, sir," he said, looking at Renzi.

They did indeed. Renzi, in double-breasted waistcoat and many-buttoned buff-colored coat together with cream breeches, elegantly flexed his rather skinny legs. This set off peals of laughter from Sarah. Kydd sat morose and overlooked in the corner.

"M'lady," Renzi said, sweeping the tall royal-blue tricorne down in an elegant bow. It was too small, but that only seemed to amuse Sarah the more. He offered his arm, which Sarah took with a gracious nod. Kydd got to his feet. Sarah looked at Renzi uncertainly.

"Miss Bullivant," said Renzi softly, "it would oblige me greatly if Mr. Kydd were to accompany us."

She glanced back at Kydd. Her eyes dropped to his lower body, and Kydd's pulse quickened. "Very well," she said coolly, looking directly at him. "Providing he follows on behind at a distance."

Kydd boiled over. "Be damn'd to you!" He thrust toward the door. Outside, he took several deep breaths and set off for the waterfront.

*   *   *

The gloomy berth-deck of *Artemis* was almost deserted, its clear sweep fore-and-aft interrupted only by a few hammocks. Kydd sat under one of the few lanthorns hung this late in the evening.

He had gone to the Solmar, which was packed with *Artemis* sailors, but they were all far gone in drink and no proper solace for wounded pride and unslaked lust. Briefly he had toyed with the idea of finding a woman to spend the night with among the throng, but something in his Methodist upbringing and a personal aversion to giving his body to a harlot stopped him.

Thus, in the way of sailors, he had returned to the bosom of his ship. For some reason he had pulled out the sea chest he and Renzi shared. Here it was, mellowing with age and sea use and carved with a mermaid cartouche that Renzi had contrived in the long days in the Indian Ocean before Calcutta.

With an unformed wish for repudiation of their friendship Kydd rummaged through its contents, each piece evoking lengthening memories. Neatly stacked along a good quarter of the chest were Renzi's books.

At random he picked one up. These were the real source of Renzi's success, his readiness with words, his effortless authority on all things. Kydd felt a stab of fury at the ease with which he had charmed Sarah. It was now past evening and well into the night—what was he doing to her now? Rage made him choke but with a force of will he crushed the thoughts. If Renzi had succeeded with Sarah, then that was his good luck. He would have done the same. The matter at hand was to get himself to the same level if it were possible—and he would damned well make it so.

Here in his hands was the key. He opened the book. The type was tiny and difficult to read in the guttering lanthorn light; the title page was flowery and embellished with intertwined pictures of animals. "D. Diderot—*On the Interpretation of Nature*," it read, together with a flurry of cursive French. Kydd leafed slowly through it: it seemed to deal in unbelievable wordiness with reason and observation, but if this was what gave Renzi the ability to speak, he would ingest it too.

He settled down at the beginning, and read haltingly, disturbed neither by the noisy arrival back on board of drunken and querulous seamen nor the raucous teasing of his shipmates. His eyes grew heavy, the words more difficult, and when Renzi finally returned on board all he could do was remove the book gently from Kydd's slumped figure and shake his head wonderingly.

Almost alone at their breakfast burgoo, Kydd and Renzi ate silently, avoiding each other's eyes. When they finished, neither rose from the mess table.

"Wish y' joy of—"

"I'm to tell you—"

Breaking off in embarrassment, their eyes met. A tentative smile spread over Kydd's features, which was quickly returned by Renzi. "The Portugee priest wishes to see me again," said Renzi, with a sigh. "A disputatious wretch, yet I will indulge him a little further, I believe."

"And does Miss Bullivant . . ."

"The young lady unaccountably wishes to be remembered to you," Renzi replied neutrally.

Kydd's voice thickened. "Last night—"

"Last night I had the felicity of debating the nature of the Chinee, the solemn imperatives of their beliefs and the impervious nature of their society with as erudite a colleague as ever I could wish."

"But . . ."

"Miss Bullivant was obliging enough to conduct me to the *casa* garden of Camões, where I looked on the rocks of his inspiration."

"She . . ."

"On conclusion, she bade me farewell, and returned with her maid, who accompanied us throughout," Renzi said flatly.

Kydd fiddled with a piece of bread, but refused to give Renzi further satisfaction.

A twisted grin surfaced on Renzi's face. "I am desired to inform you that she has been able to procure some suitable long clothes. She hopes you will find these satisfactory enough to be able to accompany us this afternoon on a visit to São Tiago."

A leaping exultation transformed Kydd's spirits. So he had not been mistaken about those glances!

Something of his feelings must have been visible, for Renzi continued, in a lazy, teasing voice, "Of course, I did inform her that you were desolated, that your watch on deck in this instance takes precedence—" He broke off at the dangerous flare in Kydd's eyes, then continued, "Of course, they are the clothes of a dead man."

For all Kydd cared he would strip the body himself, but he waited.

"Who died of the bloody flux—before he could accept them from the tailor's," Renzi finished lamely.

Eight bells at noon could not come fast enough. Liberty was granted from then until daybreak the next day in this relaxed "river discipline." Kydd and Renzi hurried off and soon were welcomed into the old residence.

The feel of silk stockings against his legs after the freedom of a sailor's trousers was odd. The nankeen breeches and the soft royal-blue coat added to the strangeness, and to Kydd it was a reminder of the flabbiness of shore life. Nevertheless, he rotated proudly before the mirror. The strong muscular definition of his body did peculiar things to the hang of the garments, but with his black hair in a neat club he made a striking figure.

He sniffed as though bored, and turning, made an awkward bow to Sarah. It brought no amusement as Renzi's had, but the sudden lift of her chin and averted eyes told him that he had her attention.

"Milady?" he said, with satisfaction.

*   *   *

"Ah Lee is curious," Sarah said. They were sitting in the outdoor garden of the Sol Dourado waiting for their tea. "She now has a quantity of gossip for her friends, I think." The little black and white Chinese *amah* with the twinkling eyes and long queue said little, but Kydd had felt the darting glances during the walk when she had followed respectfully behind.

Sarah sat opposite Kydd at the small round table, leaving Renzi to the side. For the first time he was able to take his fill of her prettiness; her characterful retroussé nose was complemented by the high, sculpted cheekbones. And the eyes, large and hypnotic: he would need determined self-control to avoid making a fool of himself.

"D'ye not find the Chinese a strange crew?" Kydd asked. He cursed inwardly as he remembered that she was governess to the progeny of a rich Chinese trader, who was now in Canton for the winter.

"Not when you make their further acquaintance," she said. Her eyes had a powerful effect on Kydd, which he tried to hide. A tiny smile curving her wide-set lips showed perhaps that he was not as successful as he hoped.

Renzi leaned forward. "One might argue that their very precepts make it impossible of a closer acquaintance," he said.

Sarah's eyes lingered for a heartbeat on Kydd, then transferred their attention to Renzi. "Sir, I am not in the philosophic line. My dealings are more of a practical nature," she said daintily. The eyes returned to Kydd, and dropped modestly.

They were underneath a hibiscus tree, which in season would have been a picture. The dull pearlescence of the winter monsoon swirled about them in the form of a fine mist of tiny dewdrops, which caught in Sarah's hair like a halo.

Kydd could not think of anything to say, and looked at Renzi. His friend lolled back, but was not at ease. He returned the look, and Kydd was startled at the stony hostility in his expression.

"I think Nicholas meant th' Chinese have, er, things in their civilization which we find difficult t' take to—I saw sights in Canton that would make y' stare," he said.

Renzi lurched upright. "I most certainly did not! I say that by their contempt for our *civilization* they have withdrawn themselves from our society and thus from all possibility of fellowship."

"Oh!" Sarah said, her hand flying to her mouth and without a glance at Renzi. "You have been to Canton? I would die to go—just the once—but ladies are not permitted." Her eyes grew yet larger, and she leant forward toward Kydd.

Flustered, he knew what was happening, but was out of his depth. In Guildford he was vaguely aware that females were one of two types; the earnest but dowdy ones you married, and the exciting ones who always turned out to be shameless doxies. Sarah looked neither—or both. And she was driving a wedge between him and Renzi.

"Why, er, yes," he said.

"Do tell me." She cupped her face in her hands. Her eyes were enormous.

There was movement to the side. Renzi got to his feet. "Pray excuse me, Miss Bullivant . . . it is not often I get the opportunity—Honrar Nuñez is expecting me. Do not trouble, I beg . . ." His voice seemed distant and preoccupied. "Your servant," he said, with a bow, and left without a glance at Kydd.

"He's sometimes a difficult fellow to understand," mumbled Kydd.

"But he is your particular friend," Sarah said immediately. "I can tell. You have no idea how jealous that makes a woman—the closeness, I mean," she said, dropping her eyes.

"We have—done much t'gether," Kydd said defiantly.

"Yet you are so different." Somehow her candor made things much easier than the delicacies of conversation before.

"What do you talk about?" she asked. "No, that's unfair. You would not be friends unless you shared something—deep," she said.

She sat back and stared at Kydd appraisingly. "You look every part a sailor, Mr. Kydd, and I do confess that before today I would rather be seen dead than talk to a . . . sailor."

"I understand," Kydd said, stiffly.

"No, I don't mean that," she said, her gloved hand coming out to squeeze his. "Please forgive what I said about sailors before, but . . ."

He forced her to feel her shame, then smiled. "It's the most wonderful thing that ever happened t' me," he said in simple sincerity.

She looked at him steadily. "There are things in this life . . ." she began.

"My father is a schoolmaster also," Kydd put in, thinking of her duty as a governess, but being a little hazy as to what that implied in pedagogy.

"Is he?" she said, looking puzzled.

"Well, not really," Kydd said, and explained the saga of the naval school.

She sat still, her eyes unblinking. At the end she sighed. "You're a very nice man, Mr. Kydd."

He was not sure if this meant his duty to his family or something more, so he compromised with an inaudible mutter.

"And a very interesting one—I demand you will tell me of your voyages across the bounding main. What marvelous things have you seen? Do tell!"

Kydd was no raconteur, his masculine directness only hinting at the loneliness and terror, the consuming bloodlust and exultation, the deeply affecting love of the sea, but it held Sarah spellbound in quite the same way as it had Cecilia. The afternoon passed, tea had come round at least three times, the fine mist insinuating cool and damp but still she would not let him go.

For Kydd, it was a dream, unreal, not of this existence. Less than a year ago he had been a perruquier in a small Surrey town, glad to be noticed by ordinary girls. Here, sitting in front of him, was a handsome woman of the world in far China who was fascinated by *him*.

Sarah stood, smiling down at him. He snapped out of his daze and scrambled to his feet. "Would you see me home, if you please, Mr. Kydd?"

"Ah, of course, er, Miss Bullivant," he said. She waited; he waited.

"Take my arm, if you please," she said primly. "It is unseemly to be seen walking at a distance."

He settled his tricorne on firmly, and held out his arm. Hers entwined and lay gently on his, and the electric soft touch of the side of her breast turned his arm into a rigid claw.

They moved off in sedate promenade. Magically, Ah Lee appeared, to follow at a respectful distance, her face blank but watchful. The touch of Sarah's arm on his was all fire and flowers; Kydd felt twenty feet tall.

He carefully matched his pace to hers, across the *praça* and into the streaming hubbub of the bazaars. As they walked, Sarah pressed closer to him, turning to speak with a flashing smile. He could manage only monosyllables in reply, but something of his happiness must have communicated itself, for she was plainly flattered. He wondered what sort of picture he made in the fine clothing he wore with such a woman on his arm, and lifted his chin in defiance. He might be a common sailor, but at the moment he was king of the world!

The road widened to a leafy avenue, and in the gathering dusk she stopped before an imposing mansion. Rearing up behind the building was a pagoda, smaller than the ones Kydd had seen in Canton, but more richly appointed. Lanterns gleamed discreetly at the entrance to the mansion; the whole smacked of careless wealth. Ah Lee scurried forward to open the door and waited inside.

Kydd's heart sank. It was self-evident that Sarah was of a differ-

ent social order, but had been amused for the length of the afternoon. It had been kind of her, but he had to be realistic.

"Thank you, Mr. Kydd. I did enjoy our tea this afternoon—you
are wonderful company, you know." Her eyes caught the soft
lantern light; they seemed to steal into his soul. She held out her
hand. It was bare, the glove had been removed.

"Er, the same f'r me, Miss Bullivant," he blurted, and shook
her hand warmly. A brief shadow flickered across her face. He
caught the expression, then realized that probably what was
wanted was a more formal exchange. He bowed deeply, but for-
got to put a leg forward; the gesture ended awkwardly and he
blushed.

He looked up again, fearing ridicule, but her face was set, albeit
with the tiniest trace of vexation. She brightened. "Do you know?
We never did get to see the São Tiago. Do you think it would be
very wicked of me to suggest that we meet again tomorrow to
remedy the omission?"

Kydd was thunderstruck.

"That is, if your duties on board your boat do allow," she said.

"After noon, we are free t' step ashore," Kydd stammered.

"Splendid!" Sarah exclaimed, clasping her hands. "If we meet at
two at Honrar Nuñez's, perhaps I can prevail on Ah Lee to provide a picnic basket."

Her mood was infectious and Kydd found himself grinning
inanely, his hat passing from hand to hand.

"Very well—until two then, Mr. Kydd," she said decisively. A
final radiant smile came that stabbed right through him, then she
swept up the steps and into the mansion. The door closed soundlessly. For a moment he stared after her, then slowly turned to
make his way back the short distance to the priest's *residência*.

There was no way Kydd could think of returning on board so
early, but equally he had no desire to join his friends at their rois-

tering in the Solmar. He paced slowly along the seafront, conscious but uncaring that a lone sailor strolling past at this hour was an unusual sight.

Sarah wanted to see more of him. The simple fact kept repeating itself, raising his hopes to levels of fantasy he knew to be foolish. At the same time he was uncomfortably aware that her proximity and physical contacts, however slight, had awakened powerful urges that in no sense could be termed honorable. One thing was certain, next to Renzi he was nothing but an oaf. He cringed at the memory of his awkwardness and lack of conversation.

Suddenly resolved, he set out for the quay where the ship's boats secured—he would return aboard and resume his acquaintance with the literature.

On the berth deck there was only one occupant, still and silent at the table under a lanthorn glow. It was Renzi, reading. Kydd slid into the seat opposite. Renzi did not acknowledge his presence, continuing to read his slim volume with great concentration.

"At y'r books still, I find," Kydd said lightly.

Renzi looked up balefully then resumed his concentration.

"The priest has tired of y'r company?" Kydd said, with more emphasis.

"He does have other duties," Renzi said.

Kydd bit off a hot rejoinder and remembered his intention. "Then I'd be obliged were you to suggest t' me one of *our* books," he said, "that would improve th' mind."

Renzi laid down his Wordsworth. "So Miss Bullivant might be agreeably impressed with your undoubted erudition?"

"So I might have th' chance of knowing somethin' more of this ragabash world."

With a theatrical sigh, Renzi leant back. Then his expression softened. "You are not—yet—a friend to logic, the rational course, but should you so desire then I have in our sea chest an old and very dear piece by John Locke, *An Essay Concerning Human Understanding,* which may yet persuade you."

Sarah was wearing light blue, with many tiny bows sewn into the skirt of her frock, and a gay lace bonnet that was very fetching.

"M'lady!" Kydd smiled, rising to greet her. Nuñez was silent, watchful as a bird.

"Kind sir!" Sarah replied, bobbing a curtsy with a radiant smile just for him. Kydd felt a rush of feeling that left him in confusion.

He collected himself and said casually, "I rejoice t' see you in looks, Miss Bullivant, if th' validity of th' inference may be allowed as experientially rooted." The bit about empiricism could come out later.

Nuñez's eyebrows shot up. Sarah hesitated in puzzlement, then her expression cleared. "You have been disputing with Nicholas," she said, in an accusing tone, "and now you mean to quiz me."

Kydd couldn't keep it up, and a wide grin spread. She was caught by his infectious glee and returned the smile. They stepped out into the street, as prim a couple as any to be seen. There was little small talk as they walked companionably together.

At São Tiago they stood on the ancient battlements and looked out to sea, to the islands and scattered ships at anchor, the bobbing sampans and serene junks. Sarah stood in front of Kydd, her bonnet held in her hands and looking outward in silence. Kydd stood close behind: the scent of her hair came up to him, the lines of her body inches from him.

As if it were some other he watched as his hands came up to take her shoulders, his head bent and he kissed the top of her hair very gently, her female scent briefly enclosing him. She froze; her hands came up slowly to touch his, still facing away, still silent.

Suddenly she turned round, but said in a quite practical tone, as if nothing had passed, "I believe you would like to see a Chinese pagoda—Thomas." Her eyes held his but moved past, over his shoulder. Kydd knew that something was happening, but was unsure, painfully aware of a thudding heart. "Come," she commanded, her grip on his arm a fierce imperative.

In a trance Kydd conveyed her back along the narrow streets the way they had come, feeling his masculinity uncomfortably, and longing with a fierce dread for what he knew must lie ahead.

Ah Lee opened the door to the mansion for them, and they entered arm in arm. "Mr. Tsoi journeys to Canton in the winter season," Sarah said, with a peculiar air of defiance. "The house is deserted."

Kydd glanced at Ah Lee, whose expression was even more blank than usual. The house was easily the richest and most spacious that he had ever entered, but had an alien look and smell with a compelling exoticism.

"We will have our picnic in the pagoda," Sarah said, and in halting Cantonese told Ah Lee, who looked shocked, but bowed once and withdrew.

Sarah steered Kydd through the vast house and out into the garden. Her arm still in his she chatted on, remarking on this Oriental bloom and that until they reached the door at the base of the pagoda. Kydd wondered what lay in the dark interior. Fiddling with the bronze latch, Sarah eased open the tiny door and held up her lantern.

Kydd started uncomfortably. In the flickering gleam he saw her face turn to him, and in his heightened state it seemed distorted, devilish, leading him on into an unknown perdition. "Come on, silly!" She giggled at his hesitation, and ducking down, entered the pagoda.

Quite used to the low deckhead of a man-o'-war, Kydd followed. The golden light of the lantern steadied and strengthened away from the evening breezes, revealing mysterious forms and carvings on all sides. He stared uneasily, the odor of cedarwood and the dust of ages acrid and strong.

"These are Mr. Tsoi's ancestors," Sarah said, then girlishly tripped around a spiral passageway at the periphery. They circled madly in a dizzying whirl that left Kydd breathless. At the very top they finally stopped, laughing. The curved roof above provided a small room, which was barely furnished with a small table and some red straight-backed Chinese chairs on a dark carpet. Many richly ornamented hangings with elaborate writing characters decorated the walls.

Taking his hand, Sarah pulled him over to a window opening and looked at him in triumph. "There, Thomas, is it not worth the climb to see this?" In the clear dusk the twinkling lights of Macao spread away over the hills, fairylike from this height. The dense, wafting fragrance of the Orient enveloped him and Kydd knew he would never forget that night. The moment hung mysteriously, enigmatically.

"Ah Lee will not be long," Sarah said, in her matter-of-fact way. "She will not stay, though, she dislikes being here." She drew him back inside, and they sat in the hard chairs, the lantern hooked to a beam overhead.

"Where do you come from, Thomas?" she asked politely.

By degrees his hot desire subsided. He had misread the situation, and if he were to press his attentions now he would suffer a stinging rebuff. Yet she had already compromised her reputation by being alone with him—he wondered why she trusted him, then remembered that she had called him "a nice man"; he didn't know if he should take this as a compliment or resent it.

The tapping of footsteps on wood began far below. "Ah Lee," said Sarah unnecessarily. The conversation tailed off until finally Ah Lee appeared with a big tray.

Kydd jumped to his feet to take the tray but was stopped by a warning cough and meaningful frown from Sarah. He sat down again in an awkward silence, while Ah Lee patiently laid out the table, her eyes surreptitiously flicking from one to the other. It was a Chinese meal, many small dishes holding hidden pleasures, and in the middle what looked like a flower vase.

"*Fa tiu*," Sarah said, pouring an opaque liquid the color of varnish into delicate porcelain cups. "A Chinese wine, best served hot." She smiled at him over her cup, and he raised his own to her and sipped. It was dense and cloying to his taste, but he felt the glow begin to spread.

Ah Lee left quietly; they heard her steps rapidly diminishing until once more they were alone together.

Sarah's eyes fixed on his face and she spoke levelly. "Do you know, Thomas, that with half a thousand bachelors out here, there isn't one I'd call a man—not a real one who's big and strong, daring, handsome."

Kydd stirred in his chair. Did this mean she really . . . "Damn you, Thomas, do you make me beg?" The tone was shrill, and had an edge of hysteria.

"Sarah . . ." he began hoarsely, but she was on the opposite side of the table and he hesitated.

She breathed deeply, then got abruptly to her feet, in the process sending the table and its contents to one side in an appalling crash of china. Kydd stood up in horror.

At first he could not respond to the passionate assault. The kiss was deep and hungry, her mouth taking his violently, her body pressed into him without restraint. They swayed, clamped together. "Thomas!" she whispered, drawing away slightly. "My darling, sweet Thomas! My dear sailor man! Do you not know we're meant to be one, my love?" Her eyes were huge and lambent in the lantern's glow.

Kydd held her in an intoxicated trance, not daring to move. Her leg interposed slowly, caressing between his thighs in an excruciating sensual invasion; his hands in response moved down her back.

"Thomas—I've never been with a man," she blurted. Her hands slid down his body and discovered his arousal. She gasped, her breath came fast and ragged; he lowered her gently to the floor.

As with a stranger's eyes he saw her tear off her shoes, and with

a flood of sexual feeling he saw her pull up her dress to the white
of knees and upper thighs. She lay on the carpet, writhing and vulnerable.

"Please, Thomas, my love, my love . . ." Her words were nearly
incoherent but Kydd was not listening. He knelt between her legs,
his head roaring at the sight of her under him, and he tore at his
breeches. His hard manhood got in the way and in a rage of frustration he ripped the cloth.

They came together, hard, savagely, their bodies moving
together in tidal surges of sexuality. The climax was explosive and
uncontrollable. She clung to him while the spasms spent themselves. "My darling, my dearest," she murmured, over and over,
clasping his body in hers with an immovable grip.

At last she released him; he drew apart and lay next to her. Wonderingly he gazed across at her, her body still racked by dying
shudders, his own knowing only a beautiful, deep satisfaction.
They lay there unmoving.

Kydd reached out for her, his arm across her bodice. There was
something infinitely endearing in the sight of the trusting pale
nakedness of her lower body, but he was becoming aware of the
night's chill, cooling the hot wetness, and he clutched at his
breeches.

Sarah stirred. "My God," she said brokenly. "What have we
done?"

Puzzled, Kydd propped himself on his elbows and tried to make
out her expression.

"What have we done?" This time it was a harsh, tearing sound,
sending cold shafts of fear into him.

"Sarah?" he asked gently.

She sat up suddenly, plucking feverishly at her dress. Her eyes
showed their whites, like a frightened horse, and his unease grew.
She lurched over to one of the straight-backed red chairs and sat
with her head in her hands.

Kydd got to his feet and covered himself, but his breech flap hung down torn and useless. It seemed futile to pretend a dignity he no longer possessed, but he softly crossed over to her. Then the sobs began, quiet and endless. Clumsily he tried to put his arms around her, but she shrugged them off. The sobs turned to weeping; a hopeless, racking female sorrow.

In all the helplessness of a man he sat motionless, waiting. The evening turned to night, the lantern guttered low. He found his coat, put it around her and resumed his vigil. Long after the night noises of Macao outside had settled in slumber, he held her while the fitful weeping continued. The silent intervals between lengthened until at last it ceased.

"Thomas," she said in a low voice.

"Yes?"

"It'll be all right if we love each other, won't it?" she said.

Kydd paused. His thoughts sped ahead. He had not even considered this, but then he realized that he could answer truthfully. "Yes, Sarah, if we loved each other of course it would be all right."

She sighed and reached for him. Her face in the dimness was a wet smear on his, but he kissed her dutifully, then gently disengaged to trim the lantern. The renewed light revealed wild disorder. Sarah stood the table on its legs again and began mechanically to pick up broken pieces of crockery and congealed food from the carpet. Kydd tried to help her.

The coolness of the night was now a hostile cold. Sarah shivered and moved to a corner of the room. Kydd found a tasseled covering and he brought it across to where she sat hugging her knees. In a touching gesture she held it open for him also. He snuggled up to her and found her feminine warmth roused him again. He dared not reveal it to her.

"I—we must plan," she said, in a small voice.

Kydd made no move, taking refuge in silence.

"Macao is a small place, people will know," she said.

"Only if Ah Lee tells 'em," Kydd said stoutly. He saw no reason to panic.

She thought. "She is discreet—she likes me. But Honrar Nuñez, he would never lie."

"And how would he know?" Kydd retorted.

"I—I could not lie to him, Thomas."

There was no answer to that. They huddled stiffly together.

"There is a way—to save—my reputation," Sarah said carefully. Kydd waited. "Thomas, you shall marry me," she announced. Thunderstruck, he stared at her. She was not looking at him but staring away dreamily into the distance. Her voice strengthened. "I will leave Mr. Tsoi's employ and you shall leave the sea, and we will set up house together, here in Macao."

"Leave the sea?" Kydd couldn't keep the incredulity from his voice.

"Of course, Thomas dear, you wouldn't want me married to a common sailor, now, would you?" He was shocked as much by the prim possessiveness in her tone as the content of what she was saying.

"But—"

"You will get used to being on the land again soon, dear." There was now a hint of asperity. "Tomorrow you shall see the Captain and tell him you are leaving the ship to settle down."

"Sarah, we are at war. My duty—"

"Fiddlesticks! Young men go to war to protect those on the land, and now you are on the land. Leave it to the others to be heroes," she said crossly.

There could be no reply to that at this time. He urgently needed to get away to think it through, to weigh the consequences of his act. "Yes, Sarah," he uttered, unable to muster a term of endearment. She looked at him doubtfully, but snuggled closer, her fingers twitching at his waistcoat.

* * *

In a dreamlike state he made his way back to the boats. Half of his being exulted, sang with joy—the other half recoiled. When he had gone to the *residência* to reclaim his sea clothes Nuñez had come to the door in a dressing robe and had seen his state.

"Had an accident, fell down," he had mumbled. The *honrar* had not said a word, but the atmosphere had been grim and reproving.

The sky in the east was just lightening when the last boat pulled listlessly for the *Artemis*. He was lucky: any later and he would have been put down as a straggler, his leave stopped. He went to his sea chest to shift into his working clothes, heedless of the lewd comments from the others. They had spent their small means quickly, had little chance of further frolics, and were curious about Kydd. He didn't enlighten them.

Pulling his striped shirt down over his head he emerged to see Renzi the other side of the chest. His face was savage, but he said nothing.

That forenoon they were paired on the painting stage hanging over the ship's side. They were to scrape back the broad yellow stripe that ran along the line of the gunports. Kydd wanted badly to talk with his friend, to let him work his logic on the situation, to resolve the skeins of worry and to come to a sound conclusion. Renzi worked next to him, his triangular iron rasping at the paintwork in vicious strokes.

"I saw Sarah last night," he tried.

"And so?" Renzi replied acidly.

"We—we came to an understanding."

Renzi's strokes ceased.

"Well, that is to say, she, er . . ." he mumbled.

"So you didn't have an understanding," Renzi said sarcastically.

Kydd flushed, but persevered: "It's not yet settled," he said lamely.

"And you want it settled. Am I to understand you wish me to advise you how best to entrap Miss Bullivant?"

A dull resentment rose in Kydd. This was his particular friend with whom he had shared so much, and who when needed was proving an obstinate enemy.

"Last night Sarah and I—coupled. She wants t' marry me."

Renzi's scraper tinkled once on the ship's side and splashed daintily into the muddy water below. His face went white, and he stared at Kydd.

"You careless lubbers!" shouted an angry figure at the deckline above. "Show a bit o' life an' get a move on!"

Kydd resumed his scrapes halfheartedly, unwilling to look at Renzi.

"I—can only tender my felicitations." Renzi's voice was distant, controlled.

Kydd said nothing, but scraped on. After a while he heard Renzi catch a replacement scraper before he, too, resumed the work.

"Thing is, I'm not sure o' the rightness of it all," Kydd continued.

The strokes ceased again. "Surely it's simple enough," Renzi replied; his voice was tightly controlled, but no longer venomous.

"No, Nicholas, she wants me to swallow th' anchor and go ashore—for good 'n' all," Kydd said warmly.

"Well, why not, pray?"

Kydd thought and could not come up with other than the truth. "I've found m'self since I've been t' sea, and don't hanker after the 'longshore life."

Renzi bit his lip. "The nub of it, I believe," he began, with a slight tremor to his words, "is whether you love her enough."

For long moments Kydd hesitated. "I don't know."

"You must know."

Kydd faced his friend. "That is th' point, d'ye see?" His earnest expression made Renzi drop his eyes. "I lay with the woman, I must own, but I cannot in all truth say before you—that I love her."

The stage swung with a small movement of the ship. Renzi sat motionless.

"So where does m' duty lie?" Kydd asked.

For a long time Renzi mechanically picked at the sea-faded paintwork. The problem was not of a class that could yield readily to logic. And without the confidence and comfort of solid reasoning at his back he felt diminished. "Duty," he admitted finally, "is a stern mistress." He was uncomfortably aware that he had been overborne by emotion in the last few days, and now he was failing his friend. There was such an entanglement of ramifications in this problem, rooted in society, personal feelings, obligation—and his own reactions.

He pulled himself together. "My dear friend, in this matter, alas, I cannot help. It distresses me, but I would rather not betray your trust with glib emollients or superficial observations. I am sorry, but . . ."

Kydd nodded once and turned back to his work.

Instead of hurrying ashore at noon, Kydd slowly climbed to the bare foretop. He could be sure of being undisturbed there, and the clean seamanlike expanse spoke to him of other things. He sat with his back against the foremast and gazed unseeingly across the anchorage.

He had lain with Sarah: that was the solid fact at issue. The question was, did he therefore owe her a moral obligation? She was a warm, passionate woman who in marriage would see to his needs and more—that was clear. But marriage, he intuitively realized, might involve more than that. A woman needed security and stability; his mind shied at the images of domesticity that this idea generated, the dreary round of politeness, social calls, suffocating conformity. And love. For some reason she had been attracted to him. But he sensed the emotional power that ruled her actions and was instinctively repelled. He himself could never relinquish control like that. He sighed, deeply. In all this, he knew that he must do what was right for Sarah, not himself. His sense of personal honor and moral duty ran deep and true—he would not be able to live with it for the rest of his life should he make a selfish choice.

On deck Cundall stared upward, trying to make out what Kydd was doing. "Foretop ahoy!" he shouted.

There was no reply. Cundall took another pull at his bottle. "Kydd, yer sad lobcock, you mopin' after some syebuck biddy? You—"

From the other side of the bitts, Renzi appeared, his eyes murderous. "Stow it!" he snapped. Rowley emerged aft onto the quarterdeck. The drunken shouts had been audible over the whole deck.

Cundall squared up to Renzi. "An' what's it ter you?"

Renzi's fist took Cundall in the stomach, doubling him up. The second, a moment later, hammered the chin, straightening Cundall before he crumpled to the deck. Renzi stood over him, his chest heaving, then moved back to the forebitts and resumed his vigil. Rowley deliberately turned and gazed out over the stern.

In the foretop, Kydd pondered on, oblivious. So what was his duty? To Sarah, that was now obvious. So he should marry her and give up the sea? If that was what she wanted. But was this decision the best one for her? What if he could not give her love, security, stability? He knew, too, from his previous experience of exile from the sea that he could never counterfeit happiness in a land-based existence, and he would end up the poorest of companions for her.

No, this was impossible, she deserved better than that. She deserved a lover who would be able to provide her with the solid, respectable marriage she needed. He felt a strange pang at the thought of another kissing her, possessing her, but the conclusion was inescapable. He felt the lifting of a dreadful cloud. In her best interests, he must be strong for both of them and refuse her. It would be hard, but any day the frigate could be released to take up her mission of war and they would part. Kydd tested the decision every way he could, suspicious that it was based on hidden motives, but it held firm. Therefore he would implement it, see it through without flinching.

Renzi saw Kydd rise, look once at the shore then descend the shrouds briskly. He busied himself at the bitts until Kydd reached the deck. "Do I take it that you are in possession of a decision?" Renzi enquired.

"I am," Kydd said, his chin lifting slightly.

"May I know?"

"I am to refuse her, I believe."

Renzi looked at the deck, doubting his ability to control his emotions. His own recent reflections had led him to place their friendship out of reach of baser human urges, and he would have suffered much pain were he now to lose it.

Kydd approached the *residência* with heavy but resolute steps. He was unsure what he would say to Sarah, but he was certain of his decision, and was prepared to bear any consequences arising from it.

Nuñez frowned and smoothed his robe. "My child . . ." he began.

"Where is Sarah?"

"She has a message for you. She is at present indisposed, but begs leave of a visit from you at her home."

"Then I shall go t' her."

The priest stood silently, watching, but Kydd did not change into shore breeches and buckled shoes. Wearing the familiar short blue jacket and white trousers of a naval seaman he made his way to the mansion. Ah Lee answered his knock and looked in astonishment at his appearance. Behind her, Sarah appeared and seemed taken aback also.

"Thank you, Ah Lee, I will receive Mr. Kydd in the drawing room."

She had dark rings around her eyes, and was dressed simply. The drawing room was large and forbidding, its dusty stillness at odds with Kydd's lively sea rig.

"Thomas, why do you not dress with more circumspection?" she asked.

Kydd said nothing, holding his sailor's hat before him and gazing at her seriously.

She seemed to pick up something of the gravity of his visit and straightened in her chair. "Nevertheless, it was kind of you to visit."

"Sarah, I don't believe it would be a good thing were we t' marry," Kydd said, looking at her directly.

Only the slightest tremble of her hand betrayed her feelings. "Stuff and nonsense, Thomas dear. You will soon get used to the land, you'll see," she said, in a feminine way going straight to the heart of the matter.

"I've tried the 'longshore life, Sarah, and it don't agree with me—"

"Doesn't agree with you? Then consider *me*. Do you propose to take me out on the sea to live?" Her voice had an edge to it.

Kydd looked dogged. "I would be a poor shab of a husband were I t' give up the sea and take up land ways."

Her eyes grew hard. "This is all nonsense, Thomas. Other men can find it in them to settle down properly, why can't you?"

He didn't reply at first, wishing he had Renzi's powers to render with precision thoughts into words. "It wouldn't be fair to you, Sarah. You deserve better 'n me."

Her eyes filled. "You simpleton, Thomas. It's you I want— need! You're a man, a strong and wonderful man, the only real man I've ever known." She hurried across and knelt by his chair, imploring with her eyes. "My love! We could be so happy together, you and I. Think of it."

Kydd felt his own eyes pricking with tears, but he sat rigid. "No, Sarah. It wouldn't be right, not fair for you."

Leaping to her feet she screamed down at him, "Not fair? Not fair for me? What about me? Why don't you ask me what I think is fair?" She stood over him, the urgency of her passion beating at him.

He looked at her sadly. Her emotion broke and she sank to the floor in a paroxysm of tears. Kydd made no move to go to her, letting waves of sorrow course through him, choking him with their burden of grief. He stood up. There was no point in prolonging the moment—the sooner it was past the better.

She heard the movement, stopped weeping and glared at him. "You've ruined me. Do you hear that? Ruined me."

Kydd looked at her wordlessly, tenderly. The tears burned and stung. She glowered. He hesitated, then turned for the door.

"If you go through that door, I—I shall never see you again." He paused but did not look back.

"Never!"

He stumbled forward.

"Thomas!" she screamed.

He opened the door and floundered out onto the street. He could still hear her despairing cries inside as he lurched away, lost in the most acute desolation it was possible to bear.

His shipmates left him well alone. Renzi squeezed his shoulder, once, then dropped his hand, unable to find a word to say about what was in his heart.

The first messages came, pleading, begging, pitiful. Kydd read each one with a set face and steadfastly remained aboard. Renzi did what he could: he went ashore, but Nuñez was "indisposed" and the door of the *residência* would not open for him.

Later a small figure could be seen at the boat landing, but the Captain had strong views about women aboard. The figure remained staring out and was still there when the cold night drew in.

For Kydd time hung heavy and bleak, but he had resolved to take the consequences of his decision without complaint. The story of his time of trial spread, and in their warm, generous manner the sailors found little services they could do for him, rough expressions of sympathy and comradeship.

Next morning, the Captain arrived aboard in a tearing hurry and almost instantly a fo'c'sle gun banged out and the Blue Peter broke at the foretopmast head. Smiles were to be seen everywhere. They were under sailing orders.

Kydd couldn't take his eyes off the lonely figure still on the quay. What agonies of mind would she endure when she learnt that the ship and he would soon be a memory in an empty anchorage? At least it was now over.

"*Haaaaands* to unmoor ship! *Haaands* to make sail!" The pealing of the boatswain's calls cut into the cool morning air, and the ship burst into life. All the well-remembered duties of a ship outward bound, the tang of sea air, the blessed imperatives of good seamanship.

At the larboard cathead Kydd found the strop and ranged the fish tackle ready for the big bower anchor. When he looked again at the landing place, the figure was no longer there. The anchor was won from the pale mud of the Pearl River, and Stirk clapped on to the tackle with him. Far above, Renzi and others cast loose the gaskets of the topsails.

"Tom, what's this, mate?" Doud, from his position astride the cathead, pointed aft. A sampan with two passengers in it was overhauling them from their quarter. There was no mistaking the occupants—Sarah and Ah Lee.

Kydd didn't know whether to cry or urge them on. Every so often one of the figures stood, swaying dangerously in the little craft and waving furiously. They were coming up fast, but the topsails on the ship tumbled down from their yards and were sheeted home with a will. The frigate bowed slightly under the bellying sails and immediately the ripple of a bow wave started.

For a time, the sampan kept with them, but as the trim frigate caught the wind, the ripple in the bows turned to a chuckle and the little boat fell frantically astern. The ship now set courses: the big driving sails flapped and banged as they dropped, but when they were set *Artemis* showed her true breeding. She lay to the winds and foamed ahead.

Kydd took one last look at the tiny figure in the sampan and sank into dumb misery. The lump in his throat was choking him, and he could hardly see.

Artemis gathered speed for the open sea.

CHAPTER 9

≈

"I allow that it was my decision, but it was th' right one, and I'm man enough I can stand the consequences," Kydd said firmly. His eyes were dark-rimmed but there was an air of tenacious resolve about him.

With the coast of China a diminishing gray blur astern, Renzi noted that Kydd had his eyes set ahead, to seaward. He deeply admired his friend's strength of mind, but he knew there would remain a sorrow that would take a long time to pass.

"But I beg you will not talk anymore of it," Kydd added.

Renzi nodded, and looked out ahead also. "It seems that we are on our way home, shipmate," he said regretfully.

"Yes."

"Back to the war."

"Yes," Kydd said again.

"Some would say that this means prize money once more, and liberty ashore in England to spend it."

Kydd turned to Renzi, who saw with relief a very small smile. "Aye, Nicholas, and you will not see y'r Peking."

Renzi laughed. "True enough. I had my heart set on meeting at least one *si fu* at the Ch'ing court." But he had learnt there was no chance at all of that. Barbarians would always be held at arm's length by the narrow, suspicious Chinese.

"We're to touch at Manila on our way back, I believe."

"It would appear to be a motion to take advantage of our presence in these waters, to show the Spanish that we have the means to defend our interests if need be."

"But we're not at war with them?"

"Not so far as I know—and the opportunity is too good to miss, sending a first-class fighting ship to remind them . . ." His words were cut off by the urgent rattling of a drum at the main hatch aft.

"Quarters!" Renzi exclaimed. However, it could only be an exercise. It was typical of Powlett to put the ship back in martial order before they had even sunk the land astern.

Stirk looked up as Kydd clattered down the fore-hatchway and hastened to his gun. "You, Kydd," he growled. "Cap'n wants th' gun captain to choose another second ter be trained up at each gun. I choose you."

Kydd's stare relaxed to a surprised smile. Stirk did no one favors where his gun was concerned; he obviously thought Kydd the best man for the job. Kydd fell back to the rear of the gun, next to Stirk but to one side.

"No, mate, yer captain fer now," Stirk said, unslinging his gunner's pouch and giving it to Kydd. He stepped aside.

Kydd took position, immediately behind the fat breech of the gun. It felt very different to know that the whole elaborate ballet of the gun crew would now take its time from him. The gun crew returned his gaze with differing expressions—boredom, seriousness, interest—but never contempt or distrust. Renzi regarded him gravely, with the tiniest ghost of a smile. Kydd's nervousness settled. He glanced sideways at Stirk.

"Go on, cully, take charge then," Stirk snapped.

"Cast loose!" Kydd ordered. After Stirk's tough growl, his own voice seemed weak and thin, but the muzzle was obediently cut free and the crew took up their positions. Kydd looked again at Stirk, but the man stood impassive, his arms folded. Kydd turned back to the gun. Ah, yes, test the gunlock. He inspected the big lock on the top of the breech; the gunflint did not move in its clamp and the hammer eased back to full cock on its greased steel with a heavy firmness.

He yanked at the lanyard secured to the gunlock. It gave positively and, with a lethal-sounding steely click, a suitably fat spark jumped across. His confidence increased as his orders had the gun crew sweating at their tasks, rammer and sponge flailing as they hauled the heavy iron beast in and out in simulated battle.

At stand easy, his crew sat wearily on deck, their backs to the carriage, gossiping, just as he had done not so very long ago.

"That'll do, Tom," Stirk said, a glimmer of approval just discernible. "Now listen ter me . . ." There followed a stream of advice, given in gruff monosyllables, ranging from using a thumb on the vent-hole to tell from the air when the cartridge was fully rammed, to firing just as the deck began dipping on the downward part of a roll to ensure that the ball would smash home directly into the enemy hull.

Kydd wiped his hands on his trousers. Now they would try three rounds at a mark—his own gun, pointed and served by him.

"Load with cartridge!" It was his first live order.

The powder monkey already had his box containing the cartridge and Renzi helped himself to the gray flannel cylinder. He placed it carefully in the muzzle and the double-ended rammer was twirled to send it down the bore.

There was a definite jet of air up the cold iron of the vent-hole, which Kydd felt with his thumb as the cartridge approached the breech end. When this stopped he held up an arm. Renzi and the others bent to their wad and shot, but Kydd had no time to watch. He had his pricking wire into the priming hole, stabbing down until he was quite sure he had pierced the cartridge, then out with a quill priming tube and into its passageway to the main charge.

A little priming powder in the pan of the gunlock to catch the spark and now the piece was loaded and primed, a silent mass of black iron waiting only for his personal tug on the lanyard to bellow death into the outside world. His palms felt moist; the eyes of the others were on him as he bent to squint along the muzzle of the gun—there were no sights. These ship-smashers were designed for close-in work, but Black Jack Powlett was merciless with those who threw away their shot by not placing their fire precisely where it would do the most good.

The sea hissed past. The waves seemed higher and more lively viewed through the gunport. They were close-hauled on the starboard tack, under easy sail, which had their side of the gundeck to weather and therefore higher. Kydd searched about the gray sea wilderness for the mark, a beef cask and flag.

Nothing. He thrust past his crew to peer through the port. Still nothing but a vast extent of sea and swell out to the horizon. He sensed Stirk next to him. Almost immediately Stirk pointed. Kydd followed the line of his arm and far, far away he caught a red flicker. "No!" he gasped. The red flicker came and went, hidden and then revealed again by the lively swell.

"No more'n a mile," grunted Stirk. Kydd's experience of battle had been of the order of a few hundred yards at the most. Powlett was not going to make it easy.

"Point your guns!" Rowley drawled. They would track the target until given the order to open fire.

Kydd took one last look at the mark and resumed his place behind the breech, looking down the long muzzle at the bearing where he knew it to be. He pointed to the left-hand side of the gun. Wong levered the handspike, his body glistening with sweat. He heaved at the truck, skidding the gun round so that the muzzle bore more toward the mark.

Kydd squinted down the gun—it was impossible! The gentle heaving of the frigate was enough to send the gun pointing skyward at one instant and then blankly at the sea the next. And the distant mark shot past the questing muzzle this way and that, as out of reach as a buzzing fly. He swore in exasperation.

Stirk eased him aside and sighted down the gun. "Not bad, be half," he grunted, "but yer've forgotten yer has a quoin." Muscles bunching, he worked at the wedge under the breech, which moved the muzzle up or down. Satisfied, he stepped back. "Has a look now, mate."

Kydd found the mark and noted that the muzzle now swept above and below the mark by equal amounts. But the ship was moving, and the mark was already off-line. Boldly, Kydd pointed to Wong again, gesturing with small downward movements as he had seen Stirk do to indicate minor changes. The gun came on target by jerks and he could see that if he could time it well, he had a chance.

The ship sailed on steadily, and he tracked carefully. Kydd took the opportunity of estimating when he would fire, that brief hesitation between triggering the gunlock, the priming catching, and the powder charge going off would translate to an astonishing sweep of movement at the muzzle.

There was a distant shout, then Rowley snapped, "Number one gun—fire!"

Seconds ticked by and then the peace was split by an aggressive bang from forward followed by gunsmoke rolling out a hundred yards or more. It was immediately blown back by the stiff wind and the gundeck was darkened by the acrid cloud. It cleared quickly and the distant plume of the fall of shot duly showed, but way to one side.

The smell of fresh powder smoke was pleasing to Kydd's senses—it was manly, keen and spoke of duty. He kept the brutish gun muzzle squarely on the tiny red flag and waited resolutely for his turn.

The next vicious *blang* and rolling gunsmoke came from the gun next to him. He tensed. The smoke cleared and a splash appeared behind the mark and seventy feet to one side, a good shot at this range.

"Number five gun—fire!"

At the full extent of the lanyard Kydd sighted down the muzzle.

It rose slowly to a wave, so he waited. It began to fall and he was teetering on the point of firing when some seaman's fine instinct made him hesitate. Sure enough a smaller, playful wave countered the first and the muzzle lifted slightly before resuming its downward sweep. He gave the lanyard a firm pull and after a brief hesitation his piece obediently thundered forth. Kydd arched his body and the maddened beast crashed to the rear in recoil, sending towering masses of gunsmoke downrange.

"Stop yer vent!" He heard Stirk's shout dimly through ringing ears, and remembered that he had to stop the flow of eroding gases through the vent-hole. It was easily enough done, but he wanted to know where his shot had gone. Staring at the jauntily bobbing flag he willed his ball on. Magically a plume rose up, almost dead in-line but sadly short.

"Blast me eyes, but that was well done, mate," Stirk said in admiration.

Kydd looked at him in disbelief. His shot so far was the farthest away.

"Never mind th' range—yer ball will take 'im on the ricochet. Not easy ter lay 'er true like that!"

With a swelling pride, Kydd stepped back and rasped, "Well, let's see some heavy in it, then, y' pawky lubbers!"

"Yair—can't come soon enough fer me, Ol' England." Cundall smoothed his shining black hair and stared morosely back at the tiny mirror, the only one the mess possessed.

Kydd was sitting on his sea chest to allow Renzi to finish tying off the end of his pigtail, now a quite respectable length again. At sea he wore it clubbed. The gun practice had broken the spell of his morbidity and he had managed to surround his sorrow with limits that enabled him to function on a daily basis.

"You're quiet, Ned," Kydd said, noticing Doud's unusual reserve.

Doud looked up. "What's ter say? All th' time we're swannin' around out this godforsaken side o' the world, some other frigate is a-snappin' up the prizes—sooner we're back 'n' doing what comes natural, better fer all."

Busily at work on a square wooden plate chopping herbs, Quashee unexpectedly spoke up. "Yer may get yer wish earlier than you thinks, Ned."

"How so, yer big bastard?" Doud said, instantly curious.

Quashee smiled. "Has yer thought? We're touchin' at Manila. What if while we've bin away the Dons have gone ter war on the Frogs' side?"

Cundall sneered. "Then we gets ter take a few dozen fishin' boats an' half a dozen merchant packets—which in course we can't take with us. Wake up ter yerself, yer ninny."

Quashee's smile grew broader. "Then yer ain't heard of . . ."

". . . the Manila Galleon!" finished Petit loudly. All looked at him in astonishment. "He's in the right of it, mates!" he said, his face animated. "Fat an' fair, sails once a year from Acapulkee in Mexico fer Manila, stuffed to the gunnels with all the gold 'n' silver they rips fr'm their colonies." On all sides around the mess table, eyes grew big. Petit continued, with great satisfaction, "An' here she comes, sailin' in, all unsuspectin' that there's a state o' war, which we o' course are obliged to tell 'em."

Happy babbling broke out, but it was interrupted by a shout at the hatchway. "Pass the word fer Thomas Kydd—Able Seaman Kydd, ahoy!"

Kydd rose. "Aye!"

"Cap'n Powlett passes the word fer Thomas Kydd!"

The mess fell silent and stared at Kydd. It was unusual to the point of incredible that the Captain would directly notice any of so lowly a station. Kydd's mind raced. As far as he was aware he had done nothing wrong and, anyway, daily discipline was the business of others. He hurried to the quarterdeck. "The Captain will see you in his cabin," Parry said sharply.

Sliding down the hatchway ladder, Kydd went aft to the broad cabin. Outside was a marine sentry. Kydd knocked carefully and heard an indistinct reply, which he took to be "Enter."

Powlett was at his desk, as usual without a wig—he never wore one at sea. His close-cropped hair lent intensity to his demeanor.

The cabin was neat and spartan, the only concession to humanity a miniature of a woman on the bulkhead and below it another of an angelic child. The rest of the room was dominated by the squat bulk of a pair of six-pounders and a deeply polished chart table. Kydd stood before his captain, hat in hand, and waited.

"Thank you, Kydd," Powlett said, finishing writing. He jabbed the quill back into the ink pot and leant back. "I have a problem," he said, in a tone that suggested problems didn't annoy him for long.

"Sir."

"You may know we lost eleven men at Macao, seven by sickness."

Kydd did not know: he had had problems of his own at the time.

"We can't replace men so easily in this part of the world." He looked directly at Kydd. "I've a mind to rate you quartermaster's mate. What do ye think of that?"

Nothing had been further from his mind. And now—it was undreamt of! He would be a petty officer, admittedly one of the most junior aboard, but he had achieved a precious step up, he had . . .

"Well?"

"I'd like it fine, sir," he stammered.

"Then you are so rated. The first lieutenant will attend to your watch and station." Powlett fixed Kydd with flinty eyes. "You are a fine seaman—I can see this, which is why I gave you your step. You have a future, but you can be disrated just as easily. See that you are zealous in your work and stay away from the bottle, and you may have no fear of that."

"Aye aye, sir!" Kydd said.

* * *

Quartermaster's mate—Petty Officer Kydd! He left the first lieutenant's cabin in a haze of joy. It was only a matter of stepping into a sick man's shoes, he rationalized, but his inner self smugly replied, *Who cares?*

Then Sarah's image flashed before him, dampening his mood. He felt for her pain. Perhaps one day they could meet again in some other way . . .

Slowly his thoughts refocused. Whatever the reason, he was now rated a petty officer. His main duty would be on the quarterdeck, as mate to the quartermaster who had the conn under the officer in command—responsibility for the helm and helmsmen. A quartermaster owed his loyalty to the sailing master, who was probably the most sea professional of all aboard.

Kydd wondered if it had been his skill at the wheel that had won him the post. He enjoyed his trick at the helm, feeling the waves trying playfully to slap the vessel off course and the live vibration of the sea transmitted up through the tiller-ropes, seeing the length of deck curving in at the bow far ahead of the helm, then gently rising and falling under his urging, the whole a connected symphony of motion. He sighed, and rejoined his mess.

"Quartermaster's mate—that makes you a petty officer," said Petit seriously.

"Yes, it does."

"Then you'll be shiftin' your mess tonight?" Petit asked.

Although new-rated, his status entitled him to join one of the senior messes, which were right aft and screened off by canvas. There were only three quartermaster's mates aboard so together they wouldn't make a mess, but he could join the quarter-gunners, the carpenter's crew, or even the élite captains of the tops.

"No, mate, I think I'll stay," he said uneasily.

"Yer a petty officer, Kydd," Cundall repeated. The others remained silent, looking at him gravely. Slowly it dawned on him.

As a petty officer, he had authority over every one of them including Petit. He couldn't stay as a friend and at the same time do his duty by the ship. And it was asking too much to expect them to treat him as an equal when he wasn't. "Yair, have to move, I guess."

Renzi was nowhere to be seen, and Kydd felt a chill of loneliness. He nodded to Petit and said, "Be on m' way by th' last dog-watch."

"Luck, cuffin," said Doud, softly.

Aft, next to the boatswain's cabin, was the screened-off mystery of the quarter-gunners' mess. He scratched on the hanging flap—a face, irritated and querulous, poked out. "What?" it said.

Kydd blurted out his situation.

"Not 'n here, yer don't." The face disappeared. The carpenter's crew had their mess snugly fashioned for themselves and did not want another intruding. An idler's mess—the cooper, sailmaker's mates and the like—offered doubtfully, but they were not watch-keepers and their perspectives of life aboard were quite different. Kydd felt he must decline. He felt rootless, an outcast, much as he had felt when he had been thrust aboard his first ship as a pressed man.

"What're you about, mate?" Stirk's voice behind made him jump. "Bin lookin' fer you half the dog-watch," he said, looking at Kydd curiously. "Gotta get yer gear shifted afore pipe down hammocks, or . . ." He pulled aside the canvas screen to a nearby mess and motioned Kydd in. "This here's Tom Kydd, frien's, quarter-master's mate, just rated."

Kydd caught his breath. Around the mess table were petty officers, men he had learnt to fear and respect. They were the backbone of the Navy, hard men in charge of fighting tops, afterguard, topmen—the élite captains of "part-of-ship." They stared up at him, some with narrowed eyes, others with a shrewd wariness. "Good t' know ye," Kydd said, in as neutral a voice as he could manage. He had no idea how to address these men, his claim to be a petty officer, one of *them*, now seeming a flimsy pretense. They did not answer.

Stirk went on, "An' this Kydd is the juggins 'oo sees a merchant hooker in a blow on 'er way ter Davy Jones. Gets 'imself streamed off in a raft from a ship-o'-the-line, jus' 'cos he thinks ter save 'er."

There was an interested stirring. "Did yer?"

"Yair. But got nothing out've it later, the shysters," Kydd said carefully.

A tall dark man, whom Kydd recognized as captain of the maintop, grunted and said, "Well, get yer dunnage then, Kydd—seems yer movin' in 'ere with us."

He felt a jet of exultation, then turned to Stirk. "You . . ."

"Quarter-gunner, jus' rated up." He thrust the canvas flap aside and called back over his shoulder, "An' we got one other *Royal Billy* in with us—cap'n of the mizzentop."

Kydd wondered who it could be, but time was short and he had his gear to shift. When he got to his old mess there were few left at the table, but with a pang he saw Renzi, standing over their shared sea chest.

"Nicholas—I, well . . ."

Renzi looked at him for a long moment. Then he spoke. "Bear a fist, y' poxy lubber!" he snapped, in a very good approximation of a petty officer's impatient growl.

Kydd could hardly believe his ears. He glowed with pleasure. "You?"

"It seems I have been raised to the felicity of captain of the mizzentop," Renzi continued, in a more normal tone, "and thus might aspire to more congenial quarters."

The mess was more snug than Kydd thought possible. Instead of being lost in the gloom of the open mess deck, the lanthorn light now shone cozily on the inside of the canvas partitions, revealing on the forward one a painted scene of a furious battle at sea in which *Artemis* was easily recognizable, and on the after one several mermaids combing each other's hair. The racks of mess-traps were more elaborate, and Kydd guessed that in other things there would be similar improvements. He slung his ditty bag with the others along the ship's side and took his seat.

"Quartermaster's mate—which watch are youse then, Kydd?" the tall dark man asked.

"Starbowlines, and it's Tom," he said warily.

"Crow, Isaac Crow," the man said. "Cap'n of the maintop. So that'd be Hallison, then, Joshua Hallison who's yer quartermaster." He chuckled. "Yer've picked a right taut hand o' th' watch there, cully."

Another petty officer Kydd knew was Mullion, larboard captain of the foretop. He had reason to—Mullion was never without his colt, a braided rope's end, which he used impartially on his men in the belief that it was the undoubted origin of their markedly faster times. He looked at Kydd steadily, then nodded and grunted, "Jeb."

The canvas flap was thrown aside and a short but sharp-faced man entered and crashed down the grog kid on the table, taking his place on one side. Kydd knew him only from afar as one whose temper was best avoided.

"Parry, God rot his bones!" he said in a grating voice, and noticed Kydd. "Who're you?" There was a visceral challenge in the tone.

"Kydd—Tom Kydd, quartermaster's mate o' the starb'd watch," he said, and felt color rising. "An' who are you, then?" he asked boldly.

The man paused, fixing him with colorless eyes. "Haynes."

"Yer glass, Kydd," reminded Crow, holding out his hand over the grog monkey. Kydd had his old pot ready, then remembered that petty officers had the privilege of taking their rum neat, not diluted to grog.

A glass was returned full of the dark mahogany liquid, the powerful odor of rum heavy on the air. Kydd raised it in a general salute and swallowed. The liquor was pungent and strong.

As they drank, Kydd began to feel the pattern of comradely warmth of his new mess. Crow asked him more about his time in a line-of-battle ship, and others put in their contribution. The lanthorn was trimmed up, and mealtime conviviality set in.

Just as the food arrived, Renzi appeared, silent and watchful. "Renzi," said Stirk briefly. "Tie-mate o' Kydd's," he added, referring to the service close friends did for each other in turn—plait and tie off the pigtail.

"Yeah, heard of 'im, Toby," grated Haynes. "With yer when you boarded the *Citoyong* through the gunports." He gave the smallest of nods to Renzi, but impaled him with his eyes.

Renzi sat, but remained quiet.

"Got a headpiece on 'im, 'e 'as," Stirk added. "We listens ter what 'e 'as to say, like."

The table held its reserve—a sea-lawyer was not a popular character to be.

Mullion broke the quiet. "So it's Manila—what's this, then?" The question was plainly directed at Renzi, and the others kept their silence.

Renzi's half-smile appeared. "We show the Dons we have the force to protect our interests, in the event a good plan while we have a prime frigate in the area." He flicked a glance at Haynes. "The Spanish are a proud race, but they have let this part of their empire decline. We will have no difficulty in impressing them here. But if we are already at war . . ."

"The Manila Galleon—we knows about that," Crow said, but in a not unfriendly tone. He opened the door across the racks at the ship's side and drew out crockery and pewter spoons.

"Then as we have no strategic interest in the place, we will quietly withdraw."

Haynes's eyes narrowed. "Yer sayin' . . ."

"If we take the town, then garrison, defend it—to what purpose? What have we won? What are we defending? There is no sense in this."

Crow looked over at Haynes with a smirk. "He's right, an' all."

Kydd was happy that no one had commented on Renzi's cultured accent. But he had his misgivings. How would Renzi fare shouting orders to his men in the mizzentop? And for that matter, he himself?

Hallison was a dour man whom Kydd remembered as having a short way with helmsmen who failed to measure up. He looked at Kydd doubtfully. "Now, lad, your main dooty is the helm, but there's a mort more t' being a quartermaster." He automatically looked up to the weather leech of the mainsail, just beginning to catch the first of the weak dawn sun. "Steer small, damn you," he growled at the helmsman, and turned back to Kydd. "All kind o' things, fr'm stowing the ballast to leadin' the boarders who are cuttin' out an enemy, 'cos we're the ones who always know how, see?" He stared directly at Kydd.

"Aye, Mr. Hallison."

At that moment sailors began to appear on deck, some bleary-eyed, others surly. Kydd knew very well what this meant but never again would he be expected to join them in scrubbing the deck.

"After end o' the quarterdeck," Hallison told him. Kydd started; then recollected himself and strode to the taffrail.

He glared about him but inwardly he was flinching. "Get a move on, you heavy-arsed dogs," he snarled. At the resentful looks of the sailors he realized that perhaps this was going too far. The men stood in front of him, shuffling their feet, resigned. "You," he snapped, picking one at random, "wash-deck hose." The man didn't say anything but went forward obediently. "Sand," he said to another. The holystones were issued and he set the line of men abreast the helm to work their way aft to the stern.

"Get those men going, th' maudling old women." Parry stomped on deck: he was in a bad mood, and wanted to take it out on the men.

Kydd had seen it before. He called, "Parry!" in a low voice to the men, who took his signal and feigned fear at Kydd as they worked hard with their holystones.

Parry glowered at the group of men who knelt amid the cold gushing water and gritty sand. At Kydd's questioning gaze he turned away to stamp forward.

Kydd knew he was under eye from Hallison, and conscientiously applied his men, knowing the little tricks they could be up to so well himself.

When they had reached the full extent of the deck, Hallison nodded and waited while the swabbers did their work drying the deck before calling Kydd over. "Good. I don't hold with startin' m'self—you'll do." Kydd couldn't conceive of wielding a rope's end on good men either. He beamed, but Hallison went on, "Cap'n will be after yer skin, lad. He wants all his petty officers in blue jackets 'n' buttons when they're on deck." He looked meaningfully at Kydd's striped shirt and knotted kerchief.

Kydd nodded. Hallison glanced again at the weather leech and said, "Go 'n' have some breakfast—be sure an' relieve me at one bell."

It was greatly satisfying, the way that seamen gave way to him at the sight of his blue jacket and twinkling brass buttons. His confidence soared as he bounded up the ladder to relieve Hallison. He had skipped his burgoo and hardtack, quickly stitching the buttons with their stout anchor to his best and only blue jacket. He would not be found wanting in any particular.

Hallison raised his eyebrows in surprise at Kydd's transformation, but did not comment. He crossed to the binnacle and reached below for the log-board. Opening it out he referred to the chalked entries. He looked at the hanging traverse board to check that it agreed and turned to Kydd. "Course sou'east b' east, good breeze fr'm the nor'west. Mr. Parry 'as the deck, Evans on the wheel. You has the conn."

"I have the conn," Kydd repeated, with beating heart.

"Petty Officer Kydd has the conn, sir," Hallison called to Parry, who looked around at the hail, but only grunted and turned back.

"Are ye ready, lad?" Hallison said gravely. If anything went wrong there would be no time for Kydd to rush below and call him—and the blame would be entirely his.

"Yes," Kydd said.

"Right. I'll have me breakfast an' be up here after." He disappeared down the after hatchway leaving Kydd with direct responsibility for ensuring the ship actually sailed where it was supposed to.

Nervously Kydd looked over the helmsman's shoulder at the binnacle. The due course lazily swam under the lubber's line. "See she stays that way," he growled, and stepped back. The whites of the helmsman's eyes showed briefly as they followed Kydd. A hard quartermaster could make a trick at the helm a misery.

Unable to prevent a grin of sheer elation, Kydd paced over to leeward, and looked down the ship's side at the wake, bubbling and hissing its way aft. He followed it as it slid away past the stern to merge in a ruler-straight line that stretched away in the distance. He drew a deep breath, strolled back to the helm and stood, arms akimbo, the picture of a taut petty officer.

Hallison returned, and took the conn. Again there was no comment, the traverse board had been properly kept up, the pegs in their holes stepping out from the center telling of the ship's progress every bell of the watch. In the swelling warmth of the sun it was proving to be a fine morning; the sea was in the process of changing from the gray-green of temperate latitudes to a deep tropic blue.

Hands for exercise was piped for the forenoon, and while Kydd watched idly from the quarterdeck, topsails were loosed and furled at a great rate. He would still be required to haul on ropes, but only at times when skilled seamanship was needed, such as when tacking ship.

Hallison touched his hat, and Kydd saw that Mr. Prewse, the sailing master, had come on deck. "This is Thomas Kydd, been rated quartermaster's mate," said Hallison. Kydd doffed his hat and stood respectfully.

"Just so," said the Master, looking at Kydd keenly. "Have you your letters?"

"Aye, sir." It would probably not be to Kydd's advantage to mention that he had acquired an intimacy of the works of both Mr. Diderot and Mr. Locke recently.

"Then this afternoon, I desire you should assist the mate of the hold when he opens it. You shall take the reckoning." He paused, watching Kydd pensively. "Have you an acquaintance of the sea chart? No? Perhaps you shall do so presently. Attend me in my cabin at four bells this forenoon."

Mr. Prewse had his cabin opening on the wardroom, along with all the officers except the Captain. This was the first time Kydd had entered the area. The Master had personal custody of the ship's charts, with the responsibility of entering unusual observations such as uncharted islands or breakers betraying a reef.

"Do you take the pen, and make a fair copy beneath," Prewse said, sliding across a hatched representation in minute detail of a section of coastline from the seaward. His extensive notes and sketches revealed the painstaking care he brought to his responsibility.

Kydd took the chair in the cramped cabin, and pulled the lamp closer. It was charged with spermaceti oil and gave a pure, clean flame, well suited to the close work. He lifted the pen and inspected it. It was the smallest quill he had ever seen, the carefully shaped nib ending in a tiny hair's breadth. He dipped it into the stone well and set to work.

"I shall return in one bell," Prewse said.

With keen eyes and hands unaffected by grog-tremor, Kydd executed a neat and clean drawing, as near as he could judge to the original, well before the Master's return. He sat quietly waiting, but his eyes were drawn to the chart underlying his sketch. "The Great China Sea" it said in large curlicued words in the title cartouche, and in smaller print was "From Lye Moon to the Philippine Islands." Modestly beneath in plain letters was, "By James Boyde, a Master in the Royal Navy, MDCCLVIII."

There was a scale at the edge and it was covered with tiny numbers, but the expanse of China and a spill of islands were clear enough. Complex star concentrations of lines were scattered randomly across the chart, lines that to Kydd made not the slightest sense. At the bottom were several views of coastlines similar to the one Kydd had just done and he bent with interest to look at them.

"The great Captain Cook never sailed these seas—yon is a poor enough thing to compare." Kydd had not heard Prewse return, and scrambled awkwardly to his feet. "No, lad, sit y'self down." He picked up Kydd's work. "Hmm—a fair hand ye have. I think we can make use of you. Kydd, is it not?"

"Sir."

Kydd's eyes strayed back to the chart. The Master's eyes softened. "I lost a good man in Macao t' the bloody flux; you show willing and you c'n take his place."

"By y'r leave, sir, I need t' get m' learning as quartermaster first," Kydd said respectfully. He didn't want to be tied to sedentary work below while the action was on deck.

"You shall," Prewse said sharply.

There was no need for the raucous thunder of the drum at the main hatch. Everyone knew they would approach the Spanish possession of the Yslas Philipinas in this cool dawn at quarters, guns run out and battle ensign swirling defiantly. If war had already been declared there was every chance that Spain would send out a squadron to their territory. That would make it a risky business to approach the deeply enclosing Manila Bay. When far inside, if there were powerful enemy men-o'-war within, a rapid escape could prove problematical.

Artemis raised land at three bells, the northern tip of the enclosing arm of the great bay. The opposing southern tip was visible a bare ten miles away, but ahead it was as if they were passing into open sea. Closer to the passage, first one, then many small fishing craft appeared. With their double outriggers and *nipa* sails they skimmed like pond insects in the calmer seas, keeping the occupants' brown skins wet with spray. They kept effortlessly with the frigate, which was under easy sail, some waving, but all clearly curious at the big warship arriving.

There was a scattering of small low-lying islands in their path, a number with isolated white buildings glistening in the strengthening sun, and an indeterminate flag flying on one.

Lookouts were posted at each masthead, and two at each top; even so the highest could not detect the inner limits of the bay within the far horizon. They passed into the wider expanse, tension mounting. They might well be fighting for their lives within the hour.

"Sail *hooooo!*" the fore-masthead lookout yelled. His outstretched arm was flung out to fine on the leeward bow. Parry hastened to clamber up the fore-shrouds, his telescope awkwardly under his arm. In the foretop he had it up instantly, trained on the bearing.

For a space, nothing, then—"Deck *hooo!* An *aviso!*" A fast government dispatch boat: she would have had no warning of their approach. As her single sail grew in definition, they saw it angle toward them. *Artemis* held her course, and the *aviso* closed to within clear visual distance, then pirouetted about and foamed back the way she had come.

The die was now cast. They approached the far side of the bay, where the city of Manila was clearly distinguishable. Every spyglass was up and trained, straining for the sight of men-o'-war.

The minutes dragged.

At last it became clear there was no danger. The long anchorage off the sleepy tropical city was dotted with a scattering of merchant ships and native craft scudding about, but not even a minor warship was to be seen.

Powlett swept his glass up and down the coast, then back to the squat, sprawling fort that was becoming prominent on the flat land. "They do not appear to be concerned, Mr. Fairfax," he grunted.

"No, sir," Fairfax said, not easing his habitual worried expression. "Then we take it they have no news of a war?"

"Keep the men at the guns, but prepare a salute on the fo'c'sle," Powlett ordered. "It would be a folly to trust the Dons, I believe."

The frigate, by far the biggest vessel in the anchorage, slowed in its approach.

"It would be their folly to take us for fools," growled Parry. "We can take the whole lot o' these should we please."

Powlett's sardonic smile was hedged with exasperation. "Have a care, Mr. Parry. You will remark the flags of these ships. I see but one with Spanish colors—ah, there we have an English, our proof there is no war." He snapped his glass closed.

A heavy thud drew attention to the fort. Smoke drifted from the embrasures. Another gun fired.

"Prepare our salute, Mr. Fairfax."

"Don't look up t' much," Doud said doubtfully, looking shorewards at the low, somnolent landscape with its fringing palms, muddy river oozing into the bay, and the maze of rickety huts on the outer fringes of the small city. Above all was the smell of the warm, heavy odor of pigs and tropical vegetation.

Around the ship hovered a dozen or more of the distinctive twin-outrigger boats, hawking strange fruits, fish and vegetables. They were kept at a respectful distance by a vigilant watch-on-deck.

"Don' ye worry, mate, it'd have ter be the first sailor's port ever without it's got its cunny burrows." Cundall had his back to Kydd, deliberately excluding him from the conversation on the fo'c'sle.

This would be the last port of call before they re-entered the Indian Ocean on their way back to England that could in any way be classed as "civilization' and Powlett would be sure to grant shore leave.

"Ye're missin' a fuckle, are ye, Cundall?" said Doud contemptuously. He winked openly at Kydd past Cundall.

Kydd felt awkward, unsure of how he should relate to his old friends in his new rating. He winked back and gave an uneasy smile.

Doud sauntered past Cundall and stood companionably next to Kydd at the fore-shrouds. "What's his grandevity think o' this, Tom?"

Gratefully Kydd took up the lead. "Nicholas? Thinks we're wastin' time. If it was war, this time o' year we'd have no chance t' catch the Manila Galleon and the prizes we'd take wouldn't be worth sailin' all the way back."

Grimacing, Doud nodded. "Thought as much. Sooner we head back, better it is fer all."

Kydd felt grateful to Doud, not so much for the friendliness but for how he had shown Kydd that he could still be sociable with old friends, and wear a different face when on duty. The bell sounded sharp behind them, a double strike. Kydd made a brief goodbye and went aft to his part-of-ship station.

"We has visitors, then," murmured one of his men, waiting at the base of the mizzen. He nodded to a merchant ship's longboat approaching *Artemis* from astern. It was pulled by four sailors who were making heavy weather of it. In the sternsheets was a single figure, from his cocked hat and breeches obviously no seaman.

"Boat *ahoooy!*" bawled the mate of the watch, Quinlan. The boat did not lie off and hail but made to come alongside immediately.

"Stand off, the boat!" roared Quinlan.

The officer of the deck, Rowley, stepped over to the ship's side. "Give him a cold shot if he tries it again," he said. A grinning seaman helped himself to a twelve-pounder carronade round-shot and held it above his head. At the threat, the boat ceased rowing and the men lay on their oars. One of the men in the sternsheets scrambled to his feet, swaying wildly. He called out but his thin, fretful voice was impossible to catch in the slop and hurry of waves against the ship's side. When this produced no response from the frigate, the man threw down his hat in exasperation and shook his fist.

"Perhaps we should allow that untutored boor to approach," drawled Rowley, easing his cuffs. "Only one to come aboard, Hallison."

When the man finally appeared over the bulwarks he had worked himself into a state. "You, sir!" he stormed at Rowley. "You are the Master of this vessel, this—this—"

Rowley waited, allowing the splutters to subside. "No, sir, I am not. Lieutenant Rowley, third of His Majesty's frigate *Artemis*," he said, with a slight bow that would not have been out of place at introductions in Carlton House.

The man stared, then resumed tetchily, "Kindly fetch him, then, if you please."

"Captain Powlett is not at liberty to see you, sir," Rowley said sharply. "He is ashore paying his respects to the governor."

"Then, sir, I shall wait." His plain dark gray and black garb suggested he was perhaps a member of the clergy.

"I should be obliged if you would state your business, sir," said Rowley stiffly.

"No business of yours, I assure you, sir—it is your captain I wish to see, and the matter is, I might allow, of a degree of urgency."

Rowley hesitated. "He may well be some time. Might I suggest—"

"I shall wait, however long it takes."

He folded his arms and glared at Rowley, who pursed his lips. "Get a chair from the wardroom," he ordered. When it arrived he thumped it to the deck and gestured mutely.

Powlett returned over an hour later, his face tight. The boatswain's calls twittered and he hauled himself rapidly up the side. "God in heaven, what's this?" he roared, at the sight of the figure sitting obstinately in a chair in the middle of the deck.

"You are the Captain?" the man said icily.

"Who the devil—?" Powlett threw at Rowley.

"Sir, this man—"

"Hobbes, Edward Hobbes. You may be acquainted with the name?"

The high, hectoring voice could not have been more calculated to inflame Powlett on his own quarterdeck, but his hesitation, more at the effrontery than at an effort of memory, gave Hobbes more time. "Or perhaps not. It is of no consequence." He fumbled inside his coat and brought out an envelope. "But I rather fancy this is." He handed it to Powlett with a drooping wrist, the fouled anchor cypher of the Board of Admiralty prominent on the envelope.

Powlett accepted it with bad grace and took out the contents to read.

"You will note the provision of 'all possible assistance from any King's ship,'" Hobbes said, with an irritating level of assurance.

"I see from this that you are a man of science, sir, who is at present engaged in a voyage of discovery. I do not possibly see how this can be allowed to affect the affairs of a ship-of-war."

"Then, sir, I will tell you." Hobbes looked around the anchorage, and pointed. "That is my ship, a brig of some species. It has split its front mast in a storm and until it gets a piece of the right kind of wood from somewhere or other it seems it cannot venture farther on the high seas." His nostrils pinched in exasperation. "My purpose, sir, is astronomical. It is essential for me to be at a point on the meridian diametrically in opposition to that of Greenwich on a date not far hence for a crucial observation, the nature of which need not concern you. Thus you will see that I am at a stand, sir, in need of conveyance to that point—to the Great South Sea I have no need to remind you."

Powlett stared in amazement. "Sir, am I to understand that you are asking me to divert the course of my vessel some two thousand miles for your sole convenience?"

Hobbes stiffened. "My convenience is not the point at issue, but that of science is. This observation adds materially to the sum of knowledge of the earth's precession, which I would have thought would interest even the meanest practitioner of navigation," he finished, in tones laced with sarcasm.

Powlett straightened. "Not possible! This frigate is a man-o'-war, not a damned—"

Hobbes leant forward and spoke in a flat, hard voice: "I have no need to remind you, Captain, that the letter is signed by Sir Philip Stephens himself, who is also acquainted to me personally. Should you be the cause of my inability to discharge my duty to the Admiralty then I have no doubt that you may very well—"

"So be it! Your letter is authority enough, but there will be an accounting of this, sir, mark my word!"

Hobbes eased back in satisfaction.

"Mr. Prewse, we shall return home east-about, by Cape Horn. Be so good as to attend me in my cabin at six bells with charts."

"Then I may instruct my assistant to convey aboard my instruments," Hobbes said. It was a statement, not a question.

"Assistant?" Powlett snapped.

"Mr. Evelyn, a most able young man. And our servants, of course."

Powlett's eyes glittered dangerously. "And your cook and washerwoman, no doubt?"

Hobbes sniffed. "There is no need to be facetious, Captain. I might remind you that time is of the essence."

*   *   *

"No liberty ashore? The slivey bastards! What right d' they have t' tell Black Jack what time o' day it is?" Haynes was pale and dangerous; Kydd kept his silence.

Renzi replied, quietly, "Every right. They're on an Admiralty mission, and we're a King's ship. But I don't believe that is the reason why we can't step off. Recollect that this is Spanish territory and they will not take kindly to our presence—there is every possibility of a fracas if we are allowed ashore."

"There'll be a frack-arse if we *ain't* allowed, mate," Crow said, without humor.

The moody silence was broken by Mullion, whose heavy jaw and brass earrings squared with his big tough hands to give an impression of indomitable strength. "Yer could be overlookin' somethin', gents," he said, a smile lurking.

"An' what's that?" Haynes snapped.

"We's headed t' the Great South Sea—an' while that ain't a prime place fer prizes, yer recollects that fer quim-stickin' it can't be beat."

Kydd's knowledge of native island people was limited to popular lurid tales ranging all the way from cannibalism to an idyllic Eden.

The rest of the mess reanimated, and talk quickened. There was a scratching at the canvas flap. Haynes, being nearest, stuck out his head with a baleful "Yeah?"

"Mr. Fairfax wants you ter vittle in them scientifical gents, Mr. Haynes," rumbled an unknown voice.

"Not 'ere 'e doesn't, cully," Haynes said abruptly.

"An' he did say youse are the smallest mess 'n' can take two easy-like."

Haynes cursed.

"The wardroom takes two, 'n' their servants come 'ere," the voice continued remorselessly. "What shall I tell 'im?"

*   *   *

The pair could not have made more of a contrast.

"Thank ye, gennelmen," said one brightly, "Ben Doody, an' I takes care o' Mr. Evelyn. Yer won't need ter see me offen," he added, his large three-cornered hat awkwardly in his big hands probably more because of the low deck-beams than out of respect. His bucolic figure beamed down on them.

The other was a pinched, crabbed man, whose drab black resembled that of a down-at-heel clerk. His first comment was a sour "We expec' to take our vittles in private, y'understands." Haynes rose slowly and advanced on him. The man backed away, but tripped on a ring-bolt and fell to his knees.

Kydd helped him up and asked, "An' who 'r' you?"

"Rance, Jeremiah Rance." He looked viciously at Haynes and added, "Servant o' Mr. Hobbes."

"Yer've got yer dunnage?" Crow said mildly, looking from one to the other.

Doody looked perplexed but Rance thumbed toward the deck outside. "Yeah, we have—outside." He stood aside to allow someone to move past to carry the baggage inside.

Nobody moved. Crow looked at Haynes seriously, but Haynes returned the look with cruel glee. "Gonna be a long v'yage home, they tells me."

"Sir, it's quite impossible—our charts are old, of th' last age. It is madness even to consider the matter!" The sailing master was uncharacteristically blunt, and Powlett glowered, but subsided. "And by this you are saying that we cannot reach their meridian in time? We must take risks, sir."

The table was overflowing with charts, and Kydd carried still others under his arm.

"Risks? The word is too soft, sir! These islands are so numerous no man has counted them! And they are of the coral kind, whose fangs can tear the heart out of the stoutest vessel. Even Cap'n Cook was near to founderin' after takin' the ground on a coral islet!"

Powlett's baffled fury was barely held in check. The main Philippine Islands ran a thousand miles north and south, a barrier to any ship from the China Sea that wanted to enter into the limitless expanses of the Pacific Ocean. "The Spaniards pass through safely enough—I have heard the name San Bernardino mentioned."

"Aye, sir, but they have the charts an' the pilots, both o' which they would rather fry in hell than let us have. Sir, it is my duty t' say, it's mortal danger to our vessel should we flog about in unknown seas looking for a passage, we have no choice but to sail endelong around."

"Three, four hundred miles north, same distance back the other side—it sticks in m' craw, Mr. Prewse—and we fail the mission!" Powlett tossed down the chart and stared in frustration through the broad stern windows.

Kydd stirred. "Sir," he found himself saying, "we have Doody, one o' th' gentleman's servants. He—"

"Hold y'r peace," Prewse muttered, gathering up the charts. "This is not business f'r you."

But Powlett turned round. "What is it, Kydd?"

"Well, sir, he says as how they got a visit fr'm the shore, some Spanish lord mayor or somethin', who was greatly anxious t' get south to the central part. He offered 'em gold dollars if they'd take him there." Kydd noticed Prewse's tight expression, but continued respectfully, "O' course, they had t' refuse him but, beggin' y'r pardon, sir, seems t' me that you could offer him a passage an' in return he sees y' safely through to the further side."

"Y' can't trust the Dons, sir."

Powlett's hand rasped on his chin as he mused. "It's a long way from Manila to the central parts. I'd wager the details of any arrangement would not necessarily need to be of concern to this mayor's superiors." He straightened in decision. "Let's get him aboard, promise of passage for money, and we'll discuss the alternative afterwards."

Rowley's minimal Spanish was barely adequate, but the minor grandee affected not to notice. A dark-complexioned man with glittering black eyes, he was extraordinarily controlled in his expression and gestures, each movement considered and graceful, but watchful withal.

Not knowing the naval salutes due a Spanish *corregidor,* Powlett had lined the entry point with as many boatswain's mates as he could find. The ceremonial calls sounded strident and clear, gratifying to the proud Spaniard. He bowed and scraped with the utmost courtesy, but was reluctant to go below with the first lieutenant; there had been few first-class fighting frigates seen before in these waters.

Stirk watched the proceedings with interest from the fo'c'sle. "Where they gonna get their swedes down? Hobbes 'as the cabins."

At that moment Crow arrived. "Aft on the gundeck—yer've not heard: it's out o' bounds ter us, worried there'll be a frack-arse." The term was going around the ship fast.

A hesitant Doody emerged by the after-hatch. Looking around he spotted Kydd and waved. Kydd grinned and beckoned him forward. "Mr. 'Obbes is in a rare ol' takin'," Doody chuckled. "Won't speak ter the Spanish gennelman, says as how we'll never get t' his meridian in time 'cos of his delay."

"Why the orlmighty rush?"

"Somethin' ter do with his instryments—has t' take readin's an' such on the far side o' the world at exactly at the same time as they does in Greenwich, but why . . ."

"Your Evelyn, 'e seems a sharp sorta hand," Crow said.

"He is! Lives fer 'is science. Seen him up past midnight, a-readin' his books 'n' papers—but he takes care an' dismisses me fer the night, bless 'is heart."

Kydd smiled. "So this cruise could be t' your liking?"

"Oh, aye! I engaged ter Mr. Evelyn t' see the world, an' I have." His broad country face beamed. "I'll have such a grand lot o' tales ter tell 'em back in the village, why, I'll not need t' buy me an ale fer months."

The sailors roared with laughter, and Doody looked about him delighted.

"Here's yer mate," Crow said, seeing Rance tramp up the forehatchway.

Sighting Doody he approached. "'Obbes wants 'is stores stowed away," he ordered, "an' he's sayin' now." Doody winked at the seamen and left with Rance.

Artemis stretched south at speed, the northwest monsoon perfect for the cruise through an inland sea past tropical islands, some hundreds of miles long, like the mountainous Mindoro, some no more than tiny sandy islets a hundred yards long. All were densely verdant, with jungle down to the water's edge and little sign of human presence.

The *corregidor* and his small party kept to themselves and were seldom seen. This was an agreeable thing for the seamen, for Hobbes had the habit of striding the decks at dawn, impeding the sailors at their cleaning duties, and he was always followed by a cloud of muttered curses.

By the following afternoon *Artemis* was slipping down the coast of Panay, the blue mountains of the interior plain to see. As the first dog-watch was struck on the bell she hauled her wind to shape course to an easterly around the southern tip of the island, and as dusk began to draw in they reached their destination, the small provincial town of Ylo-Ylo.

In the late afternoon sun, a cluster of buildings could be seen lying low and level at the water's edge, their whiteness contrasting against the inky blue of the sea, the deep green of the thick tropical vegetation, and a gathering red sunset.

"Man the side!"

The *corregidor* wasted no time in disembarking; *Artemis*'s barge was specially called away for the task. As the boat's crew pulled lustily for the shore, Hobbes watched them go, then turned to Powlett. "May I know why we are not immediately proceeding on our way? Lose not a moment, sir, we—"

"Damn and blast! We cannot stir but we have a pilot," Powlett snarled. "If the Don keeps his part o' the bargain . . ."

A tropical dusk fell and lights began to glimmer in the violet gloom ashore, the barge crew long since returned. A long bulking shadow in the sea nearby was the high brown island that sheltered Ylo-Ylo, and the peculiar odors of a foreign shore could be occasionally made out, but for want of a pilot the ship lay unmoving in the night.

The next day was only an hour old when activity was seen ashore, which resolved into a twin outrigger boat skimming its way directly toward *Artemis*. Two men were aboard, a Spaniard and a Filipino. The boat, with its single brightly colored lateen sail, smartly came about in a rainbow shower of spray and drifted up to the side.

The boat-boy flung a painter of coarse coir rope aboard the frigate and the Spaniard climbed the side. "*Piloto,*" he stated loudly, as though not expecting to be understood by the English officers.

His eyebrows lifted at Rowley's fractured welcome, to which he replied in loud but simple words.

"Our pilot, sir," said Rowley. "Mr., er, Salcedo. I think he begs that the *bangkha* be towed astern, as they will use it later in their return."

"Very well," Powlett answered.

His keen look at the man seemed to discommode him, or it could have been the sheer intimidating size of the frigate, much bigger than the usual trading vessels of the region. Salcedo was short and stumpy with an Iberian intensity, but his attempt at swagger did not convince.

He went to the side and shouted angrily at the boat-boy, who doused and stowed the sail, paying out more of the painter and doubling it around the mast. He scrambled awkwardly up the side, and as he came over the bulwark stumbled and sprawled headlong.

Salcedo's eyes flickered to the quarterdeck gathering and back to the helpless boat-boy. He snorted angrily. From inside his shirt he drew out a peculiar short coil of a black flexible substance, chased in leather at one end, the other terminating in a knobby excrescence. He lashed at the boat-boy who waited motionless on hands and knees, but when the blows ceased he looked up with a deadly hatred.

Powlett's face hardened. "Take that man forward, and see he's messed comfortably."

Prewse motioned to Kydd, who led away the boat-boy.

It seemed the logical thing. Pinto was a Portuguese, which was nearly Spain, and in the event grudgingly admitted to the language. Kydd handed the man over, his brown face and black eyes clearing at the rough sympathy his treatment had earned from the sailors.

Pinto, it became clear, knew more than a little Spanish, for he was able to explain Salcedo's curious instrument. "He was beat wi' the pizzle o' the horse," he said blank-faced. "Ver' painful but hurt th' honor more."

"What's his name?"

"He say his name Goryo—this is the Ylongos name, he come from Guimaras."

"Tell 'im we'll see him right, mate," Petit said.

By the time Kydd had reached his post at the helm the ship was at stations to unmoor ship. The anchor was broken easily enough from the sandy seabed and sail dropped from every yard. With a graceful sway *Artemis* reached out over the sparkling seas toward the eastern horizon, almost exactly halfway along the barrier of the Philippines.

The pilot stood impassive next to the wheel, but all the officers of *Artemis* and the sailing master were on the quarterdeck as well. It was hard to take, trusting the safety of the ship to one man, and there was an aura of apprehension among them.

Panay was left astern, but other islands large and small were scattered about on all sides. By early afternoon one in particular loomed across their path, and in the background the gray-blue of a continous mountainous coast in the farther distance stretched as far as they could see in both directions—a complete block on their farther progress.

Powlett was taking no chances. In the forechains, Kydd was heaving the lead, a skilled and wet job. Held by a canvas belt to the shrouds, he stood alone on the narrow platform at their base, leaning out over the sea hissing past below. He began each cast with a swing, which would get bigger and bigger, until he could whirl the long lead weight in a neat circle over his head before sending it plummeting into the sea well ahead. The line would rush out while the vessel overran the position, and when the line was vertical Kydd interpreted the depth from the nearest mark to the water—red bunting, black leather, a blue serge, or if it lay between marks it would be estimated as a "deep." It was not a job for the fainthearted. A hesitant fist on the line could bring the seven-pound lead down on an unprotected skull.

"No bottom with this line!" bawled Kydd, as cast after cast brought no sudden slackening of the line. He continued his work steadily, with the same result, the wet line rapidly soaking him.

Ahead lay the island. The officers' faces tightened as the frigate sailed closer. "This is the island of Masbate, apparently," Rowley said, in response to Salcedo's grunting. *Artemis* kept her course, anxious eyes staring forward all along her deck.

"Sir, we're standing into danger," blurted Parry, fixing his eyes balefully on Salcedo, who continued to look ahead sullenly.

Powlett glanced at Salcedo. "The passage through will be narrow and difficult, Mr. Parry. We will follow this fellow's course."

Kydd cast the lead once more. It plunged into the sea, but this time the line slackened. He hauled it taut quickly, and when the ship overtook it his hail changed. "By the deep twelve!" The deadly coral now lay seventy-odd feet below the sea.

On the quarterdeck the group of men looked at each other. "Steady on course!" said Rowley. The tension grew, and on deck seamen off watch looked at each other uneasily.

"By the mark ten!" Kydd pulled in the line quickly, hand over hand, and as he did so he caught a subliminal flicker of a paler shape passing swiftly below, followed by an indeterminate darker shape, before the sea resumed its usual deep blue-green.

It was always disturbing for a sailor to sense that things other than an infinite depth lay beneath the keel, and a coral seabed was quite outside Kydd's experience. Sixty feet, and *Artemis* drew about eighteen feet at her deepest, the stern.

Salcedo seemed edgy. His gaze was clamped as though fixing a mark, although there was nothing that remotely resembled a sea-mark on the lush slopes of the island ahead.

Kydd watched carefully. The red bunting hung wetly from the lead-line a few inches above the water. "By the deep eight!" he bawled. Only thirty feet separated the vulnerable bottom of *Artemis* from the cruel coral. Now the alternating pale and dark was common. He shivered and brought in the line for another cast.

This time it was the Master who spoke. "Sir, I should bring it to y'r attention—unless we bear away soon we will not weather the point." He hesitated then continued, "This is hard, sir, to stay quiet while we enter into hazard at the word of a Spaniard."

Powlett snapped back, "This will be a channel we are follow-ing—it makes no sense for the fellow to wreck us ashore."

"By the mark five!" Kydd's hail carried clear to the quarterdeck. Ten feet below the keel! An instant stirring among the officers, but Salcedo continued to gaze doggedly ahead.

"This is too much, sir, we will be cast ashore!"

The Master confronted Powlett, who thrust him aside. "Stand fast!" he roared.

At that moment there was a scuffle on the foredeck, and Pinto raced aft, followed by a shambling Goryo, clearly enjoying the effects of generous offerings of grog. "Sir!" panted Pinto to the Captain, knuckling his forehead. "This Ylongos, he tell me, we are condemn!" In his urgency the English wilted. Salcedo looked sharply at him and then at the Filipino.

"What?" Powlett bellowed.

Salcedo jabbered tensely at the Filipino, who shouted back.

Pinto's eyes stared wildly. "Sir, they mean to run us on the reef, and leave us as plunder fer the natives!"

CHAPTER 10

≈

For a split second there was a shocked silence, broken only by Kydd's anxious yell, "By the deep four!" Then came a burst of simultaneous action. Salcedo dived for the bulwarks and was brought to the deck with a crash by Hallison; Powlett bellowed orders that had the frigate sheering into the wind to check her ongoing surge; and all hands rushed to the side to look down into the gin-clear waters.

The coral bottom was clearly visible twenty-five feet below, a riot of colorful rocks interspersed with bright patches of sandy bottom, with just enough depth to shade all with an ominous hue. The frigate drifted forward slowly despite her backed sails. The trap had been well sprung; heading for the sloping reef with the wind constant from astern, there was no way the square-rigged vessel could simply turn into the wind and claw off.

There was little time. As *Artemis* lay hove to, Powlett turned to Parry. "Into the boat. Find a passage ahead out." He wheeled on Salcedo. "And get this villainous dog out of my sight—in irons!"

Parry lost no time in shedding his cocked hat and other encumbrances. He signaled to Doud, who went over the bulwarks and into the mizzen-chains pulling the *bangkha* up to allow Parry to board it, before following himself. The boat-boy headed over the side and emerged spluttering. He heaved himself up into the narrow craft and Doud surrendered the little steering oar to him.

Stopping only to claim Kydd's hand lead, the *bangkha* skimmed off at an angle.

Kydd took another lead-line and resumed his duty, watching the reef garden pass beneath them at a slow walking pace as the frigate drifted. He saw occasional heads of coral rising above the exotic undersea plain, their details horrifyingly clear.

Twenty feet.

All eyes were on the *bangkha,* which was half a mile off and seemed preoccupied with a particular area.

It was a fearful thing, to face the impending destruction of their magnificent fighting machine—but when it was also their home, their refuge, their everything . . . Kydd felt a cold uncertainty creeping into him. He gathered the line for another cast, but before he could begin the swing he felt the frigate tremble through his feet. Almost immediately another subliminal rumble came and then the ship's drifting was checked and the vessel seemed to pivot around slightly

He heard a grumbling scrape at the hull. Aft, the sea grew rapidly cloudy with pale particles. Sudden fear showed in every face. Then the ship swung free and continued its slow drift.

Kydd looked around for the *bangkha.* It was a mile away, at the point off the end of the large island, but it was returning with Parry standing erect at peril of being taken by the long boom. The *bangkha* whirled to a stop a few hundred yards off the bow. Parry ducked the sail and stood. At his signal the vessel's fore-topsail loosed and, with steerage way on, *Artemis* altered toward her. The *bangkha* waited, then skimmed ahead to another point.

They were still heading toward the island, but angling toward its tip, and Kydd felt instinctively that they were following a slightly deeper channel implied by a tide-scour around the point. Certainly the soundings had steadied. They passed close to the island, almost within earshot of the small group of villagers gathering on the seashore who watched in awe as the big ship passed so near. A few waved shyly, but the ship's rate of progress was so quick that they were on the other side of the island and stretching away beyond in minutes.

The coral fell away rapidly to an anonymous cobalt blue. The carpenter clumped up from below to report a dry hold and Parry was cordially slapped on the back as he returned on deck. Pinto touched his forehead and spoke to Powlett. "Th' Ylongos say, he know where we go, an' it is distant nine leagues—there he visit his brother," he said. More sail was made and, to lifting hearts, *Artemis* foamed away over the glittering sea.

"A splendid sight, Captain." Hobbes had finished his breakfast below unaware of the drama of the morning, and was now ready to take a stroll about the decks. He looked at Powlett curiously. "I see your Spanish friend has incurred your wrath. He certainly appears unhappy at his fate, raging below that he is to be sacrificed when the ship strikes the rocks." His expression was politely enquiring, but Powlett didn't enlighten him.

Ahead the impassable barrier loomed, but it soon became clear that the northern part overlapped the south, and before the noon-day meal was piped they had taken on substance and reality—and a steep channel had opened between them. It widened and there was a slight swell. The southern point drew back to reveal a small but definite slot of daylight between the two landmasses. The channel broadened more and they began breasting the swell that could only come from a great ocean, long, languorous and effort-lessly driving into the shore.

"God be praised," muttered Hobbes.

Powlett came to a decision. "Ask this fellow," indicating Goryo, "where there is water. We take the opportunity to wood 'n' water while we can."

It was a scene of tropic splendor. Kydd felt an uncouth intruder in his rough sea-clothes as he stepped out of the boat and into the sandy shallows of a sheltered bay on the inward side of the point.

"This is enchantment incarnate," Renzi breathed, treading softly on the sandy beach, as they headed for the shade of the fringing palm trees.

There was a guilty thrill in stepping onto the soil of a Spanish colony—but a very real apprehension too, for if a Spanish man-o'-war suddenly rounded the point to dispute with *Artemis,* the small shore party would necessarily be abandoned. And apart from Goryo's assurances, there might be a Spanish fort over the jungle-topped cliffs farther inland. At this very moment a party of soldiers could well be slashing their way toward them through the undergrowth.

Armed marines hastened to secure each end of the beach. Kydd was uneasily aware that, in the event of trouble, the most they could achieve would be a small delay. But that might be enough to enable them to return to the cutter, which now lay safely bobbing to a small anchor a dozen yards out, bows to sea.

The vivid island jungle, with its color and noise, distracted Kydd. He keenly felt his new responsibility for his small party. "Spread some canvas, then, you scowbunkin' lubbers!" he shouted, as much at Renzi as his own men, who stood about gaping at the profusions of nature. Renzi's party would fill the huge leaguer casks at the spring among the rocks after Kydd's party emptied them of old water and rolled them up the beach, but at the moment Renzi was wasting time standing in admiration at the scene.

Reluctantly the men began the task, stagnant water bubbling out into the golden sand. Then the cask was bullied up the beach, under the enormous palms and to the rocks a little farther along.

The leaguer would be a crushing half a ton in weight when filled, and therefore would need to be parbuckled on spars down the soft sand. There would be no laborious loading into the boat, however. Fresh water was lighter than salt and the huge casks would be gently floated out to the ship.

Kydd put his shoulder to the barrels with the rest and the work proceeded. He couldn't help darting uneasy glances at the dense foliage at the edge of the jungle, thinking of what might lie behind the thick verdancy. This land was exotic and subtly alien. It would be good to make it back to the familiar safety of the ship.

A preternatural disquiet seized him. Something round about him had changed, and he was not sure what. The hair on the back of his neck rose. The big barrel came to a stop, but the ill-natured mumbling trailed off when the men saw Kydd's face. He froze, trying to let his senses tell him. Then he had it. It was the quiet. The raucous racket of parakeets had subsided, their quarrels retreating into the distance and letting an ominous silence descend.

Kydd's eyes searched the thick undergrowth—was that the glint of an eye? An unnatural shaking of leaves? They were unarmed: if there was a sudden rush it would all be over in moments. His palms sweated as he considered what to do. Delay would only allow the hidden numbers to swell until they were ready to attack.

He yelled hoarsely at the nearest sentry, and picking up a cooper's iron stumbled toward the jungle path barely visible in the fringing growth. If he and the sentries could buy the others time . . .

Terrified squeals broke out, and into the open burst at least a dozen nut-brown children. They clutched at each other in fear, staring at Kydd with big black eyes.

"F'r God's sake!" he blazed, lowering the cooper's iron and letting his heart's thudding die down. His expression might have been suitable for crowding on to an enemy deck, but now . . .

He forced a smile. "Y'r nothin' but a bunch of rascals, d'ye hear?" he called. They stood fearfully and Kydd's eyes were caught by the spasmodic tug of a small boy at his older sister's ragged dress.

"Come here, y' little weasels!" he said, holding his hands out and clicking his fingers.

Nobody reacted until the small boy stepped forward half a pace and called out boldly, "*Pini-pig!*" before swiftly assuming the safety of his sister's skirt.

The cry was repeated by others, and more, until a regular chant began, "*Pini-pig! Pini-pig! Pini-pig!*"

The other sailors had come up with Kydd at the sight of the

children, but now they growled in exasperation. "'Oo are they callin' a pig, then?" a tough able seaman snapped.

"Take a strap to 'em, I will," said an older seaman.

Kydd advanced on them but they kept up their chant, baiting the sailors. Suddenly Pinto appeared, followed by Goryo. Kydd had not heard their noiseless approach in the *bangkha*.

"Tell 'em they're in f'r a hidin' if they keep it up," said Kydd, but already Goryo was shouting at them, in a curious tongue, more like the babble of river gravel in a stream. It had little effect.

Goryo turned to Pinto and spoke to him, sheepishly.

"He say, *el niños* very rude to foreigner," Pinto relayed on, "an' he want t' apologize for them."

The sailors glared.

"He say that when island traders come, they always give *pini-pig,* children think you are big, you have many *pini-pig.*"

Pinto prodded farther to discover that *pini-pig* was the basis of a much-prized delicacy of Visayan children, dispensed in the form of a bamboo tube stuffed with pounded toasted young rice flavored with coconut milk and palm sugar.

Laughing, Kydd unknotted his red kerchief "No *pini-pigs,*" he said softly, "but this is f'r you." He held it out to the older sister, who advanced shyly and accepted it with a bob, delightedly trying it on in different styles.

Goryo's face softened, and he murmured a few more words to Pinto, who looked at him sharply. "He say—plis excuse, they are all excite because tomorrow Christmas."

"You will, of course, be aware that this Spanish colony must be papist," Renzi said. "No heathens these." As if in confirmation, the little ones' eyes sparkled and the chant changed to "*Chreest-maaas! Chreestmaaas!*"

Kydd stared at the happy bunch: their careless joy was identical to what must be happening on the other side of the world, in England. Time had passed unmarked for Kydd, but at home there would now be the frosting of December cold, stark leafless trees and bitter winds. Here there was brilliant sun and exotic color, outlandish feast-foods—and an unknown tongue.

When he turned to Renzi his eyes had misted. So much had happened in the year since he had been torn away from his own family by the press-gang, and he knew he could now never return to that innocent existence. He had changed too much. He cleared his throat and bawled at his men, "Stap me, y' sluggards, I'll sweat some salt out o' y'r bones!"

"It's monstrous!" spluttered Hobbes. "There is no time to lose, sir."

Powlett rubbed his chin. "It is clear, sir, you have no knowledge of the Sea Service. Before we may begin our venture upon the Great South Sea we must rattle down the fore-shrouds and, er, sway up the mizzen-topmast." He turned to the boatswain. "That is so, is it not, Mr. Merrydew?"

"Aye, sir," he confirmed, bewildered.

"And this will take us until near sunset tomorrow," Powlett went on.

"If'n you says, sir."

"And therefore I see no reason not to grant liberty ashore to those hands not required." He looked squarely at Hobbes. "You may go ashore if you wish to, sir."

Hobbes snorted and stalked off.

"Pass the word for the purser. We will see if fresh fish and greenstuff can be got while we have the chance."

"Sir—"

"Mr. Fairfax?"

"Sir, the Spaniard, will you—"

"Hang him, the scurvy rogue? Do you think I should?"

It was a nice problem: without question he had been instructed in the deed, so who was the more guilty?

"Well, sir, I—"

"He has failed. He did not succeed in his purpose. We leave him to return and explain himself—punishment enough?"

"But, sir, he will implicate the savage."

"Not if it is explained to him that in such an event we will have no other recourse than subsequently to express our deepest gratitude to his superiors for his safe pilotage through the Strait, for the merest pittance in gold."

The next day most of the ship's company of *Artemis* padded down the jungle path, Captain Powlett and the first lieutenant leading with Goryo and Pinto, the rest following respectfully behind, all in their best shore-going rig. Stirk shouldered a sea chest, and was flanked by Kydd and Crow, who also carried small bundles.

There would be no danger from the indolent Spaniards on this holy day and so far from the provincial centers; Powlett could rest easy with his men ashore for a few hours—a cannon fired from the ship would have them back in minutes.

As they walked the familiar sounds of the sea fell behind, replaced by the curious cries of geckoes, the swooping mellow call of the oriole, the screech of parrots. Sudden rustles in the undergrowth were perhaps wild pigs or other, unknown species.

They halted at the edge of the village and were met by the wizened *cabeza*. His formal speech was rendered in Spanish by Goryo and in turn to English by Pinto. The words may have suffered on their journey but the sentiments were plain. Powlett bowed and they moved on into the village. The inhabitants stood in awe, grouped in the open clearing before the *nipa* palm thatched huts. To one side a glowing pit was tended by the old men of the village, whose job it was to slowly turn the *lechon*—an enormous spitted roast pig.

Gracefully shown to one side, the Captain sat with the *cabeza* at the only table with a covering, Goryo and Pinto standing behind. The rest of the men sat cross-legged on the bare earth, keenly aware of the tables on the opposite side of the clearing waiting to be loaded with food.

Stirk placed the sea chest strategically behind Powlett. It contained unused remnants of finery left over from Lord Elmhurst's entourage. At the right time it would be brought forth, but not now.

Chivvied by one of the adults a file of children approached, and shyly presented to each man a little package wrapped in a charred banana leaf. Unsure, the men looked to their Captain. Powlett gingerly unwrapped the parcel. Inside was a discolored rice cake. "*Bibingka,*" said Goryo, with satisfaction.

Kydd did likewise, and bit into it. The taste was a chaotic mix of flavors that made him gag. Powlett recovered his composure first and politely enquired of the *cabeza*. It transpired they were eating gelatinous rice with fermented coconut milk and salted eggs.

Pressed into line, the children sang. It was a remarkably unselfconscious performance, full, melodious and clear but no tune that Kydd could recognize. Renzi sat next to him, delicately picking at his *bibingka*. He didn't respond to Kydd's comment, wearing a faraway look that discouraged talk.

A hush descended. Powlett got to his feet. "Bo'sun's mate," he growled, "pipe 'hands to carols.'" Hesitating only for an instant, the man's silver whistle whipped up and the call pealed out, harsh and unnatural in the jungle clearing. "*Haaaands* to carols!" he roared.

The men stood up and shuffled their feet. "'Away in a Manger,'" said Powlett. "'Away in a Manger,'" bellowed the boatswain's mate.

Doud's voice sounded out first, pure and clear. A bass picked up and others followed, and soon the ship's company was singing in unison. Kydd stole a glance at Haynes. The hard petty officer was singing, his voice low and heartfelt. He wouldn't meet Kydd's eye, and Kydd felt his own eyes pricking at the buried memories being brought to remembrance.

The children watched wide-eyed, wondering at the volume of sound the seamen produced, but when two or three more carols had been sung, they stepped forward and drew the men over to the tables where the feast had been laid.

No matter that the comestibles were as different from their normal fare as the exotic jungle chaos from the warlike neatness of a frigate. Language difficulties happily drew a veil over the true identities of the delicious fruit bat broth, the ant egg caviar and the dog meat in *nipa* and garlic. The men ate heartily.

The children squealed in joy as they were carried on the shoulders of a fierce sailor, then thrown in the air and caught by those who in another world could reach effortlessly in darkness for invisible mizzen shrouds then swarm aloft. A red-faced Doody had them screaming in delight as he became a village pig and snorted and oinked at them from all fours. Others were chased shrieking about the compound by a burly boatswain's mate and a tough gun captain, but the act that stole the show and had Powlett's eyebrows raising was Bunce and Weems doing an excellent imitation of an indignant sergeant drilling a private soldier up and down, carrying a "musket" of bamboo.

The afternoon raced by; the drink on offer was *lambunog*, specially fermented for the occasion the previous evening from palm tree sap. This was served in half coconut shells, but its pale pink viscid appearance and stomach-turning strength gave pause to even the stoutest friend of the bottle.

Evening approached. The probable nearby presence of a volcano added violence to the red of the promising sunset, and Captain Powlett reluctantly got to his feet. "Pipe all the hands," he ordered. The shriek of the boatswain's calls pierced the din. With a bow, Powlett presented the contents of the sea chest and bundles, and in the enthralled stillness the sailors left quietly.

Artemis put to sea immediately, subdued and replete with last-minute mangoes and bananas. Men looked astern as the ship heaved to the long Pacific swells, privately contrasting the spreading gaudy sunset behind them with the anonymous dark blue vastness ahead.

As days unbroken by any events turned into endless weeks of sameness, the sheer scale of the seas crept into the meanest soul. The winds were constant from the northeast to the point of boredom—an onrushing stream of ocean air that drove them on, still on the same larboard tack, the motion always an easy heave and fall, repeating the same rhythm, surging over the great billows in a gentle but insistent advance. Onward, ever onward, they angled southeastward toward their vital intercept with the diametric meridian, the farthest they could possibly be from the land that gave them birth, and indeed farther from any demesne that could be termed civilized.

Renzi watched Kydd staring out over the great wilderness of white-dashed azure and the immensity of the deep blue bowl of sky overhead.

> *"Dark, heaving, boundless, endless, and sublime,*
> *The image of Eternity . . ."*

he intoned softly, watching for reaction.

Kydd picked up his faded blue-striped shirt, his favorite one, and resumed his stitching. The cotton had softened under the ceaseless exposure to sun and sea spray and now caressed the skin gently, but it would not take too many more patches. "Aye, but Prewse had me at th' charts again last forenoon. You'd not be enjoyin' yourself quite s' much were I t' tell you that he brought down the workin' chart fr'm the quarterdeck, and—no flam—he quick sketches in that little island we saw earlier."

"So?"

Kydd sighed. "Nicholas, we have our sea chart we navigate from, an' most of it is white, nothin' there. An' the Master is fillin' in the details as we go along. Does this give you y'r assurance they know where we are?"

Renzi hid a grin. "Dear fellow, pray bring to remembrance the fact that we bear two natural philosophers—eminent gentlemen I am in no doubt—whose study is the earth's form. We are embarked in the foremost man-o'-war of the age, and with a captain who is an ornament to his profession. What else would you have?"

Kydd's serious expression did not ease. He looked away over the vast waste of tumbling waters and replied, "An' I'll bring *you* to remembrance of what we say at church—'God save us and keep us—the sea is so big and our ship is so small.'"

Renzi kept silent and let Kydd resume work moodily with his needle. He gazed up. The mastheads gyrated against the sky in wide irregular circles, describing never an identical path but always a rough circle. The bowsprit rose and fell each side of the far horizon; the hull thrust and pulled at the body in its continual sinuous forward movement. Everything was in motion, all different, all the same.

"Grog's up soon—I'm going below," he said, offhandedly. Kydd nodded but did not look up.

The gloom and odor of the berth deck bore on Renzi's spirit. The wearisome constancy of their lives was not congenial to his nature. He had found it necessary to ration his reading, which made the books infinitely the more precious. He had taken up Goethe's "Prometheus," Cecilia's parting gift to him, and again found the restless subjectivity not to his liking—but on occasions he had seen her face emerge, ghostlike, from the pages, troubled, concerned. He persevered with the volume.

"Er, yer pardon, Mr. Renzi." It was the petty officer's mess-boy, Will, caught off guard in his scrubbing of the mess table by Renzi's early return.

"No matter," said Renzi, rummaging in his sea chest for the Rousseau. He would spark an interest in his friend for the radical precepts of the philosopher, the supremacy of Nature as the meas-

ure of all things, which would lead him to an acceptance of the
Noble Savage as the superior form of man. He brightened at the
thought of how he would present these jewels of intellect to Kydd
one night watch in the comfort of the lee of the weather bulwark.
He found the *Discours sur les sciences et les arts* and stuffed it into his
ready-use ditty bag for later.

"Get yer arse outa here, skinker." Haynes's grating voice preceded his wiry figure as he flung aside the canvas screen. Before
the noon grog issue was not a good time to be about where
Haynes was concerned.

Mullion arrived and sat opposite. His blue-black hair was com-
pressed by the red bandanna he still wore after the hour's gun practice the larbowlines had just finished. He sat sullenly but quiet.

Crow entered and immediately undid the catches of their neat
side locker, and passed down glasses. No one spoke until Kydd
arrived with the pannikin of rum, which he gave to Crow. The
copper measure filled and filled again as the tots were prepared
under the gaze of the whole mess—half a pint of best West Indian
rum to each petty officer, dark and rich.

The last of the rum did not fill the measure. Crow paused, and
looked up. In the silence Haynes's voice held whispered menace.
"Kydd—he's bin bleedin' the monkey!"

It was nonsense, of course. But Kydd knew he would have to
confront the challenge, face Haynes or back down. He didn't hesitate. His open face broke into a broad smile.

Almost immediately Mullion took it up and snorted in mock
derision. "Kydd? He's green enough, he'd let 'em gull 'im on the
measures. I'll 'ave that."

Crow's eyes flicked over to Haynes, but he passed the glasses
round.

The rum was grateful to the stomach, even if it was suffused by
the taste of half an ounce per man of lemon juice, insisted upon by
Powlett as the most reliable method of forcing the consumption of
the anti-scorbutic. The mood lightened.

"Fair makes me qualmish, seein' that devil-fish trailin' in our wake all day," Mullion rumbled. The shark had been following them for days, seldom more than thirty yards astern, its great pale bulk shimmering a few feet below the waves.

Renzi spoke for the first time. "It's interested in our gash only," he said, referring to the mush of bones and organic refuse that was pitched overside after every meal.

"No, it ain't," Haynes spat. "It's waitin'—there's some soul aboard it's waitin' for, it knows who that is, an' it's a-waitin' fer the time that's written fer 'im."

"So what d'ye want to do about it? Shark's not easy ter kill," Crow responded mildly.

"We rigs a tackle aft, streams a line an' hook with a lump o' pork, and when it strikes, all the watch on deck tails on an' heaves it aboard, holus bolus." His eyes gleamed. "An then we kills it."

Mullion grunted. "Seen one caught that way—in *Amphion* frigate in Antigua. We was at anchor, an' had one o' them big white monsters fair 'n' square b' the throat. Couldn't land it on deck till we had a purchase around its tail, an' a full luff tackle on that—what a mauler!

"Near an hour it took, mates, afore we had it on the foredeck, an' that's but half the story. Threshin' around right mad it was, near a ton o' weight smashin' an' snappin' with its great mouth open—yer could see right inside, teeth an' all." He paused in open admiration. "Then we has ter settle it. At it like demons we was, a-hittin' and a-slicin'—blood and gizzards all over the decks, twenty on us, an' still it weren't finished. Ol' Davey, he slips in the blood 'n' in a flash them teeth has a slice outa his hide."

Mullion swayed back in his seat as if backing away from the sight. Taking another pull of his rum he grimaced. "So help me, Joe, when we cut 'im open, 'is heart still beats right there in me hand—an' his tail still twistin' even tho' it's cut right orf his body!"

"What did yer find in the stomach, Jeb?" Crow wanted to know.

The table perked up in interest. Human skulls and gold watches impervious to stomach acids were not unknown. "Last night's supper" was the prompt reply, bringing reluctant grins all round.

In a reflective quiet the mess finished their rum. Haynes raised his head and looked squarely at Kydd, who gazed back forthrightly. "So where are we at now, mate?" he asked, as if in atonement for his manner before.

Kydd noted with satisfaction the assumption that he was in on the officerlike secret of their position, but in truth he had no idea—latitude and longitude were not yet in his experience, which was mainly in the fair copying of Prewse's working notes.

"We're headed f'r the di'metric meridian," he said, hoping that he had heard it right, "an' we're still a few days off."

"Di'metick who?" said Haynes, in disgust. "Never heard any who's bin there."

"The exact other side of the world," broke in Renzi smoothly. "When we get there and keep going, we're on our way back home."

The table stared at him, the implications for their isolation clear. "Been three thousan' miles on the same course since Christmas," a shadow passed across every face, "an' how far before our hook's down again?" Mullion said, in a low voice.

Renzi looked at the man steadily. "From the meridian to the nearest point of mainland to the east is about a hundred and ten degrees, say twice as far again—but that's Cape Horn. We won't trouble to linger there, so after that we'll need to cross both the whole width and length of the Atlantic Ocean before our anchor touches ground again." They looked at each other in silence, the swinging lanthorn in the gloom plucking shadows from their faces. Bearing her crew on into the unknown, *Artemis*'s decks rose and fell, her movements as regular and unthinking as the rise and fall of a woman's breast.

Crow scratched his ear. "There is somethin' by way of—compensations, mate." His companions looked up.

"We're in Fiddler's Green fer women. These islands, yer c'n buy a woman fer a nail or a bit o' iron, they're hot even fer a pretty bit o' rag. All over yer like a rash, they'll be, have ter beat 'em off with a stick—"

Kydd saw Renzi's face tighten.

"—an' they goes at it like good 'uns, no hangin' back!"

Renzi suddenly stood; his face was pale and set. They stared at him, but he left abruptly.

"What 'n' hell's bit 'im?" Mullion said.

Kydd could not believe that Renzi's usual near inhuman control had slipped on a matter of common coarseness. He got to his feet hastily and went after his friend. He found him standing at the ship's side, gripping a shroud and staring intensely out at the infinity of blue sea. "There are times when it is—save your presence, Tom—an insupportable burden to be closeted with such . . . savages, barbarians."

"It was lewd talk, is all."

"Not that! Never that! I have heard worse in the best company. No, what freezes my blood is that they believe themselves the civilized, enlightened society, and the savage your unredeemable barbarian. Nothing could be more offensive to me! Tonight we will talk of the Noble Savage of Rousseau, the irreconcilable dichotomy between nature and the artificial, perfectibility and man in a state of nature. My friend, your eyes will be opened. You will understand the sources of unhappiness and discontent in our ways, but as well you will come to know the potential human felicity in natural man."

Kydd saw that Renzi had been deeply moved and determined to pursue the reason further.

"Sir, I give you joy. We are at the farthest extremity of the world. We have intersected the meridian you so desire, and yet within span of your due date." Powlett's words were dry and sarcastic, but they did not affect the satisfaction in Hobbes's face.

"My felicitations on your consummate maritime skills, Captain," Hobbes rejoined, in like tones. "And now we have but to select a suitable point of land—an island—somewhere along this meridian to erect our observation platforms."

Powlett glanced stonily at Prewse.

"Sir, the islands are here far separated, days sailing one from the other," Prewse said doubtfully.

"The nearest one, then. Do I have to make my meaning plainer?" Hobbes snapped.

"We may raise Nukumea before evening," Prewse replied, nettled.

In deference to her condition, her increasingly sun-bleached sails and stretched rigging, *Artemis* did not tack about to her new northerly course, but took the longer, safer route of wearing ship. They would track up the meridian until they found a suitable location for the observations. Within hours a tiny dark green smudge hoisted itself above the horizon. It was an unremarkable-looking island, a little lopsided with a peak to one side and the rest relatively flat. Nearer to, they saw that the flat part was in fact a palm-encircled inner lagoon, and on the flanks of the peak was a plateau of higher ground. Pacific surf beat continuously on the bright sandy beach in a dull roar that sounded above the shipboard noises.

"This may be suitable," mused Hobbes, trying to steady a telescope against the moving deck. "Yet I will trouble you for a boat to shore. I will work a lunar to satisfy myself of our longitude."

"You have doubts of our chronometers?" challenged Prewse.

"Machines, sir, mere machines," sniffed Hobbes, "fit only to ease the life of the indolent—if they should fail, sir, you will be cast away. Trust the heavens, my dear fellow, in which there is the cold truth of the eternal to be won by the diligent."

Prewse snorted.

"Clear away the starb'd cutter, Mr. Parry," Powlett growled. "Be so good as to accompany Mr. Hobbes ashore, observe and report to me on return."

Even a quarter-mile offshore the lead-line found no seabed, so instead of lying to anchor, the frigate heaved to with backed top-sails to await the return of the boat. The eyes of the whole vessel followed its progress as it sailed cautiously along the beach. It rounded a point, but its sails still showed above the low grassy spit of land.

The angle of the sails changed when the boat checked its course and suddenly moved inwards. The sails disappeared behind a thicker clump of lofty palms. Reluctantly, the onlookers left in ones and twos, tiring of attempting to imagine what it was like ashore among the anonymous dark green verdancy.

It was trying, but there was no alternative but to "stand off and on"—sail on a course out to sea for a space of time, then reverse course to arrive back in the original position, a feat of navigation in itself.

At dawn the next morning *Artemis* met her cutter as it emerged into the open sea. "This will serve, Captain," Hobbes said, as soon as he had crossed the bulwark. He hurried below, leaving Powlett glaring at the lieutenant.

"Mr. Parry?" he snapped.

"Sir, the island would appear suitable for Mr. Hobbes's obser-vations. It is precisely on the line of the meridian. The open area you see there has a good prospect for the erection of the plat-forms, and it has adequate water." Parry's eyes showed weariness from the night spent under the stars with the acerbic Hobbes.

"Thank you, Mr. Parry," Powlett conceded.

"And, sir, if the sea state will allow it, there is a possible careenage to the south."

"Ah! Is there, b' God?" said Powlett, with interest. The chance to heave the ship down and get at the tropical sea growth on its bottom was too good to pass up. There was, besides, their previous brush with the coral, which would have damaged the thin copper sheeting and exposed the timbers beneath to attack by the pernicious teredo worm.

The cutter still bobbed alongside. "I'll see for myself. We have some weeks here at least. God's bones, but we'll not waste it."

Above the crude rafts fringing the new waterline of *Artemis*, now heaved over in the shallows in the lee of the island, the sight of her smooth verdigris-green-blotched hull was breathtaking. She lay on her side, hauled down by tackles secured to her masts. They were reinforced by additional purchases and, stripped of all possible weight, the curves of her underwater section were now accessible.

It had been a backbreaking task, removing all the frigate's stores, equipment and fittings ashore, but the seamen had been diverted by their exotic setting and the feel of dry land underfoot.

Kydd had been strangely moved by the pristine shore, with its soaring palms whose feathery fronds tossed in the oceanic air. In the thick variegated undergrowth occupying the lower levels the vegetation was wild and profuse with orchids half a foot across. A moody silence inland beckoned mysteriously.

Powlett had been uncompromising, however: while the ship was being careened it was terribly vulnerable. He fretted, stumping restlessly about, driving the men relentlessly. The work was arduous, harsh scraping and swabbing from the rafts with the sea growths and detritus raining down on them, the deep salty sea odor of it all contrasting fiercely with the rich, soft land smell.

Their sleeping place was on the higher open grassy plateau. Simple rectangular huts, made snug from the cooler night breeze with woven palm thatch in the walls, were all that was needed. The sailors slung their hammocks inside to be safe against any unknown ground-dwelling animals.

The officers had tents, while the scientists insisted on separate accommodation, in a capacious hut. At the highest point of the plateau, nothing more than a slight rise, the observatory took shape. The platform was stoutly constructed and sheltering side roofs were prepared to keep the instruments safe against rain showers.

The few marines *Artemis* carried were posted at the broad landward edge of the plateau, facing into the unknown jungle. There was not the slightest sign of human occupation and the sailors padded to and fro up the short path from the beach without any fear. And above them all was erected the tallest flagpole they could contrive, and from it, a large ensign streamed out, conspicuous and confident.

At dusk, work ceased. A large cooking fire blazed up, a welcome beacon in the dark blue night. The bubbling pots wreathed cooking smells about the hungry men. Beyond was the looming black mass of the peak in the darkness.

"Damn fine vittles!" said Kydd, with satisfaction, as he gnawed at his bone.

Renzi grinned in the companionable glare of the fire. "These are not the words you usually choose on board when we dine on this self same dish."

"No, but then I was never so sharp set," Kydd mumbled back.

Renzi moved a few yards away from the fire to appreciate the brilliant coruscation of stars in the clear night. Over the peak would soon emerge the most splendid full moon, and Renzi felt a lifting satisfaction at his condition. The young moonlight silvered the trees and huts but, as well, limned a solitary figure standing to one side. Renzi could just make out that it was Evelyn, still as a statue and staring out to sea, his face in shadow.

He crossed over to him, stumbling in the black and silver tussocks. "A glorious sight for an astronomer," he said equably.

For a moment Evelyn did not reply. When he finally turned, Renzi could see that his face was drawn. "It is—but you should comprehend that it is not my choice that I should be here." He looked toward the fire and away again. "The adventuring life is not to my taste—the privations, the boredom. My science is of a solitary kind, not to be improved by enforced socializing."

"I do apologize if I intrude," Renzi began.

Evelyn moved to bring Renzi's face into the strengthening moonlight. "You appear to have a certain . . . sensibility, if I might be so crass as to remark it."

"At present, the sea life suits my disposition. I have had my perspectives enhanced, my views of the human condition elaborated, and in fine it has been a salutary experience."

"Then I felicitate you on it," Evelyn said dryly. "The theories propounded by Mr. Hobbes are elegant and have deep implications for natural philosophy, and this is why I am here in testing them, not for any love of distant voyaging."

Renzi opened his mouth to interject, but Evelyn added swiftly, "You know that William Gooch was my learned tutor in the astronomical arts. Now I have heard that his bones lie in O-why-ee, last year murdered by savages, as was Cook before him." He lifted his chin and gestured to the invisible horizon. "Have you any idea how inconceivably remote we are?" Renzi kept silent. "La Perouse and his gallant company in the *Astrolabe* have been lost these five years. They could be cast away and waiting for rescue on any one of some thousands of islands—or then again their company might be destroyed, every one."

"Wilson was cast up on the Pelew Islands some years ago," Renzi felt impelled to say, "and the native peoples there most hospitably treated him. I remember, he constructed a small vessel and sailed away and in it he conveyed, at their request, the son of the King of the Pelews. He attended at the court of King George, you will recollect."

"And I also recollect that the poor wight breathed his last the next year in Rotherhithe and never did see his island again. No, sir! You, for reasons that must appear sufficiently cogent to you, have adopted this perilous sea life, but it is not congenial to me.

Pray leave me to my science." Evelyn folded his arms and continued to stare seaward.

Careening continued at first light on the other side of the hull. The carpenter was now able to give his full attention to the ruckled copper plating that marked their encounter with the coral.

"I shall not sleep peaceably until we are a-swim again, Mr. Prewse," Powlett muttered.

"I am sanguine that we shall be b' morning."

"Then you'll oblige me by—"

Powlett stopped short at the sudden widening of Prewse's eyes. He swung round, alarmed. Around the point swept a native war canoe, the savages rigid with surprise at the sight of *Artemis*.

CHAPTER 11

≈≈≈

"They'll be no more'n a thousan' of 'em down on us like screamin' banshees in a brace o' shakes," the boatswain said dryly. The canoe had taken in the scene of the helpless ship lying on her side, then made away with impressive speed.

Fairfax hurried over to Powlett's side. "Sir, the Feejee is accounted an incorrigible cannibal," he said, with a worried frown.

Powlett looked at him.

"They smokes the heads 'n' sticks 'em on a pole," the boatswain added.

The gunner appeared and joined the group. "Thirty-two long guns an' we can't use a one," he said, his eyes squinting at the sandy point where the canoe had slipped out of sight.

"We've got one, maybe two days t' set the barky to rights—can't be done," the boatswain said loudly. There was a general stir.

Powlett frowned: there was no glory in this kind of war. "Set the boats a-swim, Mr. Merrydew, and I desire a swivel in the cutter." The boats had been previously drawn up on the beach; now they would be streamed afloat, bows to sea and one with a small cannon. "I want fifteen stand of muskets loaded and primed, larb'd watch stand to in two hours." With a fierce look at his men he said, "Rest o' you, back to work."

It wasn't two, or even three hours, it was full evening when they came; suddenly around the point in a swarm, twenty-two impressive war canoes and swelling numbers of tattooed warriors. The ruddy glare of torches in each canoe flamed dramatically in the dusky light, adding a devilish animation.

The sailors stood to arms immediately and lined the water's edge, knowing that if the savages established themselves ashore it would be a grave situation. His naked sword picking up the glow of the torches, Parry prowled in front of them, looking repeatedly to Powlett for the word.

"No man to fire without my express order!" Powlett thundered.

Ominously there was no noise from the canoes, no war cries or yelling, just the silence of a murderous discipline. A conch shell sounded from the largest canoe, a low, powerful ululation that set the hairs on the back of the neck on end. The canoes slowly spread out in a wide semicircle, just out of musket range, clubs and spears plainly in sight.

"Here is y'r Noble Savage, then," Kydd growled at Renzi, gripping his Sea Service musket and wondering how a cutlass would stand up to a spear or club after his single shot.

Renzi gave a half-smile. "He is indeed. Can you not perceive his desperate need to defend his tiny, perfect kingdom against the rude impact of our advance?"

Snorting, Kydd replied, "I c'n see 'em well enough—an' they think we're a poor vessel capsized an' cast up on the beach, which they think t' plunder."

Lifting his head Renzi refused to be drawn. "See how they remain out of range of the muskets. They have had dealings with 'civilization' before." He lowered his musket a little and mused, "They very likely call it a 'fire-stick' or similar."

There was a vigorous discussion in the largest canoe, which contained a very fat individual sitting in a chair. He wore a high, colorful headdress. A smaller canoe came alongside, the occupants stepped out, and a more slightly built warrior climbed in followed by three others. Then it whirled about and paddled swiftly inshore.

"It's a parlay, Mr. Parry," said Powlett to the restless officer, "and I want to win time for the savants and their damn observations."

The canoe headed for the center of the beach, where the sailors reluctantly fell back. Powlett moved forward and waited, arms folded.

The canoe grounded with a hiss, and the warriors held the craft steady as the slightly built man stepped into the shallows. He wore just one garment, a sort of skirt falling a little below the knees, and had on a minor headdress. His slight build contrasted with the burly warriors taking up position on each side and he carried no weapons. The threesome paused at the edge of the water. A petty officer with a lanthorn appeared behind Powlett. The light appeared soft and gold compared with the red glare of the torches.

Slowly, the natives moved up the beach. Suddenly the slighter man hurled himself forward in a run. The two flanking him were caught off guard. Raising their jagged bone clubs they sprang forward. Flinging himself at Powlett, the man choked something out unintelligibly. Powlett snarled, "Present!" and all along the beach muskets bristled as they took aim at the warriors. They stopped in their tracks, milling about sullenly, and calling out in hoarse, angry phrases.

The sound of the man's tearing sobs sounded distressingly loud. He was curled into a fetal crouch at Powlett's feet, his body heaving. Horrified, Fairfax moved forward and pulled him to his knees. "It's a—a white man!" he said, and let him drop.

Powlett did not bend. "Can you speak English?" he snapped.

The man pulled himself together, lifting his head and looking from one face to another. He staggered to his feet, still staring at the silent faces. He reached out to touch Powlett's threadbare sea uniform. "I can that, sir," he said, his voice muffled. At Powlett's interrogative expression he straightened and cleared his throat. "My deepest apologies, sir, for m' display," he continued, his voice strengthening, "but it's been four goddamn years since I clapped eyes on one o' my own kind." The American accent was stilted, awkward.

"You are shipwrecked and now *live* among the savages?" Fairfax
asked.

The man glanced back at the warriors menacing him from afar
with their clubs. He edged up the beach, farther into the protection of the armed sailors, and continued, "Nathaniel Gurney, mate
o' the *Narragansett*—as was. Th' year 'eighty-eight, near the end
of a tarnation good season whaling, we follered a pod o' Right
whales south into these unknown seas. We let go th' hook, thinkin'
to wood 'n' water when we was tricked ashore by the natives. Only
I an' two others was left aboard, me bein' mate o' the watch." He
gulped. "Saw it all happen along shore, butchered th' whole crew
they did, then they comes for us—we're not enough to work the
ship, so we hides. When they finds us we think it's the end, but
they laughs 'n' thinks it's a big joke. So, sir, I'm guest o' the Panga
people, 'n' the private lapdog of Tofa-maulu, the King."

Powlett took it in impatiently. "Will they attack, Mr. Gurney?"

Gurney glanced at the warrior pair on the sand, threatening and
glowering. "I have your protection, Cap'n?" he said.

"Of course—you have my word."

Facing the two warriors, Gurney tore off his headdress and
flung it in the sand. This produced low groans from the warriors,
who halfheartedly threatened to resume the chase.

"When we got word of a ship cast ashore an' all arsey-versey I
thought she'd be a lost whaler, same as we, but when we rounded
the point I knew we was wrong. Ye're a frigate at least."

"His Majesty's frigate *Artemis,* thirty-two guns," said Fairfax.

"An' so I made me a break for it." Powlett coughed meaningfully. "Hold y'r horses, Cap'n, coming to it. Now they know I've
gone over to you, they'll not parlay, but they'll listen to a deal. I'm
gonna tell 'em that you're well armed and the smart move would
be t' trade for what they wants. That way they gets it without anyone gets killed."

"Very well. What articles?"

"Iron. Hoop iron off of barrels is best, they c'n shape that into

knives. Very valuable, that is. I'll need a hand axe t' sweeten the
King, but don't queer the market with too much."

"And we get?"

"You've been at sea, what, months?"

"Get on with it!" Powlett growled.

"Fruits, plantains, yams, breadfruit—set y' up in finest fettle,
they will." Then Gurney added, with gravity, "An' if you're figurin'
on staying for a spell, it would be prudent, sir, to consider to build
a stockade. Make this bit o' the island all yourn, just in case, if you
takes m' meaning."

The stockade neatly enclosed the observatory and living huts on
the grassy plateau, the bamboo palisade extending down to the
seashore on each end. The stakes would deter all but the most
determined assault, and once *Artemis* warped out and moored in
the sheltered waters of this leeward side of the island, the seaward
approach would be secured.

The canoes that brought the foodstuffs were quite different
from the lean war canoes. Large catamarans with a central platform and matting sail, they extended over the bright sea from the
larger island over the horizon, piled high with tropical harvest.
They also brought cargo of quite a different kind.

"Sir—sir!" called Fairfax, breathless with anxiety and his run
from the beach. "Sir, there are women in those canoes—quantities
of women!" The women, flowers in their hair and chattering
excitedly in their lilting liquid-voweled tongue, steered their craft
in through the rippling eastward entrance to the lagoon and
glided in to the far beach.

The men at work on the bulking hull stopped and watched the
procession pass them in astonishment. A buzz of talk began, interspersed with ribald calls, which were returned in kind by the
native girls, who waved back happily. The talk swelled to jollity
then bawdiness.

"*Haaands* to muster by divisions!" The boatswain's calls

shrieked discordantly, sending a cloud of small shrikes flying up from the thick vegetation.

On the sinuous length of beach in the lee of the grounded vessel the ship's company mustered under their respective officers, sailors in every sort of clothing in deference to the balmy warmth, most barefoot but all with some form of headgear against the strong sun. The officers were in the bare minimum of uniform and faded cocked hats, Rowley in shirtsleeves and breeches, lace at his cuff and breast, while Parry's serviceable loose shirt was unbuttoned to the stomach.

Powlett strode up. Despite the tropic warmth he wore his blue coat and laced cocked hat, sword at his side.

"Still!" The boatswain's calls pealed a single blast, and the talking died away.

For long seconds Powlett held them with his eyes, the undercurrent of exhilaration among the men ebbing under his ferocious glare. "While *Artemis* is heaved down, should an enemy sail find us here, we are dead men! I will not have us so for a single minute longer than necessary. There will be no rest for any officer or man until we are there," he gestured seaward, "at anchor, stores aboard and ready to *fight!*" Pausing for emphasis he continued, in forceful tones, "And if any man should think to straggle away, *for any reason,* I promise you most faithfully, I will take it to be desertion in the face of the enemy."

The men glanced at each other. There was sense in what Powlett was saying. There were some unknown weeks left until the scientists had performed whatever it was they were doing. The women could wait.

"Master-at-Arms!" The nuggety figure stepped forward reluctantly. He doffed his hat, an incongruous move for he wore no shirt, and with his fair coloring his body had reddened uncomfortably. Powlett's eyes narrowed and his breath hissed between his teeth. "Damn you, sir, get a shirt on!" he snapped, before ordering more loudly, "The purser and his steward only to deal with the women. No savage this side of the stockade under any circumstances. Post your guard inside, and any man who disobeys my orders I want to see before me instantly."

Despite their best efforts, nightfall saw *Artemis* still shore-bound; the big hawsers around her hull to tilt her over were gone, as were all but anchors laid out from the bows and stern. However, they would have to wait until the first light of day before they could safely ease the frigate once more into her element.

In the living huts the women's low calls reached clear and soft on the night air. They had not returned in their canoes and surely expected some response from the strangers. Kydd lay back in his hammock and listened: the warmth of the evening, the violet clarity of the dusk, the night scents of orchids, all conspired against his peace of mind. He could see the blaze of stars peeping through chinks in the matting roof, and he knew that soon a full tropic moon would set the lagoon a-sparkle with silver behind the immense inky shadow of the ship. One of the women began a soft song—cool, dreamy, infinitely beguiling. He tossed fretfully.

A cross voice came from the gloom in the hut. "Fer *Chrissakes!*"

"Shut yer face, Lofty," a second voice grumbled.

"An' all of yez, *clap a stopper on it!*" snarled another. The voices mumbled and stopped, but sounds of restlessness continued, the absence of deep, regular breathing betraying sleeplessness.

"Be buggered!" a voice said decisively. "I've a mind ter do somethin' about it." A dark shape detached from a hammock and crouched down.

"Don' do it, Toby," another voice urged. "Black Jack means it, mate."

"See yez in the mornin'," the first voice replied, fruity with anticipation.

"Rouse out, rouse out—*all the haaands!* Heave along there, lash 'n' carry, *all the haaands!*" The cries of the boatswain's mates crashed into consciousness, dispelling fitful sleep and sending the sailors automatically out of their hammocks. Bleary-eyed, Kydd stood barefoot on the hut floor.

It was dawn, only just. Outside, the night was giving way to the first shafts of light stealing across the sky. The grass was dew-dappled, a strange feeling to Kydd's bare feet, and he shivered in the cool air. Then his brain registered that this was the first time that Powlett, always considerate of his men, had reverted to sea routine while they were out of the ship. Could it be that they had sighted strange sail in the night? Renzi's watchful face next to him seemed equally concerned.

Boatswain's calls shrieked: "*Haaands* to muster! *Haaands* to muster by open list!"

Incomprehension was swiftly replaced by insight as Kydd noticed a cynical smile pass over Renzi's face. Powlett was using the regular routine of mustering the men against their entry in the ship's books as a means of detecting absconders. Sure enough, Powlett stomped down to the beach and waited, grim-faced, for the officers to muster the men of their divisions. The Master-at-Arms waited next to him, *Artemis*'s detachment of marines in their full accoutrements drawn up behind.

The subdued gray light of predawn gave way to the first signs of the golden flood to come by the time the muster was complete. Marching forward, the officers saluted gravely and muttered something to Powlett before falling back on their men. Powlett clamped his jaw and waited. The men, shaken by his controlled fury, waited also.

It did not take long. Down the path to the beach came all three absentees, shamefaced but with a hint of bravado in their gait. They separated to join their divisions, two to Rowley, the other to Parry.

"Take those men in charge, Master-at-Arms!" Powlett roared, above the cheerful morning chorus of the island. The Master-at-Arms gestured to his corporals who singled out the absentees and brought them defiantly forward.

Powlett did not even glance at them. His eyes were on his ship's company in a steely glare. "Articles of War," he thundered.

There was a stir among the men. With that single order Powlett had transformed the occasion from a familiar routine to the awful majesty of a trial—and not only this but a trial in which the evidence had all been heard. Now sentence would be pronounced.

"Article fifteen!" Powlett's voice was powerful and well suited to this duty, to judge and sentence the men of HMS *Artemis*. "Every person in or belonging to the fleet, who shall desert or entice others . . . shall suffer death . . ." The words rolled on, the same grim laws they had heard read out a hundred times on a hundred Sundays. Powlett hardly looked at the words, and finished the recitation with a snarl.

"Do you wish a court-martial?" he asked, as was his duty and the sailor's right. There could only be one answer: if they did request one, they would be obliged to remain in irons until it could be convened. That would not be until they reached Spithead, months and months ahead at best.

"No?" Powlett looked at the men in contempt. "Twelve lashes apiece. Strip!" It had happened too fast. The men stood dumbly, stupefied. "Strip!" Powlett's voice cracked like a whip. The men began halfheartedly to pull off their shirts.

"Sir—" It was the boatswain's mate; his voice was small and apologetic.

"Then get one!" Powlett bawled. Crimson-faced, the man doubled away.

The Master-at-Arms came as close as he could behind Powlett and leant forward to whisper. Powlett did not turn but growled a response.

The men, stripped to the waist, were led up the beach to one of the palms rearing up at the edge of the sand. The first was secured with spun yarn by his thumbs in a parody of the gratings that would normally be rigged for punishment aboard ship.

Powlett waited with a terrible patience for the boatswain's mate to arrive, breathless, with his bag. He nodded, and the marine drummer began a roll. It sounded tinny and unconvincing, the martial sound deadened by the expanse of sand. The boatswain's mate drew out the cat, and measured his swing. The drum continued furiously then stopped suddenly, just as the first blow landed to an agonized gasp. It was the first major punishment Kydd had seen in *Artemis*. He turned to look at Powlett and caught a flash of feeling briefly cross the hard features, a complex expression, but it could be described simply in one word: grief.

Artemis was upright well before noon, the sight of her truncated masts and hull riding high in the water driving Powlett mercilessly on. The frigate was kedged out to deeper water, all her boats afloat, every soul at work on rope, capstan or oar in the warm zephyrs.

Before the end of the afternoon watch the ship was rigged and the stores were returning aboard in a stream. In the setting sun the job was complete. *Artemis* was a man-o'-war once more, riding to two anchors and ready for sea.

"Mr. Rowley!" Powlett rasped, his relief only partly concealed. "You will take the first part of the larb'd watch and mount guard ashore over the observatory. You will be relieved in twenty-four hours." Looking upward at the new-clothed masts he added strongly, "The remainder will turn to, part-of-ship, and set this vessel to rights." For the first time in days, there was a thin smile on Powlett's face.

There was no real need, but Kydd took another rope yarn and added it to the three he was rubbing to and fro on an old piece of canvas on his knee. His work would eventually turn out to be a dolphin for the cro'jack, a simple stout rope with two eyes to prevent nip in the massive yard. There was scope for fine seamanship in the careful pointing to finish over the plain worming and parceling underneath, and Kydd relished its exercise. "Do ye not want t' step ashore, Nicholas?" he said to Renzi, similarly engaged next to him. Renzi raised his eyebrows, a sign Kydd knew to be the polite harboring of a contrary view.

Kydd saw this and grinned. He had paid attention to Renzi's earnest exposition of Rousseau's theories, but his heart had prevailed over his intellect when he had heard of the philosopher's orphaning of his own children in the interests of science, and he had lost sympathy. "Black Jack is down on us seein' the natives— do ye think he admires y'r Rousseau?" Kydd asked.

Renzi stared back frostily. "As well you can conceive, he selfishly consults the interests of his own ship, that its warlike powers are not imperiled." He laid down his yarns. "Yet I must own to a powerful longing to see, just for a morsel of time, the outworking of pure Nature on humankind. Only that," he finished lamely. Kydd suspected he was shying from the difficulty of justifying his desire to visit the shore in the face of baser motives.

They both glanced shoreward. "We're to be guard tomorrow," Kydd said neutrally. It had been hard seeing the first part of the larboard watch pile into the boats, laughing and boisterous, and shove off for the sweets of the land. But Rowley had called on the Master-at-Arms and three boatswain's mates to land with them— there would be no chance of tomfoolery.

Night drew in again. Most men chose to remain on deck in the warm tropic evening, smelling the cooking fires ashore but having to eat their own victuals, boiled to a mush by a sea-cook who had stood wondering as the unknown foods piled aboard for stowing.

As the shore became an anonymous dark mass and lanthorns were hung in the rigging, Powlett came on deck. He didn't waste time. "Cutter's crew to muster—*awaaaay* larb'd cutter!" This meant Kydd, who was bowman of the duty cutter. It was already at the lower boom, and Kydd ran out along the spar in the darkness, and swung down the Jacob's ladder into the boat. He singled up on the painter, then hooked on alongside *Artemis* to allow Powlett to descend the steps and into the boat.

There was no talking as they pulled strongly ashore. Powlett's expression deterred even the effervescent Midshipman Titmuss. They passed through the dark, phosphorescence-streaked sea in a rush, and near to the ragged line of blue-white that marked the tide-line Kydd leaped into the shallows to guide the cutter in.

Powlett stepped rapidly along the thwarts, and splashed down into the shallow water. "With me," he said briefly to the midshipman and Kydd, and plunged forward, heading rapidly for the path.

They paused, just for a moment, where the grassy plateau began. Powlett glared at the men clustered around the fire, laughing and singing. Too late, the marine sentry stumbled up and made his challenge, his hat askew and musket without its bayonet. Without comment Powlett thrust past and toward the firelight. The singing died away as he was recognized.

"Mr. Rowley?" he snapped. The men looked sheepishly at each other, cowed by the naked fury on Powlett's face.

One man, whom Kydd recognized as Hallison, detached himself and touched his forehead. "I'll find him f'r you, sir," he said, looking around before moving off into the darkness.

An ominous quiet descended, the crackling of the fire sounding loud, the men's eyes flicking about nervously. Titmuss seemed uneasy at the charged atmosphere and edged closer to the Captain. With a sudden flurry of movement Rowley arrived with Hallison, breathless and in lace shirt and breeches only, his cocked hat the wrong way around. "Sir?" he said, in guarded tones.

Powlett drew a sharp breath, then said, with icy control, "Be so good as to report your dispositions for the night, Mr. Rowley." There was a brief pause before Rowley began his report. "Damn your blood, sir!" Powlett roared, interrupting the hesitant words. "You treat your duty as a vile visit to a bagnio. Where are your sentinels? Why are these men in liquor?"

"Sir, I—I—" stuttered Rowley. Powlett leant forward, piercing Rowley with his eyes. "You, sir, are under open arrest. Get back on

board this instant." In the shocked silence, Powlett swung around
to the midshipman. "Pass the word for Mr. Parry. He is to assume
Mr. Rowley's duties ashore."

Haynes was dismissive of the whole affair. "Rowley has t' be a
right lobcock, thinkin' to bam Black Jack like that." Dice clattered
to the table. Although gambling was a court-martial offense, there
was no chance of a petty officer's mess receiving the wrong kind of
visitors without warning. Haynes peered at the dice in the light of
the guttering rush dip and snorted in disgust.

Picking them up and dropping them noisily into the leather
cup, Mullion gave a glimmer of a smile. "Can't blame a man f'r
wantin' a fuckle," he said, "an' Rowley is a man fer the ladies, right
enough. Lets his prick lead the way, 'n' he follows on behind."

His throw was vigorous, and with a grunt of satisfaction Mullion let Haynes see the result before stretching out his hand to
help himself to one of Haynes's little store of worn dried peas.
Haynes's own hand flashed out and clamped over Mullion's fist,
crashing it to the table. Surprised, Mullion looked into Haynes's
eyes. Haynes returned the look with smoldering intensity. With
his other hand he deliberately picked a pea from his own store and
carefully added it to Mullion's pile, his eyes never leaving Mullion's. "Allow me," he grated. Slowly he released Mullion's fist and
sat back.

Uneasy, Kydd broke into the savage silence. "Shipmates," he
said, "what's this that y' quarrel over a dish of trundlers?" He
stood over the motionless pair at the mess-table until Mullion
glanced up and allowed a trace of a smile to appear before relaxing
back. Haynes mumbled something in his grating voice and subsided.

It worried Kydd. It was rare for shipmates to clash in this way,
and now within a short space tempers had flared again.

For want of somewhere to go he went forward to the galley.
Renzi was proving a difficult friend while they were at the island,

and seemed to want to be alone more often than not. Around the galley were the usual crowd, enjoying a pipe of tobacco and listening to yarns and songs.

Kneeling on the deck, eyes raised to heaven in mock reverence, was a young Irishman. His round face wore a mournful aspect as he chanted an endless ditty:

> *Bryan O'Lynn and his wife, and wife's mother,*
> *They went in a boat to catch sprats there together;*
> *A butt-end got stove and the water rushed in—*
> *We're drowned, by the holy, says Bryan O'Lynn.*

> *Bryan O'Lynn and his wife, and wife's mother,*
> *They went with the priest to a wake there together,*
> *And there they got drunk and thought it no sin—*
> *It keeps out the cold, says Bryan O'Lynn.*

> *Bryan O'Lynn and his wife, and wife's mother,*
> *They went to the grave with the corpse all together,*
> *The earth being loose they all then fell in*
> *Bear a hand and jump out, says Bryan O'Lynn.*

His audience listened in happy attention, the verses following one after the other in a respectful monotone, until a slight change in tone indicated the final stanza, which was finished in a rousing climax:

> *Bryan O'Lynn and his wife, and wife's mother,*
> *Resolved then to lead a new life together;*
> *And from that day to this have committed no sin—*
> *In the calendar stands now, sir, SAINT BRYAN O'LYNN!*

Hearty chuckles met this, and Kydd felt better.

*   *   *

At dawn Powlett went ashore again, grim-faced and irritable. Stomping up the path he nodded curtly at bored sentries and met Parry coming from the living hut. He was drawn and haggard and moved wearily.

"Report!" snapped Powlett.

Parry pulled himself together. "I am truly sorry to say that some of the men straggled in the night."

"How many?" demanded Powlett. "I'll have the skin from their backs, the rogues!"

"Twenty-nine."

Powlett stopped, aghast. This was over half the watch. His hands twitched convulsively on his sword hilt before he turned abruptly on his heel and trudged down to the boat again. He was still silent as he climbed the side of his ship. Acknowledging the boatswain's calls as they piped the side, he disappeared into his cabin.

Later in the forenoon Lieutenant Rowley was summoned. He was seen to enter Powlett's cabin with a truculent expression. Words were heard from inside, hard and angry words. Rowley left with a set, pale face, stalking down to his cabin. The rest of the forenoon Powlett stayed behind his closed door.

The atmosphere aboard *Artemis* became strained and moody, radiating out from Powlett's closed door. At noon, the hands were called aft by Parry; the Captain was not present. In an expressionless voice Parry told the ship's company they would revert to three watches for liberty, one of which would be retained for guard duties, the remainder having the freedom of the island. It did not need much reflection to realize that Powlett had capitulated to the situation.

Renzi stepped out up the overgrown path inland toward the naked peak that towered ahead. Kydd followed behind, puffing at the pace Renzi was setting. They reached a broad ledge of bare rock that allowed them to look back on where they had come from. "Ah, is not that sublime?" Renzi stood on the lava rock as far forward as possible, unconsciously taking the pose of a Romantic hero, one foot braced forward, a noble brow shielded by his palm as he gazed out over the dramatic downward sweep of the foliage.

Kydd was grateful for the breeze. The day was sunny and close in the lee of the peak. Odd odors from the island vegetation and the warm smell of sun on the volcanic soil filled his nostrils. "What price y'r Diderot now?" Kydd responded happily, only hazily aware of the philosopher's existence, but knowing that it would give Renzi pleasure that he had remembered their conversation. What the man had actually said he couldn't recall.

Renzi turned on him, his face ablaze. Kydd recoiled in dismay. "Yes, you're right! That is the essence of it! We stand morally condemned—'Man is not content with defeating Nature, he must triumph over it!' "

"Why, yes, o' course, this is very right," Kydd agreed, and scratched his leg where some unknown insect had made itself known. Renzi had his oddities, but his emotional tone of late was not in character and Kydd felt some disquiet.

They resumed their upward climb and the bare gray rock of the peak presented close before them as a steep escarpment. They cast about, looking for a passage, but for some time there had been no discernible track through the scrubby vegetation. Then Kydd spied a break in the rock-face, and when they achieved this, they found that they could now see both sides of the island.

The far side was much steeper, and being to the weather side of the island the ocean surged in, smashing down on the foreshortened beach in a ceaseless assault, a constant mist of spume in a haze above the surf. Kydd could not make out anything of interest. The anonymous riot of greenery stretched away unbroken in both directions. A small bluff projected into the sea at one point, its red soil distinctive, and a small beach lay within its hook—but that was all.

Back to leeward the vista was more satisfying, the shallows

where they had careened were easily visible, and toward the other end of the island, they saw the crescent of a wide lagoon. Over a dozen canoes were drawn up on its inner beach, and one or two smaller ones lay unmoving in the lagoon itself. The occupants were fishing. Close inshore was *Artemis,* her trim lines sleek and satisfying; she lay to both anchors and appeared rocklike still, although Kydd knew her to be lively and responsive to the modest swell. The plateau was in plain sight below them, much closer to the beach than Kydd remembered, and on it within the stockade were tiny figures working on the huts and the observatory.

His eyes strayed to the beach between the lagoon and the plateau path. There were women down there, with their wares laid out, and he could see the unmistakable forms of sailors mingling among them.

"A splendid situation for our repast!" Renzi said, hardly able to take his eyes from the abundance of nature. Kydd's cloth bundle was added to the common pool, and soon they were feasting on succulent fish cooked in plantain leaves, ship's biscuit and name-less hunks of a gray, starchy substance. They gorged on fruit to conclude, and Renzi apologetically poured rum and water for their wine.

They lay back, eyes closed, letting the airy warmth and perfect stillness work on their spirits. "So, we are now at the far side o' the world," Kydd said lazily. Just bringing out the words, however, brought a flash of memory. Here was Guildford high street, the old family shop now a stationer's, the crabby windows filled with patriotic and satirical mezzotints. Gentlemen with ladies on their arm were passing by. He mentally corrected the image; the idyllic weather here had induced a summer scene in England, but of course right now it was winter, and it would be a different prospect. His mind drifted. Winter in Macao had been cold, but quite bearable. In fact, he and Sarah—he caught himself at the cold wash of remembrance, her face returned to the center of his vision, tear-streaked and pale.

He jerked awake and sat up. "Shall we return to the ship, d'ye think?" he said, scrambling to his feet. He yearned for the simplicity of the human company to be found in *Artemis*.

"No," said Renzi, decisively. His eyes remained closed.

Kydd hesitated. "The afternoon is passing . . ."

"I have no intention of returning," Renzi said. His eyes flicked open and he looked up at Kydd. "I cannot easily bring to recollection a greater peace and exaltation of mind than this prospect brings—I shall remain here until driven back by nightfall." He looked steadily at Kydd, the lines each side of his mouth lengthening.

"Then I have t' return without company," Kydd said.

"Do so, my friend," Renzi responded, without a pause.

Kydd waited, then smiled reluctantly. "Wish y' joy of y'r Nature," he said, and turned down the path.

Reaching sea level he moved toward the figures on the beach. He waved to Doud, who had a basket that he was carrying toward the informal market. Doud waved back cheerily. Kydd pressed on and saw his first native at close quarters—a man standing expressionless under a palm gazing at the chattering groups. His brown oiled body was tall and confident and he wore a fine-patterned bark-cloth skirt, which extended from a broad woven girdle nearly to his ankles. Kydd offered an uncertain smile, which brought no response.

He walked past, approaching the women of the market who sat on palm leaves laid in a crisscross. Nut-brown and strong-limbed, their noses broad and flat, they had a vitality and animal suppleness. They laughed and chattered and threw looks his way that were unmistakable. "*Ohe, papalangi!*" they teased, and Kydd grinned.

He passed by, heading for the lagoon. It was an idyllic prospect, utterly peaceful and lazy under the tall palms. He was drawn to the canoes pulled up on the sand. They were fine-lined and beautifully finished. He fingered a furled sail, made of a woven matting;

it would not stand a gale at sea, but he guessed that the canoe would head for the nearest island if it came on to blow. They would probably be wet and waterlogged in the short seas of the English Channel, but here in the broad Pacific they would respond to the spacious swells by riding up one side and down the other, fast and dry.

His attention was on the canoe and he wasn't aware of the presence of another until he felt a gentle touch on his arm. Straightening, he turned to see a native girl hesitantly offering him half a coconut filled with water-juice. Her face was open, and her quick smile widened readily at Kydd's shy response. "Why, thank 'ee," he said, uncomfortably aware that her hand still lay on his arm. "Er— is this y'r boat?" He accepted the shell and tasted. The cool young juice was nectar, and he drank again.

"*Tamaha,*" she replied happily. She wore an ankle-length colored skirt similar to those of the men but her upper body was modestly concealed by a string of pretty dried leaves and rushes hanging down from around her neck.

"Sorry, I don't understand," Kydd said, and smiled back.

She giggled, then laid her hand on her breast. "*Tamaha,*" she repeated, then touched Kydd's breast.

"Oh, well, it's Tom, Tom Kydd," he said, conscious that she did not withdraw her hand.

"*Ah—Tonki,*" she whispered, and stroked his shirt curiously. He looked down on her black hair and caught the scent of her, a head-swimming blend of coconut oil and sandalwood. Kydd cleared his throat and looked around. The man under the palm was gone, and their conversation had attracted not the slightest bit of attention from the few still on the beach.

"Um, Tamaha," he began, and fell back on his previous piece of small talk. "This is your canoe?" he asked. She seemed puzzled, so he gestured meaningfully at the craft. Her face cleared, and she slid the canoe easily into the still water of the lagoon.

He stood in confusion. "*Ohe,* Tonki!" she called, holding the canoe still and beckoning. Kydd found himself moving forward to her. Splashing in the bath-warm water, he climbed in and settled in the after part, laughing in embarrassment. Tamaha joined in the laughter, and pushing off the outrigger, climbed lithely aboard. She plied her paddles easily and the canoe skimmed out over the water.

It glided to a lazy stop in the middle of the lagoon and Kydd looked down through the crystal water to a riot of color not thirty feet down, a profusion of tumbling growths in an undulating underwater plain, the most beautiful landscape he had ever seen. He looked up to see Tamaha regarding him seriously over her shoulder. He grinned back, his reserve melting.

She lowered her head, then fumbled in the forward recesses of the canoe and came out with a palm leaf bundle. Eyes mischievous, she lay back slowly until her head lay cradled between Kydd's thighs, and her bare arm arched over to offer him a dark-colored piece of fruit. He accepted slowly and bit into it. Her eyes sparkled up at him and he felt desire mount in a betraying dull flush. He looked over the side again while he collected his thoughts, and she jerked upright again in mock exasperation.

Thoroughly discommoded, he studied the coral more closely, at which she stood up in the canoe. She looked at him once, then in a single breathtaking movement she dived into the lagoon. Amazed, Kydd gazed deep down into the water, seeing her brown body picking its way through the coral garden, her garments floating erotically free.

She found what she wanted and surfaced, water sparkling on her skin, her black hair clinging. It was a beautiful small white shell, empty and delicate, and as it took the air it became more and more intensely white. She stared at him anxiously; he accepted the gift reverently and without thinking held it first to his bosom and then kissed it before looking back into her eyes.

She retrieved her paddles and the outrigger moved purposefully through the crystal water, past the lush coastline toward the end of the crescent. It performed a neat curve and crunched up on the beach. Kydd got out and helped pull the craft clear of the water.

Without a pause, she held him by the hand and pulled him toward a rocky point. "*Lahi hakau loaloa,*" she urged. They ran together over the wet sand and up to a tiny track over the rocks. It wound around the point and past a beach to the weather side of the island, an undercut ledge of sea-roughened lava. They stood together, watching the waves approach in a long, easy heave and swell.

Suddenly, Kydd was aware of an exhalation, a hoarse, labored breathing out like a huge whale. There was a sudden thump and within seconds a giant gout of water roared up beside them and fell, soaking them. Tamaha laughed excitedly, her hair streaming. Heart hammering with shock, Kydd saw that she had lost her modesty in the deluge, her breasts were now quite bare. The water shot up again and descended once more.

As it receded Tamaha gripped his arms and looked into his face. She pointed to the blowhole once with emphasis, then slid her hands up both sides of his hips and brought them up, palms together. Kydd drew her face toward him, and gently kissed it. She looked up with a dazzling smile, and they walked hand in hand to a grassy patch in front of a cave. It was the most natural and the most desirable thing in the world. She drew him down and they lost themselves in passion.

Hand in hand they returned to the beach, and lay together in sleep under the tall palms, letting shadow patterns dance across their bodies and a warm zephyr play softly over them. When Kydd awoke, Tamaha was gone, and the sun had descended in the sky. He sat up. A griping in his stomach reminded him that he had not eaten.

He ambled along the beach and saw Mullion, who lifted a hand in recognition and passed out of sight into the thick undergrowth. Closer to, he realized that something was going on there. He followed Mullion along the path to a clearing. On a fallen palm tree sat Haynes and standing next to him was Crow, who held a gunner's notebook and pencil. Mullion crossed to Haynes, and after a low conversation he was handed an article, which he hastily pocketed.

Curious, Kydd went over. Haynes looked up. "Kydd, yer wouldn't be lookin' fer favors now, would ye?"

"Wha . . ."

"Petty officer an' messmate pays th' same." Haynes's gravelly voice held no warmth. Kydd was clearly missing something; he hesitated. Cundall entered the clearing and leered at Kydd, then went straight to Haynes.

"Two on yer account." Crow sucked his teeth and made an entry in his notebook.

"C'n yer tell us what's the goin' rate?" Cundall asked, pocketing two large iron nails.

"One nail fer short time, bit o' hoop iron fer all night in," Crow said.

"Then I'll also 'ave some iron," Cundall said, "cheaper in th' long run." A hacked-off piece of barrel iron emerged from the sack Haynes had under the tree trunk, and changed hands. "Surprises me *you* should need persuasions," Cundall said to Kydd, and left.

At this rate *Artemis* would be bled of her stores, thought Kydd, but knew in his heart that he would find it difficult to condemn. "Not t'day," he told Haynes, and left.

At the other end of the lagoon three men rolled along the beach, one clutching a bottle. Kydd grinned at their antics. "Heigh-ho!" said John Jones, gesturing with his bottle at the canoes drawn up on the sand. "An' it's *haaands* to muster—man the larb'd cutter!" The others laughed and cackled. "Look alive, yer parcel o' rogues!" His imitation of Parry was nearly perfect.

Jones went down the beach to one of the canoes. "Launch-ho, mates," he called, making ready to slip the craft into the warm lagoon. The others lurched up; a paddle around the limpid waters would be just the ticket. "An' it's one, two, six an' a *heeeavvy*," he

roared. The canoe shot into the water, but slewed sideways, sending Jones backwards into the water. The others roared with laughter but the flailing man suddenly screamed—a deathly, inhuman
shriek that paralyzed Kydd. The laughter fell away into uncertainty, the men staring fuddled and confused at the thrashing man.

Kydd hurled himself down the beach and into the water. As he
splashed to the man he saw a nondescript fish flip away on the bottom; warty, ugly, the color of mud but with glaring red eyes and a
gaping mouth that grotesquely opened and closed. The man's
body arched out of the water with pain, and Kydd's attempts to
drag him from the water were hopeless. "Y' useless bastards! Bear
a hand here!" he screamed.

They held down the unfortunate sailor on the beach and tried
to find the source of the excruciating pain. Kydd ripped off his
shirt and saw it—two small red marks under the nipple with a rapidly whitening outer area. The man's eyes bulged and his arms
beat on the sand. His breathing turned to deep gasps, and despite
the restraining weight of several men, his hands scrabbled at his
throat. His screams deteriorated to hoarse croaks. Kydd saw the
whitened area extend over the chest as the man suffocated in front
of him; the body drooped with occasional muscle twitches and the
light departed from his eyes.

The sun still beamed down, the breeze ruffled Kydd's hair playfully, but out of nowhere death had come to claim his own.

CHAPTER 12

≈

Kydd stumbled up the path to the cooking fire, its ruddy glow a beacon in the gathering dusk. He could hear the distinctive twang of Gurney's American accent and saw that he was at the center of a small group of seamen sitting together. He hurried to join them, still shocked by what he had seen, and needing human company.

"Abe, yer must've had a such a time of it—women, all the vittles a man c'd want, nothin' to do. Why d'ye want ter go, mate?" asked an older sailor.

"Aye—it's paradise here," added Doud.

Gurney didn't answer at first, looking from one to the other with his head oddly cocked to one side as if in distrust of his audience. "Yer think it is, shipmates?"

"Yair, paradise right enough," said a young foretopman.

Leaning forward, Gurney responded passionately, "I grant ye, the weather's always top-rate, an' the vittles are there fer the takin', but think on this. You don't have nothin' to do! A-tall! Yer want anythin', yer reaches out an' picks it off a tree or somethin'. You never works, never gets the satisfaction, each day th' same. Never see y'r own kind, never speak to a Christian soul—and the rest o' the world just ain't there, fer all ye hear of it. Fer all I know, King Louis may've come ter take back his Louisiana from the Spanish."

Sardonic looks were exchanged. "No, cuffin, King Louis ain't no more," Doud told him gently. "Frogs, they has a revolution o' their own, an' separates 'im from 'is 'ead."

Gurney's eyes widened. "Then how . . ."

"They has some sort o' citizens', er, parleyment—the gentry got their heads lopped off an' all, see." Doud was clearly having difficulty with the idea that someone could be ignorant of the tumult of blood that was convulsing the world.

"And we're at war with the Crapauds—they're hard t' beat on land," said Kydd, "but they can't best us at sea," he added, with feeling. He thought over other events of the last four years—the shocking mutiny on the ship *Bounty,* the Terror in Paris, George Washington becoming the first President of America, these things Gurney would learn about in time.

"Yeah, but me here with a bunch o' heathen, always feudin' and fightin', struttin' up 'n' down like." He stared gloomily at the remaining figures on the beach. "I seen sights 'd make yer blood run cold. They're murderin' heathens, shipmates."

Kydd thought of Renzi. High-minded thoughts would be no proof against the savagery of the warriors should they grow tired of peaceful trade. His thoughts drifted back to Tamaha. He would see her again tomorrow. Would she be thinking of him now? Would he tell Renzi of her? He knew that he was not immune to feminine charms—their rivalry over Sarah Bullivant had shown that. Sarah! The name caused a stab of feeling, but he had now detached that part of his past into a self-contained unit that carried her memory.

Darkness lay softly over the island, and Kydd finished the last of his meal, a boiled concoction of salt beef and yam served in a half coconut shell. Still no sign of Renzi. A buzz of talk washed about him. He lay back on the grass and gazed at the stars, thinking of nothing in particular, just enjoying the night air.

Drowsy, he went to the living hut. Their hammocks were still slung and the matting sides were rolled up to give an airiness to the warm night. As he climbed aboard his hammock Kydd saw a dark form by Renzi's position. "Nicholas?" he called softly. The form froze. "Is that you back with us?"

"Yes," said Renzi shortly.

Kydd sensed a bridge had been crossed. "Did you . . ."

"I had the transcendent experience of communicating with the savages in their innocence," Renzi said stiffly.

So there would be no revision of Rousseau's Noble Savage. Kydd wondered what form the communication had taken, given the total lack of a common tongue. "John Jones was taken by a devil fish," he said. "It was the strangest thing y' ever saw, just a single bite an' he was destroyed—Nathaniel Gurney says it was the Scorpion Fish, very bad. An' he also says as how the savage are treacherous heathens, given to murderin' each other and—"

"Gurney is a fool," Renzi spat, "an ignorant wastrel who, like us, is causing the foul corruption of civilization to lay its dead hand on these islands."

"How so?" Kydd replied, with heat. "D'ye despise even y'r own society?"

Renzi paused, and Kydd could hear his angry breathing. "I beg—we will talk no more of it," Renzi said, his voice thick.

Kydd bit off his reply and settled in his hammock.

He awoke late with a muzzy head after a night of conflicting dreams. He looked over the edge of his hammock to Renzi's, but his friend had left—as he was entitled to, Kydd reminded himself. Their spell of duty did not begin until noon.

Tamaha was nowhere to be seen, and he didn't feel like going down by the lagoon or taking the steep climb to the peak. He wandered up to the observatory platform. The observations had begun, and Kydd watched Evelyn's total concentration at the gleaming brass instruments and his quick scrawls as he added to his growing pile of papers. Hobbes glowered at the inquisitive onlookers and continued his dour ministrations.

"You, sir—yes, you!" It was Evelyn, beckoning to him while he remained bent at an eyepiece. Kydd came obediently, knowing that Evelyn was not given to idle whims. "Be so good as to advise me, Mr. Mariner. My glass has a propensity to tremble and sway in

this rather forthright breeze. It makes a ruination of my figures."
He waved at the slender brass length of his instrument up on its
wooden platform.

Kydd saw how the long optical piece was being affected by its
length. "I believe y' have here a mizzen gaff right enough, yet
wanting its rigging." He pursed his lips. "I'll return with the necessaries." Evelyn nodded, bemused at the mysterious metaphor.

Returning with a hank of spun yarn, Kydd capably set up a pair
of vangs each side of the instrument leading to its outer end from
the stout support posts of the platform. He contrived a deadeye
on one side, which allowed him to tighten the "rigging" to a harp-
like tautness. "There," he said, with satisfaction. "Do y' take a look
through y' optics now."

Evelyn bent and took the eyepiece again. "Ah! The very wonder of the age—here we have a rocklike stillness." He relinquished
the instrument and stepped down. "My thanks, Mr. Mariner."
Noticing Kydd's interest he added, "We have in these papers an
infinitely precious aggregation of data, which when matched with
simultaneous observations in Greenwich will settle once and for
all the precessional paradox."

Nodding wisely, Kydd noticed the care that Evelyn took in
replacing the papers in a polished wooden box. No doubt this
contained a final product of why the frigate had traveled so far to
this remote region.

"I have not seen your friend, er . . ."

"Nicholas Renzi."

"Just so. Presumably he is distracted in making sport with the
ladies of these islands."

Kydd tried to suppress a smile. "He is not. He has a hankerin'
after the theories of Mr. Rousseau, an' believes that we corrupt the
savage by our civilization."

Evelyn's eyebrows rose. "Rousseau? You have debated him?"
He looked out over the glittering blue ocean and continued, "For
myself, I cannot bear the bigot or his loose thinking, but in this

instance I am inclined to believe he is right, we are a plague on these people. The sooner we are sailed the better I shall like it." He swung up to the platform again. "Pray excuse, I must return to my work." Kydd knew he was dismissed from Evelyn's universe.

Parry was not the officer to accept weak excuses. Absence from place of duty was a dereliction that could not and would not be forgiven. The offender would get no sympathy from the rest of the duty watch either, for they had probably themselves been torn from willing arms to report. Kydd fretted for Renzi, who had probably wandered off in search of some marvel of nature. Possibly he had found an old native philosopher and was carrying on a deep conversation by signs. Now he was on report to the Captain who would stop his liberty or worse.

Duty ashore was not arduous. There were stands of muskets to hand, and the stockade to patrol, but against whom it was not clear. Companionable tasks included assisting the cook to prepare the evening meal, repairing the hut matting and the like. Less companionable was the sentry-go, which involved porting a heavy musket in solitude along the length of the stockade.

Supper was served out, and Kydd considered whether he should save some of his ration for Renzi. Darkness stole in, conversations became desultory and those free to do so retired to the living huts. As the moon rose, huge and magnificent, over the craggy line of the peak escarpment, it charged every object with a deep silver radiance and created myriad mysterious shadows.

Back on sentry-go, Kydd paced slowly along the stockade, peering over the top across the grassy slopes, which disappeared into shadow at the woodland edge. Nothing moved; the low soughing of the night breeze and creaks from the timbers of the stockade were all that fell on his senses. He shifted the musket over his shoulder and padded on.

"Hssssst!" It was the beach sentry, hurrying up the path. He gesticulated sharply. Kydd hurried down to the man, who was in grave breach of discipline by leaving his post. "Come down to th' beach," the man whispered urgently.

Kydd knew that there must be good reason he should go, but if he was caught—he looked back along the line of the stockade. The other sentinels were indistinct dark blobs in its shadow. He turned and plunged down the slope. At the point where the stockade met the sea he saw two figures standing together in the moonlight, which lay still and liquid on the pale beach.

"Well met, my friend." It was Renzi. His voice sounded gentle and noble but Kydd approached in apprehension for what he might find. Renzi was in native dress, a waist-length skirt and headdress of woven flowers. Next to him was a native woman dressed similarly and looking at Kydd with a palpable tension.

"Tohe-umu," said Renzi, introducing her. "She will be my wife when I settle here after you have gone."

Kydd was struck speechless. Settle? What utter madness! To cut himself off from his own kind, to . . .

"I wish to farewell you now, to let you know that I have found the contentment and fulfilment I have always craved—a union between Nature and Man that will purify and scarify the soul of the gross humors that come from artificial society."

Finding his voice, Kydd blurted, "But how will you live? You have no means, no—"

"There is no need for money or anything else. We shall build a dwelling place, and all around shall be the bounty of the good earth." His tone strengthened. "And I shall bring into the world infants who will learn humility and awe at the altar of Nature— and they then will enter their true inheritance." He turned to the woman and tenderly spoke a few native words. Her tense expression dissolved into one of deep affection that Kydd saw had no room for others.

Renzi held out his hand awkwardly. Kydd's thoughts chased each other. Once *Artemis* had sailed away Renzi would be reckoned a deserter for the rest of his days. There was no chance that they would ever see each other again. It was staggering—Renzi's fine mind wasted in this incomprehensibly remote piece of the earth. It was an insane impossibility to see Renzi tilling the soil, reasoning with the warriors. Then probably a lonely death among the savages. It was lunacy . . .

"I go now, be so good as to remember me in the years to come, dear friend," Renzi said, in a low voice. His head fell, but only for an instant. He fixed Kydd with a long look, his deep-set eyes moist, then turned and marched away.

Kydd balanced easily on the main topmast cap, a hundred and twenty feet high with only the main royal mast above him. Just below, Doud, Pinto and others were seizing a futtock stave to the topmast shrouds ready to pass the catharping. They knew their job backwards, and Kydd had no need to intervene. While they had accepted his elevation to petty officer with equanimity he found it agreeable to his natural temperament to lead with a light touch.

Far below on the quarterdeck stumped the foreshortened figure of Powlett, as irascible as a caged bear but energized by the prospect of getting to sea again. They had reverted to one watch in three on liberty, the other two watches devoted to work preparing for their voyage home in the fearsome roaring forties of the Great Southern Ocean. The only ocean to encircle the world completely, its stormy seas swept huge and unobstructed, and if there were any skimping on this work they might disappear from human ken forever.

At this height it was possible to see much more of the island, the variegated greens of the plateau and lower slopes and the blotchy bare rock faces of the peak. Kydd couldn't see beyond the escarpment and wondered which part of the island Renzi would select for his native home. He would deeply miss Renzi, and the first sea-watch especially. He had heard that the scientists had nearly completed their work, and there was a very real prospect that they would put to sea in a day or so; it would be all over by then.

Kydd touched the outer tricing line—it was worn and hairy with use, like much of the running rigging. They had only so much in the way of sea stores, and their stock of the aromatic Stockholm tar used to preserve the standing rope had to be eked out. On the fo'c'sle the sails were being roused out and checked; the action of sun and salt water on canvas had made the flax deteriorate.

It was strange to think of high-latitude sailing again, of cold and blustery winds and harsh conditions while they lay at anchor here in this balmy pleasantness. However, Kydd had a suspicion that he might grow increasingly restless at the relentless sameness of life on a South Sea island. Then he remembered that this was how Renzi would be spending the rest of his life.

They finished the job, worming and leathering for better resistance to chafing instead of the usual parceling and serving. If there were any problem in the south latitudes it would be dangerous to send men up to this height. Kydd slid to the deck by the backstay, avoiding the rows of cannon balls from the shot locker laid out in the sun for rust-chipping by the gunner's party. Powlett would not delay in having them all sweating at gun exercise just as soon as they made the open sea.

It was midafternoon when Powlett ordered the cutter away for his check ashore on the duty watch and the progress of the scientists. Kydd took his position forward and the cutter left the ship's side, pulling strongly to the shore. Powlett performed his usual run over the thwarts to the beach, and Kydd had to move fast to keep with him.

Powlett strode among the duty seamen, growling an admonishment here or a word of encouragement there. His greeting to the scientists was courteous but brief, and he returned quickly to the path back to the boat.

Suddenly Kydd stopped in his tracks and Powlett cannoned into him. "What the devil are you about, sir?" Powlett exploded. Holding up a hand Kydd strained to hear—a subliminal sound that had cut right through to a primal sense of danger. There was an indistinct commotion, and a midshipman of the watch raced down to Powlett and saluted. His face was pale with shock. "Sir— a native woman all covered with blood, an' two men!"

Powlett's voice hardened. "What has this to do with us? Are we to judge in their domestic disputes?"

"Sir—no, sir, it's a hell of a rout up there, sir."

"Very well, I'll come," said Powlett crossly. They retraced their steps, and soon caught the harsh, unhinged barks of a woman in the extremity of terror. Powlett hastened toward the growing crowd around her. She was sprawled in the grass under the stockade, hair matted and beslobbered with gore. The two men appeared untouched, but crouched, eyes bulging as they stared wildly about them. "Send for—send for the American," snapped Powlett.

"Gurney, sir," said Fairfax, wringing his hands.

"Do it!" snarled Powlett.

When the woman saw Gurney approach, she shrieked at him, her arms held a-splay. The men began to babble loudly. Gurney listened, asked some terse questions and tightened his expression.

"First thing I'm gonna do is get aboard o' yer barky, an' I advise you do the same," he said, fidgeting.

"Damn it, man, what's the problem?" The woman began wailing brokenly, beating at the grass with her fists. Powlett caught Gurney's arm and propelled him away.

"'Noo it would happen, sooner or later."

"What?" roared Powlett.

"Tubou-alohi—that's the son o' the high chief—he's kinda restless. Doesn't want t' take his old man's rule fer much longer, so he's done somethin' about it." Catching Powlett's expression he hurried on, "He's got his friends from another island t' help him— he's gotta prevail quickly, or he loses. Sends out raidin' parties, seems we have one arrived on the other side."

Powlett glowered at him. "Hands to quarters!" he ordered crisply.

The stands of muskets emptied and the seamen and marines hastily took up position at the stockade. Powlett pursed his lips. "Mr. Parry, be so good as to lead a reconnaissance party to the other side of the island and report the situation."

"Aye aye, sir," said Parry, and immediately detailed ten men for his party, including Kydd.

"Mr. Fairfax, please to muster the ship's company, have them at readiness within the stockade." He swung round and bellowed to the two scientists and their assistants still at the observation plat- form. "Pray stand ready to re-embark on my order."

Hobbes barely turned his head. "Indeed we shall not." His voice sounded thinly over the distance. "It is not convenient at this time, Captain."

Powlett ground his teeth. "Get moving, Mr. Parry!"

The party doubled over the beach, not a soul abroad, with Parry in a fierce grimace and his sword out in the lead. Kydd smiled secretly as they rushed past the blowhole, the other men flinching at the sudden gouts. They reached the distinctive red-soil bluff that Kydd remembered seeing from the peak, rustling through an over- grown path to its low summit. Parry dropped to the ground, his hand at the halt. "Silence!" he hissed. They crept cautiously to the edge of the bluff.

Below, the narrow beach was crowded with war canoes and men. The warriors were engaged in some form of ecstatic dance. They circled around a fire pit, viciously waving bone clubs and spears. At the head of the beach their prisoners, seven of them, were tied to the palms in a standing position.

Kydd looked sideways. Parry was counting carefully, assessing the warlike potential of the horde. Kydd admired his coolness, but knew even without a count that they were far outnumbered. "What d'ye think they'll do t' the prisoners?" whispered a man on one side.

"They'll probably be some sort o' slaves to th' end o' their miserable lives," Kydd muttered. It made more sense than to kill them. The prisoners did not move, probably resigned to their turn of fortune.

The counting went on, as did the circling about the fire. A conch shell bayed, a low and baleful sound, varying in clarity as the man rotated slowly around. The capering stopped. From the dancers a warrior emerged with a tall headdress and anklets of shark's teeth. Carrying a broad bone club he pranced toward the prisoners, passing from one to another, menacing each with his jagged club. He stopped before one. The club rose slowly and fixed on the man in a quivering accusation. A shout went up from the other warriors and the prisoner was instantly surrounded, dragged down the beach and thrown to the ground. He knelt, his head drooping, not a sound escaping. The warriors drew back, and in a single whirl of motion the bone club smashed the man's skull, the dull squelch carrying up to the hidden watchers.

Kydd was chilled to the core. Below him the body toppled slowly. The executioner stepped back, allowing others to move forward. Then, in absolute horror, Kydd saw butchery begin. Limbs were separated and laid on plantain leaves, strips of flesh torn and peeled from the carcass. His mind threatened to fly apart when he saw one warrior casually carrying a whole leg down to the sea to wash it. The flesh was wrapped in leaves and taken to the fire pit, where it soon left a rich aroma in the air like roasting pork.

"Retire by twos," Parry whispered fiercely. Stunned, Kydd slid back. They returned to the stockade in silence, something about their manner communicating itself to the waiting seamen.

Powlett rounded on Fairfax. "They know we're here, and they're not worried. That's not good. If they take it into their heads to make a sally, we'll be put to severe hazard." He looked soberly at Gurney. "Is it likely they will?"

"They stand t' take a lot o' plunder if they do—an' more'n that. Whoever gets t' kill a white man gets plenty o' face as a warrior. They won't attack at night, the gods don't like it, but tomorrow . . ."

Parry snorted. "We can blast them to kingdom come with *Artemis's* great guns."

Powlett glanced at him. "So we have wise shot, Mr. Parry, which knows to seek out only the enemy? At that range off-shore we cannot reach the savages without we hurt our own. No—the scientificals have nearly concluded their work, we have no further business here, and therefore there is only one course I will contemplate. We evacuate the island immediately."

Muttering began among the men, but Powlett smiled grimly. "Those who wish to linger I have no doubt will be right royally entertained by the savages." He glanced up at the sun. "We'll not complete today. Get as much of the stores back aboard before sunset as you can. Mr. Fairfax, the scientificals can remain until first light if they wish, the ship's company will take a two-watch guard. I want to be at sea at dawn."

More shaken than he cared to admit, Kydd took his place at the stockade, but his mind was on Renzi, lost somewhere in the interior. Not having any real means of communication with anyone, he would be alone at a time of appalling danger—and tomorrow was his last chance at escape.

Kydd felt tears prick, whether selfishly because he had lost a true sea companion, or for helplessness at Renzi's dire plight, it didn't matter. A thought began to force itself on his consciousness, a growing, pressing thought. He shuffled along the stockade until he found the end where it met the sea in an untidy pile of logs. "That you, Toby?" he called.

Stirk was there and grunted a reply. Dark was rapidly falling, and if Kydd was going to do anything it would have to be in the blackness of night before moonrise. "I know where Renzi is," he said, in a low voice. Stirk's eyes gleamed in the dying light of the day but he didn't reply. "I'm goin' after him."

"Yer want help, mate?" Stirk said. Kydd felt a surge of feeling: here was what it meant to be shipmates.

"No, Toby, I need y' here so when we gets back, you c'n let us back in," Kydd said. He had no plan, simply an urge to get to Renzi. He hesitated. A musket would impede his progress considerably, and a cutlass didn't have the reach compared to spears and clubs. He would go unarmed.

He splashed around the end of the stockade. "Luck, matey!" Stirk called quietly. Kydd stepped out nervously, imagining unseen eyes on him, with capture and a hideous death to follow. His skin crawled, but he went on toward the trail leading to the clearing where Haynes had held his trade and which connected with the small path leading inland.

Every bush and broad leaf that brushed his face and every root that grabbed at his ankles made his heart thump. The sky was splashed with stars, but the earth was in inky blackness. The foliage fell away—he had reached the far side of the plateau, and would be able to follow along its fringe until he reached the forest path he sought. If anyone could see him from the stockade, which was doubtful in the gloom, they would believe him to be a savage.

Here—was this the place where he and Renzi had begun their final ascent to the peak? For a minute of panic he could not recognize the area, but remembered the casuarina with its feathery leaves overshadowing the track. He plunged forward. The moist cool of the night was laced with odors of decaying vegetation and night blooms.

Things rustled and snapped. Panting loudly in the quiet of the woodland he wound his way up to where the escarpment bulked large and black against the stars. He paused, trying to remember the topography. Up here—they had seen the other side of the island from this place. Cautiously Kydd drew near. There—the other side of the island was already under the full radiance of a splendid moon, but what chilled Kydd was the distant sight of not one but four fires below. He could see some figures moving, others still, and his heightened imagination told him that frightened souls were still tied to the trees. There would be fresh meat in the morning.

He pulled away. Where would Renzi have gone from here? Only one way: along the base of the escarpment to the opposite end. Kydd struck out and after only a few hundred yards came to its end. He stepped warily, then stopped dead. Two figures appeared out of the dark, stark against the moonlight.

"Nicholas? Is that you?" he hissed. The figures stood rigid, before one broke away and approached Kydd.

"It is," said Renzi. There was a bare tremor in his voice.

"*Artemis* sails t'morrow, we can lose no time."

A plaintive voice came from the other figure, the import of the unknown words impossible to miss. Renzi murmured something over his shoulder, but then he addressed Kydd directly: "If by this you mean to persuade me to give up my decision and return to your world of hurts and unreason, then you should stand disabused. I will remain."

"This afternoon with m' own eyes I saw the savages kill 'n' *eat* their own kind—Nicholas, to *devour* a living human, an' they're here still!"

There was a hesitation, then Renzi spoke: "No doubt there will be those even of this world who will respond to Nature by profaning in the worst possible way, but that does not alter the premise by one whit that, left to himself, Man will gracefully revert to his true self, and attain the perfectibility of the spirit."

"And if y'r premise is wrong? You will tell y'r warriors they should mend their ways, that—"

"Enough!" Renzi's voice was defensive. "Logic itself will tell you that both possible sides of the human condition cannot exist at the same time, the same body. One must prevail."

"A pox on y'r logic!"

"And on rank unreason!"

Both were breathing raggedly. "Then y' will not come?"

"I—will not come!"

Kydd's anger swelled to blind rage. His muscles tensed in fury. His fist slammed out, connecting with Renzi's jaw, and he crumpled soundlessly. Whimpering, the woman scrabbled at his body, but Kydd pushed her away; she fell back to the bluff rocks, staring at him.

There was almost no time left; the savages would be waiting for moonlight on the lee side of the island before they started picking their way across the island to be in position for dawn. It might be too late now. Kydd thrust away the thoughts. Seizing Renzi's arm, he hoisted him on to his back, grateful for his slight build. He hefted him into the most comfortable position and turned round for the long trip back. The woman cried out once, but didn't try to stop him. He trudged along the track, aware that she was following blindly. Finding the path downward he hurried along it. Renzi's body was a dead weight that had him panting and straining. He wondered what to do about the woman. If she got hysterical she would certainly attract attention, and of the worst possible kind. He would have to silence her—but how?

The moon burst above the line of the escarpment. The whole island now lay still, bathed in silver. Kydd cursed and redoubled his effort. The clearing, then the beach. His muscles blazed intolerably with the strain, he would have to rest. He swung Renzi down, the body flopping untidily on the sand. He looked up and the woman froze. Panting in burning gasps he confronted her. With stabbing gestures he signed that he was taking Renzi to the ship. She nodded in mute understanding. He then signed that she could go also. She gazed at him, her face frozen—and shook her head slowly. Kydd repeated the gesture angrily. Seconds now could decide whether they lived or died. She shook her head more emphatically, then dropped to her knees beside Renzi, anguished cries racking her frame as she stroked his face tenderly.

For a mad moment Kydd considered leaving Renzi to her, but recovered, and tore him from her grasp, triggering a hopeless paroxysm of sobbing. He pulled at Renzi's arm to hoist him up, but his strength was spent. Nearly weeping with frustration and weariness, he tried again. He fell to his knees panting uncontrollably. There was a scurry of movement. He looked up and saw the woman back away in fear, and then run. He swung round, but it was too late. Dark shapes lunged across the beach toward him. He stumbled to his feet.

"Get 'is feet, then, y' ugly bastard," Stirk growled to another, elbowing Kydd aside. They staggered and lurched along the limpid stillness of the beach and finally, gloriously, reached the stockade.

Splashing round its end, Kydd felt overwhelming relief. Exhausted, he staggered after Stirk and the others who laid Renzi down on the scrubby grass. The moonlight had transformed the landscape, now dappled and lovely; it also revealed officers striding down to investigate.

Renzi twitched and groaned. The remains of his headdress still decorated his head, but the native skirt was sadly bedraggled. No one bent to see to him to avoid being associated by any implication in his criminality.

"There he is," said Fairfax severely. "The deserter Renzi! Well done, you men." Powlett frowned but said nothing.

Stirk turned his back deliberately on Fairfax and touched his forehead to Powlett. "Renzi were taken b' the savages earlier, sir, as yez can see. Seems 'e made 'is escape while they was a-rollickin' an' eatin' of each other." Stirk shifted on his feet and thumbed at Kydd. "Kydd went out ter bring 'im in, but he bein' so near knackered . . ."

Powlett looked down on the groaning Renzi. "Poor devil," he said. "Who can guess what it is he's suffered?" He stared accusingly at Fairfax. "But God be praised, he's with his shipmates now, his suffering is over."

Renzi rolled to one side, uttering something incomprehensible. "Th' experience has affected him, sir," Kydd hastened to say, "makes him say crazy things—lost his mind a bit, I'd guess."

"Get him to the ship as soon as you can, Mr. Fairfax, and tie him in his hammock. Poor wretch is not responsible for his actions." Powlett straightened. "And see that these fine men get a double tot of rum."

At dawn the woodland edge opposite the stockade was alive with movement. But at last it was possible to run boats to the ship—coral reefs made it far too dangerous at night. "Too damned smart to come round our rear by canoe," Parry said grimly. "They know we'll blast 'em to flinders from the ship if they do."

The living quarters and other temporary works were to remain; only sea stores would be retrieved. Hobbes beat a dignified retreat to the ship, but Evelyn insisted on completing his observations, the sailors marveling at his coolness at the eyepiece as yells and warlike sounds came faint but ever louder over the open ground.

"We will retire by threes, Mr. Fairfax," Powlett ordered. "The first party led by you to the ship, the second led by Mr. Parry to lie off in the boats to cover the third, which I will lead, and which will be the last to leave."

"Aye aye, sir," Fairfax and Parry acknowledged.

"And you," said Powlett to Kydd, "have my authority to remove

Mr. Evelyn and his gear by force if necessary. He is to retire as of this moment."

"Aye aye, sir." Kydd hastened to the observation platform. He mounted the platform to speak to Evelyn, and could see over the stockade to the gathering warriors. They were eddying out from the woodland edge, prancing ferociously and moving forward to strike their clubs on the ground with a battle cry before retreating.

"Sir—I have t' tell you . . ."

"They are indignant that their plunder is sailing away from them," Evelyn said, not even raising his eyes from his work. "No matter, I am nearly done. You may remove all but this."

Kydd called across a party of men to carry the instruments to the boats; Fairfax had his men embarked and pulled back to *Artemis* in good order. The savages became more bold, covering half the distance to the stockade now to perform their displays. Muskets banged away despite Powlett's orders to conserve fire for a rush, and more and more bodies lay still in the grass.

The boats returned. "Sir, the Captain . . ." Kydd tried to say.

"Yes, yes—my last reading, he will not grudge me that?" Evelyn replied testily. The sound of the war cries filled with bloody-minded hatred tore at Kydd's courage.

"Sir, my authority . . ." he said earnestly, but was interrupted by a disturbance. A group of warriors had run along the length of the stockade outside and, shielded by its timbers, had gathered suffi-cient numbers for an assault. They massed around one or two of the posts and heaved and pulled until they had loosened and fallen away. They had breached the stockade.

"Fall back to the boats!" roared Powlett, as the savages poured through. There would be no second chance, and the defenders made haste toward the shore.

Kydd swung to the ground, and looked back to Evelyn, to see him take a spear in his side. The astronomer slumped back in his canvas chair. "Damn," he said faintly, plucking at the vicious barbed weapon. Kydd grabbed a musket and fired at the thrower.

The musket missed fire with a fizz of priming. The warrior grinned and swung a bone club. Kydd swung the musket up with two hands; the club splintered against it. The musket bent uselessly, but with it Kydd crushed the warrior's skull.

In their lust to stop the ship from escaping, the savages streamed past each side of the platform, leaving the two men untouched. Kydd bent to Evelyn, who was now white with shock. "Th'—the obs-erva-tions," he whispered in shallow gasps, clutching the chair in great pain. Kydd looked down and saw the polished box, open, papers neatly inside. He grabbed it and slammed the lid, and looked up to meet Evelyn's wild stare. "Leave!" Kydd hesitated in an agony of indecision. "*Leave! Go!* That is worth more than any man's life. *Go, damn you!*" Kydd nodded, not trusting himself to speak, and fled, the box under his arm.

The last men were throwing themselves into the boats, and Kydd tossed the box into the pinnace. He looked back, but Evelyn had disappeared under a swarm of enraged savages, like ants over prey. Their barbarous weapons rose and fell, hacking and chopping. At last the bow swivel gun mounted in the cutter had a clear field of fire. It blasted out, and a storm of canister swept the scene, changing the full-throated war cries to screams.

One by one the boats from *Artemis* retired in good order, and headed back to their rightful place.

CHAPTER 13

≈

K ydd's nose wrinkled. The hog's lard was giving out, and
on the fore-shroud deadeyes he was having to work with
a nauseating mixture of fat and rancid butter. It was
essential activity, for any slackness in the rigging would result in
the destruction of a spar as it worked to and fro. Each separate
shroud ended in a deadeye, with lanniards running down to the
channel outboard to give tension adjustment, but Kydd and his
party found that such was the stretched state of the rope that now,
in addition, they had to take up the racking on the shrouds themselves. Finally, with gear well taut, Kydd was satisfied and allowed
his three men to secure from work.

Left alone, he gave a final tug at the lines, and became aware
that he was no longer on his own. He looked up and saw Renzi
standing with a set face, looking out over the tumble of blue-gray
seas.

Kydd hesitated. His sociable advances before had been repelled
with a cold intensity and he was not sure how he would be
received now. He fiddled with the loose end of a downhaul and
waited. His decisive action on the island had not been forgiven by
Renzi, who had retreated into himself, but ironically, in the week
or so since, this had been generously misinterpreted by his shipmates who were convinced that he was recovering from a mind-
scarring experience. They gave him every possible sympathy.

Kydd watched Renzi covertly, the face in profile appearing even
more solitary and inaccessible. A larger sea surged from astern,
faster than they could sail. It overtook them with a swelling and
falling accompanied by a marked lurch that sent them both staggering and reaching for a steadying rope. This simple human

impulse seemed to bring a fluidity to the situation: Kydd caught a flicker in Renzi's eye. He wandered over beside him.

"Hearty sailin' weather," Kydd said. He tested the tautness of the nearest rope. Renzi did not move away. He still faced outwards, his expression set—but his lips moved slightly as though speaking to himself. Encouraged, Kydd looked at him directly. "Mullion says as how we'll be stayin' on this same tack f'r all of three thousan' miles."

"That would be a logical assumption," Renzi replied coolly, his gaze still on the heaving seascape.

"Our gear had better be sound, I believe," Kydd added, anxious to keep momentum in the conversation.

Renzi looked sideways. "If it is not then no one will ever know—but us," he said, and Kydd could swear a smile hovered.

"A hard end t' our island adventure," he dared.

There was just a moment's hesitancy, then, "I have been considering the whole experience." Kydd waited. "It would appear that my expectations were over-sanguine in the matter of Man and Nature. The essence of Rousseau's thesis remains unaltered; timeless in its perception, sublime in its penetration—but it is subverted. We are too late."

Clearing his throat Kydd began, "But why . . ."

"It is now very clear. If even in so distant an island as this 'civilization' has come, then it must have spread its canker over the entire inhabited globe. Is there anywhere left at all on this terraqueous sphere that a true self may go to attain perfectibility? I think not." A pensive expression replaced his forbidding look. "Perhaps Rousseau would have achieved a higher immortality were he to have demonstrated a modus of perfectibility within the *mundus vulgaris*. In short, my friend, I accept that there is no longer any possibility for me to achieve a state of natural grace, and thus I bow to the ineluctability of my fate."

The smile surfaced, and Kydd responded, barely able to restrain himself from clapping Renzi on the back. "Never fear, we have a long haul ahead before we reach our own civilization, an' that at war," he said.

Renzi's face cleared. The blue Pacific rollers were now behind them, the gray of the Southern Ocean was the predominant theme, and he gazed intensely at the clouds obscuring the wan sun.

"Fierce and more fierce the gathering tempest grew,
South, and by West, the threatening demon blew;
Auster's resistless force all air invades,
And every rolling wave more ample spreads."

"Y'r Wordsworth, then?" Kydd guessed. He would have been just as happy at the fine words if it had been the village blacksmith.

"I believe it might have been the peerless Falconer, talking about the mighty ocean in his *Shipwreck,* but I may be mistaken."

Kydd smiled broadly—all was right with the world.

"Yair, second time fer me, mates," said Crow, his face animated at the memory, "an' that's twice too many fer me." He pushed his pot forward. "Worst place in th' whole god-blasted world fer a sailor, an' that's no error." The faces of his audience grew serious.

"We gets westerlies all th' way, should be quick," Mullion said.

"Aye, but we're only at forty south now an' it's comin' on ter blow—we need ter get to fifty-six south fer Cape Horn, an' there it's a reg'lar built hell." Nobody spoke. "Black squalls hit yer out o' nowhere, grievous cold, seas the size o' which make yer blood freeze ter see 'em—no galley fire on account o' the lunatic movin' o' the barky, it's no place ter be. But there's some days it's as charmin' as ever you'd want, mates, seas calm an' sun out a-shinin' on them great black rocks—but yer knows that next it's goin' ter turn on yer, like an animal, screamin' 'n' shriekin' an' out ter tear the hooker t' bits . . ."

Artemis swooped and lifted, her hull creaking and working

energetically. It was easy to imagine the result of a harsher climate, and Kydd looked about at the swaying lanthorn and slight movement of the canvas screen, and felt a quickening of his senses.

He was still affected by Renzi's labyrinthine musing on the nature of man. "D'ye know if there's any savages livin' ashore there, Isaac?" he asked, interested to see if Renzi's thesis would work at the opposite pole to paradise.

"Aye," said Crow, "that there are. Saw 'em once, an' they must be the lowest kind o' hooman yer can get. Scraggy, hair all a-hoo, mud all over, 'n' sulky with it. Don't trust 'em, any of 'em." He thought for a moment and added, "An' their women are as rough as they is—catch fish naked with a dog, they does."

Despite Crow's direful forecast, Kydd couldn't help but feel thrilled by the heightened sensations of speed and danger as they drove south. Entering the domain of the Southern Ocean proper everything was on the grand scale. Seas swelled to mountains, a quarter of a mile between peaks and higher even than the maintop in the troughs. As the following seas came on, *Artemis* would lift at the stern, going higher and steeper, until her angle down seemed a giddy impossibility, and surfing down the face of the wave in an accelerating rush before the massive swell overtook and passed down her length with a consequent sudden deceleration. Her decks filled with a foaming, hissing cataract. Then the process would begin again, a regular three times a minute.

It was dangerous on deck and lifelines were rigged the length of the vessel. If the unwary could not leap to the rigging in time, only a desperate clamping on to this stout line would give a chance while the rampaging seas invaded the deck. Every man aboard knew that with the boats griped and lashed so securely, there would be no lowering of them to rescue a man overboard—even supposing the hurtling progress of the vessel could be stopped. It would be a cold, lonely and certain death.

On the helm it was doubly dangerous. One of the massive seas coming in astern and catching the rudder at an angle unawares could slam it aside; this would transmit backwards up through the tiller ropes and to the helm, resulting in the weather helmsman being hurled through the air over the wheel while the lee man was smashed to the deck. It called for ferocious concentration on the subtle motions of the sea, and Kydd learnt much as he and others fought *Artemis* along.

If the crest of one of the gigantic waves broke it was a terrifying experience. Struggling at the wheel, the first that the helmsman looking forward would know of its approach would be a sullen rumble, rising to a rushing roar. If he made the mistake of looking over his shoulder, he would see a gigantic mass of foam-streaked sea about to fall on the vessel like an unstoppable avalanche. The spectacle was of such primeval power that it was said to be not uncommon for a helmsman to flee the wheel.

Days turning to weeks, they sailed on; the same course, the same wind from astern, each day the same wearing down of the spirit in a ceaseless fight against the danger, the motion, the discomfort. Forty degrees south turned to forty-five, then fifty and finally fifty-five south as they shaped course for Cape Horn itself.

At these latitudes discomfort turned to pain, exhilaration to dread. Skies ragged with racing scud, squalls hammering in from nowhere shrieking like a banshee in the fraying rigging, sails ripped to shreds in an instant, it was a hellish world.

At noon each day a group of officers assembled, staggering and lurching on the quarterdeck. Like the seamen they dressed in any ragged garment that could offer some proof against the weather. And almost always they dispersed afterwards without the one thing they yearned for—a sight of the sun. Without a sighting, their latitude was so much guesswork, and if this was mistaken, then *Artemis* would leave her bones on the iron-bound coast of Patagonia.

Squalls now brought a new misery. Taking in yet another reef in the foretopsail, Kydd closed his eyes to reduce the soreness of salt-reddened eyeballs as he worked at the stiff, sodden canvas. He sensed the cold feathery touch of snow. When he opened his eyes he found himself isolated in a world of white flakes, tossing and whirling around him, wetly settling on spars and cordage before being whipped away. It turned to a penetrating sleet, and in the raw, wet cold Kydd climbed back on deck in the most acute bodily misery. Even so, he could not escape. The spray bursting aboard was now half frozen; as it savagely sleeted across the deck it drew blood where frozen particles sand-blasted his skin.

Always it was a deep relief to go below and stagger along to his mess, moving from hand to hand in the wild motion, to the blessed benison of rum, age-toughened cheese and hardtack—and temporary surcease. Men sat, silent and staring, dealing with the conditions in their own way, but never complaining. That would have been the most futile thing they could do.

Sometimes the weather played tricks. The cloudbase would drop to masthead height, the jagged cloud streaming past, and heavy curtains of snow would advance rapidly to bring visibility down to feet. Then, within minutes it would pass and cloudless skies would emerge as innocent of malice as a newborn, but always accompanied by a freezing cold.

It was on one of these occasions, when the biting sleet had moved away and the crystal dome of the sky had cleared ahead, that there appeared across an infinite distance of tossing waters the distant sight of snow-capped mountains—the far southern tip of the continent of South America. The disbelieving yell of the look-out in the foretop hailed, *"Laand hoooo!"*

Men tumbled up from below, crowding the decks. Powlett appeared and stomped up to the Master, who stood with a look of wonderment on his seamed face. "God bless m' soul! My reckonin' is that those peaks are not less'n eighty, one hundred miles off, so they are." Murmurs of amazement greeted this—the horizon for a frigate was never more than twelve to fifteen miles away, and the royals of a ship-of-the-line could be seen at twenty—but this!

"Well done, Mr. Prewse! Voyage of half ten thousand miles and we're right on the nose." Powlett's satisfaction spread out like a ripple, and smiles were to be seen for the first time for weeks.

"Aye, sir, but the hard part is a-coming, never fear," Prewse said stolidly.

Brutally tired, the ship's company of *Artemis* faced the final approach to Cape Horn. The stark rock-bound land stretched across their course and was downwind to the fiercest blasts to be experienced anywhere on earth. If they found themselves in the wrong position there was little chance they could claw off back out to sea again.

At eight bells the watch changed. The short day had turned to a fearful darkness out of which came the hammering blasts with just the same ferocity as in daytime. The same dangers lurked, the same treachery, but these came invisibly and suddenly at night.

Kydd nodded to his replacement, who loomed up from the dismal gloom. His trick at the wheel always left him aching, bruised and punch-drunk with the merciless buffeting of the wind, and he felt for his lashings with relief. It was a critical time, the handover. The sea was always looking to take advantage of sleep-weary men not fully aroused to their task.

Hallison took the weather helm himself and was in the process of surrendering the wheel, while Kydd remained for a few more minutes until the new man was sure of himself. Others manning the after wheel were similarly engaged.

Some instinct pricked at Kydd at that precise moment and he snatched a glance back over his shoulder. The size of seas coming in astern could be sensed by the amount of dark shadow they blocked against the stormy but slightly less gloomy sky; rearing up was a truly huge, immense black hill of sea, which was just beginning to break. An awful, soul-chilling threat.

Kydd bawled a warning, but it happened too fast for the weary seamen. The ship lifted sharply to the watery mountain, higher than it ever had before, and as the comber broke it did so directly under her stern, sending her skidding forward at a disastrous angle. At the same time the merciless wind pressed on her topsails and heeled her over even farther. The two forces combined could have only one ending, broaching to, the ship forced around broadside to the waves, inertia rolling her over like a child's toy—to destruction.

In an impulse of pure seamanship Kydd strained to put on opposite turns at the wheel even before the slewing started, but as the vessel lay over, first Hallison, then others who had released their lashing slid and then fell to the side of the deck before disappearing under the torrent of white sea that came over the bulwarks. Audible even above the furious hissing roar of wind and sea was a heavy clatter and ominous rumble from deep within *Artemis*. Her yards now nearly touched the sea with the heel. Kydd and the two who remained with him fought the helm for their very lives.

It was Kydd's instinctive early action that saved *Artemis*. It was sufficient to tip the balance of forces in favor of sails and helm, the greater angle of rudder working with the remaining thrust from rags of sails to give sufficient way through the water to counter the broadside slewing. Agonizing minutes later the ship slowly came back erect and before the wind again.

Trembling with fatigue and emotion Kydd was finally relieved, going below to a desolation of broken gear all adrift, the surge of water swilling over the deck, and men stumbling about, utterly exhausted after their battle for the life of their ship.

A day later, a little after midmorning, the weather moderated to racing low cloud against clearing curtains of heavy rain, but the ship had been heavily battered by squalls of extreme intensity. Powlett and the Master had never left the deck, for as Prewse quietly pointed out, these squalls were born high up on the ice-clad slopes of a mountain range somewhere close by, air super-cooled and made so heavy it hurtled down the valleys and to the sea. This was proof positive that the bleak dread of Cape Horn was close at hand.

At a brief clearing of the atrocious conditions, there it was, a bare five miles away. The very tip of the continent. A low, black, straggling coast, streaked with snow, barren to the prevailing winds but darkly wooded elsewhere—a picture of desolation.

"Two points to larboard," snapped Powlett, hardly recognizable in his thick grego and woolen head covering. "We keep in with the land while we can. How far to the Horn itself, Mr. Prewse?"

"At a whisker less sixty-seven degrees west at last reckoning, we'll see it today, sir, no doubt about it—s'long as the weather lets us." With their sighting of the distant icy mountains Prewse had been able to adjust his course so that they approached by running down the line of latitude of his objective. Now they would keep with the land until they had won through to the other side.

"Coast is bold hereabouts, I believe," Powlett added, shielding his eyes from flurries of spray.

Prewse nodded. "Aye, sir, very steep to, I'll agree. A good thing, o' course, and if there *are* hazards, y' can be sure that the rock'll be covered in kelp, easy t' see ahead f'r a warning—if y'r lookout is awake."

At the mizzen cleats Crow heard the comment and muttered to Kydd, "Yair, but does 'e think that 'cos every bit o' kelp means a rock, that no kelp means no rock?" He cracked a grim smile before cinching the rope and going below.

To Kydd it was awesome and fascinating, bucketing along before the moderating swell and seeing the stark black coast slip past, the first land for so long at sea, yet knowing that if they went ashore they would find it the most bleak and windswept corner on earth.

More rain. It came in dark gray curtains of misery, washing over

the battered frigate and sending Kydd into paroxysms of shudder-
ing at the cruel wind that always followed. It cleared—and there
was Cape Horn. Kydd stared across the gray rollers at the dark
mass. One by one sailors came on deck to look, expressions ranging from loathing to fascination. Here was the reality of why they
had suffered.

From the low, nondescript coastline it swept toward them from
the north into a magnificent bluff well over a thousand feet high,
then plunged vertically into the sea as the breathtaking final point
of a great continent. Kydd watched until the grand sight disappeared into the rain squalls and sea fret, and without further ado
they passed from the Pacific into the Atlantic, homeward bound.

The bows of *Artemis* were now irrevocably directed toward England—that wondrous place whose name could send sea-hardened men into misty-eyed reverie. Kydd surveyed the little
gathering at the mess table. Sunken dark eyes and bowed backs,
introspective silences—none of them was unaffected by the experience. They had passed into the company of those few who could
say they had doubled Cape Horn.

But there was a renewal of spirit: nothing but a couple of
months of steadily improving weather stood between them and
England. The few days they had spent in the tiny anchorage in the
lee of Tierra del Fuego had broken the spell and given them back
their strength. The kelp-strewn rocks, playground of seals, echo-
ing to the cries of wheeling terns and gulls, this was a blessed
haven while they readied their vessel for her final leg.

A warm feeling had come over Kydd unexpectedly when he
looked up at *Artemis* from the boat that carried them around her
battered hull, seeking out hidden damage. Her colors were dulled,
her tar-black timbers streaked and worn, her cordage frayed and
white with salt—but this was the ship that had carried him safely
within her, across the world, to sights and adventures that would
stay with him for the rest of his life.

Crow lifted his eyes; they now glimmered with life. "We get the trades well 'nough, we'll be a-rollickin' ashore in England before th' buds o' May." His arm was still bound to his body, but at least he was not tied to a cot like Hallison and two others, who had been left helpless with broken bones after their mauling by the giant wave.

The contribution from Haynes was a grunt, but Kydd could see from his unwinking hard eyes that it would not be long before he would return as abrasive as ever.

Mullion was cast down. He had been greatly affected by the loss of his friend overside, his grip on the man's wrist not strong enough to prevent his being carried bodily overboard by the seething torrent. His last sight of his shipmate was of him flailing in the sea close by but being carried inexorably away. Mullion had stood helpless, weeping in agony as the minutes of life left to his friend had passed away out in the anonymous blackness.

Kydd caught Renzi's eye. As far as anyone could tell, apart from a deepening of the lines next to his mouth he was untouched by events, cool and considered in his words, as lofty-minded as ever. Kydd smiled. He himself had other concerns. "Could do with somethin' t' eat other than hardtack, somethin' that sticks to y' ribs."

There was a dry chuckle, surprisingly from Haynes. "Yer'll get yer meat soon enough," he said.

The others looked up in curiosity. "How so?" said Crow.

"Why," said Haynes, "th' hardtack will be manned b' barge-men."

Kydd grinned. "Let's tell ye how we used to clear the bread o' bargemen in *Royal Billy.*"

He had their attention. Every sailor was interested in ridding the hardtack of bargemen, the weevils and other life, particularly the large pale maggots that infested old ship's stores.

"Well, when we starts a bread cask in th' hold, we sets on it a plate—with a ripe fish aboard. Bargemen, they wait till it's quiet, then they swarm out t' get a taste o' the fish. All ye do then, is t' heave the fish over the side 'n' set another in its place until you've cleared the cask o' the vermin."

The cheery response and the spreading comfort of the rum was gratifying. Kydd's spirits rose.

Artemis sailed steadily north. The sun's warmth swelled, gray seas became tinged with blue, and as the frigate ranged out into the Atlantic rollers it was almost possible to put from mind past dangers and harsh times. But the ship and her company were sadly worn by the long voyage, tired by the interminable movement, jaded and soul-weary.

It was seen in so many ways. Powlett appeared on deck in the morning, but then retired to his cabin soon after, his interchanges curt and monosyllabic. On one night Kydd had gone to Merrydew, the boatswain, in his cabin to ask for some gear and had found him quite incapable with drink. The surgeon, who had no particular friends that anyone could name, was acting oddly, shutting himself away in the noisome gloom of his quarters, his meals sent to him. And the bickering between Parry and Rowley took a bitter edge, a sarcastic and barely concealed animosity.

The pleasant northeast trade winds petered out into fitful flurries all too soon after they reached the tropics; the sun was now hot and aggressive, humidity making movement a trial. Merrydew rarely appeared. He seldom spoke, his red, sweating face suffused with suffering. Kydd remembered the sun-blasted sea from the last time they had passed this way and prayed that their passage would not be protracted.

"Aye, both on 'em!" The little purser's steward anxiously awaited Kydd's response. Kydd was quartermaster's mate and was therefore among those responsible for stowage in the hold. It was shattering news: two or three of the remaining ground tier of water casks had run afoul of each other, probably as a result of their upset at the time of the monster wave, and had chosen this time to split a stave each at the point of contact. Precious water had quietly seeped into the bilge and at a stroke *Artemis*'s sea endurance was curtailed. There was no longer any question of her reaching England.

"Have y' told the mate o' the hold?" Kydd asked, but as he spoke he remembered that the old man was still lying helpless with broken ribs. Leaving the fetor of the hold he hurried up the hatchway—the Master himself would have to be informed.

Mr. Prewse was at the lee hances, in troubled conversation with Powlett. Raised voices could be heard, and Powlett's jutting chin and flinty manner augured ill for the news that Kydd was bringing.

"If y' please, Mr. Prewse," he said, holding his hat respectfully in his hands. The Master turned his calm gaze to Kydd. Unsure of whether the Captain should know from him, he paused, but Powlett's clear impatience decided him, and he made his report.

"God blast it! God *damn* it!" Powlett's rage shook Kydd, its intensity out of character. Powlett regained control. "The nearest watering?" he shot at Prewse, who thought carefully, rubbing his chin.

"Well, I—"

"We cannot go to east'd, the Spanish are probably now at war with us, we can only fall back on Brazil—true?"

"Aye, sir," said Prewse neutrally.

"Then set our course in accordance," snapped Powlett. "Closest point agreeable to the wind's track."

The closest point, thanks to the favorable southeasterly, was but two days away. It turned out to be a scrubby plain, sandy and characterless, through which a brown-stained river wound listlessly. The air was still and enervating, and with a hand-lead swinging in the chains it took hours for the frigate to work in. The watering party pulled ashore and began work; the country was unattractive and had a persistent reek as of a long-dead creature lying heavily on the air. Insects made their way out even as far as the ship, the sudden maddening sting a disagreeable surprise after so long at sea.

As soon as the boat had been hoisted in, *Artemis* shaped course seaward, but within a day there was good news. "Glory be!" said Crow. "A sou'-easter!" It was true, they would have the unseasonably early good fortune of a wind in just the right quarter to see them past Cabo de São Roque, and on past the doldrums to the northern trade winds. Every weary heart aboard lifted at the news. This would carry them into the north half of the world, and they would then set course directly for home.

"Cape São Roque," breathed Kydd. It was the last land they would see before England. An undistinguished blue-gray tongue, far to larboard: their long-awaited farewell to far-off lands and unknown perils. Soon they would be in familiar waters. "Do y' not feel it in y'r bones we are homeward bound?" he added, looking at Renzi.

Renzi looked thoughtful. "I am in two minds on the matter," he said. "On the one hand we have had the felicity of adding to the breadth of our intellects by our voyaging to the far side of the world—but I have to confess, on the other there is nothing in compass that appeals to my spirit more at this moment than the prospect of surcease, a cessation of striving, the quiet land at last. 'In thy green lap was Nature's darling laid.'"

Kydd saw his friend's face take on an enigmatic cast, and suppressed his response. His eye noted the worn ropes and frayed canvas, then wandered over the vista of glittering blue sea ahead. Seven bells sounded distantly from the fo'c'sle, and they swung out on the futtock shrouds and descended to the deck.

"Only a few weeks, then, Isaac," Kydd offered to the silent table.

"An' not a minute too soon," Haynes grated. "I got such a pain in me back 'n' legs after Cape Horn 'll take months ter shake orf."

"An' you, Jeb?" Kydd asked Mullion. The loss of his shipmate was taking its toll: Mullion seemed to have lost all appetite. He looked up. His eyes were dull and there was an uncommon lethargy in his movements. "Ter tell th' truth, I've had this headache comin' on, coupla days now."

"You should be seein' the doc, get him to bleed ye," Kydd said.

"What? That useless pintle tagger?" Crow huffed. "Ain't seen hide nor hair o' the bugger since west o' the Horn." He glanced at Mullion. "An' I heard tell it's his loblolly what set them bones," he added, "an' him without a surgeon's mate an' all." The surgeon's mate had missed the ship at Macao, but Kydd remembered the sharp-eyed young lad with the lame leg who had chosen to be a lowly loblolly boy rather than the rate of cook's mate, to which he was entitled by his injury.

A lassitude seemed to be stealing down on the ship, a torpor that was more evident in some than others, bewildering in the general lift of spirits that went with a homeward course.

"*Haaaands* to make sail!" That would be Rowley wanting to spread the weather fore topsail stuns'l, of somewhat questionable benefit to speed, given that they were going large and the sail would almost certainly be blanketed by canvas on the main. As Kydd jumped to the bulwarks with the others of his watch for the brisk climb aloft, he noticed that one of them, Millais, a reliable Jerseyman, was not with them. Instead he was looking upward from the deck, anxiously clinging to one of the shrouds. Disturbed, Kydd dropped back down beside the man. "Lay aloft, Millais," he ordered, conscious that Rowley would be impatient with delay.

Millais stared back at Kydd. "I—I can't—" he began, swayed, and then, before Kydd's disgusted eyes, vomited helplessly. Sick drunk at this hour? Millais crumpled to his knees and looked up piteously. "I don' feel s' well, mate," he croaked. The words were not slurred. Kydd felt a creeping fear and bent to help the man to his feet. Even at that distance he felt a raging heat radiating out from his body.

"Get aloft, you infernal rascals!" came Rowley's irritable bellow from the quarterdeck.

Kydd hurried aft and confronted Rowley. "Sir, that man's got a fever." He watched Rowley stiffen. It was the worst possible news. Kydd sensed a scurrying down the main hatch and guessed that the news was being spread even as they spoke.

"Sling his hammock in the gundeck forward and put him in it," Rowley snapped. It was the only thing possible. Frigates did not have even the rudimentary sick berths of a larger ship. "And tell the surgeon," he added.

Kydd touched his hat and rattled down the ladderway. The sooner the surgeon could take strong measures the better for all. The musty gloom was tinged with apprehension: Kydd had never had occasion to visit the surgeon professionally, and like most healthy men felt uneasy there.

He took off his hat and crossed the wardroom to the louvered door of the surgeon's cabin, knocking firmly. He was about to knock again when the door flew open, nearly hitting him. "You?" said the surgeon, puzzled. Kydd stepped back in surprise: the surgeon was in his usual rumpled black, but it was stained and there was a rank, unpleasant odor about him.

Kydd collected himself, and reported, "Sir, respects from Mr. Rowley, an' he wishes you t' come—he thinks we have fever aboard."

The surgeon looked at him and frowned. "Pray inform milady, Jenkins, that she must persist in the measures or I will not hold myself responsible for the outcome."

Blinking, Kydd said carefully, "Sir, my name is not Jenkins. Could y' come now? Mr. Rowley is very concerned."

"No. You will tell Lady Bassett that I have done all I can. All! There is no hope—none. I grieve for you all. Good night." The door slammed. Taken aback, Kydd hesitated.

Across the wardroom Parry emerged from his cabin, wiping his face with a towel. "What is it, Kydd?" he asked.

"Could be fever aboard, sir," Kydd said respectfully. He felt ill at ease in officers' private territory.

Parry paused. "You have seen this?"

"Aye, sir."

Striding past Kydd, Parry hammered at the door. "Doctor, we have a crisis, sir. Please be so good as to come on deck at once." There was no reply. "There is a fever on board, damn your blood!"

The door remained closed, but from within Kydd heard a desolate "No hope! None!" and a quiet sobbing.

Parry slapped the towel at his side in frustration. "We'll get nothing from that useless ninny. I'll be on deck shortly."

Fever! It was feared more than any number of enemy cannon, and with reason: in a ship there was nowhere to hide, nowhere to escape to; every man aboard must face risking his life in the unknown miasma that brought the fever.

Supper was a silent meal. Kydd slowly spooned his pease pudding. Across the table eyes followed his movements; he glared back. Haynes coughed—every eye swiveled to watch, then dropped at his savage expression. Mullion seemed sunk in misery, pushing away his wooden plate.

"A pox on it!" snarled Haynes. A twisted smile acknowledged his unfortunate turn of phrase, but he went on forcefully, "Don't sound like any ship-fever I know—an' it ain't scurvy. Could be nuthin' a-tall."

Renzi raised his head. "Or it could be deadly . . ." The table glowered at him collectively. He lapsed into silence. Kydd watched him narrowly—there was a half-smile that he could only remember seeing before battle.

Haynes tugged at his neckerchief. "Port Royal, now that's th' place fer a fever. See them soldiers arrive, chirpin' merry an' all in their lobsterback rig. A week later an' they're sweatin' and writhin' with the yeller jack, only a coupla days afore they tops their boom." He brooded. "Must be thousan's left their bones there."

"Must be a spankin'-size graveyard!" said Kydd, hoping to joke away the pall.

It was Stirk who replied. "No, mate, very small. See, they buries 'em the same day at the Palisades, spit o' sand away from the town. Come night, all these 'ere land crabs pops out 'n' digs 'em up fer a feast. Rousin' good eatin', should you get yerself a dish o' them crabs."

Kydd interrupted him. "What's this, cuffin?" He had noticed how Mullion held his head in his hands, obviously in distress.

"Me head, mate, aches somethin' cruel." Looks were exchanged around the table.

Haynes stood up. "Gotta get aloft—that scurvy crew in the foretop not done yet, I'll 'ave their liver." Crow rose, mumbled something, and they both left.

Stirk turned his gaze to Kydd. "An' you?" he said.

Kydd stared him down, then stood. "Bear a fist, then, y' hen-hearted lubbers!" Mullion was difficult to handle as he staggered haphazardly. They tumbled him into his hammock forward on the gundeck, where he lay biting off moans. Kydd saw that there were slung numbers of hammocks now, each bearing its burden of suffering.

The warm, pleasant airs on the open deck were a relief, but there was a sense of dread: the ship had turned into a prison that was confining its inmates to permit an unknown death to overwhelm them.

Kydd turned to Renzi. The half-smile was still there. "What chance . . ."

"My dear fellow, my education does not include physick. I cannot say."

They glanced aft. With a pugnacious stride and jutting chin, Powlett was now pacing the quarterdeck as if he had never left it. "I do wish, however, that the surgeon had retained but a modicum of his intellects," said Renzi, still watching the Captain. "It was churlish of him to take leave of them at this time."

*   *   *

The loblolly boy held a bowl of thin gruel over Mullion, trying to spoon it in, but Mullion twisted away his head. "Fer Chrissakes!" the lad muttered. This was no time for games, there were too many others to attend to.

"Take it, Jeb, y' needs the strength," Kydd urged.

Mullion focused his dull eyes on him. "No, mate, give it ter the others," he whispered. "This is me punishment, I knows it. 'Cos I didn't hold on ter him—I let 'im go ter his doom. He'd be aboard now an' alongside us if I'd've held on." He looked away in despair.

Not knowing what to do, Kydd took the gruel from the loblolly, who pulled aside Mullion's shirt. Kydd recoiled: the torso was suffused by a pink rash and it glistened with sweat. "That's yer sign," the loblolly said, and took back the gruel to limp over to the next man.

Suddenly gripped by an urgent desire for the open air, Kydd hurried on deck. He saw Haynes by the boat-space: he was motionless, staring out to sea, his grip on a rope bringing white to his knuckles. Kydd sensed the man's fear. "Comin' for y'r grog?" he said, in as friendly a manner as he could.

Slowly Haynes turned his stare on him. In horrible fascination Kydd saw a betraying pinkness above the line of his open-necked shirt. "I got it, ain't I?" Haynes mouthed.

There was no point in denying it. "Y' may have it, but it's a fever only, nobody died."

"You a sawbones, then?" Haynes came back, but with little spirit. He resumed his stare out to sea.

At barely six bells it was not yet time for Kydd to go on watch at the helm, but he was not ready to go below, and swung forward. Abreast the fore-hatch was an anxious group in troubled conversation; Kydd saw Petit's lined features and nodded to him. Petit came over and touched Kydd's arm. "I'd be beholden were yer mate Renzi ter help us," he said in subdued tones.

"Nicholas says as how he's no physician."

His forehead creased with worry, Petit appealed, "Yair, but 'e's book-learned, he is, knows a mort more'n he says. Say that it would be kind in 'im jus' ter step down an' clap peepers on Billy Cundall—he's very bad."

Kydd touched him on the shoulder. "I'll tell him, Elias."

Renzi snorted. "Rank superstition! If I top it the physician, it would be a mockery. I will not!"

"Nicholas, could ye not go to them? Some words o' yours, little enough t' ask, they'd bring some comfort."

Renzi frowned with irritation, but Kydd pressed on, "They trust you, an' even should ye not know the medicine, y' words will give ease."

With reluctance Renzi allowed himself to be dragged down to the berth deck, to the familiar mess of before. Cundall was lying in his hammock in the centerline of the ship, moaning and writhing. Grimacing at the charade Renzi stood beside him and the others crowded around.

"I see," he began hesitantly.

Cundall looked up at him with piteous eyes, a lost soul who barely resembled the loquacious braggart of before. Renzi took a wrist and made to feel the pulse—he had no idea what to do, so nodded sagely and let it drop. "How long has the rash been present?" he asked gravely.

"A coupla days. Will I die?" Cundall cried.

Renzi was at a loss. He had come prepared to go through a few token motions, to offer the reassurance of his presence, but he was speaking to a man who was ill of an unknown fever, asking him to pronounce sentence: life or death. He thought briefly of physicians he had seen, solemnly descending the staircase after visiting a sickroom, and asked the same question. His conscience tore at him at the prospect of laying either alternative before the victim.

He cleared his throat. "We see here as clear a case of *persona non grata* that I have yet seen."

Petit looked pleased. "Be damned! Will 'e be better?" There was a perceptible lightening of mood among the onlookers.

Renzi moved quickly to head away from the moral quicksands of an answer. "Do you steep six ounces of *Calamintha acinos* for two hours, and bathe the afflicted region every hour. That is all."

"We don' have yon *calaminthy*, Nicholas," Petit said respectfully.

"Oh, a pity, it is a common herb in England, the basil," Renzi said, in lordly tones.

"Hey, now!" Quashee pushed himself forward. "My conweniences! I have basil in my conweniences, Mr. Renzi!"

"Splendid! Its carminative properties are always useful, you'll find. I must go." Renzi left speedily.

"Cundall is in good hands, I see," Kydd said, hurrying to keep up. His open admiration for his friend caused Renzi to wince. "May I know what is your 'carminative'?"

Renzi stopped; turning to Kydd he spoke slowly but intensely. "My 'carminative' means that an essence of basil is said to be excellent for the quelling of flatulence—farting, if you will. Now pray do me the service of *never again* putting my sensibilities to hazard in this way. Physician indeed!"

It was clear that Mullion was sinking. He barely moved; the ferocious muscular pains coursing in his legs and back caused spasms that stopped his breath for long moments, his face racked with suffering. Kydd patted his shoulder. There was little he could do— he was now acting quartermaster with Hallison down, and he was due on watch soon.

Kydd left to go aft, but at the main hatch he bumped into Renzi. "Mullion is draggin' his anchors for the other world," he said. "Could ye not—"

"I could not," Renzi said curtly.

Coughing respectfully Petit appeared, standing with his hat off before him. "Thanks t' you, Mr. Renzi," he said, "an' Billy Cundall sends 'is respects, an' the rash is quite gone, now."

With a groan, Renzi waited for Petit to leave, then glared at Kydd. "So they all believe me now a master of physick."

"Aye, Nicholas," said Kydd meekly.

The number of sick had risen sharply, and there was now a significant effect on the balance of men skilled in specifics in the watches; Fairfax was constantly worrying over his watch and station bill. Kydd's temporary new rate as quartermaster was an important one. He took up position at the conn, with responsibility for the watch glass, the slate of course details and other navigational matters, leaving little time to dwell on illness.

The watch drew on, the officer-of-the-watch, Parry, unforgiving of the slightest sign of sloppiness. Later in the afternoon Rowley emerged on deck to take the air. It was not the custom for officers to promenade the fo'c'sle: the quarterdeck was their proper place. There was no alternative open to Rowley other than to begin a slow circuit of the quarterdeck, unavoidably confronting Parry on each lap. Kydd had always felt uncomfortable at the clear dislike the men had for each other, and hoped that Rowley would soon go below.

"I'd be obliged were you to keep to leeward, Mr. Rowley," Parry said stiffly. He was standing to weather, as was his right, but the effect of his order was to rob Rowley of his circle—he could now only pace up and down in a line. Rowley touched his hat with an expansive smile and exaggerated bow before complying. The rest of the watch passed silently and with acid tension.

At seven bells Powlett came on deck. Parry moved to leeward in respect; Rowley promptly went below. "Pass the word for Petty Officer Renzi," Powlett growled. Parry nodded to the boatswain's mate, who trotted forward. When Renzi reported, Powlett spoke abruptly. "I hear you are something of a physician."

"Why, not at all, sir—"

"I have no power to warrant you in any position, but you will

take on medical duties as of now, for as long as the surgeon's indis-
position lasts."

"Sir, you are mistaken, I—"

"That is all."

"But, sir, there is—"

"Go!" Powlett's voice was weary, his bearing was faltering, he looked as tired and worn as *Artemis* now was. Renzi hesitated, touched his hat and left.

Mullion died in the same hour, and Cundall's symptoms reap-peared. The forward part of the gundeck was screened off, and a windsail was rigged above the fore-hatch, but the rows of ham-mocks increased. It was puzzling: some with raging fever saw their symptoms recede almost to nothing, then return with brutal force, while others recovered, although they were now profoundly deaf. Another two died. Renzi felt trapped in the cheerless gloom of the gundeck in the midst of so much pain and squalor, as his world turned to a waking nightmare.

A boatswain's mate pulled aside the screen. His nose wrinkled in disgust—there was no way that he would enter the moaning, vomit-strewn hell. He called across loudly, "Mr. Fairfax passes the word for Petty Officer Renzi!" Straightening wearily, Renzi threw down the rag he was carrying, and with bloodshot eyes pulled the screen aside. He was touched to see Kydd look up from a bench close to the screen—he must have lingered there in support, unable to do more. Kydd rose and as Renzi went aft he tried to chat companionably with him.

Fairfax was in his cabin with Rowley. "Come in, Renzi," he said, gravely. The two officers looked seriously at Renzi as he entered, and he knew intuitively what they were going to say.

"I am sorry to have to tell you that the Captain has been taken ill of the fever." Rowley's eyes flashed nervously white. "We have endeavored to communicate with the surgeon but unhappily he is beyond reach." Fairfax sighed heavily.

Rowley leant forward impatiently. "Therefore we require you to treat the Captain using whatever you can find in the surgeon's cabin."

Appalled, Renzi gaped at them.

"Be so good as to begin immediately," Fairfax said, his worried frown deepening. "If you have need of anything—anything at all—you will get it."

"But the men are—"

"The loblolly is in attendance," Rowley said with irritation. "Go to your duties now, if you please."

"Get out!" the surgeon shrilled. "You have no right—I will inform your mistress presently!" Kydd held him back while Renzi attempted to rummage about the sad ruins of the man's domesticity. "I know what you are, you are the devil's messenger, are you not?" Kydd felt destabilized by the surgeon's high, off-key voice, at the edge of reason, and even more so when the man began to scream and clutch at him in terror. A knot of men waited outside, including a marine sentry who had let his musket fall and stood in wide-eyed horror

They escaped with the surgeon's bulky chest—a hurried search had not turned up any book worthy of the name—and rapidly made their way to the Captain's bedplace cabin. He was lying quietly in his suspended cot, his eyes closed. Renzi set down the chest carefully, conscious of the tense presence of the officers and the Captain's coxswain.

"Pray leave us. He is, er, not to be excited," Renzi pronounced. At least they would not blunder about in front of an audience. He looked apprehensively at Kydd: in all his rich and varied life he had never been in such a bizarre and helpless situation.

At his words, Powlett opened his eyes. "Renzi!" he said thickly. "Do your duty, man!"

Renzi blinked. *Do something,* his very being shouted. But if he did the wrong thing? "Does it pain you, sir?" he opened.

"Yes!" Powlett said briefly. "And this goddamned headache is oppressive to my spirit—it's pounding my brain—the pressure," he said, a tremor in his voice. Renzi noticed heavy sweat beading the rash and trembling spasms of long-endured pain. In the confined space his senses swam. He reached out to steady himself, and his hand found the doorlatch; he staggered out of the cabin. The officers gazed at him in silence. He pulled himself together and said, "Er, the loblolly if you please—I must have assistance." At least it would buy time.

The lad limped up, and Renzi drew him into the empty great cabin. "I must consult," he muttered. "What's to be done?" he asked, with a quiet dignity.

The loblolly looked frightened. "I—I don't know!" he whispered.

"But you've been surgeon's mate all this while," Renzi coaxed, "you must have seen something!"

"Not this!" He dropped his eyes. "I seen him do things, but he never showed me 'less he wanted something done."

They would not get anything from the scared boy. Renzi felt a surging despair. It was unfair to expect anything: they had never suffered a killing fever like this before. "A cruel headache. What did the doctor do for that?" It was at least doing something.

The loblolly thought and said, "Calomel." Seeing Renzi frown he added, "And bleeding, o' course."

Renzi had been bled once. He barely remembered it as he had been dead drunk at the time, but he had a dim recollection of gleaming steel and a sharp pain in his arm before he had fainted. "Can you do a bleeding?" he asked the loblolly.

"I never seen it—surgeon always did it private, like."

Renzi glanced up at Kydd, whose healthy complexion was rapidly paling. Kydd shook his head. "We must bleed him," Renzi said, and dismissed the terrified lad. Together they returned to the Captain, firmly closing the door behind them.

"We must bleed you, sir," Renzi said, trying to sound as confident as he could. He pulled open the surgeon's chest, a neat complexity of compartments containing pharmacy bottles and dried herbs. Inside the lid were clamped a bewildering array of steel instruments.

"Which one do you use?" Renzi whispered. The prospect of cutting into the Captain's living flesh was appalling. He fumbled among the contents of the chest.

"I heard y' use a fleam," Kydd interjected weakly.

"And which the devil is that?" Renzi said, in a low voice.

Powlett stirred. "Get on with it, you rogues."

Renzi's heart thudded. He selected a bright blade with a point; it gleamed evilly in the soft light of the lanthorn. He pulled up Powlett's nightshirt sleeve, baring the pale arm.

"What are you waiting for, you lubber?" Powlett's voice was a weak parody of its former self. His head twisted away in anticipation of the blade.

Renzi hesitated. He pushed the knife against the Captain's skin, which dimpled under the pressure, but he could not steel himself to bring to bear the necessary force. Then he felt Kydd's presence and steadied.

It was easy, really: the knife sank in, and dark, venous blood gouted obediently, turning the bedclothes scarlet, a spreading flood of red that seemed never to end.

"The cup, you mumping fool!" Powlett's muffled voice sounded from the pillow.

"We'll use a glass," Renzi told Kydd, and took a brandy glass— but by then Powlett had slipped into a swoon.

Shakily, Renzi emerged from the cabin. He told the waiting group what they wanted to hear and left.

Haynes died, never having left the deck once, crouched in great pain against the ship's side, and cursing brokenly toward the end. He was followed by Cundall and three others. But the last man to die caused *Artemis* the most grief.

Fairfax had the men mustered aft. "I have to tell you—it is with intolerable feeling—our brave captain is no longer with us." There were gasps and cries from the few who had not heard the terrible news. The first lieutenant's gray worry-frown deepened. "Therefore, for the present, and until we return to England, I, er, will be your captain."

There was no response from the silent mass of men. "Carry on," snapped Parry.

"You do that agin, you pocky bastard, an' I'll cut yer liver out!" Stirk's eyes flashed hatred at Crow across the table.

Crow said nothing, but he held his head very still, fixing Stirk with his hard, glittering eyes. Then Crow slowly passed his hand across his chest and began a deliberate scratch under his armpit. Stirk launched himself across the table. Crow snarled and smashed his fist into Stirk's face.

"Stow it, y' mad dogs!" Kydd shouted, trying to force himself between them. Stirk was angry and powerful, but the slighter-built Crow had a dogged tenacity that made it impossible for Kydd to separate them. It eventually ended in a panting truce and bitter words.

Kydd pulled his shabby blue jacket closer. *Artemis* was now deep into the Atlantic proper, and the first cool precursors of the north were making themselves felt. The fever had run its course, only the poignancy of empty places at familiar seats a reminder of their time of trial. He looked across at Renzi, but the sunken eyes and sallow appearance would take time to dispel. Renzi seldom spoke now.

There was a sullen lethargy about the men that Kydd found difficult to confront: he sympathized with their hard circumstances, which he shared. Since the shock of seeing the body of their captain committed to the deep, there had been a marked decline in the sense of unity and purpose; the loss of such a strong figure at the center of their world allowed it to fly apart. Petty tyrannies spread unchecked, the humbler members of the power structure suffering the most. The lack of a respected figure to distribute praise or criticism meant that the traditional engine of cohesion was no longer there—and whatever else Fairfax was, he was not a leader.

A bare ten days or less and it would all be over—but Kydd's heart was heavy. It felt as though *Artemis* herself, sea-worn as she was, was the only one staying loyal and true to Powlett's memory. His hand fell, and under cover of the table he felt for the ship's side and secretly caressed its—*her*—timbers.

The officers gathering on the quarterdeck for the noon sight stood together. Fairfax lowered his sextant and inspected it. "I make it thirty-two degrees nineteen minutes north, gentlemen. And that is a bare four hundred leagues from England." There was a favorable stir. "I will confess, a fine game pie is haunting me—perhaps in harness with a glass of decent claret not stinking of the bilge." He handed over his sextant to be stowed below, and stretched, sniffing the steady trade winds. "It will not be long now, we shall meet our families."

Kydd, at his post, let the conversation slip past. He watched the helmsman catch a wind-flaw and ease the wheel a spoke or two.

Rowley added languidly, "I do believe we shall be in time for the Season—the duchess means her daughter to be presented at court this year, and I have the liveliest recollection of Vauxhall gardens by torchlight."

"There is no likelihood of the Season for me, I fancy," replied Fairfax. "We are an old county family and there will be too much to attend to on the estate, more's the pity." He looked pleasantly at the wooden Parry. "You will be in town for the Season, or are you to be rusticated?"

Parry said with a set face, "Neither, sir." He hesitated, then added, "I believe I will visit my older sister at Yarmouth."

"Yarmouth?" said Fairfax. "Oh." He and Rowley exchanged looks, then stepped forward together in easy conversation. They halted while Rowley drew out his snuff box and laid some on the back of his hand. Before he could inhale, a playful wind scattered the grains in the air and back over Parry.

Parry's face went red. "Take your filthy habit somewhere else, sir!" he shouted.

Rowley's eyebrows rose in astonishment. He glanced at Fairfax, then allowed an expression of exaggerated good humor to accompany his urbane inclination of the head. He looked back at Fairfax and burst out laughing.

Storming forward Parry fronted Rowley, breathing deeply and raggedly. "Be damned to your popinjay ways, Rowley! Your infernal highborn humbug grates on my nerves."

Fairfax looked shocked. "Mr. Parry! I do hope—"

Ignoring Fairfax, Rowley replied coolly, plucking at the lace of his cuffs, "Sir, intemperate words do nothing but reflect on breeding."

"Mr. Rowley, this is not—" began Fairfax, his hands flapping, pacifying.

With the entire quarterdeck watching silently, Parry's face clamped in a murderous loathing. "Rowley, if you cross my bows once more . . ."

"Is this in the nature of a threat, sir?"

"Gentlemen, I implore you—please . . ."

"It is, sir!"

"Then may I take it that as a *gentleman* you are dissatisfied by my conduct?"

"*Gentlemen, please!*"

"I am, sir, damn you to hell!" Parry's voice was thick with emotion.

Rowley's voice turned silky. "Then could it be that you are looking for satisfaction in the matter?"

"Yes, I am!" Parry said hotly.

Instantly, Rowley snapped to attention. "Then, sir, I accept, as Mr. Fairfax is my witness." Turning to Fairfax, he continued, "Kindly inform Mr. Parry, sir, that my second will wait on his by sunset."

In the shocked silence Fairfax wrung his hands. "Gentlemen, can you not be reconciled? Consider, this is a ship of war, we are—"

Parry drew in a breath with a hiss. "No, sir, we cannot!" With a look of savage content, as of a monstrous burden lifted, he added, "But of course I will allow Mr. Rowley to withdraw."

Rowley turned away and studied the horizon with his arms folded.

"Then it is my most sorrowful duty to inform you both, that as there is no satisfaction offered, then the matter must come to an unhappy conclusion." Fairfax paced aft pensively and returned. "There is no prospect of a meeting until we make landfall in England. It is customary in these matters to refrain from interchanges, but in the meantime, for the sake of the ship, I must ask you both to continue your professional duties, but through an intermediary." He wiped his forehead forlornly. "May I express how deeply saddened I am by the way this day has turned out."

On into the broad wastes of the North Atlantic *Artemis* sailed, watch by watch, routines performed by rote, duties done with no heart in them. The first Atlantic gales came; once more the smash of seas and hiss of spray over the decks, racing dark clouds, deep thrumming in the rigging.

When Kydd came on watch at midnight, dirty weather had set in to accompany the spiteful blasts of the gale, rain driven with vindictive force that reddened cheeks and eyes.

He set the first helmsmen of the watch, checked the slate by the light of the binnacle and took the state of sail. It was a little surprising that the officer-of-the-watch, Rowley, did not shorten sail in this blow, for *Artemis* was straining aloft and making hard work of the beat to windward. But then again there would be few who would prefer to lose this chance to reach England the quicker.

Kydd watched Rowley standing ahead of him, huddled in grego and tarpaulin, facing into the blast, but felt no sympathy for him in his larger situation. That was a matter Rowley and Parry must resolve, and Renzi's reticence on the subject was sufficient commentary on his views.

Kydd could see forward, past the pale sails to the bowsprit plunging and rearing far ahead with a sudden bursting of spray over the fo'c'sle, and he pitied the hapless forward lookouts at the catheads. Renzi would be with the rest of the dutymen, hanking down after the customary sail-trimming at the turn of the watch. He would be able to take shelter behind a weather bulwark.

The helmsman stolidly met the bullying of the gale, his leeward mate following his motions on the other side, two men necessary in this blow. Kydd was settling down to an uncomfortable and boring watch, when against the buffeting roar of the wind he picked up a lookout's faint cry from forward. It was picked up amidships and repeated immediately, a dreadful yell—"Breakers *aheeeaaad!* Two points on the weather bow!"

A shaft of cold fear lanced into his vitals. He tensed for Rowley's order—but Rowley seemed to be deep in some sort of reverie. The officer-of-the-watch had the responsibility, and only him. "Sir!" he bawled in alarm.

Rowley seemed disoriented. "Helm hard up!" he shouted. This would instantly sheer the vessel away from the danger and away from the wind, on the face of it a sensible move. Kydd roared at the helmsmen and they spun the wheel frantically. The ship bucketed and rocked at the sudden change in direction.

Parry appeared at the fore-hatch and bounded on deck. "Belay that—hard down the helm!" he bellowed. Kydd hesitated: Parry was senior to Rowley and had every right to overrule him—except that Rowley was officer-of-the-watch and in charge.

"Quartermaster!" said Rowley, in hard tones. "Inform Mr. Parry that I am officer-of-the-watch. I have the ship."

Kydd's jaw dropped. He looked back at Parry, who bunched his fists. "Sir, Mr. Rowley begs to tell you—"

"Kydd, tell that infernal idiot that the ship stands into danger! Helm hard a-larboard!"

It was clear to Kydd that Parry's order was indeed the right one: admittedly they were now headed away from the breakers, but they were going at an increasing speed to leeward and headlong toward whatever was out there. Parry's order would have had the effect of setting the ship all aback, in stays, but at least it would stop *Artemis* in her tracks and buy them time to decide.

"Helm hard down," he snapped at the helmsmen.

Before they could move, Rowley shouted, "Avast!" He turned to Kydd, although his eyes remained on Parry. "Enquire of Mr. Parry if he is relieving me of my duties, quartermaster."

Parry's chest heaved, but before he could respond another, more urgent cry came—"Breakers to loo'ard! I see breakin' sea all t' loo'ard!" The voice ended in a falsetto shriek.

"I have the conn!" roared Parry. "Helm down—hard over for your lives!" Their run downwind away from the first breakers had placed them in mortal danger from the second. In the loom of night a continuous white line of breakers emerged to leeward and ahead; it was plain they had unwittingly run into the arms of a small bay. Agonizingly the ship's head came around again. They brought up into the wind—but the watch were not at stations to go about, and the vessel fell away to leeward, slewing hopelessly around.

It was now inevitable, and at a little after two in the morning His Majesty's frigate *Artemis* ran onto an offshore rocky ledge, part of a small unknown islet somewhere in the Atlantic.

Kydd's world dissolved into a frightful smashing, rearing, splintering chaos. He was flung down and shot forward helplessly over the lurching wet deck in a welter of tarpaulins, to fetch up painfully against the main jeer bitts.

Artemis's bow mounted and fell, and Kydd felt her hoarse shriek as she was mercilessly disemboweled by the invisible black rocks, a long drawn-out sound that tore at his heart.

Around and above him masts and spars swayed forward and gave way at the sudden stop, crashing down like felled trees, and bringing with them a man-trapping, crazy web of rigging from aloft. Her forward motion ceased, and the frigate settled to her bed of pain, her hull lifting and crunching back under the driving waves like a mortally wounded soul trying to rise up again.

Other sounds now broke in on Kydd's senses: screams of agony as men were crushed by falling spars, bubbling shrieks from below as men were drowned by the victorious sea flooding through her shattered bottom. He fought his way out from the tangle of stiff wet ropes, shivering uncontrollably with the mortal cold of deep shock. The perspective from aft had a shocking unreality: all masts were broken off short, draped haphazardly about; the ship was horribly disfigured, desperately wounded.

Numb, Kydd tried to take stock. Dying screams and screeches of agony tore at his nerves. He peered into the rain-lashed darkness, searching for familiarity and security, and through the bleak gloom he saw that they were hard up on an offshore ledge of rocks, a half-mile to seaward of a small, jagged island. But that half-mile or so was a seething mass of white-streaked, storm-driven seas. The boats on the skids amidships were smashed and splintered by toppling wreckage; there was no chance of escape there. A sense of the inevitability of his own death seeped into Kydd.

Stumbling figures in the darkness moved about the deck, shouting and calling; there was no sign of the two officers. The stricken ship continued to lift and drop in an agonizing grind, and Kydd's heart wrung in anguish at the torment even as he reached for reality to long-familiar deck fitments.

On the fo'c'sle there was a focus of movement, and Kydd felt drawn to the scene, the only evidence of intelligence in the insan-

ity. He fought and clambered over the heaving wreckage toward
it. As he did so *Artemis* was set upon by ferocious seas around her
stern. Her fine run counter was slammed from under by their
attack and as Kydd passed the stump of the mainmast, her keel
gave way. Twisted by the great forces working at her vitals, the
after end of the ship broke in a series of shattering claps of thunder. The stern portion fell at a different angle from the forward—
the decking just behind Kydd splintered across and a void opened.
The forward part remained immovable on the rocks but the after
fell away with a stupendous cracking, a series of lurches now quite
independent of the forward. Men clutching the deck on the stern
saw their doom—some slid into the ravening chaos between the
two, others were still clinging desperately as *Artemis*'s stern quarters slid backward into the violence. Kydd's mind froze in deathly
fear; unable to move, hypnotized at the awesome scene.

There were scores of bodies in the water now, tumbled and
rolled by the contemptuous seas. Released by the breaking hull,
these had been the ones asleep below; death had been forced on
them instantly. They would have had not the slightest warning of
the streaming black rocks that had brutally broken in on them.

The after part quickly receded, sinking as it did so. The few
remaining souls leaped or fell into the water. They had no chance
at all; smothered by foaming seas, battered by the pieces of black
wreckage spewing obscenely from the innards of the ship, they
were swept into the outer darkness.

Kydd tore his eyes from the sight and seized hold of his
courage. He resumed his scramble forward, crying with grief at
the hideous end of his ship and the loss of his friends. *Artemis* was
now a dismembered corpse, lying distorted and still, her bowsprit
and rags of headsails spearing up poignantly, pointing at the distant shore. He reached the knot of men on the fo'c'sle. There was
no sign of recognition, they were nameless figures working
despairingly on the wreckage with their knives. They were trying
to bind gratings and planking with ropes to make a raft, but with

only their seamen's knives they could make little progress. Kydd did not have his knife, as iron implements were not permitted near the compass. He fell back and hung from the forebitts in utter despair, looking across the white-streaked, rampaging seas rolling shoreward.

A hand clutched at him from behind, and he turned ready to fight off a mindless soul, but found himself staring at Renzi. He gripped his friend for long moments, aware of Renzi's wild, disordered state. Emotion cascaded through him.

Renzi leaned forward and shouted at him, "Lash ourselves—wait until daybreak!" Not trusting himself to speak, he nodded, and accepted the fall of a clewline cut off by Renzi. The new day would not change things, but at least they could face directly whatever was due to them.

The night wore on in a daze of cold and fear, but at about four, just as a reluctant cold dawn hinted at light, the carcass of *Artemis* shifted, grinding around to a new angle. The movement destroyed the temporary feeling of security that her motionless wedging on the rock ledge had provided, and at an hour before dawn it was clear that the end would not be long delayed.

Kydd unlashed himself—there was no point in being dragged down by the sinking wreckage—but Renzi pulled him round to face him. "We must jump," he said. His voice was strong and even, although his body shuddered with the cold. "I would take it kindly, dear friend, if you would consent to taking the end of this line." He was requesting that they be linked by a rope when they made their final leap. Kydd's eyes stung, a lump in his throat at the unfairness of it all, the unreadable harshness of fate, but he took the line and secured it to himself. "We have shared . . ." began Renzi, but did not finish. Kydd nodded and looked away.

A long, grinding rumble sounded beneath them, and the deck juddered and moved. A sudden lurch came, which sent Kydd staggering, and it was time. They slid to the ship's side, clambered to the rail—and leaped into the sea.

The water closed over Kydd, rushing and roaring in his ears, the sea strangely warm out of the cold blast of the gale. He kicked and flailed, then broke surface, briefly aware of the black bulk of *Artemis* close by, then was whirled away, spluttering and helpless. There was no question of swimming; he could feel himself in the grip of strong waves that surged and pulled at him. He became entangled in the rope that joined him to Renzi, but it was too chaotic even to know if Renzi was still attached. The tops of waves swept over him without warning and he choked on sea-water. His clothes began to hang as a dead weight, and he knew that he was going down. Thrashing desperately at the water, he breathed in the salty foam, his throat raw and burning as he began to sink.

His legs brutally hit something solid. The rising breakers lifted him up and again his legs struck. Wild with hope, Kydd frantically kicked and fought. Suddenly he was slammed against an unmistakable, sturdy, moving surface. He was carried forward, his body losing its buoyancy as it slithered and floundered across the sand. In an instant, he was aware that his direction had reversed, and he felt himself being pulled back out to sea, back into the frenzy of deep water. In a fury of self-preservation he clawed at the sand, and suddenly found himself left high and dry by the receding wave. It returned before he could do anything, but he had been able to take long, tearing breaths and was ready for the rush of water. Painfully, he levered himself out of the sea, unable to stand, merely to drag himself above the line of waves, where he collapsed, spent.

He raised his head. A few yards along was a shapeless bundle. It was connected to him by a rope, and was very still. His mind refused to accept it at first, but then, with a roaring in his ears, he shouted hoarsely. He staggered to his feet, crossed to the body and fell on it, turning it over, needing to see its face.

Renzi vomited weakly, sea-water pouring from his mouth. He lifted his head to look at Kydd with dull eyes. A slow smile crossed his features and on the tiny beach the two shipwrecked mariners embraced.

A hand touched Kydd's shoulder. He jerked round in surprise and met the eyes of a foreign soldier. *"Não se preocupe—sua vida esta salvo, pobre marinheiro,"* the man said softly.

Kydd struggled to his feet but Renzi's voice broke through weakly, "I do observe, dear friend, that the presence of this man implies two things." Coughing feebly, he continued, "First, that this island is inhabited and we are spared an unfortunate death by starvation. Second, he speaks Portuguese—probably this is one of the islands of the Azores. They are our oldest ally and thus we may believe we will soon be homeward bound."

Kydd hid his leaping happiness behind a dry smile. "O' course, if there's any officer survived, why, there'll be a mort of explainin' he'll have t' do afore his court-martial," he said with satisfaction.

"But in course, we shall be witnesses of the first order," added Renzi, "and therefore I fear our return to Guildford may necessarily suffer delay."

AUTHOR'S NOTE

At my desk is a length of rope from the seventy-four gun ship-of-the-line HMS *Invincible* that two centuries ago struck on the sands off Selsey Bill. The rope still smells of sea and Stockholm tar. I have other relics, too: a seaman's tankard, a gunlock flint, an Admiralty-issue clerk's writing kit—each one bringing that far-away world straight into my consciousness. This I value above all things—that the reader take away from my book is a perception of the reality of Kydd's world.

Some have asked how real are the incidents in *Artemis*. There is an untold wealth in the histories—but the gold is found in the letters home of a pressed man, the diary of a gunner in Antigua, the musings of retired seamen. What lies in the pages of my book is how it happened as closely as I can render it for today's readers. Sometimes the facts are more amazing than any fiction—*Artemis*'s desperate battle is based on that of the *Nymphe* and *Cléopâtre* of the time. Maillot's (Mullon's) gallant act did take place, but in fact it was the Captain's own brother, Israel Pellow, who personally laid and fired the fatal carronade shot that turned the tide.

Good fortune has played its part in allowing me to indulge my passion: the felicity of having a wife who can walk and talk the plot and characters with me, the enthusiasm of my publisher, Scribner, and the inspiration from Geoff Hunt's art. With the wider world of a naval scholarship to call upon, how can I not sit down and immediately begin the next book?

Julian Stockwin
August 2001